CAPTAIN MAROONER

Captain Marooner

LOUIS B. DAVIDSON

AND

EDDIE DOHERTY

INTRODUCTION BY

WILLIAM MCFEE

NEW YORK THOMAS Y. CROWELL COMPANY

Dedicated to

JOSEPH E. DAVIDSON

In Loving Memory

Introduction

BY WILLIAM MC FEE

IN THE LAST FEW YEARS we have had a number of crises in American shipping, and many of them have focused public attention on the subject of mutiny. For some reason this has always had a fascination for landsmen and they have tended to endow it with romantic attributes which vanished over a century ago. It must be admitted that our courts, and this includes the Supreme Court in Washington, have pandered to this romantic urge by defining even a labor strike, on board a ship tied to an American dock, as mutiny, if the crew have signed orders to obey the master's lawful commands. Merely a refusal to work, a "sit-down strike," is now included in the ban and is stated to be "mutinous behavior."

Now this is a very far cry from the old romantic conception of mutiny on the high seas. Then the word had a more precise and sinister connotation. It involved not merely a refusal to work, or a physical conflict between officers and men, but a conspiracy to seize the ship from the appointed master, and either by murder or marooning destroy the legal authority and discipline of the ship. This was the "mutiny" on the famous *Bounty*.

This was also the lesser-known mutiny on the Nantucket whaling ship *Globe,* which Louis B. Davidson and Eddie Doherty have used as a basis for their fictional reconstruction of the tragedy in *Captain Marooner*.

In 1824 whaling was one of the major industries of the infant United States. Many other industries ran on whale oil and the by-products of the vast cetacean herds of the southern and Antarctic oceans. When the news of the *Globe* affair reached Nantucket and New Bedford, that the *Globe* had been seized and sailed into unknown seas, the merchants of Nantucket petitioned President Monroe to send a man-of-war to find the mutineers and bring them to justice. The President ordered the warship U.S.S. *Dolphin* to proceed to the Pacific. In 1825 this vessel reached the lonely Mulgraves and the commander took possession of them in the name of the United States. Great Britain also claimed them and the controversy has continued to simmer in the Department of State in Washington and in the Foreign Office in London until recent times.

Numerous sources have been drawn on by the authors for this tale of the sea. For the purposes of the story this material has been cast in the form of a diary or log, kept by George Comstock, a Quaker lad and brother of Samuel Comstock, the chief boat steerer and leader of the mutiny. George actually sailed as a teen-ager in the *Globe*, and later joined the *Dolphin* when she set out to find the *Globe* and the survivors. Two of the survivors also wrote up their two years on one of the islands. The whole story is in dramatic contrast with the temperament of the narrator. The pious pacifism of the Quaker seamen forms a weird background to the scenes of violence and bloodshed, all viewed through the eyes of the youthful Quaker. George Comstock, in this novel, keeps a diary just as Richard Henry Dana did a decade later, which journal formed the basis of *Two Years Before the Mast*. Like Dana, too, Comstock came home in another ship. Both young New Englanders served under stupidly tyrannical shipmasters.

Captain Marooner, however, is fiction—but in form only. Out of the multifarious records, in the consul's office at Valparaiso, and in the United States, the authors have fashioned a tale of adventure, of murderous violence and romantic episodes which will recall Melville's *Typee* and *Omoo*.

One of the peculiar features of maritime law in those days was the lapse of time between the consummation of a mutinous outbreak and the trial of the criminals. Three years elapsed before the mutineers of the *Bounty* were hanged at Execution Dock, the place at Thames-side which was known in the pirates' lexicon as "Hope Point." It was two years before the *Dolphin* caught up with the *Globe*'s mutineers, and by that time the ringleaders had been killed.

The vast distances of the central Pacific from New England, involving a voyage around the Horn, and the dependence on wandering whalers for the transmission of mails causes us to wonder that a sea-going criminal was ever brought to justice. On the other hand, the merchants and important shipowners involved in the profitable industry were implacable in their support of the harsh discipline imposed on whaling crews, in fact on all American ships.

The story of the *Bounty* mutiny has been the source of a whole library of books, a long shelf of romances; so many, in fact, that the original narrative of events, the factual history, has been almost lost sight of by the readers of romantic fiction.

The mutiny on the *Globe*, on the other hand, has been completely forgotten, buried in the archives and old journals, since the 1830's. Messrs. Davidson and Doherty have brought the old story into the light of day again, in *Captain Marooner*, using it as a basis for a historical narrative that illuminates a page of New England maritime history.

Preface

IN THIS NARRATIVE we have undertaken to reconstruct the real mutiny on the whaleship *Globe* and the subsequent adventures of the mutineers and also of the innocent members of the crew.

To do this we have drawn entirely from absolutely verifiable sources: thus, the incidents leading up to the mutiny, the actual mutiny itself and its aftermath are based on the record of the testimony of the surviving members of the crew who were examined under oath by the United States consul at Valparaiso soon after the *Globe* returned from the Mulgrave Islands, now known as Mill or Mille Island in the Marshalls. The situations described are found in the sworn evidence of the survivors; and here, let it be noted, not one of the characters involved in this drama of the sea is fictitious. We have also fallen back on the records of the United States Circuit Court in Boston, where Joseph Thomas was tried, of the Old Whaling Library at New Bedford, of the Boston Custom House, and of the archives at Washington.

The *Globe* was engaged in the whaling industry and belonged to the island of Nantucket, Massachusetts; it was owned by Messrs. C. Mitchell & Co., merchants, of Nantucket.

It was on December 20, 1822, that the *Globe*, unable to load stores from Nantucket because of a sand bar, was obliged to leave from Edgartown, Martha's Vineyard.

A list of the officers and crew who were known to have been on board the *Globe* when the ship set sail from Edgartown on that memorable cruise is given at the end of this preface.

Most of the officers and crew who set sail from Edgartown were very young men; thus First Mate Beetle was only twenty-six years of age. Most of the crew were New Englanders, mere boys still in their early teens and the average age of the crew was well under twenty years.

In order to depict the subsequent adventures, including the cruise of the *Dolphin* in search of the mutineers and of the innocent survivors, and to relate the experiences of the latter among the natives of the Mulgrave Islands, recourse was had to the journals of Lieutenant Hiram Paulding, second in command of the U.S.S. *Dolphin* which was dispatched in search of the survivors. Lieutenant Paulding kept a day-by-day record of the events of the cruise. Access was also had by the authors to the diaries kept by William Lay and Cyrus Hussey recording the experiences of their sojourn among the natives of the Mulgrave Islands for about two years. In using the materials contained in the above mentioned records, the authors have navigated closely along the shoreline of fact.

Personnel of the Whaleship "Globe"

OFFICERS

Thomas Worth, Captain, of Edgartown, Massachusetts

William Beetle, First Mate

John Lumbard, Second Mate

Nathaniel Fisher, Third Mate

Samuel B. Comstock, First Boat Steerer

Gilbert Smith, Second Boat Steerer

CREW

Peter C. Kidder, Foremast Hand
Stephen Kidder, Seaman
Columbus Worth, Cook and Seaman
Rowland Jones, Seaman
John Cleveland, Seaman
Constant Lewis, Seaman
Holden Hewman, Seaman
Jeremiah Ingraham, Seaman
Cyrus Hussey, Cooper
Joseph Ignatius Prass, Seaman
Rowland Coffin, Cooper
George Comstock, Seaman
William Lay, Seaman

TAKEN ABOARD WHILE AT SEA

Joseph Thomas, Blacksmith, of Norwich, Connecticut

NEW MEMBERS OF CREW TAKEN ON AT HAWAII

Silas Payne, Seaman, of Rhode Island
John Oliver, Seaman, of Shields, England
Anthony Hanson, Seaman, of Falmouth, Massachusetts

Joe Brown, Harpooner, of Hawaii
William Humphries, Steward, of Philadelphia
Thomas Liliston, Seaman, of Virginia

OTHER IMPORTANT PERSONS IN THE STORY
Sally Starbuck, of Nantucket, Massachusetts
Barnabas Starbuck, of Nantucket, Massachusetts
Perdita Blanco, of Valparaiso, Chile
Michael Hogan, United States Consul at Valparaiso
Lia-Lia, native girl of Hawaii
Motake, native girl of the Mulgrave Islands
Rosita Bonheur, of France and Valparaiso, Chile
Captain John Percival, commander of the U.S.S. *Dolphin*
Lieutenant Hiram Paulding, of the U.S.S. *Dolphin*
Midshipman Ember, of the U.S.S. *Dolphin*
Buff, native of Hawaii, member of crew of U.S.S. *Dolphin*
Thomas Comstock, father of George and Samuel Comstock
Samantha Comstock, stepmother of George Comstock
Hon. Joseph Story, Justice of the United States Supreme Court,
     assigned to the United States Circuit Court, Boston
George Blake, of Boston, Assistant U.S. Attorney
James T. Austin, of Boston, Defense Attorney

Chapter One

NOV. 3, 1822. A fine clean day with strong winds blowing; a joyous, bracing day. The streets of Nantucket are full of dancing oak and maple leaves, and the pungent smell of their burning. I watched some old ladies burning leaves this morning, then strolled down to Barnabas Starbuck's storehouse at the wharf. It had been cleared for the barrels of whale oil aboard the *Globe,* which has just come into port with its hold filled. I watched the line of men rolling the barrels along, like so many beetles pushing their balls. They sang as they worked, songs born of the sea.

Cyrus Hussey was sitting on top of the woodpile back of the storehouse, pretending he was on the deck of an outward-bounder and steering a course by the stars. I knew that because he held the axe as though it were a tiller.

I filled my lungs with the smell of new wood, a much better smell than that of burning leaves or pure sperm oil in barrels; and for want of something better to do, I asked Hussey to let me chop a few staves. I liked the work, and might have made a sizable pile had not my brother Sam stepped out of the Starbuck home and come to talk to us.

"Going to the dance?" he asked. Hussey, who was staring out at the whaler, lost in dreams, turned quickly, and the keys that hung from a chain attached to his belt clashed musically together. The un-Quakerish greeting surprised him for a moment. Then he said he'd like to go, but hadn't been invited.

"I'm inviting you," Sam assured him, smiling his peculiar coaxing smile—a flash of white teeth gleaming in pleasant contrast to the rich tan of his face and the sun tints in his black unruly hair. Sam can get anything he wants with that smile. He makes everyone his slave, man, woman, child, and dog. Even I, his brother, who know him better than anyone else, I think, feel obliged to him when he smiles.

"Maybe you can help us," he went on. His tone was confidential, a gross flattery. Hussey beamed to think such a man as Sam Comstock would seek assistance from him—Sam the harpooner, the man of medicine and surgery, the navigator, the hero of a hundred adventures in far-off lands and waters!

"I'll do anything I can," Hussey said.

"We haven't found the right location," Sam confided, frowning a little as though acutely aware of his absolute dependence on young Hussey. "We've looked at Peleg Gardner's storehouse, but the cooper hasn't finished repairing it. Neighbor Coffin's shanty is full of grease, and the try-pots are in the way. If we could use Starbuck's loft—"

Cyrus, who had been chopping all morning without raising a sweat, suddenly oozed perspiration through all his pores; he shivered.

"He'd kill me!" he whispered.

Sam smiled again, and put a friendly arm over Cyrus' shoulders. "Don't be afraid," he said. "We'll reef the windows aft, and keep all hands quiet. Old Barnabas is hard of hearing anyway, and he'll never venture around forward. That reminds me. I'm sailing with the *Globe* next voyage, and I know Captain Worth could use another cooper."

"Would he take me?" Hussey asked.

"I'll speak to him," Sam promised. "You'll get along fine on the *Globe*. Why, a young man of your ability ought to command a third mate's berth on his second voyage, in which case your lay is doubled."

He pronounced the word mate in the barbarous accent current on Cape Cod. "Met." It is but one of his ways of winning people to him.

"Here's the key," said Hussey, and offered his soul as well.

I threw down the axe and watched him walk away, Hussey tall and thin and awkward, his red wrists and hands falling far below the edge of his sleeves, his head bent and cocked to one side to accommodate Sam's voice; Sam, shorter than Hussey, but twice as broad across the shoulders, moving with the sinuous grace and roll of a ship's cat.

Both wore the somber gray of Quakers, but whereas one was but a humble gangling member of the Meeting, the other was a personage of distinction, and his garb the uniform of an aristocrat. Sam was ever a figure of adventure and romance, beautiful and thrilling beyond the telling. Not a man nor a woman nor a child but stopped to look at him, I noticed, and pause in what he had been doing, and draw in deep breaths as though his lungs ached for sea air.

True, some devout members turned righteous backs on him, after they had filled their eyes. True, some women stood turned to stone. But the eyes of girls brightened at his coming, and their little mouths opened, and their wet teeth shone; and the brightness remained in their faces long after he had passed.

Poor Hussey. Like so many others I know, he will be Sam's forever.

And forever he will serve the sea. But I should not pity him. He loves the sea, has always loved it. His talk has ever been of whales and whaling, and ships, and storms at sea. He loves the sea as I love books, and trees, and fields, and rocks, and friendly houses, and a steady-burning flame at night beside my bed—and Sally Starbuck.

It was shortly after I left the woodpile that I saw Sally.

She was coming toward me down Judith Chase's Lane; and I knew her, but denied it fiercely. I knew her walk, the way her arms swung, the motion of her dear blonde head. I began to tremble, like Hussey talking to Sam. I told myself, oh so heatedly, that it wasn't Sally, it couldn't be Sally. Sally was in Boston, had been in Boston these three months.

But it was Sally, a little taller, it seemed to me, a little sweeter, a little prettier, a little more like the great lady I had always fancied her. It was Sally, and I could hardly speak to her, could scarce thank her for this diary she brought me, could hardly endure the exquisite embarrassment of looking at her.

Sally. Seventeen now. Sally in a russet dress and a scarlet cape that matched the colors of the flying leaves!

Coward that I am, I fled from her. After a few words I turned and ran, my heart thumping against my ribs as though it were terrified, my breath caught in the brambles of my throat, as my heavy feet were caught in the weeds and the tall clumps of dying grass.

She was laughing as I fled; but it was a kindly, sympathetic laugh. Angels must laugh that way, sometimes, at things we mortals do. Why did I run? I never ran from her before. Why did I nearly die of terror? She was always as close to me, and as dear to me, and as natural to me as my right hand.

Seventeen! Why are girls always older than boys, even when their years are less? Why was Sally born two years ahead of me? Had it been two thousand, I think, I should feel easier about it. Yet, perhaps not. In some old tome, I should some day come across a drawing of her. And I should feel the same pain of her in my heart, know the same ache of realizing she is not for me, and never was, and never could be.

A Methodist. Old Barnabas Starbuck's granddaughter.

These things I could overcome. But the two years? How can I ever surmount them?

Why did I run from her? Because I knew? Because I realized? Because I cannot stand the torture of loving her, and knowing she will never be mine?

"There's a deal of laughter in the lass, poor thing," my father used to say of Sally, when he saw us together, "but she means no harm to anyone."

Poor thing indeed. I have never read in all the books in my father's house, in all the books in Nantucket and New Bedford and Falmouth and Edgartown, any story such as mine; a girl like Sally, bright and warm and radiant as the sun, and a poor fifteen-year-old lout of a Quaker, terribly, hopelessly, body-and-soul in love with her—so steeped in the impossibility of his love that he runs from her as though she were the plague.

Ah poor thing! Poor thing indeed.

Chapter Two

NOV. 5. Bright, but with a hint of winter in it. Sam is packing his sea chest for the voyage. Medical instruments, medicines, herbs, pills. And guns and knives and other weapons. Axes, beads, a bolt of gaudy calico. Probably no other man ever set out on a whaling voyage so peculiarly equipped.

What do these things mean? That he will desert ship at the first South Seas island? He has always wanted to be the head of a savage tribe, "sultan and pope and absolute czar," as he says, to reign with a rule of iron, to lead his faithful slaves in victorious war on other savage tribes.

Perhaps I should speak to Father. Still, Father thinks it better that Sam spend his days at sea than here in Nantucket where there are so many temptations for him. He does not trust Sam in the store. Money disappears mysteriously from the till. Wine evaporates from the wine pipes—yet does not wet the floor of the wine cellar. Sam spends too much money in the tavern. He spends too much time with dubious women. His name has become a scandal to all of the Meeting of Friends. Perhaps it is wisdom that guides Father. And yet—

"Thee was always a whining, puling, sly, oversuspicious and under-bold little bookworm," Sam berated me when I came into his room and saw the queer treasures he was packing. It pleases him sometimes to use plain speech. Perhaps he does it but to plague me, for I never use it. If we say "thee" and "thy" to God, why should we address mere men in these words?

"But keep thy mouth shut and thine eyes blind, and I'll not disturb thy smug green piety, Brother George," he finished.

Upon which he smiled that charming warming smile of his, and put an arm around me, and pressed me gently to him.

"Don't mind me, lad," he said. "It's whale oil talking in me, and whale's blood, and—and a frump of a woman that gives me no peace."

How I used to adore this brother of mine! What stories I made up about him. He was the hero of every book I devoured, of every tale I tried to write. Now—yet perhaps I wrong him. What does a fifteen-year-old boy know of men, especially such a man as my brother?

He began to talk of Captain Worth, newly promoted from first mate. That man must be kin to Satan, if all Sam says of him is true. But Sam is as neat at embroidering, in his way, as Sally herself.

"He was the burliest, sullenest, most iron-handed mate on the seven seas before he froze his fingers. It was nothing for him to storm into the forecastle, lance in hand, and hurl the blade at any-one who didn't jump at his command. He killed a man like that, I've heard—drove the point clean through him, the way Eskimos spear fish."

"Why sail with such a man as master?" I couldn't help asking. Sam laughed, and patted me on the head, as though I were a child.

"Mates are all like that," he said, "on all American ships. Especially on whalers. I hate whalers, and whalemen. But this time—"

He didn't finish what he meant to say. He started again to pack; and I went strolling through the town. But I didn't see Sally.

NOV. 7. A night of gritty stars. They held the dance last night in Barnabas Starbuck's loft. The *Globe*'s crew tacked a few flags here and there and festooned the rafters with canvas. Sam picked up some ship lamps, and some from the old lighthouse. He had Hussey bore holes in a lot of barrels. The lanterns were placed in these barrels; and the barrels, suspended with light cordage, served as chandeliers.

There were more chandeliers than lanterns, so a number were equipped with sperm tapers. The floor had been holystoned, the cobwebs had been removed, the windows had been cleaned. The place was gay and inviting—but there was the smell of oil permeat-ing it. Even the wind that came in through the open windows didn't help. The men didn't mind the smell. They were so used to it they didn't even notice it.

At the last moment Sam remembered he had no musicians. John Lumbard, second mate on the *Globe,* gibed at Sam for his forgetfulness, and several men laughed. Sam didn't like it, I could see, but pretended to enjoy the joke on himself.

"There's a fiddler on the *Lyra,*" Lumbard said.

Sam and John and Cyrus Hussey and others of us went immediately to the whaleship, tied up not far from the *Globe,* and boarded her. Sam's shouting brought the head of a colored man up from a hatchway.

"Come up, gut-scraper," Sam cried, "and bring your fiddle. You're wanted ashore to play for a party."

The colored man was frightened as he caught sight of Lumbard's pockmarked face in the lamplight. I felt sorry for him. But there was something amusing in his fright. He said he dare not leave the ship, whereupon Sam and Lumbard grabbed him, pulled him up on deck as easily as though he were a baby, and Sam went below for the violin. Lumbard held the captive, and booted him several times.

"Lemme go," the colored man kept saying. "Lemme go. Ah's only a po' Nigge'. Ah cain' fiddle fo' white folks nohow. Ah gotta stay aboa'd. Ah gotta. Dem's o'de's, suh. Cap'n's o'de's."

Sam handed him a half pint of real "ginniwine Jimmecky," undiluted. The colored man—William Humphries—poured the liquor down his great throat, shuddered, smacked his lips, beamed, and bowed his head to each of us.

"Huh! Dat smacks!" he cried. "Yah! Yah! Yah! Dat sho' smacks!"

He slapped his mighty thigh with his mighty right hand. He finished the rum in two swallows and tossed the bottle over the side.

"Ah's finished wid de bottle," he said, "and ah's done wid de ship. Us goes."

He looked scornfully about the deck, and spat.

I watched him for a long while, fascinated, as he sat on a chair against the wall of the loft, tuning up his instrument, and playing it. He was the first Negro I had ever seen. I'd read about them, of course, and seen pictures of them. But until then I had no idea they were such huge creatures, that their teeth were so white, their skin so satiny, so shiny, and their voices so rich and powerful and sweet. Nor had I thought they were so humble, so tremendously eager to please, so good-natured under rough treatment. And yet this man had danger in him too.

He played well, surprisingly well. A man such as this could never have been taught to play save by himself.

I was so absorbed in watching Humphries, and speculating about him that it was almost with a sense of shock I realized people were dancing all about me, and some standing against a wall were singing, and some were keeping time with the heels of their heavy boots.

And there was Sally. In Sam's arms.

Her sweet, round face was looking up into his, with a look I'd never seen on it before—a blindly trusting, openly adoring look. Mouth parted. Eyes shining. And Sam's face! Soft, tender, fond, yet fiercely passionate.

I couldn't bear it. I hurried out of the loft. I hurried down to the wharf, and past the ships, and far along the shore. And I wept. I am not ashamed to record it. I wept like a boy who has lost everything dear to him. I was too hurt to care whether anyone saw me or not.

She was in rose-colored silk. A nosegay of bright flowers nestled over her heart. A wine-colored bonnet, such as no other girl in Nantucket ever saw, dangled by its ribbon from Sam's forearm.

I sat on a rock, a cold wet rock, and took a mournful pleasure shouting her name to the dark and the wind and the sea. And the wind mocked me, and the sea mocked me, echoing her name, "Salleeeeee! Sall-eeeeee!"

I didn't know Sam was aware she had come home from Boston. I had said nothing to him of meeting her. When did he see her? What did he say to her? And she to him?

She always had a fancy for him, I remember now. Even when she was a little girl. She always wanted to hear the stories he told me. He was always a hero to her. He was always a man. I was never anything to her but a little boy, a child two years younger than herself.

A man must have killed a whale to be a man in this town. Sam has slain dozens of them. Perhaps if, like me, he'd never seen Leviathan— No, she would still adore him, as so many women have.

I am afraid for her. She'll break her heart. God help her.

DEC. 1. Sam has bought many kinds of seeds for the voyage, even pumpkin seeds. Why? Certainly not to feed the whales with.

DEC. 2. I must go down to the sea in ships. I cannot stand it here. To see Sally now, to stroll with her, to talk to her—even with Sam away—I could not. It would be torture.

Ah, yes, there's a deal of laughter in the lass, poor thing. I passed her home last night, and heard her laugh. And Sam laughed too.

I shouldn't be jealous. I shouldn't be afraid for her. Even Sam could never harm her. Why am I such a child?

Chapter Three

DEC. 4. Clear and cold. As dismal a day as I remember. I have at last made up my mind. Three years is a long, long time. But I shall be eighteen when I come back. And it may be that I shall come back alone.

What is Sally to such a man as Sam? Is she the "frump of a woman" he spoke of a few days ago—the woman who would give him no peace? Impossible.

She gives me no peace either. That is why I am going to sea in the *Globe*. I could not endure it here, even with Sam gone. I should always be the little bookworm in her eyes. He would forever be the heroic adventurer.

I should be thrilled, realizing I shall have adventures to rival those of my brother Sam—even more exciting adventures, it may be. Yet I am not thrilled. I am actually frightened at what lies ahead of me —and more than sad for all I shall have to leave behind.

And it seems to me that what I am doing is as futile as Sam's pumpkin seeds—that I will be the same when I return as I am now, even if I have slaughtered all the whales in the Atlantic and the Pacific.

DEC. 15. At sea. Cold. Sally came to see us off this morning. And she looked so little, standing in the shadow of her grandfather, and so pretty, and so forlorn—the tears streaming down her face—that I fled the deck. I had been standing with Cyrus Hussey. She saw me. She waved her hand—her pink-mittened hand—and smiled. Then she looked away from me, looking for Sam.

Sam was below at the time, I think. At any rate I did not see him on deck. Nor did Sally. Of that I am sure.

Three years! God help me!

DEC. 16. We are ashore! We were hardly out of the harbor when an accident happened to the rigging. We had to put back to have the damage repaired. Gilbert Smith, who is boat steerer next to Sam, says it is a bad omen. And so say others of the crew. But I cannot see in it anything but good fortune. I shall see Sally again before the *Globe* is ready to sail.

My father embraced me, after the first moment of surprise. His eyes were dulled with moisture. I burst into his store, as soon as we had arrived from Edgartown, and blurted out the news of our accident. I never saw such a glow of happiness on any human face—not even on Sally's as she looked at Sam, dancing with him in her grandfather's loft. I really think that if I broached the subject, Father would do all in his power to keep me home with him. But no. I must go to sea. I must.

DEC. 21. At sea. Rough, and bitter cold. I have almost recovered from my first seasickness, and have learned a chanty.

> When the waves dash high, and the sky grows black,
>   And pale lubbers crawl below, sir;
> The whaler mounts on the old whale's back,
>   And darts his lance as he goes, sir.
> Oh for the life of a whaler, oh!
>   Yo, ho, and a heave, ho, he!
> Hauling here, bawling there,
>   With a yo, ho, ho, and a heave, ho, he!
> Steadily, readily, greasily, merrily
>   Goes the whaler's life at sea.

It is a fine song, especially when sung by all hands. Gilbert Smith taught it to me. Smith is old. He must be all of twenty-five. And he has peculiar ways. But I like him. He's a kindly man. "Friend George," he calls me.

Strange that we two good Quakers should have gone together to a Methodist meeting. Very strange, now that I think of it; yet at the time it seemed only natural and right.

We met, in our Quaker clothes, that Sunday morning after we put back; and after giving each other good day, Gilbert Smith suggested a stroll.

"God has made a grand day for a stroll, Friend George," he said, "and we have time before the meeting."

We were astonished to learn, when we neared the Methodist house of worship, that we had strolled overlong, and would be late for the Quaker service.

"But the Methodies worship Him too," Smith pointed out. "Better to be in time for the Methodies who start later, than tardy for the Quakers; and thee knows the Methodies will never press two Quakers for a penny. It would be unbrotherly, and un-Christian."

There was a queer smile in his mild blue eyes.

"And after the services, Friend George," he said, "I shall walk with Barnabas Starbuck, whilst thee makes converse with the girl."

A landward breeze was blowing. The surf was booming, spray shooting up off the sides of whalers rocking in the harbor, and the sea crawling nigh to the weeds behind the churchyard.

'May God forgive me my sins,' I thought, 'but I must see her, even in a Methodist meeting.' We entered unobtrusively, and took seats in the rear, and listened to the Methodist minister, the Reverend Eliphalet Coffin, a shad-bellied old man, a former whaling captain, as he expounded the gospel.

It was some time before I saw Sally. I found her through a sudden glimpse of her grandfather's profile. Wrinkled, stern, masterful, implacable, miserly, that face. Sally's face next to it, sad, and beautiful, and sweet, was turned toward the face of the preacher.

The girl and the old man sat next to the memorial window, donated by Starbuck, a beautiful stained glass with an image of our Lord stilling the waves—and through one broken pane I caught a glimpse of tall masts swaying in the wind.

Underneath the window, on a gilded plate, were the words, "Sacred to the memory of Miles Starbuck, who, in the bows of his boat, was killed by a sperm whale off the Island of Tahiti, Oct. 2, 1819."

I couldn't see the plate where I sat; but I knew the words well. I was present when Barnabas Starbuck first wrote them down. He was seated at his desk, his face as inscrutable as it was now, and Sally and I sat together in a big chair and wept together for her father.

What the Reverend Coffin said I knew not for watching Sally and her grandfather and trying to read their thoughts. Once I saw the old man staring at the memorial window; once I saw him put his hand tenderly, I thought, over Sally's.

It was a long sermon, and there were many hymns, the words of which I had never heard; yet it seemed but a short time until we stood outside the House of God, and Starbuck took a pinch from his jeweled snuffbox and sneezed with the suddenness and fury of a volcanic eruption, and greeted Gilbert Smith and me with vehemence and surprise.

Smith began to talk of the accident to the *Globe*, and Starbuck forgot his granddaughter. So we strolled together behind him, and at a little distance.

How pretty Sally was in her lavender gown and pleated bonnet, the French coat trimmed with fur, and the dainty muff that held her hands! How often I've seen her in lavender! It's the most fetching color in the world.

We smiled, and touched hands, and spoke a little; but it was not until we reached her home that courage came to me.

"Sam had to stay aboard," I said. And then I added quickly, "You love him, don't you, Sally?"

"Yes," she said. She was so proud of it, so glad of it!

"You've always loved him, haven't you?"

I had to say it. I had to.

"I've always loved you both," she answered softly.

This time it was she who fled; and I who stood looking after her.

"Thee has said good-bye?" Gilbert Smith inquired as we trudged through the narrow streets. "I have a feeling thee will see her again. But thy brother—" He shook his shaggy head from side to side, solemnly. "Thy brother is a man of violence. And there is blood in his pumpkin seeds that will grow foul fruit."

"Blood?" I said.

"Aye, blood, and no blood of a whale, Friend George, I venture."

As we neared his home, Gilbert's little dog, a white fox terrier, came running toward us. Gilbert caught him up in his arms, and patted his shivering sides. Then he unbuttoned the top part of his gray coat, and thrust the creature into the warmth of his bosom.

"Thee's cold, little Daniel," he said. "Yet thee can warm me when no other can."

Daniel is the pet of the ship. He can say his prayers and do other tricks. Smith says he understands every word one says.

"Pray, Daniel," he commands. And Daniel, upon the word, sits back on his haunches, closes his eyes, droops his head, and puts his forepaws up in the attitude of one rapt in devotion. When one says "Amen," he leaps quickly up, and begins to frolic in an abandon of joy.

I too have prayed like that. I have been rapt. And hope has leaped up in me, and frolicked with as joyous antics—only to die, never to rise again.

Sally came to the wharf in Edgartown as we were casting off; and found us at the rail together, Sam and me.

"God bless you," she called. "God bless you and keep you both, and bring you back safe."

Suddenly there was a narrow strip of water 'twixt ship and wharf, and gradually it widened; a dirty, greasy, green strip of water, with the sun glinting on patches of oil and turning them into so many rainbows. Then there was only a blur where Sally was, and whitecaps on the water, and a wind whistling past my ears, and Captain Worth calling orders in a tremendous, angry voice.

Good-bye, my dear. I know, somehow, I shall never see you again.

Chapter Four

JAN. 20, 1823. Cool and calm. A month or so of sailing. More than a thousand miles of travel. Ever since New Year's day, until this morning, it has been storming. And never a sight of a whale.

I have been so seasick I wanted to die. That passed. I am becoming more or less a real sailor. Yet I am still homesick.

I still dream of Indian Row, and Judith Chase's Lane, and Orange Street, and Stone Alley, and the elms running uphill from Straight Wharf to Uppertown. And Sally, in a lavender dress, sitting near a lilac bush in her garden, her little fingers playing over her needlepoint work, her eyes on the ivy that crawls across the red bricks of her house—seeing not ivy at all, but a whaling ship at sea. This, although it be winter, and Nantucket buried in snow.

The food is very bad. The water is rancid. Captain Worth had it stored in old oil casks. I wonder if he drinks that water himself; or has he a private supply? I wonder more and more about him. He isn't the man I thought him. I do hope nothing happens to him. Yet, the way the crew talk, or rather whisper, I'm afraid. He must know they hate him. But he doesn't mind, if he does know. At least he's brave. And he's a whaler. Everybody admits that.

I liked him. I liked him very much the first time I saw him. I thought him a godly man, standing there with his legs apart, his stumps of hands in his coat pockets, and a benevolent smile on his face. He was just what a sea captain ought to be, I thought, tanned, wrinkled, tall, lean, built to hold to the deck in any wind, four-square and forthright, a plug of finecut in his mouth, laughter and strength and tolerance in his sea-green eyes.

"So you're Sam Comstock's brother," he said.

"Yes," my father answered—and how afraid I was that father would offer to shake hands! "This is my son George."

"A likely boy," Captain Worth said. "Maybe he'll be a boat steerer, a harpooner, like his brother."

"He's a little young," my father said—using the tone he employed always in bargaining with someone. The horse was a trifle old, he'd say, but still stout in limb and wind for all that. The gun was a little old-fashioned, maybe, he'd admit, but its sights were true, and there was still a deal of good shooting in it. He was going to add that I was a little young, but strong and willing, and eager to go to sea on a whaler. But Captain Worth didn't give him a chance.

"Of course he's young," he said, and laughed. It was a nice, fine, man's laugh. "I like 'em young. Most of my crew are young—fine young scamps out of Falmouth, Nantucket, Martha's Vineyard, and New Bedford. Anywhere from fifteen to nineteen, every man jack of 'em. The finest lads in the world, sir, the very finest. I'll make whalers of them too. They'll be men when they come back. Yes sir. Men!"

All the time I was studying the captain I was wondering about his hands. Sam had told me the captain had no hands, merely stumps. He'd lost his fingers years ago on a voyage into the Arctic. He'd been the only one out of a ship's boat to survive. All the others had frozen to death; but Captain Worth had lost only his fingers and his thumbs. They'd been frozen stiff as icicles, my brother had told me, and had come off like chalk, one by one, as he'd knocked them against chunks of ice, against the gunwale of the boat, or against each other.

I still don't know whether the story is true. I've never seen the captain that his hands weren't in his jacket pockets. How he eats, how he drinks, how he does any of the things a man must do with his hands, I do not know.

I've seen him many times since that December day; but I've never seen him smile again, nor heard him laugh. He curses the men. His voice is savage, loud, shrill. It makes one jump.

JAN. 23. Still rough, but it doesn't affect me now. If only the men would stop talking! They are all surly. They are all sullen. They are all afraid.

William Lay confided to me tonight how he came to be here. Starbuck heard the noise in his loft that night, the music, the stomping of feet, the singing of men, the laughter of girls. He sent Lay to investigate, and Sam, taking him for a spy, rushed him aboard the *Globe* and thrust him into one of the big oil casks in the hold. There he remained all night. He could stand erect. He could sit down. He could jump up, but not high enough to lift off the lid. He couldn't climb up the inside of the cask, for it was coated with oil. His handsome blond hair was matted and soaked with dirty oil, his clothes were wet and foul, and he was most uncomfortable and most indignant; but when Sam smiled and explained it was all a joke, he forgave him readily and even offered to stay on board.

Starbuck, Lay says, went to Magistrate Folger, and stamped and fumed and pounded his cane on the floor, and bellowed and threatened, and finally had a warrant issued for Lay's release. But it was too late. The *Globe* had already left Nantucket, to ship supplies at Edgartown. Lay showed me the warrant, and I laughed at its peculiar phrases—"a certain William Lay whom divers unknown youths, not having the fear of God before their eyes, did bung-up within a certain oil cask, an unsavory operation and a most unChristian trespass upon the liberty of said citizen."

But afterwards I did not laugh. It occurred to me that we are all bunged up in this oil cask of a ship, and here we must stay, God help us, until we are delivered. And, the way the men talk, and act, the way they look at the captain, and the bad food, and the bad water, it makes me think some dreadful act of violence will deliver us soon.

And Gilbert Smith's words haunt me— "Blood? Aye, and no blood of a whale, Friend George, I venture."

Chapter Five

JAN. 26. At sea. We saw two whales yesterday, shortly after dawn. I was awakened by cries from aloft. "Buh-loes!" It sounded just like that. "Thar buh-loes!" Long, loud cries that got under my skin and made me shake with excitement. I knew what it meant. "There she blows!" A whale. A sperm whale. I swung out of my hammock, dressed quickly, and rushed up on deck. The rigging was black with men, and most of them were yelling.

"Two sparm whales," Third Mate Nathaniel Fisher told me as I passed him on the companionway. "'Bout three miles off."

Captain Worth crowded on all sail. We gulped down a hasty breakfast, and got the boats ready for lowering. I was still shaking with such excitement that I got in everybody's way. I couldn't help looking at those whales, frisking on the surface of the water, blowing up little jets of steam. It was a fine morning. The sea was almost calm, and the rays of the rising sun were staining the clouds and the water.

While I watched, both whales flipped up their tails, and disappeared into the cold red and silver depths of the ocean—leaving a patch of white water where they had been.

"Sounded," said William Lay, who stood next to me by the rail.

I laughed, because I had wanted to say the word myself. That's queer, isn't it?—how all boys want to pretend they are grown up in the presence of other boys. Neither Lay nor I had ever seen a whale before. Yet both of us wished to impress the other with our qualities as calm and seasoned old whalers.

"They'll breach again," I said. Then Lay laughed.

In half an hour the whales reappeared, but now they were about four miles away from us. The wind was light; we were losing in the chase.

"Lower away!" bellowed Captain Worth.

We made a rush for the boats. I was frightened—a little. Suppose I did something that wasn't right! Suppose I turned coward! Suppose I found myself not strong enough to row—and had to let someone else do my work!

But nothing happened. At least nothing I had feared. I went in the captain's boat, the bow boat, with my brother Sam as boat steerer. I saw nothing of the whale now—since I sat at an oar with my back to him. I pulled, and found it not so difficult to pull in unison with others as I had fancied.

Our boat was in the lead. All I could see were the other whale boats, sails fluttering in the slight wind, the men pulling in rhythm on their oars—and back of them, rising and falling on the breathing bosom of the sea, the great ship with its tiers of canvas.

The *Globe* fell far astern as we rowed. The other whale boats, setting their sterns'ls, went by us—and now there was nothing to see but miles of glinty green water, and a flight of gulls, and the rays of the sun slanting down through a rift in a mass of gray-black clouds.

Suddenly the wind stopped blowing. The running sea stopped running. We were in the middle of a still, dead calm.

"There!" my brother's voice cried suddenly, making the blood leap in my veins. "She blows! She blows!"

"You've run past him," Captain Worth said, and swore a fearful oath.

Instantly Sam swept the boat around, and I saw one of the whales. The boats of Mates Beetle and Fisher were bearing down on him,

Beetle under mainsail, gaff-topsail, and stuns'l. Beetle was nearest him, Fisher about a mile astern. The monster was a quarter mile or more to Beetle's larboard, and heading across his bow.

"Spring to it," the captain roared. "Jerk her up!"

We rowed furiously, racing against our own excitement. For a few minutes I lost sight of the whale. Then he was close by—a mountainous object shooting a column of water high into the air. I saw his hump plainly, cutting through foaming water. Then I saw his head, a tremendous head. It was bigger than our forecastle. It was gray spotted, and shiny black. Each gray spot was bigger than the top of an oil barrel. And then I saw his flukes—broad enough to span our quarter-deck—sweep up and up and up into the sky, pitch black against the clouds. They seemed to blot out the sun, and cast a shadow over the entire ocean. Up, up, up they went—and swiftly, gracefully, majestically down again into the deep.

I couldn't speak, even to say "Sounded." It was the most beautiful thing I had ever seen, the most thrilling.

We were so near Beetle's boat that I could hear his grunt of disgust and disappointment.

Hours of rowing followed that awe-inspiring vision of Leviathan, minutes of bailing, and minutes of munching hardtack and swallowing water. We raised our stuns'l and jib, to catch a freshening wind —and now it was the captain's voice that cried, "Thar blows! Thar blows!"

I looked over my left shoulder and saw him pointing. I saw the stump of his right hand. I shuddered, involuntarily, and turned my head quickly—but could not shut out the sight.

We were moving slowly now, and I knew we were astern of the whale, creeping up on him. Suddenly I heard him spout. It was a sound like no other on earth—stirring, echoing.

"Whuff!"

And then the hiss and swish of power as the jet of mist went upward.

"Whuff!"

A gust of wind from a cavern; a catapult of breath to shake the sea itself! I felt the boat rock, as my heart rocked, at the sound.

I turned my head. I couldn't help it. And there was my brother, naked above the waist, ready to hurl a harpoon. The muscles stood out of his broad back and his long arms. One bare foot was pressed hard against the bottom of the boat, the other solid against a thwart. The iron was in his right hand. He drew his arm back, slowly, slowly—so slowly I couldn't breathe. And then he hurled the weapon, and I saw it sink deep—"chock up to the hitches."

Before I could breathe again Sam had thrown a second iron—and blood was matting his hair and running in little streams down his back.

"He's fast!" he cried.

I was frightened, seeing the blood. But it wasn't Sam's blood. It was the whale's. Gore was shooting out of the black and gray hump, even as steam was shooting out of the spotted head. The whale frightened and sickened me with his pain. His flukes rose and fell, rose and fell, and his gigantic body writhed and twisted and thrashed, and beat the water into froth. Everybody in our boat, and in Beetle's—which had come up to starboard—shouted with joy. Everybody but me.

The suffering monster sounded suddenly. One moment he was there before me, shaking and coloring the sea. The next moment he was gone, and the waters were calm, and clean. Then I noticed that the rope, the line, was running swiftly, hissing and smoking out of the tub, spinning like mad around the loggerhead, and flowing out of the bows into the sea.

"Wet line," Captain Worth shouted. "Wet line."

I had forgotten. But, at the captain's shout, I remembered my duty and seized a bucket of water, I poured it over the line. The smell of its burning was strong in my nostrils. I was amazed at that. I didn't know, I couldn't comprehend, that friction was at work on that rope—though I should have known. So many, many old whale-men had told me all there was to know of ropes, and the speed at which they travel when a whale is on the other end. Without that water the rope might have burst into flame!

The line ceased smoking, began to slow. Captain Worth stood up, a lance held tightly between his two stumps. Sam hauled in the line. He hauled it slowly, at first, then swiftly. It was slack. The whale had escaped. The irons had drawn.

I was sorry for Sam, seeing the chagrin on his face; yet I was happy too. I had such an admiration for that whale, and the heroic fight he had made.

But almost immediately we saw him breaching, half a mile away, heading NNW. We pursued again. Again we came close to him. Again Sam hurled an iron into his hump. His flukes shot up, poised high above us, and fell. There was a report like the crack of thunder. Our boat rocked as though it must founder. Water splashed upon us like torrential rain, blinding us, stinging our eyes. Sam, with the second iron poised to throw, stumbled and fell—but hurled the iron truly in spite of everything.

Once more we were fast. Once more the sea was lashed to fury and churned to foam and blood. Once more the wounded beast sought refuge in the depths, and the line hissed and smoked.

Presently, as though a volcano had spewed him up, the mighty creature broke water close to us. He surged up big and awful as a tower. He dropped to the floor of the ocean, facing us, and came toward us, his jaws opening and closing. His mouth was as big and open as Uncle Shadrach's barn door, as big as our own attic at home, as big as a church. His lower jaw glistened with teeth, and the huge sockets in his upper jaw, into which those teeth fitted, stared at me like so many fierce and hungry eyes. I think I tried to scream. But I was too terrified to utter a sound.

A moment more and he would have swallowed us down, boat and men and weapons and line and sails. But he never reached us. While he was still a few yards from us he raised his flukes, and slid down out of our sight.

"He's loose again," Sam said. He was not excited, merely puzzled. He looked at Captain Worth.

"Four irons drawed," the captain said. "And you call yourself a harpooner?"

"The blubber was too rich and soft to hold them against the strain of the line," Sam excused himself. "The irons went in, sir. You saw that."

"I saw a hundred bar'ls get away from you," the captain answered. "That's what I saw."

He had dropped the lance, and his hands were again in his pockets. It was getting dark now. I wondered where the day had gone. The lights of our ship showed far away. On the rim of the sea.

We pulled for them with aching muscles and bodies wet with perspiration, blood, and green salt water.

Chapter Six

JAN. 28. Rain. The new man's name is Joseph Thomas.

I thought he was dead. He had probably been in the boat for a week or more. If he had any companions with him they must have died of hunger and thirst. Maybe they went crazed and jumped overboard. How Thomas survived I don't know. Maybe by catching flying fish. Sometimes they leap into a boat, Sam says.

It was awful to see the man naked, breathing through his ribs. I shall never forget that. I shall never forget his eyes. Dead man's eyes. He looked Spanish to me, or Portuguese. With all those whiskers on his face, and his skin peeling where it wasn't tanned, he looked certainly some kind of foreigner. But his name is Thomas, and surely that is American.

Did he tell his name to the captain, I wonder? Or did he write it? For all I know Captain Worth may have made up the name for him.

If it hadn't been for the fog we might never have found him. Thomas might really be dead now, drifting around in the open boat. He might have passed the *Globe* without seeing us, without being seen.

Maybe he's not a mute. The fact that he hasn't said anything to a soul aboard the *Globe*—unless it was to Captain Worth—doesn't mean he can't talk.

There's something mysterious, something eerie about the man, something ghostly. Looking at him makes me shiver.

We were chasing a whale when the fog shut down on us. We lost the whale, and found Joe Thomas. He was lying in the bottom of a boat. It was a boat from the whaler *Linda* of Falmouth. Sam threw him a rope, meaning to tow him. But the man was too weak to catch it. He couldn't even try. Sam had to maneuver our boat alongside, then jump down, pick the man up in his arms, and get back into our boat.

"He's dead," I said. I didn't want to touch him. His mouth was open, and his eyes were open. My skin crawled. I'd never seen a dead man.

Sam thrust him into my arms. I held onto him all right, though the boat rocked under me. I didn't feel his weight because of the intensity of my emotions. I placed him upright on a seat, quickly, to give my hands relief from the contact with his cold and clammy skin. Lay produced a little water in a tin cup. Thomas could scarce drink it. Weird noises that were not human came through his cracked black lips. He stared at us with his dead eyes, then slept, slumping a little on his seat.

Captain Worth had steaming grog administered to him, and a bit of salt meat. Mate Fisher brought him some dry clothes from the slop chest, and assigned him a hammock in the forecastle.

JAN. 30. I am still throbbing with my experiences of this morning; and surer than ever that dire things are brooding over this ship.

We had pulled up to a whale, coming from his stern in order to keep out of his eye, and Sam had fastened one iron to him when he stood on his head, smashed his flukes down from the sky upon us, and disappeared into the sea.

It happened so swiftly I hadn't time to pray. Before I quite realized it, and while the boat was being overturned, I saw that my right foot was caught in the whirring, smoking rope that was going down, down, down with the whale. I knew I should either have my leg torn off or be drowned. Sam saw my plight a second before I did. Fortunately he hadn't hurled the second harpoon, had it still in his right hand. Quickly he brought the edge of it down on the rope, cutting it in two. The next moment we were in the water.

I couldn't thank him then, nor until a long time afterward; for I was trembling so with the narrowness of my escape that my teeth chattered; and besides, the one thought paramount in my mind was to cling to the overturned boat. I clung to it so that I could hardly let go, even when Sam and the others were trying to right it. I must have forgotten I can swim.

One of the crew, poor Joe Prass, had both legs broken. He says the whale's flukes did it. I don't wonder at that. Second Mate John Lumbard took him into his own boat and hurried him to the ship.

We managed to recover most of the equipment that went overboard when we capsized; and presently we set out again after the whale. But though we pursued him for miles, and saw him blowing every little while, we never came near him again.

It was while we were going back to the ship that I had an opportunity to speak to Sam, and he laughed and pushed me away. Then he sat down close beside me and whispered.

"It was nothing," he said. "Only, I couldn't afford to lose a man. I'll be needing you on my side soon."

At first, I thought, foolishly, that he might be hinting at mutiny, something desperate at least in which he and others would contend against Captain Worth. But then I remembered all the strange ambitions of which Sam has talked, and was properly ashamed of myself. No, it isn't mutiny that's in his mind. It's only that boyhood dream of being king of some balmy island in the South Seas. It's nothing worse than desertion. And I'm sure he'll get over that. For all his wildness, there's still much good in Sam.

FEB. 1. The bread was more than half moldy today. And I was told that more than three-quarters of our potatoes have rotted. Two of the crew are down with scurvy. Prass will be set ashore in Oahu.

His legs are in splints. He'll recover. But he'll always walk with a limp. No more whaling for him.

FEB. 10. Nearly two months; and we have not yet caught a whale. There is talk that we have a Jonah aboard. Joe Thomas. They forget we had the same bad luck before he came aboard. Perhaps it is because he is still a mystery that the crew talks of him thus.

It is certain that he has sailed on whalers before. He knows how to splice a rope and do a turn at the wheel, and he's a most capable blacksmith. Yet, as one watches him, beating on the anvil, shaping harpoons, straightening lances, or forming iron hoops for the oil barrels, one sees in him something sinister and extraordinary. Sparks fly. The bellows roars. Flames light up his drawn, lean, whiskered face, his dull eyes, his tight-shut mouth, his long sharp nose, his skinny arms. Lights and shadows play on the background of his rude leather apron. I wonder what thoughts beat against his brain, as his hammer beats against the red-gold iron.

Yesterday he gave Sam the harpoon he had with him in the small boat when we found him. It is made of the finest Toledo steel. He put it in Sam's hand and walked away. Sam thanked him. He made no answer. He never answers any question. He never talks. And in his eyes there's always that look of one who has died.

FEB. 12. Despite our Jonah, we caught a whale today. A big one, but not a very big one. Sam put two irons in him. Gilbert Smith, boat steerer in Mate Lumbard's boat, put two more into him; and Captain Worth, holding a lance in his stumps of hands, took out the beast's life neatly and quickly. He raised the weapon above his head, held it horizontally for a moment, then greased it into a spot behind the fin. A red geyser exploded out of the wound. The whale tumbled and fought and lacquered the green sea white. But gradually his efforts grew feebler and feebler, and presently he rolled "fin out."

It was blowing stiffly, and quite a swell set in. Night was coming on. We secured the whale, set our lights, and started back to the ship. Our water was gone. There was nothing to eat but a few crusts of bread. There were sharks all around us, nipping our oars as we pulled them through the water. It was nearly ten when we reached the vessel.

We made the whale fast alongside, with its head aft. While we were putting a weighted cord around the narrow part forward of the flukes, Mr. Lumbard's boat was beset by a huge shark. Smith killed him with a harpoon, crying, "Back into hell, thee devil, thee."

"Thomas," Captain Worth called. "Joe Thomas."

Thomas came silently across the deck from his smithy and stood looking down on us.

We waited, but Thomas made no answer.

"Git yourself a lance," Captain Worth said, "and keep night watch. These damn sharks'll eat up all our ile before we git it aboard."

There must have been fifty sharks at least. Fins would cut through the surface. Great gray monsters would leap right out of the water, teeth gleaming in the light of our lamps, and tear off chunks of blubber and flesh. I shuddered to think of any man's being made to stand and fight those voracious devils.

I didn't believe I had heard the captain aright. Where was a man to stand? "In a boat?" I asked Sam, in a whisper.

"He'll stand on the whale, of course," Sam said, "and patrol it."

"And if he falls?" I said.

Sam only shrugged his shoulders.

Second Mate Lumbard fastened a rope around Joe Thomas, pulled it up under his arms, and lowered him down to the carcass of the whale.

"If they get too much for ye," he said, "give the line a yank and we'll haul ye out of danger." He turned his pockmarked face on me. "You and Hussey stay here and watch him," he ordered. "Yank him up whensoever he's a mind to come."

I held a lamp for Thomas to see by, as the rope let him down. It was a feeble glimmer—yet enough to show me those slithering, cruel-mouthed scavengers; enough to show me the terror on Joe Thomas' dead face. I almost dropped the lamp.

Chapter Seven

FEB. 13. O, Sally, if you could only see the *Globe* at night, with the tryworks—the great ovens amidships—blazing high, changing the black of night to the red and gold of sundown, making red devils of the men!

They are all naked to the waist, shining with oil and sweat, and flecked with soot. Everything is red, fiery red, gleaming red, liquid red—even the sea and the sky. Last night, far off on the horizon, I saw what must have been another whaler with its try-pots flaring. It must have been that—but it looked like a grinning jack-o'-lantern.

I was awakened at daylight by three loud raps on the scuttle—a few hours after I had gone to my hammock following our capture of the whale. I rushed to the rail, but Thomas was no longer there fending off the sharks with his lance. He was gone, but the sharks remained.

Immediately after breakfast the huge cutting tackle was hoisted to the lower masthead and slung from tremendous straps. Then the stage for the cutters was swung out over the side; and the tackle, with the blubber hooks fastened to it, was hauled out over the gangway. The mates, Beetle, Lumbard, and Fisher, with monkey ropes around their waists—fastened from inboard—went out on the cutting stages. They were armed with keen-edged spades. Beetle yawned through his massive walrus mustache, his head high in the air, as if trying to overtop his taller mates. Lumbard picked his teeth with a quill, his pitted face impassive as a mask. Fisher stood staring down at the carcass below him and the sharks that worried it. His hand cupped his crumpled ear, as if to catch the swish of their tails.

Not one of them seemed to think his perch was at all perilous, or that the work he was about to do was of the least importance.

Gilbert Smith was lowered down by ropes onto the carcass. Lumbard cut a place between neck and fin, and Smith inserted the blubber hook. We on deck bore the purchase of the tackle to the windlass, and heaved it taut. Beetle and Lumbard and Fisher worked away methodically, cutting off the head, severing the lower jaw first.

It was twelve feet long, that jaw, and a line of great sharp teeth marched about it. There must have been more than forty teeth, each jutting four or five inches out of the flesh, but I didn't have time to count them.

The head, secured with chains, was left in the water astern, and the mates now began to slice the blubber into long narrow spiral strips, the "blankets." As the mates cut, and the strips unwound, the whale turned and turned—like a ball of string under the claws of a kitten—and the sharks became more daring.

By midafternoon, while the blubber was still coming aboard, we had the tryworks hot, had cut some of the blanket pieces into chunks, known as "horses," or "horse pieces," had cut these again into lesser bits known as "books," and were feeding them to the flames.

As I stood in front of the try-pots I had a curious sensation that

I was in danger. I swerved quickly, almost slipping on the oil-covered deck, and turned to see Captain Worth bearing down upon me.

"You, George Comstock," he said.

His eyes were bloodshot. His thin narrow lips jerked at the corners. There was the smell of liquor on his breath.

"Git a bucket and scoop up the ile in the scuppers," he commanded. "Can't waste any ile. This damn carcass will make little enough as it is. Git."

I got.

It came on to blow shortly after I began my new task, and Beetle sent some of the crew into the rigging.

"Storm acomin' up," Hussey said, passing close to me. "They'll be h'istin' the whale's head soon."

I didn't answer, for at the time I thought I was going to be sick again. The ship was careening to starboard, bending to the weight of the blanket pieces, as they came aboard, and the weight of the whale too; and the sea was rocking her in a way my stomach didn't like.

It darkened suddenly; and the sea increased in violence. I bent to my work steadily, for the scupper was running with oil; so much so that, no matter how many buckets I took out of it, it always seemed half full. I heard the captain bellowing now and then; and, looking up, occasionally, saw him darting here and there like a crazy man. He's grown a beard since we set sail, a stringy reddish that stands out straight to the fore. It was this beard that always caught my eye, so red it is, so wispy.

Suddenly I looked up, with some astonishment, to see that beard pointing at me like an accusing finger; and above it those bloodshot eyes bearing a hatred I cannot describe.

"Yes, sir," I said. I felt guilty of some heinous offense, but knew not what it was.

"For'ard," he shouted at me. "I don't call twice!"

I looked forward, and saw what I should have seen before, had I not been engrossed at my task. The head of the whale, adorned with chains, was coming up out of the sea, not astern now, but forward. The carcass of the whale was gone. The sharks were gone. The crew was hauling in the head, or what was left of it, and I was needed at the windlass.

I hurried forward, slipping a little on the canting, oil-covered deck, and took my place.

Third Mate Fisher began to sing; and we all took it up. "Yo, ho, heave, ho, he!"

The ship almost went over on her side, so great was the weight of that head we held at the end of our puny rope. She groaned in protest. She screamed that she would break her back. She cried out in every beam, in every spar and sail, that the task set for her was impossible.

Captain Worth stood to one side of us, crying "Heave!"

His hands were in his pockets, his head thrust forward like a turtle's, the beard blowing toward us like a flame.

"He's crazy," one of the men said.

"He's drunk," another answered. But we heaved, and we heaved again and again, until our arms ached, and our backs ached, and the sweat rolled out of us like grease.

Up, up, up, inch by inch, came the head. It was at the rail; but the rail seemed almost at the water's edge.

"Heave!" cried the captain. "Heave! Heave!"

We had long since ceased to sing; for we had no breath to sing with. It was all we could do to keep our places on that precipitous deck, and to maintain our grasp on the rope.

Suddenly one of the men cried out in a great deep voice: "Damn you for a madman and a miser! You'll drown us all. Cut her adrift or we'll careen!"

We almost let go our holds at this boldness.

Captain Worth took one step forward, and his hands flew out of his pockets.

"Who said that?" he cried.

But the next moment a great sea struck the ship from the larboard side, and the head of the whale came aboard, and fell with a great crash to the deck as we let go the rope.

The vessel shuddered as though she'd struck a rock. All of us went flying this way and that way about the deck. Even the captain lost his footing.

But in another moment twenty hands or more were scurrying to the starboard rail, securing the head there with chains and ropes. And no sooner had this been accomplished than the mates were shouting orders, and every man of us save the man at the wheel and the harpooners was going up aloft.

It is late now, and we are hove to. We have secured everything as snug as could be. We are riding out the gale nicely; but we still maintain a list to starboard where the mighty head is chained. Two ships' crews could pitch horseshoes on that head, were it level, or play at bowls. A chaplain could hold services there, and preach to a goodly congregation. Yet Gilbert Smith asserts it is a small head for a whale. "A small head, Friend George, but full of spermaceti, as thee will see on the morrow."

"Aye," I said. "But who was it called the captain madman and miser? Who was it damned him?"

"If I knew, Friend George," he said, "I would tell no man. Better for that man that he had never been born."

Chapter Eight

FEB. 15. The storm continues, with intervals of extreme violence, and frequent lulls. For two days we have been trying out the blubber, boiling it, and putting the oil into barrels, so that, until tonight I have had no opportunity to set down anything that has happened. Tomorrow we cut open the head, and drain it of its spermaceti, more or less as a well is drained. The spermaceti is contained in the case, or upper part of the head. The rest of the head is known as the junk; and it is rich in blubber. Smith says there may be twenty barrels of oil in that head. There were fifty in the carcass.

The men were playing cards in the forecastle a little while ago when Smith's dog Daniel came scampering in. Stephen Kidder, brother of Peter Kidder, had picked him up and was petting him when Smith arrived.

"Ungodly man," Smith shouted, "put down that dog. I'll not have him smirched with thy card-playing fingers."

Kidder immediately released the animal. There was a cynical look on his hawklike face.

"Down on thy knees, Daniel," Smith said, "and pray for mercy for thy sin."

The dog obeyed joyfully, going back on his haunches, lowering his head reverently, and covering his eyes with his little forepaws.

"Ill fares the ship," said Smith, waving his hands like Preacher Coffin, "where men beguile their idle time with the devil's work, and show a bad example to boys and dogs, Amen."

At the last word, Daniel leaped up and wet his master's hands with eager tongue.

Sometimes the men tell stories of whalers, of singing whales and fighting whales, of ships sunk by whales—as the *Essex* was sunk a few years ago—of men swallowed alive, of whalers rowing thousands of miles in little boats; of whalers eating their comrades to keep themselves alive. These tales I like. But sometimes they speak of savage women encountered in the South Pacific isles, and of women met in various civilized ports, and of women left at home. This I cannot bear.

Two of them were talking of women as Daniel prayed, knowing they would shock us Quakers.

"Come, Friend George," Smith said, "let us walk out where we can be cleansed of filth by all the winds of God."

It was so that we witnessed the scene on deck.

There was a man standing with his back to us as we came out of the companionway. He was standing erect, swaying as the ship swayed, his bare feet holding fast against the billows of oil and water that poured over them, gazing at the head of the whale, his raised hands clenched, his voice lifted in a scream that cut through the roar of wind and wave, and the groan and creak of timbers.

"Damn all whales," he cried. "Damn all whalers. Damn all stinking whaleships. Damn all whaling captains. Damn all men who go to sea—to eat swill and drink poison, to be beaten, to be scourged, to be starved and cheated and killed by madmen and misers."

Smith put his hand on my arm, and shoved me back so that I might not see the man.

"There be the man who damned the captain, Friend George," he said. "And there comes thy brother toward him."

Over Smith's right shoulder I could see Sam making his way to the starboard rail. In the eerie glow of the still-burning try-pots, I could see his face distinctly. It was a happy face, a triumphant, gloating face. It made me a little sick to see it thus.

"Quick, Friend George," Smith whispered, "thee and I must not be found here. We must not bear witness to mutiny."

We started to go, but I turned and got a glimpse of Sam, his arm around the man, helping him aft over the treacherous deck. They went, not as ship's officer and mutinous seaman, but as two friends. Later, on deck alone, going to take my trick at the wheel, I stopped and looked at the captive head. In the glare it seemed to be alive, and horribly menacing. Its near eye burned with malicious fire.

FEB. 17. I have passed through a nightmare I cannot properly record. I had scarce turned in, after being relieved at the helm, and was just falling asleep when there came a cry from above, and a clap of thunder. The ship pitched to larboard, righted itself, and listed again to starboard. I fell out of my hammock, and found half a dozen others on the forecastle floor.

"All hands on deck," someone shouted to us from above.

We rushed through the narrow door, like schoolboys at recess time, pushing and clawing at each other, and scurried up the companionway. At first I saw nothing unusual, save the steward, who was standing to one side at the top of the companionway, clinging to a stanchion.

"The whale!" he shouted. "She's broken her bonds and come alive. She's breaching on the deck. Thar blows! Thar blows!"

His eyes were dilated with terror, and his hand shook as he pointed. I looked, and saw the head of the whale, loose and on the rampage. It was as animated as though it had indeed come back to life; and many times more menacing than it had been in life.

Rain beat down on us, and a sharp wind cut through us; but we stood there by the companionway for many minutes, silent, unmoving, unaware of wind and rain.

"She's looking for her body," the steward shouted. "She's looking for her lower jaw. We're all dead men. We can't escape."

Sam, who had come up from nowhere, struck the steward so savagely the poor fellow crumpled to the deck, sliding toward the larboard rail as the vessel lurched.

The huge mass of blubber and bone did indeed seem resurrected and bent on vengeance. It had the leap of a tiger, the relentlessness of a serpent, the stealth of a cat, the spin of a top. Now and then it seemed also to possess the reasoning power and the determination of a man.

It was in about the center of the deck when I first saw it, pausing as though to reflect on the proper course of mischief. The vessel tilted to starboard. Down went the head, smashing into a mass of barrels neatly stowed by the rail. It broke their stout oak ribs and their iron hoops without effort. Oil gushed out of them and was caught by the wind to spatter us all and wash the deck—and make the captain bellow with anguish at the loss.

Back the head sailed to larboard. The steward leaped nimbly up with a cry of fright, and went into the rigging with the agility of a cat.

A section of the larboard rail had gone overboard, I saw now. That explained the clap of thunder I had heard. The whale's head had caused that damage—probably sending eight or ten barrels through that rail.

It was headed directly for that breach in the rail, but the action of the steward seemed to startle it, to make it aware of the danger of going overboard. It paused a moment, then veered, and wantonly plowed into fresh pastures of oil barrels.

As I watched the ship-shaking monster, spellbound and helpless, Gilbert Smith's dog Daniel rushed by me and went barking bravely to the assault.

Immediately Smith started after him, but the pitching of the vessel, the oil-soaked deck, and the rain that fell like little whips, shot his feet out from under him.

"Come back, Daniel," he called. "Come back."

Captain Worth, and Mate Beetle, and all the other officers were bawling at the same time, and the dog could not hear his master's voice.

The whale's head eluded the dog, crashed into a number of oil casks near the starboard rail and spun around. Daniel slipped in the oil, caromed into the berserk head, and bounded back again.

There came a sudden lull in the wind, a treacherous stillness on the sea. Some of the crew rushed toward the avalanche of blubber, stout ropes in their hands. But they had scarce approached when the wind bore down again. The head leaned back as if to spout through its blowholes, then leaped and charged. The men went crawling and scampering out of the way, like so many water rats before the surging tide. The head slid back to larboard.

"Block it!" Captain Worth screamed. He stood near the wheel, water dripping from him, his sharp-pointed beard outthrust and wavering—as though the strong fingers of the storm were pulling at it. "Block it!"

We gathered up what things were handiest, empty barrels, broken barrels, mattresses, blankets, coils of rope, try kettles. We tossed them in front of the head; but to no avail. The deck was too slippery to place these objects rightly; and we could not always judge the direction the head would take.

When we did manage to place them properly, the head slid over them without pause, crushing the barrels and the kettles as though they were children's toys. We were afraid it would smash into the foremast. We were afraid it would sail aft and demolish the try-works. We were afraid it would crash through the deck and sink the ship. At every leap, at every fall, the vessel shook as though it would go to pieces.

Yet, despite our fear, we enjoyed the antics of the dog. It was great sport for him. He attacked and nipped. He retreated. He jumped aside. He slid away. Now and then he paused to shake himself of the oil and water in his hair, and to bark. Now and then he cocked his head to one side, his tongue darting in and out, and considered a new attack.

Smith called to the dog again and again, but could not make himself heard. Finally he sank to his knees, his left arm around an oil barrel, and began to pray.

Daniel, intent on his play, didn't see this at first. When he did, he went back on his haunches, as he had been taught, bent his head reverently, and put his forepaws over his eyes. Before I could cry out a warning, before anyone could make a move to save him, the ship tilted sharply. The dog slipped to starboard. The whale's head slipped too and crushed out his life.

But, thus taking vengeance on its annoyer, the whale was blinded to its own danger. No sooner had it killed the dog, then it saw the breach in the rail ahead of it, and the open sea beyond it. It was too late then. The whale could not have stopped itself. No power on earth could have stopped it. It tried. I saw it try. But, before it could do more than try, it was over the side, splashing into the ocean with a great splash.

I became aware of two things then simultaneously, and I can't say which affected me the more, the captain jumping up and down in infantile rage and screaming that he'd lost "thutty bar'l o' sparmaceti ile," or Gilbert Smith's holding the crushed and bleeding body of Daniel in his arms, and whispering to it, coaxingly, urgently, "Amen, Daniel. That's all, Daniel. Open thy eyes, Friend Daniel. Didn't thee hear me say 'Amen'?"

FEB. 18. Calmer today. We have repaired all damage to the ship. Joseph Thomas has been placed in confinement somewhere in the hold.

After breakfast, all hands were called aft; and Captain Worth, apparently sober, but with his eyes more bloodshot than I have ever seen them, paid us his respects.

"Scum!" he screamed. "Do we hunt whales for sport? Do we have ile to throw away? Are ye from Nantucket and Falmouth and New Bedford, as I thought? Or are ye off-scourings from some heathen port I wot not of? Surely ye are the poorest, stinkin'est, slimiest bilge that ever put out in a whaler, and a set of mutinous dogs!"

On and on he went, his eyes taking fire, it might be, from his stringy beard.

"Some one o' you," he screamed at last, "filed loose them chains that held the sparmaceti to the rail. Some one o' you did that dee-lee-berately. Whoso that man be, let him step for'ard!"

No one moved. No one breathed aloud.

Our silence, our wooden attitudes, our astounded, or obstinate, or defiant faces, the something we felt but did not outwardly express brought his hands out of his pockets, made him dance up and down.

"Speak!" he roared. But no one spoke.

Suddenly he ceased to dance. His berserk rage seemed to pass. He thrust his hands back into his pockets. Something like a benevolent smile came into his face.

"Joseph Thomas," he said. His voice was calm, soft.

Joseph Thomas left the ranks and went a few steps toward him. "Your chains were rotten," the captain said. "They would have parted, even if no mutinous hand had filed them. Through your slovenly work we've lost over thutty bar'l of ile, and almost the ship too and every man aboard. From the time you first set foot on this ship we've had nothing but misfortune. If it warn't that I know it'd kill ye, I'd have ye seized up in the riggin' and flogged 'til the blood spurted out o' your eyes. Naw, I won't kill ye, as I'm a Christian man. But I'll find a way to punish ye. And until I do—"

He motioned Beetle and Lumbard to come to him. He whispered to them, and left the deck. Thomas stood where he was until the mates led him below.

FEB. 19. The sea is so violent even the stoutest fear to go on deck. I have been seasick again, and terribly homesick. Can't think of anything but home, Father in his store, Sally. We are going around Cape Horn, to the Sandwich Islands. If only I could get letters there. Or just one letter. Some whaleship that left home after we did may have mail. Saw a ship yesterday far off on the horizon.

FEB. 22. George Washington's birthday at home. Still sick. This is a blessing in some ways, as I cannot eat.

FEB. 23. It is said that Captain Worth means to maroon Joseph Thomas on some island.

MARCH 1. Off Cape Horn. Somewhat recovered from my recent sickness. The storms continue, and grow in fury.

MARCH 2. Calm this evening, but with tremendous swells. It was calm last night, but toward daybreak the wind freshened. At eight o'clock we took in topgallant sails and double reefed our topsails. At nine we close-reefed the topsails and sent down the royal yards and mast, to scud dead before the wind. At ten o'clock I was relieved from the helm, and the ship was broached to. Then a terrible wind struck us in the quarter, knocking the captain's boat from the crane, carrying away the main topmast backstay, and doing considerable further damage. The head of the foremast was broken off an inch below the cap, the mainmast cracked in three places, and the main topmast wrecked. We are leaking a little, there being eighteen inches of water in the hold. We are running for Valparaiso, Chile, the nearest sizable port.

MARCH 4. Calm and bright. Joseph Thomas was marooned this morning on a funnel-shaped island off the coast of Chile. God be good to him. And God forgive us all.

I was at the rail, looking at the island, a bleak pile of rocks jutting out of the sea. I saw the boat lowered, saw Mate Beetle get into it, followed by Stephen Kidder and Rowland Jones, whose pasty white face was paler than usual. I thought the captain was sending the boat ashore to look for turtles, or birds' eggs, or possibly fresh water. Then I saw Joseph Thomas get in.

No man of the crew said a word as the boat shoved off, though, I suppose, every one of us wanted to. We didn't dare. To ask for mercy would be useless; to protest would be considered mutiny.

Thomas stood up in the prow facing us.

"Good-bye," he cried—and immediately I knew the voice. It was the voice of him who cursed the whale's head; of him who called the captain madman and miser.

He shouted other things, but we didn't hear them, for the oars were carrying him swiftly away, and the wind was against him; but Kidder told me later that he said he hoped some day "to be in a small boat with the captain, adrift and miles from shore, when he would kill him and salt him and eat him—as he had eaten other men—and use his hide to shelter him from rain and sun."

I had a glimpse of Captain Worth's face as the small boat rowed away. There was a pleased expression on it, a self-satisfaction terrible to see. He had picked the right man—dumb though that man pretended to be.

Kidder gave Joe Thomas a knife, on leaving, and Jones gave him a handkerchief, with which he may wave to any ship that chances to pass. The island, they tell me, is uninhabited; and, so far as they could see, has little vegetation and no water.

"The sea cast him upon our mercy," said Gilbert Smith, "and the sea reclaims him."

"You do not feel a little guilty, Friend Smith?" I asked.

"Aye," he said, "even as thee, and all the others. Did I not say this ship was cursed? But let thee not feel guilty, Friend George.

'Twas none of thy doings. And let thee not talk. Murder abides in the prattle of little boys at sea."

Chapter Nine

MARCH 8. Ashore at Valparaiso. A bright day.

This is a beautiful and ugly and quaint and fascinating city; though I have seen little of it. The motion of the ship is still within me, and I find it difficult and tiring to walk. The people are swarthy, gay, polite, Indian, Spaniard, Portuguese, English, and American, and queerly dressed. Even the Americans here seem different from those at home.

We sailed into the semicircle of a bay two days ago, and were becalmed. We ran up the Stars and Stripes, and the U.S. Sloop of War *Vincennes* sent boats out to tow us to an anchorage. The next morning some officers of the sloop came aboard to survey the ship and pay their respects. We are badly in need of repairs, and may be here a week.

This morning the captain gave us shore leave, and Gilbert Smith and I strolled through the streets of the town together, going first to the American consulate where I left some letters to be mailed home on the first ship, then along the narrow strip of beach, where we sat for a time and looked at the barren hills to the north and talked.

Here, it would appear, all is play. There are cockfights, horse races, bullfights, billiard and gaming tables; but I saw none of these. What interested me most were the half-naked Indians carrying great burdens on their heads, the gauchos—colorful men on horseback— the oxcarts, the curious animals that look a little like camels and may be llamas, and the row of grogshops on wheels.

These grogshops were the first foreign things we saw. They had been drawn up along the beach to welcome us.

"See, Friend George," Smith commented. "The devil has equipped them with wheels so they can follow a man all day."

Smith disapproved of every man we saw.

"Every one of them," he said, "has a knife concealed about him, and waits for a chance to plunge it in thy back."

We saw two women drop to their knees in front of a shrine, at the sound of church bells, and bend their heads and pray.

"Idolaters, Friend George," Smith said.

But the attitude of the women must have reminded him of his dog, for he turned his head away quickly that I might not see the wetness of his eyes.

It is very hot here, and there is much dust; and there are awnings that shelter the fronts of all the stores, awnings propped up on poles, which give a curious effect to each street.

In the harbor there is a Chilean ship with an Irish name, the *O'Higgins*. It is the flagship of the Chilean commander, an English gentleman, Lord Cochran.

Chile is now an independent country with a virtual king at the head of it, one Bernardo O'Higgins. It is probably for him the ship was named.

I talked to a man driving two laden burrows down the main street. He was most polite. He boasted he was pure Indian, and had no Spanish in him. The Spaniards are not liked here. He also told me of an earthquake that shook this city some few months ago. I was trying out my Spanish on him. Perhaps he was trying his English on me. However, we understood each other.

SUNDAY. A beautiful morning, but what day of the month it may be I neither know nor care. Time means little here in Valparaiso since I met Perdita. She's a delightful girl, a real friend. Her hair is black. Her eyes are black. Her skin is like old ivory, and she wears a silver cross in the hollow of her neck, a little cross on a silver chain. She's the daughter of Captain Blanco, Captain Worth's friend.

Captain Blanco came aboard the *Globe* a day or two after we entered the harbor, and invited Captain Worth to have dinner with him ashore. I met Captain Blanco as he came up the Jacob's ladder, and directed him to the cabin. I liked the man. He was fat, round, short. He wore gold earrings and made me think of a buccaneer.

He understood my inadequate Spanish, apparently, for he patted me on both shoulders with his soft fat hands, and beamed with a sort of pride in me. I can't describe it any better.

"So young," he said in English, "and so good a linguist. Would you work for me? I need a boy like you. Always I deal with the English and the Americans; and my people speak little English. I'd pay you well."

"I'm signed on here," I said, "thank you."

That afternoon Captain Worth ordered me to take a small demijohn to Captain Blanco's home. It was no trouble to find the house, as it sat on a hill overlooking the bay; but it was a hard steep path for one unused to climbing hills.

The house is, I think, the most beautiful in the world, built out of white stone—or stone that has been whitewashed—and lying around a patio or garden, in which grow the strangest shrubs and flowers and trees. There are bird cages everywhere, and in them the most brilliant feathered creatures I have ever seen.

While I was talking to Captain Blanco, Doña Perdita came in with a dish of strawberries. With some ceremony Captain Blanco introduced her. I wondered at that, having read in books that there is always a duenna in Spanish homes, and the daughter of the house is never introduced to strange visitors, especially English or American young men.

Perdita was short and slight, with lips redder than the berries she held in the dish, and with the bloom of the rose dyeing her cheeks. Her wealth of black hair was held back by a high jeweled comb, and a straggling wisp curled over each eyelid. She held one merely by the twinkle in her dark eyes; and, as she smiled and showed her lovely little teeth, bells chimed joyously inside one. Girdling her pretty throat was a chain from which dangled a silver cross that looked like the Roman numeral one bisected by the same number. Her figure seemed somewhat shorter than Sally's and she appeared a bit younger.

She helped us finish the strawberries, and then—as though it were the usual thing, suggested she might guide me about the city. I felt no shyness with her. I didn't at all want to run away. I didn't feel myself growing awkward and dumb, as has happened to me when Sally smiled.

We strolled toward the harbor, and she let me know she was aware of her father's wish to use me as an interpreter. She begged me not to be so hasty in refusing. She is so friendly, so nice, so pretty, so good! I had to promise. Of course, I can't accept. I must go on in the *Globe*. I must, some day, go back to Judith Chase's Lane, whether Sally will welcome me there or not.

This afternoon Perdita came aboard the *Globe* with her father, and I showed her about the ship. She was thrilled with it, especially with our weapons. I introduced her to Sam, seeing there was no way out of it. If he impressed her as he has impressed other girls, she gave no indication of it.

He gave her his most winning smiles; but inasmuch as he has never learned Spanish, he was at a disadvantage. He could not tell her anything about himself, except through me.

"Does she speak English?" Sam asked me.

I laughed at him. I said, "No. Not one word."

It is possible Sam has reformed. But of that I am not convinced. And this girl is much too nice for him, much too fine. There is a purity in her eyes I never expected to find outside our own Meeting. And she's so in love with life! When one tells her of the whale, and the battle it gives a boat's crew, her eyes shine like Chilean stars—and the stars are brighter and nearer here, and much more mysterious than they are at home.

I have written three letters to Sally since we arrived here. But I have not yet told her of Perdita. Perhaps I should. If she could experience a feeling of jealousy—even in the slightest degree— But no. That's done. That will never be.

MARCH 15. Valparaiso. I should have accepted Captain Blanco's offer. There is nothing but trouble and misery now ahead.

Captain Blanco was aboard us last night, drinking with Captain Worth, and I was present in the cabin as a sort of interpreter, though I was scarcely needed, when the steward ushered in a midshipman from the *Vincennes*.

"The commodore wishes to see you at once, Captain Worth," the officer said. And I didn't have to translate that. "You are to come immediately, with your log and the muster roll."

Captain Worth, who had thrust his hands into his coat pockets on the officer's entrance, got himself up now by putting his right elbow on the table and using it as a lever.

"My compliments to the commodore," he said, smiling. "Assure him I shall attend him early tomorrow morning."

"The order brooks no delay," the midshipman replied. "I am sorry, captain. You must come at once."

Captain Worth looked surprised and not a little troubled; and his eyes swung away from those of the naval man's.

"Find Sam," he said to me.

"He's gone ashore, sir," I reminded him.

Captain Worth was annoyed.

"Yes, yes," he said. "I remember. Go get the log and the muster roll. This is pretty highhanded treatment to an American whaleman. George, explain to Captain Blanco that circumstances—matters of state—compel my abrupt departure. Beg him to excuse me, and say I will wait on him early tomorrow at his office."

He turned to Captain Blanco, and smiled and wagged his chin whiskers in a sort of apology as I translated. I pretended not to know that Captain Blanco spoke better English than Captain Worth.

In less than half an hour we were aboard the sloop of war, and a sailor brought us straightway before the commander, a man of more than middle age, and of severe dignity.

He eyed the captain sternly, saying nothing for a long while. Captain Worth tried to speak, but could only stutter. He wanted to ask if he could sit down; but seeing no chairs about, changed his mind. Or so I judged.

"Captain Worth?" the commander asked.

"Yes," said Captain Worth. "Yes, sir."

Again the commander eyed him coldly.

"I've heard of your habitual drunkenness," he said, after a few moments. "I've heard of your bad usage of the crew, and certain threats you made against them. You have a bad record, Captain Worth a very bad record. I am ashamed to call you an American. But what I want to know is about a man named—" he hesitated, looked at a paper lying on his desk—"named Joseph Thomas."

The captain was startled. For the first time I noticed his Adam's apple.

"He deserted," he said.

"Be so good as to let me see the log," the commander said to me. I gave it to him, and he riffled the pages for a moment until he found the entry he sought. He tossed the book on his desk.

"So it says in your log," he said. "I hardly believed that. Isn't it true you had this Thomas rowed to an island and marooned? You call that desertion?"

Captain Worth had no answer. His face was white as a whale's belly.

"You rowed him out to a desolate, uninhabited island, and left him there, without provisions, without shelter, without arms. A dose of six and thirty would be just the thing for you; and, by God, if I had my way you'd get it, and I'd send you home in irons. You will return to that island as soon as possible, Captain Worth. You will take that man off and bring him here. And pray God he's still alive and well, so you'll not have to answer a charge of murder."

At the word murder, the captain's body shook, and I distinctly heard his teeth chatter. They were still chattering as we pulled back to the *Globe*. But the lights of our ship stilled them, brought him back a modicum of courage and defiance.

"There's a traitor aboard us," he said, "an informer. I'll find him. Aye, I'll find him. I'll never rest until I do. And I'll punish him fittingly—murder or no."

I heard his teeth sound again, uppers grinding grittily on lowers, and heard him repeat—"murder or no."

Chapter Ten

MARCH 16. Rain. Torrential rain. A nor'wester shaking the sea. The men surly and sick from Valparaiso grog. We're making for that funnel-shaped island to take off Joseph Thomas if he be still alive.

A strange day, not yet to be understood.

Early this morning Captain Worth bade me accompany him ashore to act as interpreter. He must pay a call on the American consul, arrange for a supply of vegetables and meat, and settle the repair bills and port charges.

We stopped at the consulate first, and I was made to wait outside in the driving rain, as the captain had no need of me within. It was thus I met the consul, a pleasant, red-faced Irishman named Hogan. He came through the rain leisurely, minding it not at all, and smoking a cigar that was as wet as his face. He greeted me cordially, asked my name, and flattered me no little.

"A whaler!" he cried, shaking my hand vigorously. "We talk of the hardy Norsemen, the Phoenicians, the early mariners, stout men in flimsy boats, the earliest explorers of the deep. But let me tell you, son; in all the history of adventure there never were such men as our Nantucket whalers—kids, mere kids, schoolboys putting out in little boats to kill great whales, venturing into the jaws of monsters, trusting their lives to an inch of planking, roaming the whole world of water, discovering new lands, fighting—but come in, come in. Why do you stand out here in the rain?"

"Captain's orders, sir," I said.

"Damn your captain," he cried. "He's like all the whaling masters I've ever met, no doubt. What's his name?"

"Worth, sir."

"Worth! The *Globe!* Damn his avaricious brutal soul to hell! I'll deal with him. Watch his face when he comes out. I'll have him breathing sulphur, damn him. I've heard of him. Worth!"

Hogan breathed a great cloud of smoke into his lungs, and blew it out again gustily, and stomped angrily away from me, into the consulate.

Captain Worth emerged quite hastily, and within a few seconds; and, as the consul had predicted, he was breathing sulphur and his face well repaid the watching. We walked rapidly to a ship chandler's in the market, where the smell of the meat we purchased nauseated me.

"Surely, captain," I cried—unable to stop the protest—"you'll not let them unload that poisonous mess on us."

"Poisonous?" he answered, acridly. "This is good meat, well-seasoned. It wants but a bit more spice to make it fit. And I've paid dearly for it. Look ye, this is a damned un-Christian country for a Yankee, a land of robbers. I have no cash. I have no credit. I must pay for everything with ile. Ile, mind ye—and at only forty cents! Ah, they'd take my life's blood if they could. Ile at forty cents. And were it not for Captain Blanco—"

I was glad we were going to see Captain Blanco again, for I was sure I'd find Perdita with him, and have a chance to say good-bye to her. We trudged through the narrow streets near the water front, little rills rushing across the toes of our boots—and sometimes reaching as high as our ankles.

But Captain Blanco was strangely agitated as he greeted me. He scowled, and his swarthy face paled. He seemed furious, yet he showed us a controlled politeness and even a forced cordiality. I must have committed some terrible blunder, some awful breach of etiquette. But, though I have examined my conscience again and again, I cannot think what it is.

He called in his own interpreter, let Captain Worth know he did not want me in his office, and dismissed me summarily, but with the utmost courtesy. Then, as I was leaving, he thrust into my hand a double-tangent quadrant. It was such an exquisite thing, and the giving of it was in such direct opposition to his manner toward me, that I was struck dumb.

One hand tugging at his black mustache, and his cheeks flushing as though in anger or resentment, or plain virulent hate, he said softly:

"My daughter wishes you to have it. As a parting gift. Adios, senorito."

"Perdita," I said. "May I see her? I must thank her. Is she at home, captain?"

"No, no," he said quickly, his eyes flashing dangerously. "She is ill. She is very ill."

I bowed, and went back into the rain. For sometime I wandered about, trying to solve the puzzle thus suddenly thrust upon me. I thought perhaps I could solve it only through Perdita, and determined to call upon her. I went, therefore, to the market to buy her a present, and after much peering into assorted stocks of merchandise, and much talk to greedy merchants, bought a Spanish comb that would look exactly right in her jet-black hair.

I had it carefully wrapped, and held it under my oilskins all the way up the hill. It was treacherous walking, for the rain had washed gullies in the hillside, and great holes in the path; and streams came cascading down with force enough almost to bowl me over, and great gusts of wind now and then sucked the breath out of me.

I was panting as I pushed through the gate into the patio. It was quiet there, though the rain beat down. There was no wind. The bird cages had been taken inside the house, and the place, though full of gorgeous flowers and waving, dripping trees and shrubs, had a vacant, eerie, melancholy look.

I stood a moment, breathing hard, and looking all about me.

I saw Perdita sitting in a wide-open window, her head resting against the white stone, her eyes closed, her right hand pressed to her cheek as if she were in pain. At first I thought she was asleep, but a sharp spasm in her shoulders told me otherwise.

"Perdita," I called. "You're crying! You're really ill?"

She was startled. She jumped up, stared at me with widening eyes. Her face paled, as her father's had, then reddened.

"Don't come in," she cried. "Don't come near me."

And suddenly she turned from me, and ran; and the whole house echoed with the raucous screams of birds.

It was not heartbreak on her part. There had been no love between us. Only fun. Only laughter and singing, and her white teeth gleaming with joy, her black eyes sparkling with happiness. No, she was not in love with me. She was not grieving at my departure.

What have I done to her, or to her father?

The oil was moved ashore this afternoon. The provisions came aboard. Captain Worth returned shortly after dark, drunk and cursing.

And I shall never see Valparaiso again—nor poor Perdita.

MARCH 21. Calm and bright. Near noon we anchored about a mile off the island. Captain Worth, Mates Beetle and Lumbard, and Gilbert Smith went ashore, looking for Joseph Thomas.

"There was no habitation or shelter of any kind, Friend George," Smith told me. "We found a few brackish pools of water, a number of birds' eggs, and Joe Thomas' monkey jacket. It was torn almost to shreds. Well, the sea gave him to us; and the sea's taken him back again, no doubt; but I'm glad this matter be not on my conscience, nor on thine, to haunt us nights."

APRIL 19. Calm and very hot, with light winds from the southwest. Have sighted no whales since leaving Valparaiso. I am not too sorry, for I have become absorbed in the study of navigation. A whale might interfere with my lessons.

Perdita's quadrant inspired my new study, and Mate Beetle's generosity of time, and patient efforts, have fostered it. Thus the long hours that have hitherto been filled with thoughts of Sally, with homesickness and brooding and speculations of what is to become of us all pass swiftly and profitably.

It is most queer that I should go to sea against my better judgment—and really against my will—only to find a tutor such as I should never have found ashore. And what a classroom the *Globe* has turned out to be! Lessons on the deck, with the tar oozing out of the seams, the sails flapping overhead, the sea murmuring—and at night the great stars hanging low, and answering to their names as Beetle points them out.

Beetle is a solemn, dour man with long black hair, a thick wiry half-moon of whiskers about his round red face, a fat round body, and enormous hands and feet. His English is as slovenly as anybody else's—yet he speaks both Latin and Greek, and has a profound knowledge of mathematics and of all things pertaining to the sea and ships. He's harsh and bullying at times, easily enraged, superstitious, and painfully shy. If I could only open wide the door of his mind! But he keeps it locked and bolted, as though he feared thieves. He rarely opens it, and then but a trifle.

MAY 1. Off the Galapagos Islands. Calm and bright and frightfully hot. Most of the crew were up early and ashore for the tortoise, which grows to such tremendous size here. They are easy to capture. One merely turns the creature over on his back—with the help of three or four strong friends—and there he is, helpless. We found great quantities of them, some weighing six hundred pounds or more. It required four men to carry the biggest to the boats.

"They make a very delicious steak when broiled, Friend George," Gilbert Smith told me. "They'll live for six months or more in the hold of the ship, without food or water. How would thee like to be a turtle? They have their own water supply stored away, their own internal reservoirs."

Men are smiling and excited again for the first time since we put into Valparaiso. The meat we have been served has been so bad we had to hold our noses as we ate it—and some of us have refused to eat it at all. But now—roast turtle steaks! There must be a hundred or more creatures crawling about in the hold. We are assured fresh meat for many days.

MAY 5. A dark, rainy, cheerless day. We're bound for the Sandwich Islands. There may be mail there. There was none at Valparaiso, but we scarce expected any. We are sure to meet other whaling ships at Oahu, however; and it is almost certain one will have letters from home. For some of us.

MAY 6. Rainy and dark. Captain Worth ordered Cook to serve the meat in pies. It was such a revolting dish that even the most timid of us shouted angrily that we would not eat it. We went in a body to the cook, each carrying his pie. We gathered up all the pies in the galley, and threw them overboard one by one.

Captain Worth came running toward us, actually running, his beard afire with wrath.

"What is the meaning of this?" he demanded. "Mutiny?"

"The meat stinks, sir," I said. "We threw it overboard."

"Stinks, does it?" he said. "And you have the audacity to stand there and tell me so to my face?"

It might have fared ill with me had not Sam, my brother, and Gilbert Smith come up and whispered to the captain, plainly interceding for me, and for the others.

"Stinks," the captain repeated. "There's no difference after you've eaten a thing, whether it's sweet or sour, whether it stinks or smells like a damned little vi'let."

"We have turtles below, sir," I said. "Can't we please have turtles to eat?"

He looked at me a long time, his face expressionless, then looked at the others.

"Why, yes," he said softly. "You'll have turtle meat hereafter—and nothing but turtles. But—remember—you asked for it."

With that he turned and walked away.

Turtle!

"Turtle steaks," says Cook, "got so much juice in 'em you should eat 'em in the small boats—they sprays so when you clamps your teeth on 'em."

I can hardly wait.

MAY 10. A perfect day. A beautiful day. The dark blue of the water and the light blue of the sky. A whale that will give us a hundred barrels.

We sighted the whale early this morning, going leisurely to leeward, and pulled for him miles and miles and miles. For more than five hours we kept to the course, Beetle pleading with us, scolding us, cursing us, bullying, until, completely exhausted I peaked my oar.

I could not help it.

I expected Beetle to do something drastic, but he merely laughed at me. Had Captain Worth been in the boat, as he usually is, I'm sure he would have cursed me. But for weeks he has been too drunk to get into the boat.

"George Comstock's calved," Beetle roared, and gave orders for the others to peak oars.

Holden Hewman, red cheeked and panting, with his red hair matted on his perspiring face, looked at me gratefully and said, "Thank God." Cyrus Hussey grinned and squinted up at the sun, probably trying to figure the time. Lay winked and lay back panting. Sam began taking off his shirt.

Holden Hewman was the most spent of us all, for, being afraid of a whale, he saves his grog allowance and drinks it all at once—just before the boat is lowered and the chase begins—thinking thus to fill his heart with courage. The long pull and the heat of the day had taken the alcohol, and the bravery, out of him and had left him limp.

"Who's got the water?" he said.

I was reaching for it when I saw Perdita's cross, hanging from a black cord around Sam's neck.

I dropped the water bottle and stared; and, though I tried not to show it, I must have let my brother see something of the emotion I felt. It looked so obscene on his bronzed hairy chest—the dainty thing that had looked so sacred lying against her throat.

"Well," he said, with a rough tenderness, "well, don't cry about it."

What I would have replied I cannot imagine, but at that moment Hewman screamed "Look out!" and with such alarm that I turned to him and saw him point with trembling finger out to sea.

All day the whale had had his fun with us, like a dog that loves to be chased. Now that we had stopped, he had turned and was chasing us.

Beetle, shouting orders, took his place in the stern; and Sam stood up in the bow, one iron in his hand, the other placed carefully at the side of his right foot.

The great creature came across our bow, playfully.

"Now!" Beetle cried, and Sam threw the iron, stooped, picked up the other one, and gave that to him as well while he was still stunned at our treachery.

He did not sound. He splashed the ocean with his flukes, and ran. Straight west he sped, carrying us after him, the spray whipping our skins, blinding us, smothering us, soaking every stitch of clothes.

It was perhaps an hour before the whale slowed, and spouted blood. He died as we pulled up alongside him, and it was unnecessary for Beetle to touch him with the lance.

"Well," Beetle said, "you had your fust Nantucket sleigh ride, boys. Bet you never went so fast in all your lives afore."

We had a long wait before the ship came sailing up to us; and though Sam sat down by me, I did not look at him. I dared not.

"Don't take it so hard, lad," he whispered.

He jerked the cross, breaking the string that held it, and tried to press it into my fingers. I winced. I could not endure the touch of his fingers. I drew my hands away, and the cross fell on my lap.

I flung it overboard, into the peace and immensity of the sea—but not all the water in the sea can wash it clean again, nor hide the shame it symbolizes.

My actions angered Sam. He would have struck me had it not been for Beetle.

"Peace there," the mate bellowed. "Whatever your quarrel, ye'll not settle it here, ye two."

Sam muttered something under his breath and left me. I could feel him seething. And I was not surprised to see him, a moment later, snatch up a harpoon and hurl it savagely into the body of a shark that had come near, attracted by the blood of the whale.

I am sorry I threw the cross overboard. It was a silly, boyish, spiteful thing to do. Yet I could not keep that memento of a girl's betrayal; nor could I let Sam keep it.

How could he do it? The man that Sally loves!

Chapter Eleven

JUNE 10. Turtle. Turtle. Turtle. But never roasted, never fried, never seasoned, never anything but boiled. There is no taste to it. It is far better than the rotten meat. And yet, in its own way, it is as bad. Or worse.

This is Captain Worth's revenge. Cook has orders to boil a turtle every day for the crew—after cutting the best parts into steaks for the officers. Cook boils the oil out of it, skims it off the top of the pot, and puts it aside. Eventually it goes into the barrels of spermaceti; and some day will be sold as pure spermaceti oil.

"What can we do?" I asked Gilbert Smith.

"Do?" he said. "Thee asked for it, Friend George. Did I not hear thee say, 'Can't we please have turtles?' Well, take heart. The turtles diminish every day—not one by one, but, mysteriously, two by two, as the animals went into the ark."

"Two by two? How do you mean? One for the captain, and one for the crew?"

"No. One turtle is killed each morning. It does for the entire ship. Every night another turtle vanishes. The captain has set spies to find out how. Be careful, Friend George, and let thy friends be careful too."

"You mean someone is stealing a turtle every day, and eating him?"

"Eating him? One man eat a turtle, Friend George? One man carry him up from the hold? What are thee thinking?"

"A conspiracy!" I said, delighted.

"A bad word," said Smith, making a wry face. "I like it not. Let thee say rather that some godly men are halving the captain's sins of fraud and avariciousness, throwing overboard half the turtle oil he'd otherwise palm off as spermaceti. But woe to them if they be caught, Friend George. Let thee drop a hint here and there, softly."

"Half the turtle oil," I said, "and half the boiled turtle that would be served to us. But, how do they get the tortoises up from below?"

"Ah," he said, "it is too bad thee's not speaking to thy brother."

AUG. 15. Land at last! How eager I am to go ashore! I am too excited to sleep. Surely there'll be a ship there with mail for us. It's taken us so long to get here. It seems years.

The Sandwich Islands!

About four o'clock this afternoon we caught the odor of heliotrope, far off shore. It was like a whiff of paradise. Soon afterward John Cleveland, a sturdy little fellow with a voice that sounded like a big foghorn, cried from the crow's nest that he saw a school of black fish on the lee bow. But actually they were canoes, filled with naked men and women, beautiful, strong people, bringing us potatoes, sugar cane, yams, cocoanuts, bananas, and fish, for which we traded pieces of iron hoops, nails, and other articles worthless to us. Surely these islanders are the happiest and nicest people in all the world. I hated to see them go.

Tomorrow morning—no, today, in a few hours—we shall go ashore on Oahu! I have prayed there will be at least one letter from Sally waiting for me there, though, if there is, it will only torture me!

AUG. 18. No mail. No mail of any kind. Except for Sam. But I really didn't expect any; so I am not at all disappointed. Sam says Starbuck has bought the *Globe*. I feel a bit closer to Sally. Her grandpa owns my ship.

I wish I could live forever in this garden of God. I've never seen so beautiful a world—precipices rising straight out of the ocean, gorges, waterfalls foamy as beaten egg whites, flowers so beautiful and fragrant they hurt like exquisite pain, birds of brilliant feathers and the fire and the smoke of volcanoes. I trembled with ecstasy.

Early this morning, shortly after we had anchored, Lunalilo, a local chief, came aboard with his three wives. He's a funny little man, with the roundest, fattest, most impressive belly I have ever seen. His wives are fat too, but all three of them rolled into one would scarce equal the displacement of his paunch. I stood marveling at it, and the little dimple in its center, until Gilbert Smith introduced him as an old friend of his and Sam's.

Lunalilo and his wives brought garlands of flowers and necklaces of colored beads which they threw around our necks. They were almost naked—like the natives who visited us last night. Still, there was no affront to modesty. We had expected them to appear thus. We thought their nudity delightful. Smith, however, hinted to the chief that he and his good wives should be more fully dressed when appearing among white men.

The chief smiled. He explained to his wives. They all left us; to return an hour later in their ceremonial clothes. Lunalilo was wearing a pair of cotton stockings—his toes sticking through them—and a high silk hat that was mildewed near the brim. The women had only added more flowers to their costumes.

On this visit the chief invited the entire crew to a feast at his palace. We agreed eagerly. After so many days of boiled turtle we were frantic for any new variety of food. He promised us roast pork!

I sat beside Mate Beetle as the meat was served.

"Pork," I said. "Roast pork! Actually roast pork!"

The words were music.

Beetle grinned and pointed to the pigs' heads all about.

"If you hadn't seen them pigs' faces," he said, "you'd never a-knowed it was pork, now would you?"

"No," I said, and went on eating.

Long after I had eaten my fill I sat and watched Beetle. I had heard many tales of his prowess as a trencherman, but had never seen him in action. Still I had heard it said that he had once eaten an entire ham to settle a wager in the Spouters Inn. And I had been aboard the *Globe* only a few days when I learned of the elaborate measures Captain Worth took to protect himself from Beetle's rapacity at meals. Cook told me about that.

"Cap'n's handicapped," he said, " 'cause he has no fingers. He's got him a spoon, with a ring on it, 'stead of a handle. He sticks the stump of his right hand through the ring, and he can eat good as you and me that way. Everything served him has to be cut up fine, and served separate, so Beetle he won't git it. When I makes pies, though, your brother Sam he looks after Cap'n's interests. No sooner do I put a pie on the table than Sam he harpoons it and divides it six ways with Cap'n's compasses, so's Beetle he can't cheat. Beetle he don't like that none, but your brother Sam he jus' laughs at him. He don't care for Beetle, Sam don't."

Beetle ate with the steadiness of New England rain and the earnestness and zeal and unhurried persistency of a Methodist preacher talking of hell. It was delightful to watch him.

After a time, a long long time, even Beetle was satisfied. He heaved aside a bone he had picked clean and turned to me, smiling oddly.

"How'd ye like the roast terrapin?"

That is, I thought he said "terrapin."

"*Terrapin?*" I asked.

I must have shown I was puzzled for he laughed heartily, hands on his quivering belly.

"Yes, sir," he said. "Roast terrier. Or maybe it was spitz or hound. How do I know?"

"Dog?" I ventured. "That was dog meat?"

"And very good too. You'll remember Gilbert Smith excused himself. I suppose eating dog would have reminded him of little Daniel."

I didn't feel so good now myself.

"Dog's nothing," Beetle said. "Once I attended a banquet in the Society Islands, and thought I was eating dog—until I saw a human head acting as the center piece."

Later Gilbert Smith confirmed the mate's statement. "Sure they eat dogs," he said, "the heathen! The cannibals! But what can thee expect of people who burn men and women for sacrifice? See yon hill? There was an 'imu ahi' there not long ago, an oven for burning people to please the gods."

"Probably witches," I said. "They must have got the idea from dear old Massachusetts."

"God forgive thee that remark," said Gilbert Smith.

Today I met some of Lunalilo's children, including his daughter Lua.

AUG. 20. The *Phoebe Ann* of New Bedford, the *Pocahontas* of Falmouth, and the *Palladium* of Boston are in port; but none has any letters for us.

The *Lyra,* which sailed for the Japan coast last week, will surely have mail; but we may never find her. She left Edgartown a month after the *Globe.*

This I have from William Humphries, who was the cook aboard the *Lyra,* the colored man who played the violin at the dance in Barnabas Starbuck's storehouse. Cyrus Hussey found him playing his fiddle on the beach, and brought him aboard the *Globe.* He claims the *Lyra* deserted him; but Captain Worth believes he deserted the *Lyra,* and refuses to have anything to do with him.

Lunalilo's daughter, Lua, is a beautiful girl, scarcely fifteen. I saw her again today in her canoe, poising it skillfully on the inclined plane in advance of a wave, shooting as fast through the water as a fish. How she maintained her position at such speed, and avoided breaching to and upsetting, I don't quite understand. It must be a delicate adjustment of forces, an uncanny sense of balance, good judgment, skill with the paddle and something more.

"Aphrodite!" I called aloud. I couldn't help it. The sheer beauty of this island goddess coming to me thus out of the sea foam set my legs running toward her.

She leaped gracefully from the canoe, and came to me through the shallow waters, shaking the spray from her black flower-decked hair, from her naked shoulders and arms. She was as fragrant as she was wet, and as happy and sparkling as the waves themselves. We held hands and laughed together, for no reason at all.

I knew but a few words of her language, and she not a word of mine; yet we conversed as old friends, we who had never seen each other until two days ago. We spent some time in her canoe, skimming over the waves, laughing as the water splashed us, crying at the albatrosses that flocked about us. We climbed a hill together, treading on flowers, walking through trees and ferns. We strolled to the top of the Punch Bowl, to the crater, where she sang me a little song; a very sad little song that I attempted to repeat later to Mate Beetle. He translated it thus:

Oh thy fiercely flaring fires, Keaka;
    Thy sky-ascending tongues of flame!
Tabu incense, scattering ashes,
    Sacrifice fire, engulfing flame!

Lua had pressed my hand as she sang, and the laughter went out of her face.

"You see," Beetle explained, "she's afraid of them fires, afraid they'll git her someday. Same time they're holy to her. Maybe they burned up a lot of her ancestors."

The dour look left him for a moment and his hazel eyes smiled oddly into mine.

"There's other flames women's afraid of, lad," he said, "'specially naked little island women that think white men are gods. Be careful; men gits burned as well as women."

I almost laughed aloud. What should I do? Cast down my eyes when I meet Aphrodite on the beach? Walk with my arms folded and my thoughts on the niceties of killing a whale?

True, Lua is a little pagan, and I am a Quaker. True she is all but naked, and I've never seen feminine nakedness before. Yet she is as modest as any Quakeress in Nantucket; and when modesty and beauty walk together in one bare body, why should a man beware?

Chapter Twelve

AUG. 21. Captain Worth is enjoying life ashore. He knows little of what goes on aboard the *Globe*—nothing of what his crew is doing. He does not realize that seven of the men have deserted, including Sam.

I wonder if it is here that Sam intends to plant his pumpkins. What shall I tell Sally?

AUG. 22. Tonight we had an adventure, Gilbert Smith and I, and I am still throbbing with emotion.

We were looking for deserters. We were coming down a hill, Smith a few paces in front of me, when a man leaped out of the darkness.

I did not see what happened until it was over, though I did hear Gilbert's voice.

"Friend, thee does wrong to attack me. I be a man of peace. Leave me now lest I be tempted to hurl thee over yon cliff."

I heard the sound of a scuffle, then Gilbert talking again.

"I made thee a promise, Friend. It would be a black sin to backslide on it. Thee must go over the cliff."

He was panting when I came up to him, and there was the sound of a great commotion just below us.

"I have killed him," Gilbert said. "Surely I have killed him in his sin."

"He makes a deal of noise for a dead man," I answered. "And he swears loud Christian oaths."

We stretched out full length on the road and peered over the rim of the cliff. At first we could see nothing. But soon we realized that not one but a number of men were camped below us.

There was a fire burning near a group of huts, and presently I saw a man rush to it and pick up a firebrand, which he held high and circled about his head.

Then we were able to understand a little better what had happened. Smith had hurled his attacker through the thatched roof of a hut just beneath the cliff. The fellow had apparently come hurtling down into the midst of a party, who took him for a clumsy robber. They were pummeling him now, we could see. And they were cursing him—in the English of New England.

We got up, brushed the dirt off our clothes, and went on down the hill. Neither of us said a word until we neared the dock. Then Gilbert asked the question I was afraid he would ask.

"Thy brother was one of those we saw?"

I did not answer.

"And the man with the light," Smith said. "Saw thee his face?"

"Aye," I said. "It was Joe Thomas."

AUG. 23. The canoes put out this morning. A great fleet of them, making great white marks on the blue water. A war party. Chief Lunalilo was in the first boat, everybody says. And Sam was with him.

Gilbert Smith tells me there were others of the crew in the war party. I did not see them.

"All the deserters were there," he said, "except Holden Hewman. He is about to marry, Friend George. An island woman. A pagan. An idolatress. A naked hussy with flowers in her hair. The devil's own spawn. He must be saved, and thee must help me save him."

"Not I," I could not help but answer. "I hope you do not find him, Friend Gilbert. I hope he marries the girl and stays in this paradise. Why should you want him back on the *Globe*—to work like a slave, to eat swill, to submit to the murderous whims of Captain Worth—?"

"Softly, softly, Friend George," Gilbert whispered. "Thee must not model thyself on thy brother."

I did not understand, and I felt a hot anger at his words, a fierce desire to defend my brother Sam—and a great curiosity to know what had prompted Gilbert to speak this way to me.

"Ah," he said with a sigh, "thy brother was once a crusader, even as thee, Friend George. But the devil and Joe Thomas took him to the top of a hill and showed him a new world that he might make his own."

With that Friend Gilbert left me. •

AUG. 24. Captain Worth has come aboard, almost sober, and in a murderous mood. And he has heard of the desertions.

"I want them scamps," I heard him shout. "I want 'em dead or alive. Beetle! Lumbard! Fisher! Smith! Comstock! Sam Comstock!"

There was silence for a moment, and then I heard him call again, "Where's Sam Comstock?"

"He's ashore," Beetle said, "no doubt huntin' them deserters."

"I saw him with two guns on, sir," said Smith.

"Guns," cried the captain. "That's it. Guns. Why don't the rest o' ye do the same? Beetle, issue guns to all the officers. Tomorrow at daybreak round up the crew, and bring back every man jack o' them blackguards. If they won't come peaceable, shoot. And when ye shoot, remember a crippled whaleman's no damn good to me. Better a dead deserter than a crippled whaler. Six o' them. And Prass makes seven. There's a curse on this vy'ge, a bloody curse."

Later Gilbert Smith sought me in the forecastle, and took me aside. "Thee will go with us tomorrow," he said, "to hunt thy friends."

I said nothing, but he read my thoughts.

"We be men of peace," he said, "but thee must consider this—does not God love a dead whaler better than a living idolater?"

I shuddered at that, and tried to divert the conversation.

"What did the captain mean, saying, 'Prass makes seven'?" I asked. "Has Prass deserted?"

"Prass? He can barely walk. He's to be put ashore tomorrow, to make his way home as best he can. We must get someone in his place. In all, we must recruit seven men here—unless—"

"You don't think we'll find the deserters?"

Smith shook his head gloomily.

"It ill becomes a man like myself to say it," he whispered, "but pity overcomes me for these runaways. We'll take none of them—except of course, young Hewman."

I couldn't help saying, "I wish the whale had broken my leg, as well as Ignatius Prass's."

"So," Smith went on, "we'll have to shanghai half a dozen men—and it's only the devil's own that's ever shanghaied, Friend George. Only the devil's own."

"Half a dozen? You intend to get Holden then—and only Holden?"

"Peace," he said fiercely. "Hold thy tongue. Six—and maybe seven. If thy brother does not return in time—"

"He'll return," I said; but I was far from feeling confident of that, and the boat steerer knew it.

"Aye," he said. "I fear it. He'll return—with friends."

And he quoted from Luke: "Then goeth he, and taketh to him seven other spirits more wicked than himself . . . and the last state of that man is worse than the first."

Chapter Thirteen

AUG. 25. Her name is not Lua, as I had first thought. It's Lia-Lia. I don't know how to spell it. It means "star of stars." Star of Stars! Her eyes are little stars. Black shining stars.

It was too hot to sleep in the airless forecastle: so I had dressed and come up on deck. I was leaning on the starboard rail, looking at the spangled sky, and across the waters at the dark hulks of ships, and the line of the shore beyond, a white blurred line that gave off music if one listened.

My nostrils were filled with the smell of the land; and yet, it seemed as if I were sitting in the sun, watching the whalers in Nantucket Bay, smelling the smell of the oil in Barnabas Starbuck's storehouse, and talking to Sally. At the same time, I was thinking—"All these months and no word from her; all these ships in the harbor! They must have brought hundreds of letters from Nantucket and Falmouth and Edgartown and New Bedford—but not one brief note for me."

I saw the canoe coming toward the *Globe,* but it meant nothing to me. It was just a canoe. I saw the girl coming over the rail. There was nothing strange in that. She was just a naked island belle with flowers in her hair and around her neck, coming to trade fruits and vegetables.

But she saw me and recognized me at once. At least I suppose so, for she came running toward me, laughing and calling my name, a gay sprite with shining eyes. I was actually startled, for I had forgotten all about Lia-Lia. The moment she had vanished from my sight, that moment she had ceased to be. Yet suddenly here she was again, endowed with life, and placed dramatically before me.

It was not until Mate Beetle approached that I emerged from my peculiar trance.

"So you came on deck because it was too hot below," Beetle said sarcastically. "Lad, I'm afeared you're growin' up. Maybe that's a pity, and maybe it ain't. But the old man'd skin ye alive for this."

"Talk to her, sir," I said. "It must be something important that brings her here."

I could see in her face that she had something to tell me. Something that ought to make me happy. I suppose it was the emotion within her I sensed, the eagerness expressed in every move of her lithe little body. A blind man could tell that she was welling over with joy of some kind.

"Quite important, I dare say," Beetle said. "Gal couldn't sleep, thinking of young George Comstock."

He turned to Lia-Lia then, and spoke to her jestingly at first, then with mounting seriousness.

It was tantalizing to stand, ignorant and mute, and listen and watch, and wonder. Lia-Lia was all excitement and happiness. She couldn't stand still a moment. She looked constantly from Beetle to me, from me to Beetle. Her hands made pretty gestures. Her feet danced. Her body swayed. Beetle stood stolid, chin thrust forward a little, fists moving slowly up his ribs and slowly down. At first his voice was light, bantering, indulgent; but quickly a new element crept into it, and I began to be afraid for Lia-Lia.

"What is it, Mate?" I asked. "What does she say?"

Beetle ignored me, went on questioning the girl.

'Her father's been victorious in battle,' I thought. But no. She wouldn't have come out here at this hour just to tell me that. I thought of all sorts of things.

"Well," Beetle said at last, giving me a most peculiar look, a long scrutiny that embarrassed and slightly enraged me, "it seems there's a marriage feast ashore, and you've been invited."

"I'd like to go," I said; and at the word Lia-Lia seized my hands and started to pull me away.

"Sure," Beetle said, grinning. "Go ahead. I'll tell the old man you had my permission. Lower away, lad."

How very buoyant we were, we two, flying over the water to the wedding feast. How we laughed, and shouted, and sang! There was nothing in all this beautiful world but joy and laughter.

We went smashing through the surf, laughing above its thunder, frightening the birds that circled above us. We dragged the canoe high up on the sands, just as the sun burst over the rim of the world. We ran hand in hand until we had to stop for sheer weariness of running. We went slowly then, Lia-Lia stopping every little while to exhibit a dancing step or two, and twist her body around in exultation.

Up a rather steep incline we went, and into a house wherein was a *lanai*, a sort of bower, a little garden brought indoors. Here the happy couple were to stand, and pledge themselves to each other. A fragrant altar, a colorful altar—yet it made me think of a bleak little Methodist church with no flowers in it at all, and severe hard benches, and a stained-glass window with a tiny hole in the pane, and Sally and her grandfather there on a Sunday morning, their faces turned toward the pulpit wherein an old whaling captain thundered passages from the gospel.

There was a crowd in the little house, a crowd of girls and women, talking and laughing in happy excitement. Every now and then I caught the names Kalua and Waimaka.

Lia-Lia danced up to a smiling fat woman, dragging me by the hand, and explained who I was.

"These all sisters and friends of bride," the woman said, beaming on me. "Waimaka and Kalua, they marry here. Be husband and wife ever after."

She took my other hand and dragged me to the door. She pointed to a house nearby.

"See?" she said, "New house, Kalua—Waimaka. Bridal house. You marry. You have house too."

She giggled and hurried away from me through groups of flower-decked nymphs; and I looked into Lia-Lia's shining eyes.

I cursed myself. I hadn't meant to make her love me.

I turned from her quickly, to spare her any knowledge of what I felt, for I thought she could read my eyes, as I had read hers. Then I saw Holden Hewman standing there, dressed as an islander. This was Kalua.

He looked at me as I had seen him look at a charging whale,

terrible fright in his eyes, his mouth agape, his Adam's apple quivering horribly.

There was a pretty native girl standing proudly at his side, her hand in his. Waimaka. One of Lia-Lia's sisters. She was looking at Holden's weak profile, openly adoring him.

Until then it had never occurred to me that a white man was to be married here, one of my own shipmates. Until then I hadn't realized that Beetle had used me to spring a trap.

"Run," I said. "Holden, take the girl and run."

He tried to answer but could not.

"Beetle knows," I said. "That's why he let me come. I've probably been followed here. Run. There's still time."

" 'Run,' says thee, Friend George?" I heard Gilbert Smith's voice asking. "Thee gives bad counsel."

He was back of me, in the open door.

I bent my head, guiltily. I could not turn around. I could face neither the righteous boat steerer nor the sinful seaman. In a way I had betrayed them both, the one through stupidity, the other through sentiment.

"Get thee dressed," Smith cried in his sternest tones, "thee deserter, thee follower after heathen gods. Put decent clothes on thee, and at once. And thee, Friend George, get thee back to the ship."

Waimaka threw herself on Hewman, screaming like a mad woman.

I edged my way through the crowd of angry, frightened, puzzled wedding guests, and looked suddenly into Lia-Lia's face.

She stood near the door, quiet, her big eyes staring at me, her hands hanging limply at her sides.

She said no word. I slunk past her, past Gilbert Smith, out into the open where some of the crew waited, rifles in their hands.

A great feast had been prepared beneath the trees. There were fires burning, and underground were ovens that threw off savory smells. There were women there, staring at us, women frozen into the attitude of wrapping smoking food in great cool leaves.

I went past them all, sick at heart, took my place in one of our boats, and waited.

Holden was handcuffed when they brought him down. He did not look at me. We rowed to the ship in profound silence.

Chapter Fourteen

AUG. 26. Still at anchor.

I woke out of a dream, a nightmare of tribal warfare, to find Sam pulling, gently, the lock of hair that habitually falls over my forehead. Thus he used often to wake me when we were both much younger.

"Come up on deck," he whispered.

There was a slight wound under his right cheekbone, and he limped badly. But he made light of his injuries. He smiled that old smile of his that always put me under his spell, and slipped an arm around me as though there had never been any bitterness between us, and never would be again.

"You are hurt," I said.

"It's nothing," he tried to assure me. "I got brushed by a war club. That's all."

"But your leg?"

"Only a bad boil."

We sat aft, by the starboard rail, silenced—for a little time—by the majesty of the flaming stars. Sam filled his pipe and lit it, holding the lucifer until it almost burned his fingers; then gently blew out its flame and threw it overboard.

"The war is over," he said. "We beat the enemy, killed a lot of their men, burned a village, took some captives. But—Lunalilo's dead."

I had a mental picture of the fat, genial, little chief. I remembered him as I had first seen him, with his three wives. It seemed impossible that he was dead.

"I could marry one of his daughters now," Sam said, "and be the chief. Some day I could be king of all the Sandwich Islands. Every ship that came in here would have to pay me tribute. Every sailor who wanted grog, every whaler who wanted to quit the sea—"

"You are going to desert!" I said.

"No," he said. "This isn't what I want. Life here isn't so different from the life at home. The same kind of men make life hard here as they do in New England. If it isn't 'ile' that drives them here, it's still the ambition to pad their fat bellies with more fat, to pile up money, and to become kings by making slaves of others."

He puffed his pipe for a long while.

"Men like Starbuck," he said, then, "men like Worth. Men like most of those you know in New Bedford, in Falmouth, and a dozen other towns. The leading citizens, so-called. The self-righteous masters of New England!"

"What about them?" I asked. He was silent so long I thought he had forgotten them.

"God, how I hate them!" he said. "And how they hate me, and all the things I'd like to be. Men who have thoughts only for ile, for rum, for tobacco, for black slaves, for their proper places in the town hall, in the church, and in the home.

"Arrogance. Greed. Ambition. Ruthlessness. What they have done at home, they will do here in these islands. Pious, God-fearing, man-killing men, like Worth, will make life here as narrow and dreary and awful as the life we know at home. They bring a curse to the earth, even as they have brought it to the seas.

"No. Not here. Let me live on some friendly island that has never known the likes of Worth or Starbuck; where no captain feeds me rotten meat, dares curse me, dares drive me, dares scourge me with the cat or the fist of a bully mate, dares put me ashore on a barren island that I may starve myself to death or take my life with the sharp blade of the knife he furnishes me.

"Let me grow up with simple people, good people. Let me teach them how to make life even simpler than it is on these islands. Let me teach them how to grow, say, pumpkins in a cornfield. Let me sow potatoes in their fields. Maybe pumpkins will not grow in certain climates. Maybe they will. We shall find out.

"Let me teach them how to make war successfully, if there must be wars. Let me give them arms. And let me teach them what I can of medicine, games, religion, law—whatever I can teach them. Someday I shall be king of people like that—not a slave on a dirty whaler."

Listening to him talk, I was a child again. He had spoken just so when I was six, or seven. I recovered some of the adoration I once had for him. And I remembered something Gilbert Smith had said— that he was a crusader.

I started to say something of the sort, but no sooner had I mentioned Gilbert's name than Sam's attitude changed. He grabbed my arm, and hurt it with his fingers.

"Gilbert!" he said. "I did hear that he had been attacked on the island. Was he hurt?"

"No," I said.

His fingers immediately released their pressure. He smiled again. "That is good," he said. "And I heard something about you and one of Lunalilo's daughters."

I didn't know what to say, so I said nothing.

"You are a sentimentalist," he said. "You like girls—but as some men like sea shells. You don't want to kiss them. You don't want to do anything but talk to them, or laugh with them, or run them races down the beaches. I guess you're still just a little boy. But—you don't know what you do to them! It never seems to have occurred to you that girls are different than boys—that they are inflammable. You set them afire—and are aghast that they get burned. It wasn't my fault, back there in Valparaiso. It was yours, really. You walked away from the little señorita—when she wanted someone to make love to her. She didn't care for me. And yet—and yet it wasn't her fault, either. A woman isn't a doll. And a man like me isn't a boy."

I wanted to talk to him of Sally, but I dared not. He was planning on deserting Sally, evidently—for, if he were to establish his island kingdom he must, of necessity, leave Sally where she was. But to mention this—I could not.

Sam got to his feet, dropped the dottel of his pipe into the water, and reached his right hand down to lift me up.

"Where did they put Holden Hewman?"

"In the hold," I said.

"Aft?"

"Yes."

"Good night, George. And don't talk in your sleep."

AUG. 27. They buried Lunalilo this morning. They buried him at sea. His coffin was placed in a canoe, so Beetle told me, and rowed by six kahus, as they call the chief's retainers, far out into the brine. There the coffin was weighted and sunk.

Two men had been selected to keep the dead chief company in the other world. They were to be put to death and thrown overboard with the coffin—but when the time came for the funeral procession to set out from shore, only one of the two could be found. He was there, but he wasn't any too anxious to die. He pointed out, reasonably it seems to me, that if, according to the ritual, two men should be killed to honor the chief, then it must be two men or none.

He said he would consent to die, if one of the kahus died with him. Otherwise, no. The chief would be very angry to see only one slave come out of the shadows to tend him in the other world. He would make it hard for that one man.

He argued so skillfully that his life was spared. The other man—Brown is his name, Beetle says—will be killed, I suppose, on general principles. That is, if he is found.

Incidentally, Holden Hewman has escaped from the hold, aft.

And Captain Worth has ordered the ship's officers to recruit seven men to replace the deserters.

To recruit— That means to shanghai!

AUG. 28. We will put out to sea any day now. We sold some barrels of oil this morning to a Spanish merchantman. In exchange we received gold doubloons, two linen shirts, a canoeload of vegetables, five kegs of rum, a box of tea, gunpowder and shot, and 100 piculs of sandalwood. Captain Worth is quite pleased with his bargain, and has gone ashore to "celebrate."

The money was delivered in eleven sacks. Beetle and I were given the task of counting it, and then placing it in the captain's sandalwood chest.

I counted the beautiful coins and arranged them in piles, and rows of piles, while Beetle made entries in the captain's account book, writing with his left hand.

I fell adaydreaming of Spanish treasure, the pirate ships, the golden galleons of the Spanish Main, and the loot of burning towns, when something darkened the port—throwing a shadow on the gold. I turned and saw, in the porthole, a dark scowling face, one made more than ordinarily frightful by reason of livid scars that ran up both cheeks and across the great hooked nose.

'Blackbeard,' I thought, 'or Captain Kidd, or Morgan!'

Then fright changed to wonder. We were high above the water line. Was the pirate standing in midair? Was he standing there at all? Was he a ghost of some long-dead plunderer? Did he actually exist?

He did, for he leered at me and scowled at Beetle.

"Beetle," I cried. "Look!"

Beetle looked, and started up. The pen dropped from his hand. Whereat the face laughed, and spoke.

"A man who writes with his left hand," it said, "will meet someday, a right-handed hangman."

Instantly then the face shot upward, followed by the body that belonged to it. Beetle looked at me as if he'd seen a ghost.

When I found I could move my legs I went to the open port and twisted my neck so I could look upward. There were ropes over a pulley arrangement above me, and a boatswain's chair was swinging to and fro.

I laughed, in my relief.

"Just one of the carpenters repairing the side of the ship," I said. "He went up in a bosun's chair."

"Oh," said Beetle, sitting down again. "But what did he say? He saw all that gold. What did he say?"

"Something about a left-handed man," I answered.

Beetle sprang up again.

"I'll rope-end him," he cried. "I'll tear him apart. I'll—I'll—"

Then he saw the humor of it, and resumed his seat, grinning.

"Well, we've work to do," he said. "And when we're through here, we've orders to bring the captain aboard. Go on with your counting. But that throat-cutting rascal did give me a turn, I don't mind saying."

Chapter Fifteen

AUG. 30. We have some new men aboard.

One is Joe Thomas, the dead man. He was dead when he came aboard the *Globe* out of the fog and the sea. He died again when we marooned him. And here he is once more, as dead as ever.

We found him yesterday in a grogshop, Captain Worth and I. We were looking for Sam. That is, the captain was looking for Sam. We went to a number of grogshops before we located the right one. It was a filthy place, dark, full of smoke, full of rough and loud talking men, full of nauseating odors.

At first we could make out nobody. After our eyes had adjusted themselves, we saw Sam at a table near the bar. Three men were with him. Sam saw us, whispered to one of his companions, and stood up. His companion stood up too. Joe Thomas!

Captain Worth almost screamed. He took a backward step. His stumps of hands came out of his pockets, scurried quickly back again. His red beard fluttered madly.

"Aye," Joe Thomas said. "The man ye put ashore to die. The man ye marooned on a rock in the sea. Joe Thomas. Did ye think me a haunt, Captain Murder?"

"Joe Thomas!" The captain said the name again, but in a different way. "It was—it was only a matter of discipline. I put back for ye, the day after I put ye ashore. But—but—but—"

"But me no lies, Captain Marooner," Thomas shouted. "I know the black heart of ye. I know whaling skippers. Ye're all alike. Poison mean. Greedy for ile. Ye'd drink it if ye could. Ye'd let it circulate in your veins, if so ye might—and brag among yerselves which had the better ile. Ile! More to ye than blood—especially the blood of yer men. Damn all whaling skippers. Damn ye especially. And, had ye two hands like a man—"

"Stop it," Sam said. "Stop it, Joe. The skipper's all right. He *did* turn back for you."

"Did he now? But not the *next* day; nor the next *two* days. Three days I stayed on that island before a schooner rescued me. Three days! Without water. Without food. Three days and three nights until I saw the schooner! Discipline, says ye, Captain Worth? Some day ye'll learn the meaning of the word."

"Peace," Captain Worth said, in an unctuous voice. "I tell ye I never meant ye to perish there. And I'd have ye join the crew again. I'll double your lay, that I will, Joseph Thomas."

Thomas reached behind him for his whisky glass. He downed his drink and threw the glass at the captain—and almost hit him.

"Away!" he said. "Out of my sight before I knife ye. Ah, ye let me have a knife on the island. Ye remember? A sharp knife. To take my life with, if I wished it. Out now, afore I use it on ye. Haunt me no more, double lays, or triple lays, Hands Without Fingers or Thumbs. Get out before I kill and eat ye."

But Joseph Thomas is one of those shanghaied aboard us. He came in the bow boat with the others.

The bottom was filled with them, all stupidly drunk—or drugged.

"Grab hold of them swine and bring them up," Captain Worth shouted as the boat came alongside.

One of the men showed fight, seeming to realize what was happening. Beetle struck him, knocked him to the deck. Blood gushed from the fellow's mouth. Blood and oaths. He is the man of the bosun's chair, the fearful man who looked in at Beetle and me as we counted the Spanish gold. His name is Silas Payne. He had a gun in his pocket, I was told today. Perhaps that is why Beetle struck him.

The third is an Englishman named Oliver. He was smiling when he was hoisted up on deck, and he was singing an obscene ballad— in most horrible English. Beetle cooled him too.

Another is Humphries, the colored steward of the *Lyra*. Apparently he didn't have to be shanghaied. The fifth is the native who ran away to escape being buried at sea with Lunalilo, the chief. There are two I haven't seen yet, one named Hanson and the other with the queer name of Liliston. I wonder what they are like.

Gilbert Smith helped me carry Silas Payne to a bunk in the fore-castle, then led me to a secluded spot near the tryworks.

"We were cursed when we set sail, Friend George," he whispered; "now we are doubly cursed. Did thee look well at those wharf rats, those deserters, those thieves and murderers? I am afeared thy brother picked them for no good."

We spoke in whispers, although nobody was near to listen.

"Maybe you are wrong," I said. "Maybe you but imagine terrors. Certainly these men have been ill used, but—"

"Nay, nay," he said fiercely. "I be not imagining, dear friend. I speak from knowledge of this sort of scum. Murder is abrew on this ship, Friend George. I knew it when I looked again upon the wicked face of Thomas Joad."

"Thomas Joad?"

"Aye. His name is not Joe Thomas. It is Thomas Joad; and he is thy brother's evil genius."

He seemed astonished that I had never heard the name of Joad.

"Thee has not lived in Nantucket," he observed. "Thee has lived in a cave lined with books. Perhaps thee's never heard either of the whaler *Clemency Grant?*"

He was wrong there. I had heard of the whaler. I had seen her lighting up the sky and the sea. And had I not seen her thus, yet would I have remembered her name, for she was the first vessel on which Sam went to sea.

I was eight or nine. It was late at night. I heard people shouting, men running, women screaming. I woke and looked through the window of my room, and saw the whole sky ablaze and shot with thick black smoke. Then I noticed that even the ocean was burning. Last of all, I saw the ship itself, with the flames rising from her. A ship outlined by the fire that destroyed her. I dressed quickly and ran to the docks.

The small boat I did not see until it was a few feet from the sands. I ran to the boat, and there was Sam. He was one of a dozen or so, but I saw only him. His clothes were soaking wet and smeared with heavy oil. His hands and face were black and slimy; but I knew him.

"Were you on the *Clemency Grant* at that time?" I asked Gilbert.

"I was one of the crew. A boy then. Little older than thee be now. And I have been silent until now—when it becomes me to speak to thee. For thine own good."

He looked nervously all around before he spoke again.

"The *Clemency Grant!* The whale ship that was the damnation of many, including her captain, Phineas Spence."

Captain Spence, Gilbert said, was more of a beast, if possible, than Captain Worth. He worked the men harder, with less rest. He served food that was much worse than any mess aboard the *Globe*. He was even more careful of every drop of oil than our skipper; and more careless of the lives that produced the oil.

Yet nothing untoward occurred until the day Captain Spence ordered an old sailor named Eliphalet Hood into the rigging.

There had been violent storms for the best part of a week. All the men were exhausted through work and exposure, and on the point of mutiny. Futhermore, Hood, who was covered with boils—the effect of the rotten meat—and who had been injured by a fall, was unfit for duty.

When he heard the skipper order the old man aloft, Sam stepped forward and offered to go in Hood's place. The captain struck him such a blow that he lay unconscious on the deck, and might have been washed overboard had not Gilbert brought him below.

Tom Joad, Sam's friend, was angered out of his senses by the captain's brutality, so that he called on God, in a piercing voice, to strike the captain dead! Immediately he was seized by the mates and beaten unmercifully. Then Captain Spence ordered that he be flogged.

Meantime Eliphalet Hood went aloft. What happened up there Gilbert did not see. All he could tell me was that the old man suddenly slipped, cried out, and fell into the tossing sea. The *Clemency Grant* went on without him.

Joad was whipped the next morning, with all hands watching—including my brother Sam.

"Sam wept," Gilbert said, "even as thee would weep to see a friend's back flayed open with the cat. And he made a vow—to me and others—that he would, someday, make Captain Spence pay for this savage cruelty."

Gilbert was silent. So was I, though of course I felt like urging him to continue. I thought, for a time, that he was not going to tell me any more. But he was only choosing the right words, I guess. He wanted to impress me with a warning, and to give me a lesson in right thinking and in right conduct.

"In the main," he said, finally, "thy brother's thought was good. It was good in itself, Friend George; but the motive that inspired it was evil.

"Sam Comstock proposed that all those common men who went down to the sea in ships, the men of the whalers and the men of the fast merchant ships, band themselves into a guild—into a strong brotherhood that would assure all crews of decent food and decent treatment.

"This idea, Friend George, I seconded with all my heart. American seamen be not sheep nor cattle to be worked until they drop, to be fed with slops, to be beaten with stripes until, perhaps, they die. They be not inferior creatures to be exploited for the enriching of their betters. Nay, they be men with souls. They be as true Americans as those who own the ships and those who captain them.

"There is a greed on the part of shipowners and masters that is unseemly; that takes no account of the danger to a seaman's body or soul; that recks not of storm or calm or the absence of fat whales; that seeks only ile, ile, ile—and all the ile that can be put aboard a dirty craft.

"Aye, the idea I seconded indeed. And I still believe in it.

"But it was not the good of all that inspired thy brother to this conception, dear friend. It was revenge that put the words into his mouth. Not the sense of justice, but the hope of getting even with the captain, and his ilk."

Again my friend was silent; savoring, I think, the taste of the future in which men would band together for justice—and obtain it.

"Of all the men who discussed thy brother's thought," Gilbert continued, "only Tom Joad declared it childish. It could never be, he said. It would be impossible to band together such gadabouts as American sailors be. And, if it were possible, it would take a hundred years or more.

"Then, he said, there was the law to be considered. The law was ever for the rich and powerful, never for the poor and weak. What could we expect from politicians except stricter laws?

" 'Have we friends in Congress?' he demanded. 'Barnabas Starbuck has. So has Phineas Spence. So has every other ship captain, and every shipowner. And what would they do while we were organizing our little brotherhood—getting in touch with those ashore and those on the seven seas? What think you? Would not there be laws against such a brotherhood? Aye. It would be called mutiny. It would be called treason against the god of mammon. It would be called a desecration of the dollar.

" 'Can you weigh the blood out of my back against a gram of oil that can be sold on the market, Sam Comstock? Can you weigh the loss of Eliphalet Hood, and the destitution of his widow and his children against a barrel of prime sperm oil to be stored in Barnabas Starbuck's storehouse? Let us not be silly. Let us take our revenge while we can.' "

This time Gilbert was silent so long I could not help but prod him.

"What did Sam say to that?" I asked.

"He said," Gilbert answered, "that Joad was right in part—that indeed it might take a hundred years to effect a brotherhood. And he added that it did seem wrong that men should suffer in the meantime. What else he said I know not, for I was summoned on deck. And never since have I talked with either thy brother or his evil genius about the rights and wrongs of seamen.

"The voyage continued after Joad's flogging. Without incident. It was only on the night we were coming into port, Friend George, that anything out of the usual occurred."

"The fire," I said.

"Aye," Gilbert said. "The fire. It broke out in the hold, aft, where many barrels of prime sperm oil were stored. I was nearby at the time. I smelled smoke and made my way aft in an effort to locate it.

"My way was lighted suddenly by fire. Several of the barrels had been broached, Friend George. By a whaling spade, I fancy. And the fire was even then beyond control.

"I hurried to find the captain. And I found him. Dead in his cabin. His head had been opened by a whaling spade, which was lying near his body. It was the spade Joad used. He had fashioned it himself. He was ever the clever blacksmith, Thomas Joad—or Joseph Thomas as he now calls himself. I would know his spade among a thousand."

"And you think Sam helped him?"

I was so carried away by horror that I spoke aloud. Gilbert shushed me, and looked all around again.

"Nay, nay," he said. "To this day, I am convinced, he believes that Captain Spence went voluntarily down with his blazing ship. I have never forgotten his words to me as we rowed ashore in the small boat.

"He was sorry, he said, that he had not seen the anguish on Phineas Spence's face in the light of those blazing oil barrels. That he swore, would be recompense enough for the loss of his lay. Nay, rest assured, thy brother had no part in setting the ship afire, nor in the murder of the skipper. The point is that he rejoiced in the burning of the oil; that he thought it a fitting revenge."

I did feel better. But Gilbert had not finished.

"And thy brother rejoiced openly when he learned that Captain Spence was surely dead. He rejoiced in drink, Friend George, and in such fashion that all Nantucket was scandalized.

"Before scores of men in the Lilac Lantern, Friend George, thy brother Sam arose and drank a toast to 'that devil, Phineas Spence, cooking in hell now in his own ile with all his smug and righteous companion skippers.' Now, perhaps, thee knows why so many men and women in Nantucket look upon thy brother with a holy horror."

"But are you sure Joad killed the captain?" I asked.

"No, Friend George," he said. "That I am not. Yet I may add that, of all the crew, Joad was the only one who swore he would never again go to sea, and the first one to ship out on a whaler. The guilty flee, Friend George, when no man pursueth.

"Joad fled, and for years we saw him not. Thy brother went his way alone, but something of the venom of Joad was left in him. And then—behold the hand of the devil!—one day they come together again, in a fog at sea; thy brother and his evil genius.

"And now, for the third time, they are united. For the devil's doings.

"There be evil days ahead. Thy brother has ever been a man of violence; and, though there be many crimes I would not impute to him—still, with these riffraff hellions to whisper temptations into his ears, who knows what will become of him?

"Do thee watch and pray. The seeds are growing. A little time and they will bear crimson fruit."

SEPT. 1. At sea. Clear and calm.

We left Oahu last night, on the flood tide.

And there was a girl on the beach who screamed and screamed—a girl who took to her canoe at the last moment and followed us far. Sam was right. I have hurt her more than Sam ever could.

Lia-Lia the forsaken!

I wish I had never seen her.

Chapter Sixteen

SEPT. 15. On the Equator. Hot. Calm. Tar oozing out of the deck. Scant winds. I am sixteen today. Sixteen going on seventeen.

A queer spot for a birthday surely, a whaleship stuck in the middle of a flat green-blue sheet of glass; all of us nearly naked; dead sails overhead; a blinding sun; no clouds moving; and hardly a sound to let a man know he is alive.

Back home there would be presents, and hearty handshakes, and boys slapping me jovially on the back. "And one for good luck." And Father sighing. "Thee is growing, laddy, yet thee has still to eat another barrel of flour before thee is a man." And Sally!

Has she grown? I wonder. I have. I'm at least two inches nearer the stars; and several inches wider across the chest.

There would be a party in my home. And Sally and I would wander along the beach, after it was over. We'd look for shooting stars, and we'd sit and talk and listen to the murmur of the waves. She's only a year older than me now—yet in a month she'll be eighteen. Two years my senior again.

Father always intended to send me to a school in Boston when I was sixteen. Ah well!

Why should any boy long for the sea? A desolate, cruel, lonely existence. An unnatural life. Romance? Adventure? I used to think sometimes, long ago, sitting on the wharf with Sally and watching the ships come in—I used to think that someday, when I was grown up, I might find all these things on the sea. How long ago that was!

We're all such forsaken, desperate, helpless creatures—even the strongest of us aboard. We each seek some escape—some in scrimshaw work, some in putting their thoughts on paper, some in drink, some in talking and dreaming of women, some—like Sam—in plotting little wars, in dreaming of island kingdoms, in veiled talk of bloody deeds they might accomplish.

How many nights since I left home have I wept myself to sleep out of sheer loneliness! I was ashamed of that, thinking it cowardly and weak, a sign that I lacked character. Yet I have seen other boys weeping in their hammocks—and I have watched the men who are too old to weep give way to their weaknesses in manner just as futile.

My sixteenth birthday; and as full of melancholy as could be. Not even the memory of Sam and the terrified turtle can cheer me, though I doubled up with laughter at the time.

It was the last of the terrapins. He weighed at least three hundred pounds. Sam had been elected by the rest of the crew to throw him overboard. He had secured the shell-back with stout rope, and was carrying him on his back, when he slipped on the oil-smeared planks in the hold and fell.

I was half asleep when I became aware that someone was standing over me, whispering my name. I blinked open my eyes, and saw Gilbert Smith, a bull's-eye lantern gleaming on his face. He was strangling with restrained laughter.

"What is it?" I asked.

"Come with me, Friend George," he said. "I'll show thee something."

We sneaked quietly up to the deck, which was untenanted save by the man at the wheel, stole swiftly forward along the larboard deck, and thence down to the hold by means of the forward companion.

There was a deal of noise, a thumping and straining of great bodies, a whacking and a thrashing around, and Sam's voice cursing.

At first I could see nothing but the barrels of oil and water stowed in the hold and lashed. Smith was shaking so with silent laughter that the light in his hand flashed crazily on these.

It was not until he stopped laughing and put the light on Sam that I saw what was happening. There lay my brother, bound with four or five lengths of stout hemp to the back of the monster turtle. He couldn't get up. He couldn't unloose the rope. He could merely beat the planks with his fists and the heels of his boots, and bang his head down on the shell of the turtle. The latter was moving this way and that, at will, bumping Sam's head and hands and feet into barrels and stanchions, striving to get away from him.

"I was going to carry the fool thing above and drop him overboard," Sam explained, "but I slipped and fell, and I can't get up. And I haven't a knife to cut myself loose. Don't stand there laughing. Get a blade. Cut me free before this fool animal butts my brains out."

SEPT. 20. Calm. No wind. No sign of whales. No cry of "thar blows" has come from the masthead since we left Oahu. The crew are talking again of Joseph Thomas, saying he is the "Jonah." He pays no heed to them. As once before, he is deaf and dumb. He avoids us all. If we speak to him he looks at us with his queer eyes, looks at us as if we weren't there, looks through us, and passes on.

Only two of those we took aboard at Oahu are at all human. One of these is the Negro, Humphries. He is, by far, the best-natured man aboard. He is the steward. He takes the place of Cook who jumped ship at Oahu. He steals food from the galley and passes it around to the boys, Lay, Hussey, Jones, Columbus Worth, and me. He is always smiling or laughing, always talking of playing his violin for us, "some night when cap'n he ain' so drunk." Humphries is a wonderful storyteller.

He was born on a Mississippi plantation, a slave. He ran away. He hid himself on a river packet bound for New Orleans. There he stowed away on an out-bound merchantman. He's been all over the world. He has a wife and six children in Mississippi, a wife and two children in Gloucester, and a wife in Oahu, he says.

"Ah loves de sea," he says. " 'Cause why? 'Cause it's free. 'Cause it

don' need no hoein', no pickin', no nothin'. 'Cause Ah gits along fine
on a ship. Soft jobs. Good nourishments. Plenty fish. Plenty brine
beef. Plenty whale meat. Ah, dat's it. Whale meat. You know what
makes me strong? Whale meat. Dat's it. Dat smacks! And whale
milk. Yassuh! Ain' nothin' in all de world put stren'th in a man like
whale milk!"

He laughs until the sails shake.

"Man, man," he roars, "bring me a she-whale an' Ah'll sit up all
night milkin' her—and spit in de sharks' eyes if dey gits too close."

The other appealing newcomer is the native we call Joe Brown,
whose nimble feet saved him from escorting Chief Lunalilo into the
other world. He came aboard us with nothing on him but a loin cloth
and a string of blue beads. He danced with joy when he was given
an outfit of "white man's clothes," and crossed himself again and
again. I imagine he is a Papist, for he crosses himself every time he
goes aloft.

He wore his trousers wrong-side to the first day; and wouldn't
change them until Second Mate Lumbard lashed him with a rope's
end.

His eyes shine with excitement and pride. He's working with the
white gods—actually one of them. And when he returns to his people
he'll have tremendous prestige—enough to wipe out the shame of his
desertion. Only Smith disapproves of him.

"Aye, Friend George," Smith says. "He's gentle and willing. I grant
thee so much. But for all the Christianity he professes he's still a
heathen—and the spirit of Lunalilo haunts him day and night. He's
a good man aloft—and better than thee with the harpoon. But with
all that—he's still an idolater, and no one to be trusted."

The others of those we shanghaied—Silas Payne, John Oliver, Anthony Hanson, and Thomas Liliston—strike as much terror into me
as does Joe Thomas.

Payne especially terrifics me. He is a thin, gaunt, dark New Eng-
lander, a sullen, vicious, shambling, scar-faced man. He is terrible
even when he smiles and says something meant to be funny.

I turned the grindstone for him this morning while he sharpened
spades, harpoons, and lances. It was tedious work.

I sat on the weather side of the quarter-deck with the sun glaring
full in my face, making me blink. Finally I shut my eyes tight. I
kept turning the creaking wheel for hours. At least it seemed hours.

It was an odd experience. The sun on my face. Colored lights
dancing before my tight-shut eyes—something like a tropical imitation of the Northern Lights—and in my ears the noise of the stone and
the shivering of the steel.

Wheeze! Bzz! Bzz! said the stone.

Cling. Zzzzz! Cling! Zzzzz! whined the blade.

All the time I seemed to be another man, looking at myself, seeing an overgrown boy, sunburned and freckled, his face and clothes smeared with whale gurry, his duck frock blackened, his trousers torn and patched, and thick with grease and oil, and his Scotch cap, its bright colors blurred with time and oil and spray, pulled down over his eyes. Yes, I was looking at myself, and at Payne, his gray eyes squinting at the steel he was edging. I was looking at us both, and feeling afraid of Payne, and sorry for myself.

Now and then I shifted, under the intensity of the sun's rays, and opened my eyes a trifle, and watched the sparks fly from the grindstone, and mirror themselves in Payne's fierce eyes. And, perhaps because those Northern Lights were still playing tricks with my eyes, each spark turned into a drop of blood; each shivering kiss of blade on stone became a man's last sigh.

After a time these fancies went out of me, and others took their place. The ship was turning, as I turned the wheel. The sea was turning. The whole world was turning. Judith Chase's Lane went by me, tilting, whirling, end-over-end. Sally's face went round and round in a circle. My own face spun before me, now dipping in the sea, now moving through the thinning clouds, now whirling in the blinding glory of the sun.

Somebody tapped me on the shoulder, and the world, and the faces, and the ship stopped turning; and I heard Sam's laugh. I opened my eyes, and saw him, not turning, but weaving.

"You've been turning that stone for half an hour, and nobody's using it," Sam said.

"Where's Payne?" I asked, trying to adjust my vision.

There was something bright in Sam's hand. It hurt my eyes to look at it.

"Gone and left you rocking the stone to sleep," he said.

It was a surgical instrument my brother held.

"It's a lancet," he explained. "I'm going to open my foot. You'll have to help me. Still groggy? We'll wait a minute then."

We walked aft, and sat in the shade and talked, until the dizziness left me. Then Sam handed me a sort of hook with a delicate spring attached to it. He thrust his foot out, and I saw it was badly swollen.

"Why don't you get the captain, or Lumbard, to lance it?" I asked.

"I'd sooner die than ask them a favor," he said, boiling up in sudden anger. "And they'd as soon kill me as not."

At that he kneeled on his left knee, holding his right foot flat to the deck, and split it open with his lancet, after which he attached the hook device to the parted flesh.

"Hold it," he said. "Keep the wound open."

I trembled so that he swore at me. The sight of blood, the bare tendons, the grinning bone, and the vile matter that seeped out with the blood weakened and chilled me. I all but retched.

Sam's anger flared high for a moment, then subsided. He smiled at me. He laughed gaily—though I supposed he was in terrible pain.

"You remind me of Phineas Spence's widow," he said, not looking up from his work. "She heard I was bringing surgical instruments aboard. I guess all Nantucket heard it. She stopped me on the street and asked me about it. 'Yes,' I said. 'I'm something of a surgeon.' 'Could you cut off a man's leg?' she asked me. 'Madam,' I said, 'I could even cut off his head, if that were necessary.'"

All this time, while I held the flesh apart, Sam was scraping the bone—a sound that still chills me whenever I remember it.

"All right now," he said, finally. "Reach into my right coat pocket and fetch out what you find."

It was a leather box, wrapped in a piece of sail cloth.

"Open it," he said.

I opened it, and looked at a row of needles, one of them threaded with catgut. Sam took it from me, placed it on the deck beside him, removed the hook from his foot, and, without further ado, began the task of sewing up the wound.

"Shouldn't you wash it first?" I asked.

"Bah," he said. "Am I a woman? A little bandaging. A few days. And that foot will be as good as ever."

He bade me go to his cabin for a clean bandage, "and a bottle of sassafras tea you'll find in my trunk."

I was eager to obey—to get away from the sight of that butchery for a few minutes. I found the bottle, but I'm sure it wasn't sassafras tea. It smelled like rum. I didn't begrudge it to him. I was almost tempted to swallow a little of it myself.

One thing I noticed in his trunk. Most of his weapons have disappeared. But the pumpkin seeds—and other seeds—are still there.

OCT. 2. Calm. Wind from the SW. It will rain this afternoon. Heading for Fanning's Island. The brine has run out of the beef barrel. The beef is putrid. Oliver, a bandy-legged little man, grabbed the pan out of Humphries' hands as he came in with it.

"Cor!" he said. "Hit stinks to 'igh 'eaven. 'Ow can a man stomach that?"

He rushed to the rail with the mess and threw it overboard.

"Ain' my fault," Humphries said. "No suh! Cap'n say dat beef good enough. Cap'n say salt it and boil it. Cap'n's o'de's, suh."

"Get out and bring us decent food," Payne shouted, "or I'll cut your black gizzard into ribbons."

Humphries, for once without his grin, began backing out, nodding his head.

"Yassuh! Yassuh! Ah do what Ah cain, but, cap'n, suh—"

"The captain will speak for himself," Captain Worth said, appearing in the doorway as suddenly as a devil summoned by witchcraft.

Behind him bulked Mate Beetle, with a long net in his hand. In the net was a chunk of the stinking beef. Beetle must have fished it up out of the water.

"Throw the meat on the table, Mr. Beetle," Captain Worth said. "There's plenty of brine in it now. They'll eat it."

He took us all in with his cold bloodshot eyes.

"Damned swine," he burst out. "Throwing away my good food. Tender insides, I swan!"

We said nothing. He kept glaring at us for a time.

"Who heaved it over?" he demanded. "Who dared?"

No one answered.

The captain glared at the steward, who turned almost white.

"You know, Humphries," he said. "Who did it?"

Humphries fell to his knees.

" 'Fo' God, Cap'n," he cried, "Ah didn't see. Ah tripped. Ah fell. When Ah riz—gone beef!"

The captain grunted and turned from him in disgust.

"You'll finish the barrel," he said to us, "spoiled or not. When that's gone—you'll get turtle meat again. And if any damned rascal of ye complains, or whimpers, or wastes another bit of food aboard this ship, by thunder, I'll have him flogged."

Payne waited until captain and mate were well forward. Then, seizing the slimy meat in his bare hands, and making an awful face, he hurled it through the port.

"Blast his eyes," he growled. "Wait 'til we git to Fanning's Island!"

Liliston, with outthrust jaw and hairy ear, towered over Payne and he nudged him sharply. Payne ceased talking. He and Liliston stared at each other, then turned and glared at us. Lay, whose magnificent head of blond hair contrasted sharply with Liliston's hairless head and chin, seemed possessed of a flash of intelligence.

"Why can't we troll for fish?" he asked. "I got some hooks."

We had fresh fish for dinner.

Chapter Seventeen

DEC. 15. Calm. Sultry. Just a year ago today we set out from Edgartown. A whole year gone. A wretched, wasted, lost-forever year! A futile year. We caught few whales. We are almost as empty of oil as we were when we set sail. How much longer will it be until we get our fill of oil—and turn back home?

Or will we ever get back home?

DEC. 16. Calm. Sultry. Captain Worth has lost sixteen silver dollars. Every one, including the mates and the harpooners, has been searched. The entire ship has been searched. The money has not been found. But the captain has confined Joseph Thomas below.

On suspicion!

I can imagine the captain welcomed this opportunity to punish Thomas. It may be, many of the men feel, that he merely *said* he lost the money.

DEC. 24. Calm. Soft breeze from the south. Up in the rigging tonight I saw a halo around the moon. I mentioned it to Sam.

"Beautiful," I said. "Especially for Christmas Eve."

My first Christmas away from home really—for last year I was so seasick that Christmas came and went without my knowing anything of it. My first real Christmas at sea—and there was a halo around the moon!

Sam laughed at me.

"Don't be a fool," he said. "Don't you know that is caused by clouds full of ice crystals? These reflect the beams of light. There's nothing mystic about it."

At midnight the ship's bell rang out Christmas tidings, brassy clanging notes on the sharp sweet air.

"Merry Christmas, Sam," I said. There was a shameful lump in my throat. It was so strange, so sad, to be so far away from home on Christmas. There should be many bells ringing, church bells and sleigh bells. There should be waits singing in the snow, and squat stone houses, and bare black waving trees, and lights shining out into the darkness; glad, friendly, beckoning lights.

But there was only the calm sea, and the little wind, and the bright moon with the halo about it, and the feeble sound of the ship's bell, and Sam's voice saying "Christmas! Will you never grow up? Merry Christmas! What's merry on this tub? Merry Christmas—and a storm coming up!"

DEC. 25. A rough sea, with dark lowering clouds. And yet, somehow, we made a Merry Christmas of it just the same. The men had decorated the forecastle before I came off watch. There was an extra sperm lamp suspended from the center deck beam, swinging to and fro with two huge wicks blazing in it. It shed aroma and warmth as well as light. It actually made the dark hole cheery. And they'd put up part of a whale's jawbone, hung it with green seaweed, and thrust sperm candles into the sockets, to make a Christmas tree.

"Me'y Christmas," shouted Humphries as I came in. He sat in his hammock, half-naked, mending a hole in his flannel shirt—already full of patches. His dark skin glistened in the lamplight.

"Merry Christmas," the others called. Hussey and Columbus Worth were smoking pipes Lay had made for them out of a sea elephant's hollow tooth. Lay had one for me too, a beautiful piece of carving, with a penguin's quill for a stem.

"Merry Christmas!" I shouted, and shook hands all around.

No, not all around. Payne, standing in front of the mirror was trimming his beard with the sharp edge of Sam's harpoon. Liliston and Oliver, sitting apart, talking to each other, did not look up as I came in. They were chewing tobacco, and spitting between whispered sentences.

A queer picture of a Christmas scene. Add to it naked arms and legs stuck out of berths, half seen through the smoke, the glimpse of a bearded bronzed face here and there; and, hanging from pegs, a collection of dripping sou'westers, monkey jackets, stockings, shirts, and trousers—proof that men had been up during the night battling with the storm which blotted out the bright moon and its halo.

Later, Humphries, a white jacket over his patched shirt, served hot food, and hot rum toddies.

"Cap'n's o'de's," he said. "Rum toddies, fo' all today, and a Me'y Christmas."

After dinner, while we gathered around the "Christmas tree," Humphries tuned up his fiddle and played some Christmas carols.

Mate Beetle came down and lit the candles. Every time the hatch was opened the candles went out. Every time the candles went out we laughed, or cursed. All through the singing Payne and Oliver, straddling opposite ends of a chest and thrusting out their feet to keep the chest from rolling, played checkers.

It brightened a bit in the afternoon, and services were held under a tarpaulin on deck, Gilbert Smith reading verses from the Bible, Humphries playing hymns, and all of us—or most all of us—singing at the tops of our voices.

Captain Worth stood by, hands in his pockets, smiling as benevolently as a bishop. Joe Brown, the native, blessed himself again and again, and wept every little while, and danced, and now and then cried out, "Christ born! Christ born!"

The captain promised us roast ham and plum duff for supper; and all of us danced like that simple brown man, out of sheer joy.

But when Humphries went to the barrel of hams, he found someone had been there before him. There was nothing in the barrel but a few ham bones, with fringes of meat upon them.

We thought, at first, that the captain was feigning anger. But we were wrong. His fury was so tremendous he almost fainted. I've never seen a face turn so white, nor eyes gleam with such red malice. He shook, even to his stiff red beard. He thrust the palms of his hands hard against the rail of the bridge and it seemed to me they shook the entire ship.

It was many seconds before he spoke.

"We have a cannibal among us," he said then. His voice was the more effective inasmuch as it was calm and low and cold when we had expected it to be hysterical with rage.

"A filthy swine who eats the flesh of his fellow swine. Raw! Well—" he paused and spat—"well—I shall find him."

He turned to Humphries.

"We still have terrapins," he said. "Have two brought up, and roasted."

"Two, suh?" Humphries said. "Only one dar, Cap'n. Ah counted him. Only one."

Forgetful that he had no fingers the captain tried to catch up a harpoon and throw it. It fell as he touched it. He jumped up and down like a mad man. He foamed at the mouth. He cried out, but what he said we couldn't understand.

"For'd," Beetle cried. "For'd every man o' ye. Christmas is over."

Who ate that barrel of hams? I can think of only one man who could have done that. Mate Beetle. I wonder how long it took him.

JAN. 1, 1824. New Year's day. God keep me from another year such as the one that has passed. God give us whales and send us home again. God give me another sight of Sally. I can ask no more.

JAN. 23. The *Lyra's* here. The *Lyra* of New Bedford. I feel as excited as a child. I hardly know what to say, where to begin. It's the next best thing to going home. It's like a wonderful dream come true.

She came up suddenly, that blessed old whaler. Humphries, who was in the crow's nest, spied her first, and took her for a whale.

"Dar she breach," he called out, his voice shrill with excitement, his arm pointing SSW. " 'Bout eight mile, suh. She breach ag'in. She breach and breach, Cap'n, suh; but she don' blow."

"Breach but don' blow," the captain mimicked him angrily. "What the hell kind of whale is that?" He bade Beetle hand him his spyglass. He hurried up to the main top, going as nimbly as any boy, and turned the glass in the direction indicated by Humphries.

"A whale ship," he cried.

"Sail ho!" came the cry from the foremast.

There is no greater thrill than speaking another ship at sea—and having it turn out a friend.

In less than an hour we knew the oncoming craft to be the *Lyra.*

"Mistuh Comstock, suh," Humphries whispered to me, catching me by the arm, "Ah's in trouble, Mistuh Comstock."

"Yes," I said, "you deserted the *Lyra,* didn't you?"

"Yassuh," he said. "And now, if day cotch me, Cap'n Joy, he'll skin me alive, suh. What'll Ah do, Mistuh Comstock? What'll Ah do?"

"Have an accident," I said, trying not to laugh—yet there was much of comedy in the frightened gray face. "Fall down, skin your knee—anything to give you a chance to stay below."

I didn't mean it seriously, of course. But Humphries took me at my word, and "accidentally" ran a harpoon through the calf of his right leg. It was not a serious wound, but enough to take him below with Captain Worth's profane permission.

We all burst into cheers as the *Lyra* came close. The men on the *Lyra* cheered too, and sang, and waved their hats to us. Soon we were all singing together, frightening the sea gulls with our noise—

> Heave him up, O he yo!
> The captain's bawling louder.
> Raise his flukes! O he yo!
> The steward's making chowder.

It was no time at all until we were cutting through the water in the waist boat, Sam, Captain Worth, Beetle, Columbus Worth, and I. The two captains greeted each other with salty oaths and gales of laughter. The rest of us shook hands with old comrades, and tried to hold our emotions in check.

The mail bag came up out of the *Lyra*'s stomach, and letters rained out of it—one for Sam in Sally's writing. I knew it was hers the moment I saw it. My heart rose up and fell. I wanted to snatch it from Sam. Sam thrust it, unread, into a pocket of his monkey jacket!

I waited, hoping there was a letter for me, not believing it when all the letters had been sorted out, and there was none with my name on it.

After supper aboard the *Lyra* we had a social smoke, and swapped experiences, and lies. The one I liked best was told by their steward. A flying fish, he said, had flown right into his frying pan that morning, and winked at him. It had the loveliest blue eyes, "with lashes that long."

He's raising it for a pet.

Chapter Eighteen

JAN. 25. Calm and bright. Still "gamming" with the *Lyra*.

This morning we witnessed a weird tragedy.

We sighted a whale. The *Lyra* saw her at the same moment. We heard her lookout singing, "Thar blows," at the same time Beetle bellowed, "Bul-lows! Bul-lows!"

We lowered, hurrying with frenzy to beat the *Lyra*'s boats. We rowed, and the *Lyra*'s men rowed, stroke for stroke. We strained our backs, Captain Worth lashing us on, needlessly, with curses and threats. He didn't seem to know we needed only this competition to make us exert ourselves to the utmost—that we did our best not because of him but in spite of him.

We began to pull ahead. Our boat took the lead. Lumbard was right in back of us. The first of the *Lyra*'s boats was but a foot behind Lumbard, and on his weather side.

How we pulled! The thrill of the race still courses through my veins, and the sound of the captain's voice crying "Pull! Pull! Pull!"

We pulled until the sweat blinded us, until our arms were numb, and our throats dry. Our brains reeled, and the ships grew smaller and smaller and gradually vanished from our sight. We pulled, and Lumbard's men pulled, and so did the first of the *Lyra's* boats.

"Sounded," Captain Worth cried. "A ninety-bar'l sparm whale! And a calf! Pull now. Pull!"

He sniffed, as though smelling out the hiding place of mother and son. He bade us rest. We rested. Lumbard's boat shot by us on the starboard side, and the *Lyra's* boats passed to larboard.

We wet out throats and mopped our faces, and sucked in air. We took off our shirts and let the hot sun dry our perspiring skins. Sam munched on a piece of bread. The captain sniffed and sniffed.

Third Mate Fisher's boat came toward us slowly, barely creeping over the face of the sea. Joe Brown stood in the prow, harpoon in hand. Fisher was in the rear, steering, which was odd because the mate and boat steerer assume these positions only when the whale is close.

As I looked, the whales breached, half a mile from us, but not a hundred yards from Fisher's boat. Captain Worth had his back turned, and was sniffing the sea in front of him.

Mother and son! They fascinated me so that I never thought of singing out. If anyone else saw, he was as speechless as I. It was beautiful to see the two frisking on the surface of the calm blue sea, the mother fondling her baby—actually fondling it. It was such a little fellow—for a whale—and its spout so tiny!

It happened in a moment. The sun shone on Joe Brown's harpoon. Water spouted from the baby whale—water that quickly turned to red. The mother whale charged the boat, jaws open. The men leaped overboard, all but Joe Brown.

I saw him outlined against a fleecy cloud that was pasted on the blue horizon, his second harpoon poised. And then I found myself jumping over and swimming toward him, fast.

I heard men shouting. I lifted my head from the water, and looked around. Where Joe had stood, awaiting the mother whale's fury, there was only white water and the wreckage of a boat!

Lumbard's boat rescued all those in the water, except me. I swam back to the captain's boat, and Sam helped me over the side. We pursued the whale, and caught her just as the sun was setting. Sam put two irons on her. It was not difficult. She showed no fight. Her calf was dead. I think she was glad to die. We didn't even have to lance her.

We could not tow her, for the sea had roughened, and we were almost exhausted with our long pull. At least I was. That swim had been almost too much for me. We put irons into the dead monster, to mark her as ours, put a drag on her to buoy her up, placed a cable around her flukes, and made it fast to a small kedge to anchor her; then left her for the night.

All the way back to the ship we speculated on the fate of the men who had been in Fisher's boat. I wondered also about Joe Thomas. At least, I thought, even if he were still living on bread and water, he was fortunate. He would not have to spend this night fending off sharks from a whale's carcass.

Lumbard standing huge against the rail of the *Globe*, hailed us as soon as he heard the sound of our oars. His voice came clearly across the waters.

"Fisher's boat smashed, sir. Whale chawed it in half, and swallied down Joe Brown."

I hadn't had a chance to save the poor devil. But I am glad I tried. It was worth the scolding from Sam and the reprimand from the captain.

After supper, Gilbert Smith intoned a passage from the Twenty-Third Psalm, and we stood by, bare heads bent. Green pastures and still waters and a sad drum beating—and later, Smith's solemn voice saying, "A good man, Joe Brown—a good harpooner, but nevertheless, a heathen to the end. 'Lunalilo' he called out at the last. 'Lunalilo, mercy!' He escaped his old chief once. He couldn't do it again. A heathen, Friend George. Thee realizes that. Yet I feel our God will smile on him. He was only half a heathen after all."

JAN. 26. Have just come off watch after a mysterious conversation with Cyrus Hussey, who stepped into my path as I was relieved at the wheel.

"Laugh at everything I say," he begged me. He looked all about him, furtively, as though ghosts in the shadows might overhear. I laughed, but I was startled.

"Get word to Beetle or the Skipper," he said.

I laughed again, and Hussey laughed with me. He laughed loudly, nervously, warning me someone was coming. I turned and saw that it was Sam.

"It just dawned on me," Hussey said to Sam, "that George is taller than me. A whole inch."

"And I was saying that Cy's hair, that used to be a sort of brown, is bleached yellow as a girl's," I said.

Sam took Hussey's arm and walked away with him. He did not smile. Hussey's face, I noted, was ghastly. He had tried to tell me something. Sam had prevented him. I must see Hussey later today. There was a warning in his face. A definite warning.

Chapter Nineteen

FEB. 21. Calm. No wind at all. The calm that follows violence. The peace that follows death.

I am not sure this is the 21st, yet computations from the log book of the *Globe* show it must be. It seems months since my last entry in this little book. I have aged years. Sally is no longer two years my senior. She will never be as old as I am now.

If only I too had died!

It is a tragedy for one to survive a tragedy—and harbor it forever in the mind. Perhaps it will help a little to record it here, honestly and fully, as I remember it, and as parts of it were told to me. I shall begin then, with the morning of January 26, when we were still gamming with the *Lyra*.

On that day all the boats were mustered early, and we pulled for the whale we had killed and marked and buoyed the night before, the mother whale that fought so valiantly for her calf. After less than an hour's work with the oars, we arrived at the approximate spot, but found no buoy. After some minutes' searching, however, we located our drag, took the lines from it, and arranged to weigh the whale. At the first tug all of our irons came up, some with little patches of blubber adhering to them.

"The sharks," Sam said. "They got here first."

Captain Worth rubbed his palms together and spat into the sea.

"The Jonah's with us again," he said.

There was something about his voice, though it was calm and unaccented, that made me study him. There were lights in his eyes that matched the color of his beard.

"Seems like," Sam said. "There's not a barrel of oil left in that carcass."

"A Jonah," the captain repeated.

We pulled back to the ship in silence.

Beetle was on watch when we came aboard. Humphries stood close to him, his big eyes mirroring something of our mood.

"Bring up Joseph Thomas," the captain ordered.

Beetle whirled on Humphries.

"Don't stand thar, grinnin' like an ape," Beetle shouted. "Fotch him up."

Humphries sped away without answer, vanishing down the companionway forward. He returned in a few minutes alone.

"Cap'n Wo'th," he said, "Mistuh Thomas he say 'scuse 'im; but he ain' finish his breakfast yit, suh."

The colored man was visibly frightened.

"Ain't finished his breakfast, ain't he?" the captain said quietly. "That's too bad. That's much too bad." He licked his thin lips with his tongue. "Go back and say I require him on deck at once."

Humphries went, running. He came back, panting.

"Cap'n, suh, Mistuh Thomas say he ain' feelin' well. Mistuh Thomas say he wouldn't come on deck even fo' God."

The captain made a sign to Beetle. The mate went down the companionway, and returned, dragging Thomas after him, his hand gripping the seaman's shirt by the neck.

"Here's Mister Thomas, sir," Beetle said, "taken in the middle of his bread and water."

Thomas struggled to free himself, and Beetle slapped him; not hard, it seemed to me, but with sufficient force to shake him. Had not the mate held him so tightly, Thomas would have fallen from that slap.

"Mind how you handle me," Thomas cried.

Beetle was so astonished at the words that he let go his hold, and Thomas wavered on his feet. He put his hands to his neck, as though to cleanse it of Beetle's touch. His shoulders twitched—narrow, stooped, cadaverous shoulders. His cheeks flushed.

"What did you say?" Captain Worth asked mildly, taking a step toward Thomas, and thrusting his stumps of hands into his pockets. "Perhaps I heard ye wrong."

"You'd better mind how you handle me," Thomas repeated.

"So," the captain said, and not taking his gaze from the man, spoke to Beetle. "Seize that man up, Mr. Beetle. Seize him up and spread-eagle him! Twenty-five licks with a rope's end."

"Ye'll pay for this," Thomas cried in a queer frightened voice. "Aye, ye'll pay, ye stinking, stingy scum. I'd like to see ye swimming in the try-pots, and them boiling and bubbling with oil. I'd like to see ye cooked, and your skin shriveled and dried so I could use it as a mat to stamp and spit on."

His flushed cheeks paled as Beetle and Lumbard seized his arms. A fit of coughing shook him.

"You're not going to flog him?"

The words came out of my mouth before I realized it. Without warning, Beetle struck at me with a rope's end. Beetle, who had so patiently taught me, who had sometimes treated me as though I were his son!

"Mind your own business," he said savagely as he struck.

The rope's end hurt. But it was a lesser hurt than his sudden anger.

Beetle slipped irons on Thomas' wrists, and marched him to the quarter-deck, Lumbard following. On the quarter-deck Thomas' arms were lashed to a ratline from the starboard side, and Lumbard ripped his shirt up the back, and tore it from him in two pieces.

The narrow ribs stood out of the flesh like hoops on a barrel; hoops that contracted and expanded prodigiously, as emotion alternately pressed and released them.

"Call all hands aft!" Captain Worth cried, his voice anything but calm. "Come down from the masthead, you. And you, Peter Kidder, come down from the lookout."

The captain stood bareheaded on the break of the deck, hands in his pockets, and waited until all had swarmed up from below, and down from above. I glanced around, not wanting to watch that pitiful bare back. I saw Sam and Gilbert Smith standing near the mainmast. Smith seemed to be praying. Sam was smiling.

"He looks like—like he's glad," a voice whispered in my ear, the voice of Columbus Worth, the captain's nephew. Worth was staring at Sam in disdain and horror. I had been shipmates with Columbus for over a year now, but I knew him scarcely at all. He was my age, or younger, a frail, slim, bright, good-looking boy. Lay and Hussey were his friends; they called him Chris. He had always seemed to avoid me. I never knew why. But now I thought I had the answer. He had always feared and detested Sam, and wanted nothing to do with him—or with his brother.

"It's just his way," I whispered. "You never can tell how Sam feels by looking at him. He looked just like that when he lanced his foot."

"Maybe," he answered. Then he asked, "Will Uncle really flog him? He can't stand it, can he? He's nearly dead now. This will kill him, won't it? Why must we watch?"

"Silence!" Captain Worth roared, pointing his beard to every one of us, it seemed. We stood rigid.

"Lay on!" he said.

Beetle had rolled up his sleeves. He was holding a length of rope, spliced and knotted, in his right hand. At the word of command, he took his stance, swung the rope twice about his head, then brought it down upon his target. I shut my eyes before it fell; but I couldn't shut my ears to the victim's screams.

"My God!" I heard Rowland Jones say. I felt his right hand grip my shoulder. I opened my eyes and looked at Columbus Worth. He was pale—a queer pale. His skin looked like the white of a fish's belly, but there was a greenish tint in it. Jones was behind me. I could not see him, did not want to see him.

After a time Joseph Thomas stopped screaming, and involuntarily I looked at him. His back had been flayed open. He was unconscious. His legs had buckled at the knees, and his head had fallen forward. He was hanging limply from the rigging. Only the lashings on his outstretched arms held him up.

Beetle had given him fifteen strokes. Now he relinquished the rope to Lumbard. And that young giant plied it with a vigor Beetle never had, so that before long the rope was dripping with blood.

Ten strokes Lumbard administered. Before he had finished, Columbus Worth was vomiting, over by the rail, and Jones was gripping me with both hands, hiding his head against my shoulder.

Beetle cut Thomas down after the last stroke. Lumbard sloshed a pail of salt water over his bleeding back. Sam went forward, picked his friend up, and bore him to the forecastle.

Jones let go his hold on me as Sam walked by us. He staggered away, toward the rail.

As I followed him I saw a little black dog on the quarter-deck, sniffing at the red wet wood. I hadn't seen him before, but later I learned that he was Humphries' pet. Humphries had brought him aboard at Oahu, and kept him confined in the galley.

"Get out of here," Captain Worth cried. The dog looked up at him and wagged his tail. But the captain was in no mood for play. Before anyone could guess his action he had advanced on the animal and kicked him brutally in the ribs.

"Whose cur is that?" he demanded.

The dog ran, limping and whining, through the crowd of seamen, looking for his master and finding him, clawed piteously at his boots.

"Yours, Humphries? Get him to hell out of here, and keep him out."

"Yas, suh," Humphries said, bobbing his head and showing the whites of his eyes. "Ah rescued him f'm the cannibals, suh. Dey was goin' to cook and eat him, suh. He didn't mean no trouble, suh. No suh."

He took the dog in his arms, and hurried away; and I was not surprised to see Gilbert Smith following him.

The crew of the *Lyra*, Captain Joy, and some of the mates came aboard the *Globe* after dinner. Captain Joy proposed a wrestling match, and offered a pound of tobacco to anyone who could pin his first mate's shoulders to the deck.

"The prize is mine already, sir," Lumbard said, stepping forward.

"Mr. Lumbard got a letter from home yesterday," Captain Worth said, smiling at Captain Joy. "He's a father now. That's why he's so cocky, Captain. But cocky or not, he's good. I'll wager a keg of Jamaicky he falls your man two out of three."

"Done," said Captain Joy and called for his champion, a tremendous brute named Bingham.

The two men stripped to the waist, and squared away at each other. Lumbard, tall and gawkily built, his arms reaching down below his knees, made frightful faces at his adversary. The latter studied Lumbard calmly, and contemptuously. He seemed easily the more powerful of the two. He was better built, more graceful, and far more agile than Lumbard. And he was so confident of winning that those of us who had placed wagers on Lumbard wished we hadn't.

Lumbard had never been popular with the crew. He was a surly, brutal, coarse-speaking man. He delighted in kicking men and boys out of his way when he was hurried, or knocking them down when they didn't jump at his orders. We bet on him only because we knew his strength.

Suddenly Bingham leaped at Lumbard. Lumbard's enormous hands shot out. His great feet shifted. Bingham went up into the air, came down with a thud that seemed to rock the ship, and lay where he had fallen.

"Two out of three," cried Captain Worth.

Captain Joy shook his head.

"I have need of that man, Captain," he said. "Once is enough."

Mate Fisher stepped up to the two captains.

"If you have anybody else, Captain Joy," he said, "I'd like to try him."

Again Captain Joy shook his head.

"I have no one else," he said. "Bingham is my only wrestler."

"Too bad," Fisher answered.

"I'll wrestle you," Sam shouted. "Two falls out of three. Five dollars in gold to the winner."

Fisher smiled, laughed aloud.

"One fall," he said. "And no wager. I would not rob a shipmate."

"You're afraid to bet," Sam cried. "You know I'll throw you."

He tore off his shirt. Fisher tore off his. They stood for a moment eying one another. They were evenly matched, I thought. Though Sam was a head shorter than Fisher, he was much wider through the chest. He was hard and hairy. Fisher seemed soft and flabby. His chest was almost devoid of hair.

They circled about each other for a moment. Then Sam gripped Fisher's hand, and hove sideways with all the strength of his being, thinking to pull his foe off balance. Fisher smiled, as one might at a tiresome child. Then he pulled Sam to him roughly, hugged him quickly, squeezed him of air and sprawled him out on the deck.

Most of the crew laughed to see Sam down; but anger steamed up in me. Sam rolled his head from side to side, glaring at his jeering friends, then leaped to his feet and aimed a blow at Fisher's jaw. The mate caught Sam's arm in midair, held it a moment, then used it as a lever with which to spin him around and around. Sam fell, dizzied, and couldn't get up for a time. Fisher stood over him, breathing easily—not even winded by his exertions.

I went to Sam, helped him up, picked up his shirt and handed it to him. He didn't see me. He looked all around for Fisher, but everything was a blur to him, apparently. He couldn't stand still. His body reeled, as though it must begin to rotate again. He didn't see Fisher, I am sure, but he saw a big man stripped to the waist, and he addressed him.

"I'll get you for this," he said. "I'll get you."

Payne and Oliver and Liliston came thrusting through the crowd. Payne shoved me to one side. The three surrounded Sam and led him away. I stood there a moment, not knowing what to do.

"Let him be, Friend George," said Gilbert Smith. "Thee can do him no good. And he may do thee hurt, he be so furious."

"He's my brother," I answered.

"Aye," Smith said. "More's the pity. Go to him then, but never forget I warned thee."

Chapter Twenty

SAM had not gone to his cabin. I found him in the forecastle with Payne and Oliver and Liliston. Humphries was there too, but at a little distance from the others. And Joseph Thomas lay in a nearby hammock.

"You should have knifed him," I heard Payne say.

Oliver broke in with his horrible cockney voice. " 'E 'ad no charnce," I heard him say. "Not a bloody charnce." His voice was a whine that made me shudder.

"It's my bad foot," Sam said. "I slipped."

They stopped speaking when they saw me. They stared at me, openly resenting my intrusion. Payne had suspicion in his eyes. Oliver's mouth flew open, baring his rodent teeth. Liliston and Humphries were palpably uneasy. Thomas Joad, or Joseph Thomas, looked at me as though he were afraid. Sam glared.

"I slipped," he repeated. "I tell you my foot slipped."

"That bad foot of yours," I said. "You could scarce stand on it a few days ago. Is it—are you—?"

I began to stutter foolishly, as I always do when my brother looks at me like that. I felt hot and cold. I knew my cheeks were burning with embarrassment.

"Don't be making excuses for me," he said. "Everybody knows I slipped. What do you want here?"

"He's a damned spy," Payne said.

"Take that back," Sam said.

Payne muttered something I didn't catch, though the tone was apologetic. Sam put his arm about me and drew me to him, and smiled at me. I all but cried.

"Listen, all of you," he said. "This is my brother, and who calls him a spy will answer to me. Understand? Beetle cut him with a rope's end today. You saw that. That finishes that fish head."

Then Sam patted my shoulder gently.

"I'm all right, George," he said. "Get out of here now."

I was halfway up the companion when I heard him ask, "You going to the captain's cabin with me tonight?"

Joseph Thomas answered the question. "I ain't saying now. I'll talk about that later."

Why should he take Thomas to the cabin, I wondered? To ask for medical aid, I thought. Salve for his wounds, and a few days' rest in which to heal them.

Beetle stood near the companionway as I came on deck. It was evident he had seen me going below, and had waited for me. I began to smart all over with resentment. I pretended I had not seen him. But he walked beside me aft, and it was impossible to pretend.

"How the fellow sulks," he said. "All for a bit of rope's end that had no malice in it."

"It stung just the same," I answered hotly. "I asked you a simple question, and you struck me."

"I'm afeared I did, lad," he said. "But a boy needs a taste of the hemp to keep him humble. I've seen men speared for less than what you said. When the skipper gives an order, no common hand should question it. Some mates would have bashed in your skull instead of flicking you gently with a rope's end."

"Don't apologize," I said.

"What airs we give ourselves as soon as our voices change!" he said, more amused than offended. "Ah well, there'll be no lessons then tonight?"

"Not tonight," I said, trying not to cry—for I was between rage at him and pity for myself—"nor ever again."

"That's a long time, lad," Beetle said, his fat face half vexed, half amused. "We'll talk it over tomorrow."

He bowed clumsily and lumbered away.

Captain Joy was making his adieux to Captain Worth. One of the *Lyra*'s boats had already left the *Globe*. I could see it walking like a spider over the blue waters. The other boat was waiting. I watched Captain Joy go over the side, then sought out Gilbert Smith. I had need of his philosophy.

I found him midway of the lee rail. He was holding the steward's dog on his knees. He had doctored its hurt and covered it with a bandage, and he was stroking the dog's silky ears, and talking to it in the voice he had used in speaking to Daniel. He eyed me with some reproach as I threw myself down beside him.

"Thee has quarreled with Beetle," he said.

I admitted that was the truth.

"He was thy friend," Smith said soberly. "Thee brought his rope on thee with too much exercise of thy tongue."

"Must a rope's end answer a simple question?" I asked.

Smith answered me obliquely.

"The skipper has but a modicum of respect for the mate. The men fear Mr. Beetle, but think him merely a hog, considering only his belly and his manners. Thee might shudder to see him at table, his knife blade piled and dripping with food, and to hear the great noises with which he ingests his victuals. And thee might laugh too. Thee might think him a brute, seeing the lusty strokes he gave Joe Thomas. Thee might suppose him an untaught child, hearing him speak. He is a child. Despite all his erudition and his abilities, he is but a child. Still, child or no, he be a man, an able man, an older man than thee— and one of thy friends."

He let the dog lick his hands.

"A child," I said. "Does a child tear open a man's back with a rope?"

"Aye, if those be his orders. A child obeys, Friend George."

I had begun to feel ashamed of my conduct toward the mate, and had half determined to go to him and forgive and ask forgiveness. But a sudden recollection of that flogging on the quarter-deck stiffened me.

"Then we are all children aboard this ship," I said.

Smith smiled gently.

"A man may be a child," he said, "and a child may become a man. Do thee be a man, Friend George, and let who will be children."

After a while I went to supper. And some time after supper, I went on deck hoping to run "accidentally" into Mate Beetle, and patch up our quarrel. But I did not see him.

At eight o'clock, Captain Worth came on deck and had two reefs taken in the topsails. At nine he prepared to go below.

"Keep her by the wind until two o'clock," he bade Gilbert Smith, who was in charge of the watch. "Don't tack until the other watch comes up."

"Aye, aye, sir," Smith said. "By the wind, sir."

"And on tacking," the captain said, "set a light to signal the *Lyra*, so she can tack with us, and keep us company."

"Aye, aye," responded Smith.

The captain looked all around him before he vanished, his beard examining all heaven with distrust. He stared some little time at the *Lyra*, lying in the path of the moon, then sighed as with weariness, and left the deck.

I stayed by the rail, wanting to be alone. At ten o'clock, Sam came up. Smith gave him the orders and went below. I took my place at the wheel. The night was calm and warm. The moon was very bright. The stars were clear and brilliant.

Soon sparks of phosphorescentlike fire fell into the sea. They fell like rain. They glittered there and grew, and spread. Presently the whole heaving bosom of the ocean was covered with gems. I was so overcome with the beauty of it that I forgot Beetle and all connected with him. I was sailing through the starry fields of heaven. I was gliding over a rising and falling field of luminous daisies, and making up words wherewith to describe the wonder of it to Sally.

About ten-thirty Lay came by with a bucket. The captain had sent him for shaving water. He tossed the bucket overboard, and I witnessed a pyrotechnic display of color and light such as I never dreamed of. He brought the bucket up, dripping liquid fire.

"Nice," he said, lingering a moment by the wheel to stare out at the glowing sea. "What do you suppose it is?"

"Sea animalculae of the luminous order," I said, repeating Beetle's words of weeks ago.

I had no more resentment against Beetle now; only sorrow that I had been rude to him. Sam came up, interrupting my reflections.

"Keep her a good full," he said. "She's too damn high in the wind."

She was a good full, and not too high, and he knew it. He walked away, frowning; and I fancied his defeat in the wrestling match was still rankling in him, making him unreasonable.

"All right, Sam," I said. "I'll keep her a good full."

Then I forgot him, and went back to the glories of the shining sea, exulting in them until a few seconds before twelve, midnight.

I reached for the rattle to wake up my relief then; but before I had a chance to shake it, Sam came rushing at me, a boarding knife in his hand.

I saw the moon reflected on the blade, and thought, for a moment, that I had fallen asleep at the wheel and was in a nightmare.

"Don't sound that rattle," Sam said.

A lump formed in my throat. My face became clammy with perspiration.

"If you make the least bit of noise," he said, "I'll send you straight to hell and damnation."

To show me he was in earnest, he raised the knife and brought it hissing past my neck. I stepped back, involuntarily, and dropped the rattle.

As abruptly as he had appeared, Sam left me. I saw him a moment later, a lighted lamp in his hand, going into the steerage.

I picked up the rattle and, again, clumsily, I dropped it. It made a noise. Immediately, Sam was at my side and the edge of that terrible knife was pressed against my throat.

"Must I kill you?" he said. "I told you not to make a noise. I meant it. Give me that rattle!"

I gave it to him—and he passed it to one of the men who had come up behind him, Payne, Oliver, and Humphries. Humphries was holding the lamp. Sam lay down his knife on a small workbench that stood near the cabin gangway. Payne picked it up. Sam had an axe in his hand.

Sam went into the cabin. The lamp went with him, throwing its light on the back of his head and his wide shoulders. Payne and Oliver faded into the shadows of the gangway for a moment, then Liliston came backing stealthily out. The moon shone full upon him, frightened him. He turned and scampered aft.

That odd feeling of being in a nightmare, that had come to me with the first sight of the knife, took possession of me again. And yet, at the same time, I knew it was no nightmare, but cruel reality.

The captain was in the cabin, and Beetle, and Fisher, and Lumbard—and possibly Gilbert Smith.

Sam and his friends were sneaking in to them, armed; and I was there at the wheel, helpless with fright and horror. My knees gave way. I tried to cry out, but no sound came from me. I could not even pray.

Chapter Twenty-One

I HEARD a sound that had, at first, no special meaning for me, a sound that came from the cabin. My mind was so numbed with horror, I suppose, that it required time to make any new impression on it.

It was like the sound of an axe upon a tree. It made me see—as one sees things in a dream—Sally walking through the trees that border Judith Chase's Lane, myself walking nervously at her side, and both of us watching Sam swing his bright blade into the bole of an oak.

But suddenly the scene appeared to change. Now I was in Barnabas Starbuck's storehouse with Cyrus Hussey. I was helping him chop staves. He was sitting on top of the woodpile, looking over my shoulder at the masts of ships tied up to the wharf. I was breathing in the smell of the sea, and the odors of tar, and oil, and burning leaves, and the fragrance of new wood. I heard the rattle of keys that hung on the chain fastened to Hussey's belt. I heard Sam's footsteps, and saw him enter, and heard him say, "Going to the dance?" And now he had the axe, not I. And Hussey was trying to warn me of danger, but didn't dare, because of Sam.

These things seemed strange and foreign to me. I couldn't understand them. I looked about me now, and saw neither Sam nor Hussey near me. The wheel was in my hands. Overhead were the brilliant stars. All about me was the sea that quivered and shone with fire.

Again I heard the sound of the axe. And now I knew what it meant. I shut my eyes. Spasms seized me. I retched.

I waited, the sweat pouring out of me, sweat that seemed cold as ice water. I heard Beetle's voice, and knew he was pleading for his life, though his words were indistinct. Again I heard the thud of the axe.

Again and again I heard it.

I wanted to scream, but could not even whisper. The axe fell no more. There was silence for a long time. A very long time.

Eventually Sam came stealthily out of the shadows, toward me. He had something in his right hand. I thought it was the axe. But actually it was the lamp. It had gone out. He was coming to relight it at the binnacle.

'He has gone mad,' I thought. 'He'll kill me too. He's coming to kill me.'

For a moment I was glad. I wanted to die. I wanted to have the horror over and done with. But as my brother came nearer and nearer the fear of death grew stronger in me. I could not die, I tried to assure myself; I *would* not die.

And Gilbert Smith? He must not die either.

"You won't hurt him?" I asked. "You won't hurt Gilbert Smith?"

Sam's chin was blood spattered. He wiped it with a bloody hand. He glared at me.

"Why are you crying?" he demanded.

"I'm afraid," I confessed. "I'm afraid they might kill me too."

"They?" he said with a sneer.

He lit the lamp then, and hurried from me.

I heard voices, and the report of a musket. I jumped at the sound. The smell of powder smoke sickened me anew. I heard the rending and splintering of wood, the sound of a door broken forcibly off its hinges. I heard Lumbard scream. I heard the musket roar again. Then all was quiet.

It was still quiet when Gilbert Smith appeared on deck.

"Save yourself, Friend Gilbert," I bade him. "They've killed the captain and the mates. They'll kill you too."

"God save us," Gilbert said.

"Fly," I pleaded.

"Fly?" he said softly. "Whither, Friend George?"

"To the *Lyra*," I said.

"I cannot swim," he answered. "And could I, there is one I must not leave to be butchered."

"Who?" I asked.

"Thy young friend Worth, the captain's nephew. Thy brother will murder him surely if he be not hid."

I felt shame that I had not thought of Columbus Worth and his safety before this. I had thought but of my own skin, and Gilbert's.

"Aye," I said. "Columbus Worth. And Lay. And Hussey. And the Kidders. And Rowland Jones. Hide them all."

Smith put his hand gently on my shoulder.

"Keep up they courage, Friend," he said. "And pray!"

With that he left me.

He had scarce gone when Sam appeared on the quarter-deck, and gave his first command.

"Mr. Payne," he shouted, "get all hands aft to make sail."

"All hands on deck," Payne called, knocking loudly on the scuttle.

Rowland Jones came up from below, as frightened as I was. The Kidders were just behind him with Lay and Hussey, and others.

"Columbus Worth," Sam called.

There was no answer, and in the pause I began to shiver again.

"Where's Columbus Worth?" Sam shouted.

No man answered him.

"Where's Smith?" Sam asked.

"Here," Smith shouted, stepping forward calmly.

Sam hurried toward him, came face to face with him opposite the mainmast, holding up the light to scan his face. Smith was not frightened. He was not agitated in any way. Sam saw that plainly. The scowl vanished from his face.

"Are you for me, or against me, Smith?" he asked, in a voice that seemed perturbed.

"I am willing to do aught thee wishes me to do," Smith said.

"Go forward," Sam said, "and set the fore-topgallant sail and flying jib."

"Aye, aye," Smith said, and started to obey. Sam stopped him.

"You're actually with us?" he asked.

"I'll do what thee requires," Smith answered simply.

Sam shifted the lamp to his left hand and threw his right arm jubilantly around the boat steerer's neck.

"If you're with us," he said, "God's with us. Divine aid is assured us!"

Did Sam really believe that God had blessed his bloody work? Did he actually think the Quaker's meek compliance with his orders was proof of God's blessing on murder?

Impossible—unless he had become mad.

He nodded solemnly to Gilbert.

"I am the captain now," he said, and strode away.

"Have the bodies hauled up," he commanded, "and let them be heaved overboard."

All these things that I have set down above I saw and heard. This is the truth, so help me God.

Chapter Twenty-Two

FEB. 22. Fair, with a stiff west wind.

All the things I shall relate hereafter I heard from others. I set them down for any trial that may be held—should we at last reach America. But I do not offer anything as evidence. Some of the incidents I shall relate were told me by truthful men. Other incidents were supplied by such as Lawyer Witherspoon might term untrustworthy; yet I have reason to believe even these men told the truth.

God help us, this is the story as it came to me.

FEB. 28. This is what Humphries told me:

Sam killed the captain, splitting his head with two blows of the axe. The captain, slumbering in his hammock, never woke. Payne stood by with the boarding knife, but it was not needed. Humphries held the light, but his hand shook so that Sam was angry. He took the lamp from him when it was time to kill Mate Beetle.

Payne's long knife ripped into Beetle's flesh, and the mate wakened. He had been so deep in sleep, apparently, that at first he could not comprehend what was happening.

"What is it?" he asked. "What is it?"

With that he got up. He saw Payne and the knife. He saw Sam, with an axe in one hand and a lamp in the other. Then he must have realized what they meant to do.

"Silas!" he cried. "Sam! Don't kill me. Don't."

Suddenly he seized Sam by the throat and tried to use him as a screen against Payne's knife. Sam was taken by surprise, so that the axe and the lamp both fell from his hands. The lamp rolled, still burning, across the floor. Humphries picked it up and lifted it high to light the struggle. What ghastly shadows it must have thrown. What frightful faces it must have revealed.

"You murderous devil," Beetle said. "You treacherous, mutinous dog. Kill me in my own room, would you? Well, I'll kill *you!*"

Sam punched with his free hands, then tried to jab his fingers into Beetle's eyes. But the wind was going out of him under the pressure of the mate's rough hands on his neck, and he had no strength.

Payne got the axe, thrust it into Sam's right hand, and jabbed at Beetle with the knife. Beetle, fearfully stabbed, let go his hold on Sam, and turned toward Payne. Sam used the axe.

The man was hard to kill, Humphries said. He did not die until Payne ran the boarding knife for the last time through his body.

After some moments the trio went to the stateroom occupied by Lumbard and Fisher. Sam tried the door and found it locked.

"Bring the light close," he commanded.

Humphries was shaking violently. The light went out. It was then Sam came to the binnacle.

After he had relighted the lamp, Sam went into the cabin, took down two muskets, loaded them, tipped them with bayonets, and went softly back to the locked door. Oliver, meantime, had joined Payne and Sam. And Humphries thinks that Liliston was close by.

Oliver had been standing guard outside the cabin when Worth and Beetle were killed, ready to give the alarm should any of the crew come near or any interference threaten; and Liliston stood not six paces from him.

Sam gave one of the muskets to Payne. The lamp he again entrusted to the steward.

"Hold it steady now," he said. "If it goes out again, your life might go out with it."

Evidently Lumbard heard Sam's voice. He called out to him.

"Are you going to kill me?"

Sam cursed. And then the murderers heard Fisher's voice.

"Are you going to kill me too, Sam—because I beat you fairly?"

Sam aimed the gun in the direction of Fisher's berth, holding the muzzle a few inches from the locked door, and fired.

"Any one hit?" he asked.

"You've hit me in the mouth," Fisher answered.

"Good," Sam said. He ordered Payne to lean his musket against the wall.

"Comstock!" Lumbard shouted.

Sam did not answer. He hurled himself against the door, then stepped aside to let Payne do the same.

"Comstock? What's the matter? You can have anything I've got. Anything! Just let me go down into the fo'c's'le! Let me jump overboard!"

"Not yet," Sam answered, and threw his body once more against the door. The thin wood shrieked for mercy. Payne hammered on it with the butt of his musket, splintered it. Sam sent his shoulder against the wood a third time, and the door broke and ripped from its hinges. He caught up the musket, made a thrust at Lumbard with the bayonet point, tripped, and pitched headlong into the stateroom.

Before he could get up, Lumbard had him by the neck. But there was blood on Sam's neck, and Lumbard's hands could not maintain their grip. Sam squirmed loose. He leaped up, and found himself looking into the barrel of the musket, and staring at the bayonet that must have glinted sinisterly in the lamp light.

Fisher held it, held it steady.

"Never thought you sich a detarmined devil, Sam," Fisher said. His mouth had been torn by the bullet, but he spoke distinctly.

"Ah nea'ly yelled," Humphries told me. "Ah was so skeered when he say dat. Blood talkin', Mistuh Jawge. Jes blood. No mouf. He din have no mouf at all. Blood bubble and gush and talk. Yas suh. Nea'ly shake me to pieces."

Sam figured that Fisher didn't know there were so few men in the mutiny, didn't know the musket in Payne's hands was not loaded, didn't know he could retake the ship merely by pulling the trigger.

"Just lay down the musket," Sam said quietly.

Fisher hesitated for a moment, then put the weapon in Sam's hands. Sam stared at him.

"You fool," he said. He wheeled quickly around, and slit Lumbard down the middle.

Lumbard fell. Sam drew out the bayonet, and turned to Fisher, watching the big man's terror.

"You remember my promise when you threw me?" Sam asked him. "I said I'd get you. Well, I've got you. You're going to die."

Terror went out of Fisher. He gave Sam a look of contempt. He turned his face to the wall. "At least I'll die like a man," he said.

Sam held the muzzle to the back of Fisher's head and pulled the trigger.

"You've killed him," Lumbard said. "Don't kill me. I'm a married man and a father, Sam. I just got a letter yesterday. I'm the father of a little girl. You won't kill me, Sam. For her sake, Sam."

Payne jabbed the bayonet through him.

"I'm a bloody man," he cried. "I've got a bloody hand."

He held the point against Lumbard's neck, and slowly lowered it. That is Humphries' story.

I was below when the bodies were brought on deck. Captain Worth, the first to die, was the first cast into the sea.

Gilbert Smith stood by, ready to hold a burial service for the dead, but Payne ordered him below. Sam was in the cabin at the time, and for a moment Gilbert thought of appealing to him. But he changed his mind in the face of Payne's anger.

"No prayers for these damned swine," Payne said. "No service. Let them poison the sharks."

Lumbard, though he had been transfixed so many times, was living when he was heaved into the sea. What strength there was in that poor bleeding carcass! What pathetic hope! What desperate courage!

They brought him up on deck with ropes, as they brought up the body of Fisher. Joe Thomas, standing by, spat in his face. He thought the man was dead. So did the others.

But Lumbard caught the plank, as they put him overboard, and clung to it. And he cried out in a loud voice—almost as loud, Gilbert thinks, as the Man crucified between two thieves.

"Comstock," he cried, "for my baby's sake, have pity."

His windpipe, I have been told, was but the shred of a windpipe; yet his voice was clear. Perhaps it was only the imagination of the frightened men and boys that made it seem so loud, so clear.

"Pity," Joe Thomas said. "He wants pity."

With something of an effort he stamped on Lumbard's fingers.

Lumbard gave up and slipped into the sea. In a moment, Humphries called from aloft that the man was swimming.

"Swimming?" Payne said. "It isn't possible."

"Dar!" Humphries cried, pointing. "He swim! He swim!"

Payne saw him then, saw that he was trying to reach the *Lyra*. "Lower away the bow boat," he ordered. "After him."

The cranes were swung away. A boat was partly lowered.

"You, Hanson, Oliver, Peter Kidder," Payne ordered. "Spring in. Get that man."

But he thought better of it. These men might row directly to the *Lyra*. They might betray him.

"Never mind," he said. "Let him go. He'll drown. Hoist up the boat. Set a light in the mizzen rigging as a signal for the *Lyra* to tack. Set all sails. Keep her a good full. Jump to it, whalers! Jump!"

It must have been shortly before this that I stole into the "crocheting" room, a tiny room near the windlass, where the wives of former captains used to while away the hours sewing.

I went there to be alone, to muffle, if I could, the sound of the axe thuds I had heard. I closed the door softly, fell full length on the floor, and wept my fill.

As I lay there I became aware of the smell of lint and wool and lavender, vague smells that conjured up visions of many motherly women. I thought I could see them, hear them talk to me. I thought I could see my own mother among them, and I thanked God she had died when Sam and I were children. I thought of her, and I thought of Sally. And thinking of them made me weep the harder.

I was still crying when Humphries backed in through the door, and turned, and spoke to me.

"Dar now," he said. "Dar now, Mistuh Jawge, dat ain' no way fo' a big boy to ca'y on. No way 'tall. Ah seed you th'ow up out dar; and Ah seed you creep in hyeh. Ah knowed what to do right off. Yas suh! Ah made some hot tea fo' you. Come on now, Mistuh Jawge. Drink it hot. Daid men don' haunt nobody. No suh. And dem daid men had to die, yas suh."

"Go away," I cried out. "You helped kill them. You're a murderer. Don't touch me."

He laughed, tolerantly, and set a pewter mug of strong tea on the chair near the door. He sat down beside me, and clasped his hands around his knees.

"You and me's friends, Mistuh Jawge," he said. "And Ah on'y held de lamp. Mistuh Sam, he say, 'Come 'long or Ah cut you' th'oat.' And dar Ah is, holdin' up de light. But, don' cry fo' dem. You seed Cap'n kick mah dog. You seed Beetle and Lumbard whup Joe Thomas. You seed Fishe' th'ow Mistuh Sam. Dey's daid. And us is free. Us'll live lak kings."

Humphries had been my friend. I had always liked him. He had always been kind to me, given me little delicacies filched from the pantry, played his fiddle for me, jigged for me, told me stories of his wanderings, his wives, his queer adventures. Yet now I feared him.

Chapter Twenty-Three

MARCH 1. Still calm.

Humphries continued to stick to me like a burr. In tones almost as dulcet as the strange music that flowed from his fiddle, he diverted my thoughts from the horrible killings that had turned my insides. He caressed me with his words in much the same manner as a mother would soothe her scared child.

"Ah knows a island whar Mistuh Sam kin be de king," Humphries said. "And Mistuh Smith kin be de haid o' de church. Ah could be de haid o' de church dar now, did Ah resurrec' a fellow lak Ah promised."

He told me then how he had been shipwrecked, years ago, on one of the Society Islands. He was the only survivor of a whaling crew of twenty-six, and because of his stature and his clothing the natives did him honor. He stayed there a long time, learned the language, proclaimed himself a god.

The chief's son died, and Humphries told the father not to grieve. He would restore the boy to life, but in due time.

"Dar was war and famine in de land," he said. "Dem people wasn' eatin'. Ah wasn' eatin' mahse'f. So de boy's death was Providence. Yas suh! Providence. Ah told his pappy dat widin thutty days Ah would resurrec' de boy. But Ah laid down rules.

" 'Buil' a lil house fo' de boy,' Ah say to de chief. 'And buil' a big house fo' me. Ev'y day bring de bestest food in de land. De boy got to eat on'y de bestest food whiles he's resurrectin'. Else will he be defunk all he's life. W'en he eats his fill, dat boy goin' to riz up and walk home. Yas suh.' "

"And the chief believed you?" I couldn't help asking.

Nor could I help reaching out for the steaming tea, and sipping it, as Humphries talked.

"Dey buil' de houses," he said. "Dey bring me de fat o' de land. Dey bring me mo' wives dan Ah kin put to wuk. Yas suh. Ah guess Ah was the husbandest man in de whole world.

"Ah was haid o' de church. Ah was a powe'. And den a old whale ship come 'long and anchor in de bay."

"And then?" I said.

"Well, Ah figu'ed Ah could swim out to de whaler in de night and jine up, and live on pickle beef and spoil' potaters. Or Ah could live high two weeks mo'. But Ah re'lized dat if Ah didn't resurrec' dat boy, de chief'd give me a chance to resurrec' mahself. And so Ah swum."

Somehow, as the colored man talked, my aversion and horror lessened, and some of the old feeling of friendliness I bore him began to return. He was a murderer; but murder meant little to him. And he was only a tool of Sam's.

By this time, dawn was creeping in through the partly opened door. Humphries smiled on me now, showing all his white teeth.

"Us free now, Mistuh Jawge," he said. "No mo' whalin'. No mo' pickle beef and spoil' potaters. No mo' wuk. Us going to de islands and live lak kings. And all Ah did was hol' de lamp."

I went out and scanned the horizon. The *Lyra* was nowhere to be seen. I walked about the deck until I heard the cry "All hands aft."

Sam was there, awaiting us. He sat on the vise bench, a cutlass in his right hand, a pistol lying close beside him.

"If there's anyone you like better than me for captain," he said quietly, "you have a perfect right to choose him."

The canvas flapped loudly in the silence. The ropes hummed. The sea roared. We stood and shuffled our feet for a moment.

I heard a whisper behind me. "Yer as good as 'e be, mitey; an' yer'd mike a sight better captink." It was Oliver, speaking to Payne.

Sam must have heard the whisper, though I doubt he knew exactly what was said. He must have heard something though, for he reached out quickly for his pistol.

"Since you all wish me to be your captain," he said, "you must swear to obey the laws I have here in my hand.

"One. If anyone sees a sail and fails to sing out at once he shall be put to instant death.

"Two. If anyone refuses to fight a ship to keep her off, he shall be put to death as a traitor; he shall not be hung, but bound hand and foot, and boiled in the try-pots in boiling oil.

"Anyone not wishing to abide by these laws does not have to sign them, but might stand to one side."

"I'll sign," Payne said.

He walked forward. Sam placed the paper on the bench. Humphries brought pen and ink. Payne stooped and signed. One by one the rest of us followed his example. Then we made our seals.

At Sam's direction those who had taken part in the mutiny made red seals after their names. The rest of us made our seals with black ink.

"Now each of you swear to uphold these laws," said Sam.

We all swore. All but Gilbert Smith.

"I give my oath only to God," he said. "I'll not swear, but thee may take my word, if thee will."

"All right," Sam said. "Now I appoint Mr. Payne first mate, Mr. Humphries second mate. You, George, will be steward. Now, George, you and Hussey clean out the cabin."

I shall not dwell on the noisome and ghastly aspects of our task. We worked fast, the sooner to be done. We were still at work when Sam strode in, with Payne, Oliver, Humphries, and Joe Thomas. They sat at the table, and drank toasts to themselves. Sam ordered rum served to all hands, and later, when most everyone was feeling the effects of the drink, he ordered us to throw overboard "everything that smells of whaling."

Harpoons, lances, blubber knives, boarding knives, tackle, hoops and staves, even the bricks of the try-pots and the barrels of oil on deck and in the hold were heaved into the sea.

"Ho ho, heave ho he!" men sang as they pulled the tryworks to pieces.

"Yo ho, heave ho he!" they sang as they rolled out the barrels of oil—oil for which we had sweated and agonized and risked our lives. I had visions of a dead man floating on the sea, his red beard pointing at the sky, and his white lips muttering: "Ile! They're throwing away my ile!"

Gilbert Smith paused at my elbow to watch the work of destruction.

"The sea gives, Friend George," he said. "And the sea reclaims."

"Is Columbus safe?" I asked him.

"I think so," he said. "He's somewhere in the hold. They've searched the ship for him, but they haven't found him."

Joe Thomas staggered across the deck to us. He was very drunk.

"Damn all whales," he said. "Damn all whalers. That I have lived to see this day!"

He drank from a bottle and hurled it over the rail, and staggered away. As we watched him there came that familiar cry from aloft.

"Thar blows! Buh-loes! Buh-loes! A sparm whale two p'ints off the larboard quarter."

With one accord we rushed to the rigging. And there we halted.

"Fools," Payne roared. "We're done with whaling."

And so we were. Our tryworks down, our try-pots gone, our weapons overboard, we were indeed done with whaling, done with honest work and adventure, done with purpose. It was a rude awakening, even to the least of us.

We clung to the rigging, and watched the whale. It was floundering in a most unusual way, lashing the sea into acres of foam.

"It's fighting something," Smith said.

As we came closer we noted that the sea was reddening. We saw the whale leap half its great length out of the water, and saw a smaller fish fastened to his under jaw, a brown-backed, white-bellied fish that might measure twenty feet. It had a jet black dorsal fin.

"Another killer," Smith whispered. "It'll keep a strangle hold on the whale, until the whale dies."

"If I had a gun I'd kill that little fish," I heard someone say. "It'd be an easy shot from here."

"If we could only lower a boat," another man sighed.

But we were done with that.

"It's fun to catch whales," someone else said, "the greatest fun in the world."

But we were done with fun.

We watched the whale as long as we could, knowing it soon must give up the unequal struggle against its pigmy adversary, and roll "fin out."

"The only part of the whale that little killer wants is the tongue," Smith said.

"Strange," I replied, "how such a comparatively tiny fish can murder so huge an animal."

"Aye. And a ship is larger than a whale, and the men on it craftier and more dangerous than all the whales in the sea. Yet one man can take a ship, as thee has seen."

"And another can take it from him who seized it first," I said.

"Payne?" Smith asked.

"Payne. And Oliver after Payne. And after him—"

"Payne," he said, thoughtfully. "Thee's right. Yon's a sinister man. And Oliver—a whining, wheedling, conniving knave. The first to grumble, and the last to serve. A bilge rat! Aye! Payne. And then Oliver. And then?"

"No!" I burst out. "I'll not stand it. I'm not going to be a slave to these murderers. I'm not going to live with them. I'm going home, Friend Gilbert. I'm going to take the ship. Will you help me?"

"Aye," he said calmly—as calmy as though he did but agree that it might rain.

"There are a dozen men at least who'll help us," I said.

"Patience," he cautioned me. "And do thee let me work out the details while we wait. Could thee kill a man, Friend George—for home—for Mistress Sally?"

"Yes," I whispered, but I was frightened.

"It may not come to that," Smith said. "But if so be—so be it."

Chapter Twenty-Four

THRICE the ship had been searched for Columbus Worth. Once he had been seen below, creeping aft to the run, and Payne had fired at him. But he had escaped.

Sam had tried to track him down with Humphries' dog. But the animal was no bloodhound. He scampered away from Sam, wagging his little tail, and disappeared.

"Mistuh Chris," Humphries said, "he loved dat dog heaps, suh. Yas suh. Dey's togethe' down dar, Cap'n Sam. Find de dog, find de boy."

"I'll kill them *both*," Sam swore.

One of my first acts, as the new steward, was to steal down into the lower hold with a bowl of food for Columbus Worth. But knowing of Sam's threat I had to take great care that I was not seen by any of the mutineers.

It was very dark in the lower hold, and I dared not light a lamp. I thought I might have been followed. A light, in such case, would surely have betrayed me.

I stumbled against barrels of food, tripped on coils of hemp, and on old sails, bumped my head against low-lying timbers, caught my ribs on the sharp corners of great wooden boxes.

"Chris!" I kept whispering, "Chris, it's me, George."

After a time I heard the whimper of a dog. And so I found young Worth. He was lying exhausted at the foot of a water barrel. The dog was in his arms. He had had nothing to eat in three days. His right shoulder had been grazed by one of Payne's bullets.

"All right," he said hoarsely, when he saw me bending over him. "Kill me. I don't care now."

"I've come to feed you, not to kill you," I said quietly. "Can you sit up?"

"I'll try," he said.

I put the bowl into his hands, and watched him eat. That is, I listened to him eat. It was too dark to see him. I heard the dog eating too.

"Water," he said, after he had swallowed a few bites. "Did you bring water? I must have water."

I handed him a bottle, and listened to him drink. He must have poured some into the hollow of his hand, for I heard the dog lapping up water too.

"There's a barrel of water here," Worth said, when he had finished the bowl. "I'm leaning against it. It's full. But—I couldn't get at it. I found the bung. High up. Right near the top. I pushed it in. But I couldn't get the water out. I couldn't tip the barrel. I hadn't strength enough. I used part of my shirt, dipping it in, sucking it, washing my wound with it. I thought I was going to die here, and be eaten by rats. If it hadn't been for the dog the rats would have chewed me to pieces before this. Thank God you came."

I was serving breakfast in the cabin when Liliston stalked in, holding Chris by his wounded shoulder.

"Here's yer prisoner, Cap'n," he said, grinning proudly. "Found 'im in the lower hold. I heered the dog yippin', and I went down there, and there he was. Damn dog got his tail caught atween two bar'ls when the ship rolled."

Chris was pale as wax, but he held himself straight. And though Liliston's grip must have pained him dreadfully, he made no moan.

"Where's the dog?" Sam asked.

"Still down there, Cap'n," Liliston answered, his grin broadening.

"Let the boy alone," Sam said. "Go down and get the dog. And see you don't kick him. Men who kick dogs on this ship come to no good end."

He turned to Worth.

"You stole your uncle's pistol," he said.

Worth shook his head and began to shiver. It wasn't fright. It was the reaction. He had been almost numbed with the cold dankness of the hold. It was warm here in the cabin, and bright and dry.

"Well, just the same," Sam said, "you've got to die. We can't have any tattletales on board."

"This boy's no tattletale, sir," Gilbert Smith said gently, getting up out of his chair and standing before Sam. "And he has done naught to merit death. Thee knew his father, sir, who died in a whale boat off the Azores. Thee knows his mother, too. I will stand surety for him, Sam Comstock. Thee may kill me if any harm befall because of him."

Worth's shirt, that portion of it that hid his right shoulder, was badly discolored with old blood stains. Now new bright red stains appeared in it.

Sam, seeing them, threw down his knife and fork, pushed back his chair, and walked toward him. He ripped the shirt off the shoulder and examined the wound.

"Yes, Gilbert," he said. "And I knew his uncle."

"And thee knows me," Smith said simply.

Sam turned to me.

"Take him to his hammock," he bade me. "I'll be down presently to dress the wound. Has he eaten?"

"I am not hungry, sir," Chris said before I could answer.

Sam waved us away and resumed his place at the table. But at that moment, Chris tottered and fell. Humphries, whirling out of his chair, caught him in his arms.

"Ah'll take him, suh," he said.

Oliver was indignant.

"Yer the second mite, Mister 'Umphries," he said. "Yer got no business acarryin' a spy."

"Ah *is* de secon' mate," Humphries answered. "And who is you?"

Stephen Kidder laughed in derision, and Oliver flew at him with a knife.

"Yer carn't smirk at me," he said. "I'll cut yer 'eart hout."

Sam threw his empty cup. It caught Oliver on the ear. He dropped the knife, and turned, blinking in surprise.

"I didn't mean nothink, sir," he whined.

"On this ship, Mr. Oliver," Sam said quietly, "all disputes must be settled according to the laws of honor. By dueling."

After breakfast we were mustered aft. Oliver and Kidder were made to appoint their seconds, and to choose one of two pistols which Sam had loaded.

"Repent of your sins," Sam bade them. "And make your peace with your Maker. Then take your places."

He bent down and drew a line with a piece of chalk. Twenty paces away he drew another line. When the duelists were in position, he gave each of them a weapon, letting Kidder have first choice.

"I'll count," Sam said. "Fire when I say three."

Kidder, tall and thin, was shaking like the shaft of a harpoon in a dying whale. Oliver, squat and square, could scarcely stand. His eyes were shut tight.

The pistol fell from Kidder's outstretched hand and discharged. It happened so suddenly, I jumped.

"I'm shot," Oliver screamed, falling flat to the deck. " 'E got me in the leg. I'm dyink. Ow me poor missus!"

"Better let me blindfold you," said Sam, tying his handkerchief over Oliver's eyes. "Then you won't faint, seeing your own blood. George, get me my surgical instruments. Hurry."

He gave me a wink that countermanded the order—a wink that shocked me, so genuinely funny it was.

He pulled off Oliver's right boot, slit his trouser leg, and tore off his sock—at the same time making signs to all of us not to laugh.

"Terrible," he said. "You'll have to lose that leg. I'll have to amputate it. Either that, or let you die."

"Me leg!" Oliver whimpered. "Ow me leg!"

Sam stood up.

"Wood's scarce," he said. "I can't see how we can make you a wooden leg. Stand up on the legs you have."

"I carn't," Oliver whimpered. "I carn't. It'd kill me."

"Stand up!" roared Sam.

Oliver sprang up. Sam took the bandage off his eyes then, and laughed aloud. Most everybody else laughed too.

"Those guns were loaded with blanks," Sam said. "I wouldn't waste lead on cowards like you."

He whirled Oliver around, and kicked him savagely.

"Get out of here, both of you," he shouted, turning to Kidder. "And if I hear of any more nonsense I'll shoot the pair of you."

In the afternoon of that day, Sam came down to treat Worth's shoulder. I stood by, holding a basin of hot water.

"The wound is slight," Sam said. "You'll be all right in a day or so—fit enough to hang. Where's that pistol?"

"He didn't steal it," I exploded. "You know he didn't. You just want to kill him! You want to kill us all! What's happened to you, Sam? In the name of God—"

He seized my wrist, and such an expression of fury came into his face that involuntarily I stepped back from him.

"What do you know about that gun?" he demanded.

"You gave it to Humphries," I said. "You're just pretending Chris took it, so you can murder him. All right, murder me, too."

Sam released my wrist. He finished dressing the wound. He put a clean bandage on it. He gathered up his tools and put them in order in their case.

"Come with me," he said grimly.

Humphries was in his quarters when we got there. He was sitting on his bunk, cleaning the gun. Sam took it from him. It was the captain's.

"Ah heard somethin', suh," the Negro said, his eyes rolling in terror. "Ah's skeered. Yas suh."

Sam thrust the weapon into his coat pocket.

"Where'd you get it?"

"Ah found it, suh."

"Found it, did you? Why didn't you give it to me?"

"Ah heared somethin', Cap'n, suh. Mistuh Smith and Mistuh Pete' Kidde', dey goin' to riz up and take de ship. Yas suh. Ah's skeered."

Sam stepped outside the little cabin and bawled for Payne.

"Mr. Payne," he said, "guard this man. George, find Smith and Peter Kidder. Tell them to report to me in my stateroom. Right away."

I waited outside the cabin, worried, sick at heart, and terribly frightened, while Sam talked to Peter Kidder and Gilbert Smith. It was true they had spoken of retaking the ship. So had I. So had Lay and Hussey and Coffin and Jones, all of us who didn't want to wear forever the brand of pirate and mutineer, who wanted to go back to our decent lives, our homes, our dear ones.

What would become of us?

The conference lasted more than an hour. Smith and Peter Kidder came out together. They passed me, saying no word. But there was a sort of dumb fright in Peter's moist, calflike eyes.

"There will be a trial, Friend George," Smith managed to tell me later.

"For you?" I asked. I had to clutch at a rope to keep me up.

"Nay, Friend," he answered sadly. "To try yon poor untutored savage, and to hang him."

"No," I said. "Oh, no."

"There be no help for it. The Good Book bids us tell the truth. But, mark thee, if I tell it, I doom myself and others with me, a dozen and more decent, innocent, Christian men and boys. Better a murderer swing in the air, than any one of them. Aye, when thee weighs them in the balance, Friend, the black man dies."

We could hear Humphries singing as we talked, a great rich voice that stirred us cruelly.

> Oh Lawd look dow-own.
> Look down and see Thy suhvant Daniel,
> Ringed 'round wid feahsome li-ons.

"We can't," I said. "We can't let Sam hang him, Friend Gilbert."

"Peace," he said fiercely. "Yon is a mutineer, a murderer, a son of Belial for all his psalm singing. Would thee sacrifice thy friends for him?"

The singing stopped, and we heard the sound of Humphries' fiddle.

Gilbert fell to his knees and prayed. And I did likewise. When I looked up, I saw Sam pacing the deck, head bent as though he were worried. He wore a sword. And two pistols were tucked into his belt.

At dawn, all hands were summoned aft to witness trial and execution. Humphries was brought forward, his hands tied behind his back. He shambled ahead, searching every face for a sign of friendship. He was terribly afraid.

"Sit him there on the chest," Sam ordered. "Smith and Kidder, sit on either side of him." He waited a moment, then began to interrogate the prisoner. Humphries made answer in a low voice, kept shuffling his feet. I could see only the whites of his eyes.

"It appears," said Sam, when he had finished asking questions, "that William Humphries has been accused of a base and treacherous act, in loading a pistol for the purpose of shooting Mr. Payne and myself."

"No, suh," Humphries muttered. "No, suh, dat ain' right. Ah heared somethin', suh. Ah was skeered."

"Such an offense must not go unpunished," Sam continued. "The prisoner must be tried by court martial. I will appoint three judges. Mr. Payne, Mr. Oliver, and Mr. Thomas. The prisoner may appoint his own judge."

Humphries looked up at that. He saw me and tried to rise, but could not.

"Mistuh Jawge," he cried piteously. "Mistuh Jawge, you be mah judge. You save me, Mistuh Jawge!"

I shook my head. I knew I could not be an impartial judge.

"Mistuh Coffin den?" he said humbly. "Please Mistuh Coffin."

Rowland Coffin nodded.

"Having been tried," Sam said, "the jury will now render their verdict of guilty or not guilty. If guilty, the prisoner shall be hanged to a stuns'l boom, rigged out eight feet up on the foreyard. But, if not guilty, Gilbert Smith and Peter Kidder shall be hung from the afore-mentioned gallows."

I looked at Smith and at Kidder. They sat impassive on the chest. Back of them, and Humphries, I saw six men with muskets.

"Guilty," Rowland Coffin said, hanging his head as though he were ashamed. "Guilty," said Payne and Oliver and Thomas in one voice.

They led the Negro forward, put a cap over his face, tied a rope around his neck, and directed him to sit on the rail. He did not struggle. He did not speak. He obeyed every order as though there was nothing else he could do.

"Every mother's son of you take hold of that rope," Sam shouted. He held a fourteen-second glass in one hand, his cutlass in the other.

"You've got fourteen seconds to live, Humphries," he said and turned the glass so that the sands began to run. "Have you anything to say before you meet your Maker?"

How fast the sands raced!

"I'll give the signal," Sam went on. "When you hear the ship's bell, pull. Anyone refusing to obey, I'll cut down with this sword."

Faster and faster ran the sands. I let go of the rope. I fell on my knees, sobbing.

"Little did Ah think Ah was bo'n to come to dis," Humphries began. And the cutlass clanged against the bell, and breath came swiftly and loudly out of throats, and hemp creaked.

I covered my face with my hands and cried the harder.

I was still crying when the rope was cut and the strangled body dropped splashing into the sea—the sea poor Humphries had loved, "'cause it don' need no hoein', no pickin', no nothin'—'cause it's free."

Sam's arms lifted me. Sam's hands sat me on the chest, where, a few minutes before, Humphries had sat and listened to the mockery of a trial.

"Don't take it so hard," Sam said. "He deserved it. He was a thief, he stole the skipper's sixteen dollars. Not Joe Thomas. He let Joe Thomas be flogged for that. That's why I made Thomas one of his judges. Humphries confessed that. He gave me the money. Besides, it was either him or Gilbert Smith who took the pistol. And I need Smith. I'm going to make Smith chaplain. And his first job will be to hold services for the old man and the mates."

"Services!" I cried.

I laughed hysterically and clutched his arm.

"Shut up," he cried. "Shut up, you sniveling milksop."

He sprang up and stood glowering at me for a moment, his fingers whitening on his sword hilt. Then he turned on his heel and strode away.

I went to the pantry, and found Humphries' dog, tied to the stove. Someone had leashed him there, that he might not see his master die. As I freed him, Smith came in with Humphries' violin and bow.

"He left his fiddle to thee," Smith said. "Thy brother sent it by me."

Then Gilbert took a package from his pocket and began unwrapping it.

"And this is for thee too," he said. "I got it in Oahu, and meant to take it home. But do thee eat it now, or it will spoil."

It was a little piece of hard candy.

When I looked up to thank him, Gilbert was gone.

Chapter Twenty-Five

ON February 7, we stood in with one of the Kingsmill group of islands; and a number of natives came out to us in canoes. They offered us beads made of shell, but had no food. We went on, passing through the channel between Marshall's and Gilbert's Islands. On the morning of February 8, we luffed to, and sent a boat toward one of the Marshalls, but the natives looked hostile and the boat put back. Some natives swam out to her, and Payne gave orders to fire on them.

The swimmers dived under water, and made for shore, but some were killed and others wounded.

The boat was nearing the *Globe* when Payne saw a canoe with two men in it, making for the shore. He gave orders to overhaul it, and as soon as it came within range he stood up, aimed, and fired.

The natives held high a few strings of beads and a jacket made of some kind of flags—offering all they possessed for their lives. Payne must have realized they were unarmed; but he wantonly fired again. I saw one of the natives fall into the bottom of the canoe, writhing convulsively, and the other leap overboard and swim.

"How much longer must we wait?" I cried.

"Until we reach the Mulgraves," Smith whispered. "We're headed there. Thy brother knows those islands. The natives are friendly, and rich. There he will plant his pumpkin seeds. There he will set up his kingdom. There, when opportunity lends a hand, we will retake the ship. Until then, patience."

On February 11, we raised an unnamed island, stood in, sent a boat ashore in command of Payne and took off cocoanuts, fresh fish —and women.

Since the night of the mutiny there had been little discipline aboard the *Globe*. Sam kept us all with him in the cabin where we were idle, fearing we might conspire against him unless we were continually watched. The mutineers drank all the time, sang ribald songs, told stories of the murders over and over again, played with their greasy cards, chewed tobacco, and smoked foul-smelling pipes. The cabin reeked with smoke, and stunk of tobacco spit, spilled rum, and perspiration.

There was no discipline at all the night the women came aboard. It became a saturnalia for which I have no words. We stood off shore most of the night—while the men drank, fought viciously over the women, and howled like wolves until they dropped, one by one, from drink and utter exhaustion. We stood in at dawn, and landed all the women but one—the one Payne locked in his stateroom. A pretty girl who might be seventeen.

MARCH 4. Calm. On the morning of February 14 we arrived at one of the Mulgraves and cruised about, seeking a landing place. It was a rocky island, beautiful beyond imagination in the red and gold of the dawn; palm trees and breadfruit trees waving us a joyous welcome; the shore fringed with laughing, singing, shouting, copper-colored men and women.

Sam anchored and sent a small boat to cruise about. A little flotilla of canoes came out to us, some of them equipped with sails. Presently dozens of men and women were stalking up and down the deck, graceful, gay, good-looking people. They wore garments made of dried native grass about their loins. They wore these garments fore and aft, leaving their sides bare. There were flowers in the women's hair, and wreaths of blossoms about some of their heads, and necklaces of delicate shells around their throats. Some had bracelets and anklets of shells. All had rolls of green leaves sticking out of slits in their long ears.

They looked at everything, touched nothing, smiled at every one of us, spoke to us in their native tongue, and offered us fruits and shells and beads.

A little girl, who might be twelve or thirteen, offered a cocoanut to Liliston. He was very drunk. He looked at the cocoanut as though it annoyed him. He threw it away, grabbed the girl and tried to kiss her. She screamed in fright.

Liliston laughed at her, caught her arms and twisted them cruelly. It was more than I could bear. I ran forward and struck him. He staggered back and the girl pulled free. He jerked out a knife, but I hit him again before he could use it. I hit him full on the jaw.

I had disliked and feared this man since the first time I saw him. He was tall and spare and ugly, a surly man with an outthrust jaw that never seemed able to grow a hair, and ears that were the hairiest I ever saw upon a man.

He fell and lay insensible at my feet.

"Motake," the little girl cried.

She looked at me as though I were God. She knelt at my feet and embraced them.

"Thee has done wrong, Friend," Gilbert said solemnly, coming up from behind.

He bent over Liliston and examined his face.

"Thee's nearly broken the fellow's jaw," he said. "Go now, and take the little heathen with thee. And drop her overboard. There's danger in her for a Christian lad."

"Motake," the girl said again, rising, and smiling on me.

She was a lovely child, with beautiful, even, white little teeth. They looked lovelier than the white flowers in her hair or the white shells about her slender throat. She had shiny, liquid brown eyes, exquisite delicate features.

"What does 'motake' mean?" I asked.

"It means 'good,'" Gilbert said. "It means 'thee's wonderful.' It means 'get rid of her for thy soul's sake, Friend George, and instantly, before thee be again ensnared.' That's what 'motake' means."

The girl took my hand and led me aft toward a group of her people, talking merrily. They closed about me, evidently praising me. They touched the buttons on my jacket. They touched the corner of the handkerchief that peeped out of my pocket. They loaded me with beads. They forced a shell into my hand, and indicated I was to dip it into a queer-looking, delightful-smelling mixture one of the women held out to me. It was breadfruit meal, and it was delicious. It was spread thickly on a fragrant green leaf. I dipped the shell into it. They laughed gaily as I ate.

The boat returned, reporting no good landing place had been found. It was dispatched in the opposite direction, and returned just before dark with no better luck.

Sam decided to stand in until we got regular soundings. Then he anchored within five rods of the shore, on a coral rock bottom in seven fathoms. The ship was moored with a kedge astern, the sails were furled, and all hands retired to rest, save Oliver and Lay, who were assigned to anchor watch.

On Sunday morning, February 15, Sam announced we had arrived at our destination. All stores and supplies must be taken ashore, and the ship burned and sunk.

"What shall we do?" I asked Gilbert.

"Wait," he answered.

Most of the men were set to work to construct a raft out of spare spars, so that the stores could be the more easily conveyed ashore. While it was building, Sam ordered Hussey and me to row him to the beach.

He left us alone on the shore, as he went forward to seek out the chiefs. The beach was of pure white sand, and the sun shone on it. It was strewn with beautiful shells. Back of it was the sweet green of the trees, and back of that the shimmering white pinnacles of cool mountains that turned out to be only clouds. All around us were laughing, beautiful, curious women and girls.

"I tried to warn you," Hussey said. It was the first time we had been alone since the morning of January 26—the first time we had spoken to each other.

"I know," I said. "It wasn't your fault."

He scratched his curly, golden head—the beautiful head that all the girls were looking at—and sighed.

"I'm with you, you know," he said.

"I know that too," I answered. "I'll give you the word when we're ready."

We rowed back to the *Globe* with six fat chiefs. All of them glistened with cocoanut oil. One of them was wearing a very old coat that had once belonged to a white man—a very thin white man. Dinner was served in the cabin, and Sam gave each of his guests a present. He presented a pair of fish hooks to one, a barrel hoop to another, a hatchet to the fattest and most important.

"You'll spoil them," Payne complained, his great nose quivering with anger. He spat tobacco juice and wiped his heavy black beard with his scaly hands.

"I'm master here," Sam answered.

Payne snarled and his little eyes burned, but he said no more.

When the darkness dropped upon us, we rowed the chiefs back, and they made us stay to supper.

Fires burned everywhere around and women sang, and queer music came from all about us. We ate roast pig served on banana leaves, and girls crept up to us and watched as we ate. Feeling little fingers touching my arm, I looked down and saw "Motake" laughing in the firelight. I moved part way off my mat and she moved part way onto it; and we laughed aloud together.

Sam looked at me in disgust.

He sprang up, made his apologies and his excuses, and bade us row him back to the ship.

Next day the raft was completed, and anchored between the ship and the shore. One end rested on the rocks. The other was kept to seaward by the anchor. The unloading then began, supervised by Payne. Hussey and I rowed Sam ashore, that he might see to the disposition of everything.

Two boats brought the articles from the ship to the raft; and from the raft the stuff was carried onto the shore. As the supplies accumulated, Sam began the erection of a tent and ordered that a second raft be constructed by laying spars upon two boats and placing boards over the spars. This raft could be floated well up on the shore with an incoming tide.

During the first day, most of the sails were taken to the island, including the mainsail, the foresail, the mizzen topsail, the main-topgallant sail, the topmost stuns'ls, the mizzen-topgallant sails, and the boat sails. The flying jib was thrown overboard because it was torn.

Next we unloaded casks of bread, barrels of flour and beef and pork, casks of molasses and sugar and dried apples, vinegar, rum, pickles, cranberries, coffee, chocolate, potatoes, onions. Tow lines, coils of cordage, lance warp, balls of spun yarn and worming, the stream cable, the larboard lower anchor, the ship's tools, and such lances and harpoons as hadn't been thrown overboard were rafted ashore with the food supplies.

The money in Captain Worth's old cedar chest—the silver of Valparaiso and the gold of Oahu—went ashore secretly in the small boat. Secretly, and in the dead of night. Sam and Payne carried it into the boat. And I rowed them ashore. I alone. Sam stayed ashore. I rowed Payne back.

On the second day, various chests of clothing went ashore, and I stood by, making inventory of them.

It was about noon when Oliver came aboard, sweating profusely. He went immediately to Payne.

" 'E's miking 'isself very free with the clothes, 'e is," he said. " 'E's givin' them 'out to hevery bleedin' beggar hashore. Like ha bloomink kink, 'e is. Miking friends at hour hexpense, I calls it."

"I see," Payne said. "Go back and tell him if he doesn't stop, I'll go ashore. Tell him I don't like that. He's stirring up the natives against us, getting them on his side. I'll not have it."

Oliver started away.

"No, wait," Payne called after him. "I'll go myself."

I rowed him ashore. He went directly to Sam.

"What is this?" Sam cried. "Mutiny?"

"I have an interest in these articles," Payne answered. "So have all the others. And you give them away."

"If you, or any other man, want anything of me," said Sam, squaring his shoulders and glaring at Payne, "we'll settle it by our rules of honor."

"That's just what I want," said Payne. His eyes glittered in triumph. Triumph! He had maneuvered Sam into this position.

Men quit work on the raft, and edged up quickly. Liliston. Coffin. Thomas. Hanson. Oliver. Where Oliver came from, I don't know. He was not in the boat when I rowed Payne ashore; yet here he was now at Payne's elbow; his eyes glittering like Payne's.

"I'm ready now," Payne added.

"All right," Sam said. "I'm going on board for a few minutes. We'll pick swords when I come off."

I rowed him to the *Globe*.

"You're a fool," I said. "He'll kill you. If he doesn't, Oliver will."

"Shut up, milksop," he answered.

He made a little speech to the men on board, questing for a vote of confidence, yet not asking for it. There was only silence.

Sam was exasperated.

"I'm going to leave you," he said. "I'm joining the natives. Look out for yourselves."

He went for a moment into the cabin, returning with two swords. With one of them he slashed the air.

He held the blade aloft, theatrically. "This shall stand by me as long as I live," he cried out. He sheathed the blade and bade me row him back ashore.

Chapter Twenty-Six

MARCH 5. Continued calm.

"You see where my tent is?"

I was rowing Sam ashore and couldn't see it. But I said I did.

"I was going to build a church there," my brother said. "I was going to build a town. I had the site picked out. I was going to build homes, a council chamber, a market building, a palace. Now they can do without."

"You always wanted to be king of a South Sea isle," I couldn't help saying. "King and sultan and pope."

Sam smiled at me as he used to smile long ago. But I remembered his red sins and hardened my heart against him.

"Come with me, George," he said. "I will be king. I'll own all these islands. I'll have a tremendous army. You'll be second in command. Payne—once Payne's out of the way—"

"No," I said. "I want to go home."

His smile faded. He looked tired and worn and sad.

"Home!" he said.

He drew in a deep breath and we said no further word to each other.

He pulled off his shirt as we reached the shore and strode across the sands. It was only then I saw the tent. We stopped close to it. Payne, also bared to the waist, came slowly forward. Behind him were Oliver and Liliston.

Sam held out two swords, hilts forward.

"Your choice," he said.

Payne took one, and smiled. It was the first time I had seen anything other than a scowl on that scarred, thin, fierce face.

Men of the crew came strolling up from all about. Two boats put out from the ship. Natives stood everywhere, all men. Some of them had spears. There were no women any where in sight.

"Ready?" Sam asked, placing his left hand behind him, and extending his sword toward Payne.

"Aye," shouted Oliver. " 'E's ready to cut yer bleedink 'eart to fish b'it, 'e is."

Sam spat on the sands.

"And you," he said, "when I get through with your hatchet-faced master, I'll make you sing through your windpipe—like Lumbard did."

Oliver's mouth flew open in surprise and fear.

"Carn't a man 'ave 'is little joke?" he cried. "Yer knows 'ow it is, mitey. A man says things 'e sometimes doesn't mean. Yer carn't tike it amiss like that, yer carn't."

"Like Lumbard did," Sam said again. Oliver shook and fell backward in haste.

Payne tried to take advantage of the situation. He lunged at Sam. Sam's blade met Payne's in the nick of time to turn it, his feet stirring the white sands.

The blades rang and flashed and swished, in thrust and lunge and parry. The duelists grunted and panted. Sweat ran down their bodies. Sam pressed forward, always forward. Payne retreated, cautiously, never losing his frightful smile.

His attitude, and perhaps his skill too, exasperated Sam. He leaped and slashed at Payne, and Payne stepped back. Sam thrust as though the sword were a harpoon.

" 'E's no bloomink w'ale," cried Oliver, taking heart. "Yer carn't 'arpoon 'im. Watch yer hown windpipe, mister. Hit's you will be singin' like Mite Lumbard. An' wot'll yor ning, I hovik's prid?"

Oliver's remark roused Sam to fury. He took it out on Payne. "Fight," he roared. "Don't dance a hornpipe, goatface. Fight!"

Payne sharpened his derisive smile, and kept on the defensive. Sam sprang at him, slashing right and left, reckless and contemptuous. Payne sidestepped, feinted, then reached nimbly out and pricked Sam's left ear.

Now it was Sam who staggered backward, ever backward, and Payne who took the offensive. His blade made vicious, fiery, little circles. Men were shouting, cheering, cursing. Oliver was jumping up and down in his excitement.

Suddenly Sam's bad foot met some obstacle in the sand and gave way. He fell on his left knee, and his right arm moved in desperate arcs to fend off death. Payne stood over him, his sword darting forward and back like an adder's tongue, waiting to strike.

Sam picked up a handful of sand, and flung it upward into his adversary's eyes.

"Foul!" cried Gilbert Smith. "A plain foul, that. Put up your swords now, like Christian men, and call a truce."

"No truce," said Sam. He was on his feet again, and he would have attacked the half-blinded Payne had not Smith put a deterring hand on his left shoulder.

"Away, psalm-singer!" cried Payne, rubbing the sand out of his eyes. "Stand aside or I'll run you through."

"As thee will," Smith answered.

Sam stepped back, and raised his left hand high.

A harpoon came shooting out of some bushes higher up on the beach. It struck the sand at Payne's feet, throwing up a glittering white geyser, and stood there, quivering. All of us who were nearby could see Sam's initials carved in the shaft.

"So," Payne said quietly. "One of your natives hurled this dart at me when you gave the signal."

"And if he'd thrown it as I taught him," Sam said, "it would have torn out your entrails."

Oliver scampered away as fast as his fat bowed legs would let him, but Payne stood fast, sword waiting.

"Treachery," he said. "I might have expected it."

He looked from Sam to the natives back of him, looked at their spear points, looked at the crew.

"Well?" he asked.

"I'm done with you," Sam shouted. "All of you."

He sheathed his sword, and strode into his tent, beckoning to some of the natives. They followed him through the flapping canvas door, and emerged with muskets, fish hooks, packages of seed, a lance, a hatchet, and all the surgical tools.

Sam's ear was still bleeding when he came out of the tent. He had combed his hair, put on a clean red shirt, placed a necklace of gaudy beads about his throat, and shoved two pistols into his belt; but he had not deigned to dignify his wound by dressing or bandaging it.

"You've made your choice," he said, addressing me. "So much the worse for you."

We watched him go, painting red spots on the dazzling sands. Some of the men cursed him, but most of us were silent.

"Back to the ship, you men who belong there," Payne bellowed, taking command. "There's still a lot of stuff to be unloaded. Oliver, see that I have a tent of my own here. Liliston, fetch my woman ashore. From now on, I'm staying here."

I went back to the ship with Smith and Lay and Hussey and Peter Kidder and Columbus Worth.

"Thy wound is healed?" Smith asked Worth.

"Aye," Worth said. "It does well enough."

"Thee can swim?"

"That I can."

"Should thee be ashore tomorrow night, thee could swim to the ship?"

"Aye, and further."

"And thee?" he asked each of us in turn.

"Aye," each of us said.

"Then I will contrive it for tomorrow night," Smith said.

"Why not tonight?" I ventured.

"There's a deal of work to be done yet, Friend George. There is much confusion on deck that needs seeing to. There are provisions to be hid, and arms that must be secreted. We dare not try tonight. And we dare not tarry beyond tomorrow night. Ye all understand the time?"

"Aye," we said.

That night I was ordered ashore, to stand guard over the tents, to pace the sands with a musket in my hands, to cry out every so often that all was well. I didn't mind it so much. The world was quiet. There were only the sands, the water lapping on the beach, the murmur of trees in the wind, the moon, the wheeling stars and the ship.

A bleak spectacle she was, a pitiful wretched derelict with a few rags of sails clinging to her rigging, no light showing aboard her, no sounds coming from her over the rippling waters.

And yet, I thought, that ship would carry me home.

I thought of Judith Chase's Lane, and Sally coming to meet me. I thought of my father's store, and him there, listening to my stories of horror. How could I tell him? How could I tell Sally?

All night I walked the sands, and listened to the music of wind and wave and trees. All night I wavered between the excitement of retaking the ship and starting home, and the fear of arriving home. All night I made excuses for Sam, thought up lies whereby I might soften his conduct, might somehow explain what he had done.

At times the knowledge that I might actually see Sally again, and my father, got the better of me, so that I almost shouted or sang aloud. And then I would be afraid that at the last moment something would go wrong, that I would be left ashore while the *Globe* went on without me.

Toward morning, when the stars had begun to pale and the first sign of light appeared in the gray sky, I thought I heard a rustling in the bush. I was in such a state of nerves I pointed the musket in the direction of the sound and cried a shrill, "Who's there?"

There was no answer, only a more definite rustling.

"Come out or I'll fire," I cried so loudly I woke up half the men. They rushed out of the big tent, grabbing up what weapons they could—thinking, as I did, that the natives were attacking us.

Seeing my shipmates, I took courage and went into the bushes. I found a girl there, crouched and fearful.

"Motake," she said. "Motake."

I recognized her then, and laughed and took her hand and brought her into camp.

Payne came running from his tent.

"I'll teach her," he cried. "Bring her here."

But when he saw the girl clearly he frowned.

"Oh," he said. "She's not my woman. My woman's gone."

"This is a friend of mine," I said. I could not call him sir.

"What's she doing here?"

"I don't know," I said. "I can't speak her language."

"Motake," the little girl said.

"Something's frightened her. Oliver, go fetch Smith. He speaks a lot of island tongues. She's come to warn us of something. Hurry up."

Oliver hurried away and Payne ordered Hanson to serve breakfast. We had finished the meal and I was urging the girl to drink some coffee when Gilbert Smith arrived.

"Thee does wrong, Friend George," he said, "to poison heathen girls with bellywash such as that."

He smiled at her gently and questioned her in several dialects before she understood. Then she talked long and earnestly and Smith listened.

"She says Sam Comstock is inciting her people to rise and massacre us," he said. "He is not in the village now. He went deep into the woods last night with the elders and most of the warriors to hold a powwow."

"Ask her if she's seen my woman," Payne said.

Smith questioned the girl at length.

"No," he answered.

"She lies," Payne shouted, jumping up. "Oliver! Liliston! Bring me a gun. Get guns yourself. And blank charges. Mind you, nothing but blanks. We haven't too many real bullets. We can't spare lead. Hurry. There's nobody in the village but women and children. My woman's there and I want her."

"Nay," Smith protested. "Thee will stir up ill feeling in yon village. Thy wench is not worth that."

"Silence," Payne said. "You forget your place, Mister Smith."

"Aye," said Oliver, "an' 'e's jealous of yer too, if yer harsk me, the psalm-singin' 'ypocrite. 'E wants 'er for 'isself, 'e does."

Motake looked at Payne and Oliver, and huddled close to me.

"Tell her it's all right," I whispered to Smith. "She's frightened. Tell her she'll not be hurt. Nobody in the village will be hurt."

Smith told her. She smiled and seized my hand. She looked at me with shining eyes and said, "Motake." Then she leaped up and was gone before anyone could stop her.

"After her," Payne shouted; and three men ran heavily through the sand.

It was not long until we heard the shots. We could see nothing, for the village was hidden by trees. But it was easy to picture the terror, caused by those loud reports, among these simple, primitive people.

Soon Payne and Oliver and Liliston returned to us, shoving a woman before them.

Sam's harpoon was still standing in the sand. Payne drove it further in with the butt of his musket, then put the woman's arms around it, and handcuffed her wrists. Oliver handed him a rope's end. I started forward to protest, for I could not bear to see a woman whipped. But Smith seized my ankle and threw me.

"Oh," he shouted, "did thee fall?" And in my ear he whispered, "Anger them not, Friend George, for the love thee bears thy friends. Do not endanger our plans."

"But to whip a woman—"

"Aye, it be monstrous; but thee must murder half a dozen men to save her."

Payne, busy plying the rope's end on the woman's soft brown flesh, was a sight so terrible that I thought of killing him. It would not have been a sin. At least I felt so at the time. Her screams went through me like knives. The blood pounded in me. And shame suffused me that I should sit there and do nothing.

Payne beat her until the blood spurted from her flesh, until she fell to the foot of the shaft, until her screams died into little whimpering moans.

"Take her into my tent," he bade Oliver then, "and chain her to a tent stake."

"Aye," said Oliver, yanking the harpoon out of the ground. "Yer mide 'er a proper wife now, yer did. A bit of a rope's end is good for the best of 'em, I halways s'ys." He picked up the woman and carried her into the tent.

"And now," Payne said, addressing us, "what'll we do to Samuel Comstock when we find him?"

We looked at him, silent everyone.

"I'll put it to a vote," he said. "You, Liliston. How do you vote?"

"Hang him," Liliston said, grinning at me.

"You, Hanson?"

"Shoot him."

Each one voted for death, until the question was asked of Smith.

"Thee will excuse me," Smith said gently. "I'll have no part in voting the death of any man."

"And you," Payne said, scowling at me. "What do you say?"

All the time I had been wondering what to say. Now I said it without thinking.

"Fools," I said, "hasn't there been enough murder? Aren't you satisfied? Kill him, Mr. Payne, and one of the crew will kill you. Besides" —and here I had a sudden inspiration—"if you kill him, you'll never find the gold and silver in the captain's chest. He's hidden it."

They surged forward at this, eying me with ugly looks. What might have happened is easy to imagine. But at that minute, Oliver spied Sam approaching a few yards away.

My brother was coming leisurely, and he was alone.

"'E's 'ere," Oliver cried, and darted into Payne's tent for a musket.

Chapter Twenty-Seven

MARCH 1. A brisk wind from the SSW. I shall never know exactly why Sam returned to us at that moment, nor why he returned alone.

He had attained his ambition, such as it was. He had made himself the head of an island tribe. He had his army of natives. In time, he might have made himself something of an emperor of the savage islands.

Did he suddenly regret his desertion of his white companions? Did he think that with his charming smile and his gracious manner— and a few tactful words thrown in—he could once more bend Payne and Liliston and Oliver and the rest of us to his will, make us his subjects?

Did he, so soon, find that he needed us as much as he needed the natives? Did he come only to bargain with us for such things as axes, clothes, or varieties of food?

Or had he, as Gilbert Smith suggests, repenting of his wickedness, come to make peace with us and urge us to sail for home?

"He was a man of moods," Smith says. "He was a man who needed praise, men around him who thought well of him, men to advise him, to guide him, to defer to him; not slavishly as the natives do, but out of good will and good common sense."

Whatever my brother's motives may have been, he came toward us alone, unarmed save for the cutlass in his hand.

He saw Oliver but paid no attention to him. Never had he looked more the aristocrat, the hero, the demigod. Never had his smile been so winning.

There was a general rush for weapons as he came nearer and nearer. The chest of gold doubloons and silver dollars was forgotten in the fear of him, in the lust to kill him.

"Sam," I shouted, "go back."

But he didn't hear me, for at that moment Oliver fired. Ludicrously he fell over backward at the discharge of his own gun.

Sam continued walking toward us, as though nothing had happened. Liliston fired from behind the tent. And then Payne fired. Sam, unhurt, came briskly on, waving his sword in a manner meant to be friendly.

"Don't shoot," he called. "I'll not hurt you."

Payne fired a second shot and Sam stopped. He staggered. Liliston fired again. Sam fell.

" 'E's shammin'," Oliver said. " 'E's pl'yin' fox."

Payne ran out, an axe in his hand. I watched it all as though it were a drama in which I was not concerned. I had wept bitterly when Sam killed Captain Worth and Beetle and the other mates. I had wept when he hanged Humphrics. But now I could not cry.

The white sands turned red about him. The incoming tide licked at the heel of one outthrust boot. A monkey chattered nervously in a tree high above him. The wind blew sand on his still body.

And Payne's axe fell, glittering in the sun.

"With a haxe 'e killed the skipper," Oliver shouted. "With a haxe 'e dies. Aye. Now let 'im slit me windpipe if he carn."

There was unholy glee in Oliver's voice; but I felt no resentment toward the man, no more than I'd feel toward the words of a villain in a play.

They sewed Sam up in canvas, his sword at his side, and dug a grave in the dry sands high up on the beach. They lowered him into it and shoveled the sand in a heap above him.

I watched the sand cover up the canvas shroud, and listened to its whisperings, and remembered other sands on beaches at home—and two boys running hand in hand across them, laughing for the sheer joy of being alive.

" 'I am the resurrection, and the life,' " Gilbert Smith said solemnly, reading from a worn and grease-stained Bible, " 'he that believeth in me, though he were dead, yet shall he live.' "

Gilbert's voice was queer, unnatural, strained. Somehow it reminded me of Sam telling me stories as we sat on the wharf near Barnabas Starbuck's storehouse and looked at the ships and the sailors and the circling gulls and the sun shining on the surf.

Gilbert spoke of green pastures and still waters; and Sam's voice had whispered to me of savage tribes, and pumpkins shining in the jungles, and a white boy leading armies and making himself a king.

"Those who die in the Lord," said Smith; and I remembered Humphries, the poor savage who once promised to resurrect the son of an island chief. It was not Sam who lay there under the falling sands. It must be Humphries. Sam was somewhere in the mountains, or the deep green woods. He was planting pumpkins. He was bringing civilization to the savages. He was making himself king of all the Southern Seas.

Smith paused, and thrust the Bible into a pocket of his coat, and looked up into the serene blue sky. He called out in a loud voice a name that whipped me back to realities.

"Captain Worth!" he called.

The shovels halted in the sand. Men gasped, stared at one another, stood motionless.

"William Beetle!" Smith cried in the same loud tones. "John Lumbard! Nathaniel Fisher! William Humphries!"

It was a dreadful moment for us all.

"I implore you," Smith continued, in a gentler voice, "show mercy to your comrade, come at last to join you."

"Drum beat!" shouted Payne.

I looked around in dull surprise. I hadn't seen a drum taken ashore. Yet there was Hanson, with a drum suspended by a cord around his neck, the drumsticks poised.

The drum rolled, an ironic tribute of glory to the dead.

"Salute," said Payne.

Oliver, Liliston, Joseph Thomas, and Peter and Stephen Kidder lined up beside the mound, aimed their pieces at a white cloud floating serenely in the blue, and fired. The sound went echoing like a lost soul through the far-off blue horizons of the island.

"Now stamp down the grave," Payne ordered. "Level it off. No one must know there is a grave inside the camp."

"Aye," said Oliver. "Stamp it is, sir. An' right merrily too, says I."

"Aye," shouted Liliston and Oliver, stamping and dancing and spitting streams of tobacco juice upon the mound. Oliver started to sing and the others took it up.

> With a stamp and a ho, and a yo heave ho.
> Yo ho, heave, ho he!
> Towing here, ye-hoing there,
> With a yo, ho, ho, and a heave ho he,
> Steadily, readily, greasily, merrily,
> Goes the whaler's life at sea.

I watched. I listened. It all meant little to me.

Gilbert sat down beside me and began to carve an epitaph on the shaft of Sam's harpoon.

"Mind them not, Friend," he said softly. "Yon dancing fools be only frightened and half-drunken men. Thee bears up well. I know thee loved him. I know the blow is hard. But his was a stormy life, and the storm is over. How old was he, Friend George?"

"He was twenty-three," I said.

Dinner was served at noon, but I ate none of it. After dinner I rowed Smith to the *Globe*. Payne had ordered him to bring ashore the two binnacle compasses.

"We cannot leave without a compass," I whispered.

"Patience," Smith answered. "I've hidden one of the binnacle compasses. The other one, and the hanging compass in the cabin, I shall fetch ashore. Payne will not know the difference."

"When do we leave?" I asked.

"Half past nine sharp."

"Do the men know?"

"All of them. But some are fearful. There is not food enough aboard, they say. We'll never make it with these few sails, they think. And thee, Friend George—Payne's watching thee. He noted thee did not eat thy dinner. See that thee acts circumspectly tonight at supper —else he may detain thee ashore."

I ate my share of food at supper, and forced myself to laugh aloud at something Gilbert said. And as I laughed, I felt a hand thrust into mine. The little island girl was at my side.

"Motake," she said.

"What is she doing here?" Payne demanded.

"She comes to warn us," Gilbert said, after he had talked to her. "Her friends plan an attack on ship and shore tonight."

"The devil!" Payne said.

"It would be well to post sentries, armed with muskets; and we should have at least six men on the ship."

Payne nodded.

"You and Thomas will guard the ship, but I can't spare four more men. Take the two Kidders and Hanson. That's three. I need all the others."

"Aye, aye," Smith said.

Payne turned to give orders to Oliver and Liliston, and Smith took the opportunity to whisper to me.

"Kiss the child, and see thee does it well."

I threw my arms around Motake. I was awkward at it. And the girl was shy and ignorant of kissing. She struggled and my kiss fell on her broad, flat little nose. I amended this, however, kissing her fairly on the mouth; and this time she didn't struggle. On the contrary she twined her arms about me and fairly screamed, "Motake!"

"Desist," Smith shouted. "I will not have such scandal in my presence. Unloose this heathen wench that threatens thy immortal soul. At once!"

I let my arms fall, but the girl still clung to me.

"Ah," said Gilbert sadly, turning to Payne, "let me keep this brand from the burning this night. Let me keep him aboard, away from this child of Belial."

Payne laughed, and others with him; and coarse jokes flew about me. I bent my head in seeming shame, but the little girl purred like a kitten gorged with its first rich cream, saying again and again, "Motake."

"Nay," Payne said. "I need him here tonight. Early tomorrow he must take us to the treasure his brother buried."

"For his soul's sake," Smith entreated. "I'll have him ashore before thee's waking in the morning." And for his own soul's sake, I suppose, he added—"If it be humanly possible."

"All right, all right," Payne said, scowling. "See that you do. Take him with you."

The girl followed us to the boat, weeping now; sensing, perhaps, that she and I were being forever parted. She came swimming after us. We did not stop. She called to us. We paid no heed. But we could not get rid of her. Shortly after we went aboard, she came over the rail and rushed into my arms.

"Kiss her good-bye," Smith said. "I'll tell her thee will see her tomorrow—if it be humanly possible."

I kissed her. She said, "Motake," leaped overboard, and swam away.

Smith passed a bottle of rum to Joseph Thomas.

"It may be cold tonight if there be a wind," he said. "This will do thee good."

"Wind or no wind," said Thomas, "I was never one to shun the rum. Thankee."

Thomas turned to me and his dead eyes laughed at me. He pulled out the cork with his teeth and spat it over the rail.

"To your first kiss, says I," he said. "Thankee, says you. And many more of them, says I. Thankee again, says you. And the same to you, Joe Thomas."

He drank deep. In an hour he went below. At seven o'clock, Gilbert followed him, saw he was fast asleep, and went about collecting arms. He returned on deck with one musket and a handful of cartridges, three bayonets and a number of lances, which he placed near the starboard rail where we could get them if we had need of them. A handsaw he placed near the windlass. Picking it up, I saw it had been well greased. Next he went into the cabin, found a hatchet, and placed it handy to the mizzenmast.

We went into the rigging then, thanking God the night was dark and there was no moon. We loosed what sails we had left and turned out the reefs.

We worked as fast as we could, Gilbert and I; but excitement chilled and stiffened our hands, and the moon rose before we were done.

"Hanson," Gilbert called, "Stephen Kidder."

They came to him like shadows.

"The bunts of the sails are yet confined aloft by their gaskets," he said. "Go aloft, on the foreyard and the foretopsail yard, and let fall when I give the word. Thee, George, take the helm. Peter Kidder, thee and I will take the foretack."

It was half past nine when everything was ready.

"Let fall!" Gilbert shouted. He picked up the handsaw and cut the cable.

"But the others," I cried. "Gilbert, the others are not here."

"We dare not wait," he answered. "The moon is rising fast. They'll see us any minute now."

"Lay," I shouted, reckless of who heard me. "Hussey! Worth! Jones! Coffin!"

They might be swimming toward us. They would hear me, in such case, and call out to me. I stood up and listened, putting my hand to my ear. But I heard nothing save the sound of the wind and the thunder of the surf.

"Wherever they are," Smith said, "they are in God's hands. There we must leave them."

With the cable cut, the ship paid off quickly. Her head was off the land. The wind hit us. The flying jib flapped and filled upon the other tack, with the sound of a cannon. The ship vibrated to her keel.

Gilbert took up the axe and cut the hawser. The *Globe* came right into the wind. The rudder slammed. The hull heaved and shivered. The sheets moaned in the blocks, all the sails filling.

Easily, smoothly, the ship moved through the swell. We were at sea. We were going home.

Tears of happiness streamed down my face.

"Thee sees that star?" Gilbert asked, pointing at it. It was a bright star, low down on the horizon. I saw it, but it was all streaked and blurred.

"Steer for that star. And cry no more, neither for thyself, nor thy brother, nor thy friends marooned with savages and mutineers. Only boys cry, and thee's a boy no longer. Thee has not killed a whale. But thee's drunk rum, and held it well. Thee's hit a man and all but broke his jaw. Thee's kissed an island girl. Thee knows somewhat of navigation. So thee's coming home from thy first voyage as first mate.

"Aye, thee's a man now and men don't cry."

"A man," I said. I wiped my eyes with my sleeve, and tried to laugh.

"Aye, a man. And thee's homeward bound to Nantucket. Which reminds me, Friend George. In thy brother's inner pocket, before I sewed him in his shroud, I found this letter."

It was a letter from Sally; just a friendly note. And there was a postscript, which still sings constantly in my mind.

"I am enclosing a note for George. Don't forget to give it to him."

What did she write in that note Sam never gave me? It tantalizes me that I do not know. I may never know. For, though we are homeward bound, I may never see her again.

"Hope not too much," Gilbert has advised me. "For what awaits us, Friend George? I'll tell thee. A perilous voyage. Starvation, it may be, if we cannot put into some island—and that would be dangerous, seeing we be but six. And, if we survive, and reach home—it may be a hangman's noose that welcomes us."

"I am not afraid," I made bold to say.

"Thee be not, but I be," Smith said. "We be but six, and one of us a desperate, ungodly man. I fear Joe Thomas still, I tell thee. We have few provisions. We have little water. We may die of thirst or hunger or starvation, or Joe Thomas' lance. We may not be able to fight the seas. We must endure much, alas, to go homeward to our hanging."

"But why should they hang us?" I asked.

"How can we prove we are not bloody mutineers worthy of the ropes around our necks? I doubt not that was the reason the others did not come—they feared the rope as I do."

"Would you have remained on the island?" I asked.

"To be slaughtered by the savages, white or brown? Nay. 'Tis better here. We may founder. We may die any one of a dozen awful deaths. But we shall die free men, Friend George, and with free consciences. We will not die with mutineers and heathens."

I had no answer for him. I kept steering toward the star.

Chapter Twenty-Eight

MARCH 8. A fine fresh day with moderate winds and a clear blue sky. There is not a ship in sight. The sea is as empty as the sky, and we as lonely and fearful as a star blazing its way through infinite reaches of space.

We are making for the mainland of South America. The sails flap gently, like the wings of tremendous condors. The sunlight on the water dazzles me with its brilliance and its promise. The air has the feel of spring in it, and the smell of Nantucket—the smell of green grass growing under a young girl's feet.

I feel like caressing the wood of the ship as though it could respond like a horse or a dog, as though it might increase its gait to humor me. Yet I am as one still chained to the nightmare of Payne's vicious face, Oliver's smirking lips, and the wistful looks of Hussey and Lay and Coffin and Jones and Columbus Worth! How is it that God left them on the island that we six might be saved?

I think it may be they stayed behind so as not to excite Payne's suspicions by their absence; that they voluntarily marooned themselves that we might get away. And I think they might have been afraid that the *Globe*, robbed of nearly all its rigging and almost all its food and water, would never get to any port.

MARCH 9. Wind still moderate and cool. There is a leak in our water tank; and Peter Kidder, who was ordered to stop it, complained there was a Jonah still with us, meaning Joseph Thomas. We have but twelve gallons to last us perhaps three weeks. It will take that long, I think, to reach the next group of islands. We are rationed to one small cup a day. Also we have rationed our food.

MARCH 10. It rained this morning and we caught some water in the folds of our sails. But when we tried to drink it, we found it salty. The sails had so much salt incrusted in them the rain had turned to brine. This afternoon the sun blistered the seams on deck, and we knew thirst indeed. It was all I could do to refrain from helping myself to another sip of water.

I looked down and tried to forget myself in what I saw, through the clear water, on the bed of the sea. The brightly colored plants, the luminous fish, a huge shark, a hideous yellow sea snake. But how can a man forget thirst, or hunger, in any spectacle? In the midst of my reverie I was roused by Anthony Hanson's shout "Thar blows!" It was a whale all right, and the old excitement gripped me again.

MARCH 10 (later). Joe Thomas has found rum somewhere in the ship. Gilbert—I must learn to call him Captain Smith hereafter, since he actually is the captain now—removed Joe from the wheel because he was obviously unfit to steer, and motioned me to take the wheel.

"Damn all sea captains," Thomas muttered, "ye included, Captain Smith."

Captain Smith made a search of the hold. He found a cask of rum, more than half full, and ordered that it be removed for medicinal use.

MARCH 11. Continues sunny and hot. Joe Thomas was caught at the water tank; and, when apprehended by Captain Smith, he threw the cup in the air. Captain Smith caught the cup with one hand, and Thomas' jaw with one fist.

"Stand guard over this man while I go below for the irons," he bade me. Whereupon Thomas rose and said there was no need of that, he would do as the others did hereafter.

"If thee was not so sadly needed in the work," Smith said, "thee would find imprisonment in the cuddy aft. But if thee tries to be a man—" He walked away without finishing his sentence.

MARCH 12. Fair and still hot. Despite our close rationing and our careful watch on the water tank, most of the precious liquid has dis-

appeared. All our lips are cracking, except Joe Thomas'. Thomas has
found some kind of drink, evidently. Perhaps there is more rum in
the hold. Close to noon this morning I came across him sharpening
his long sheath knife. When he saw me coming he stepped on the
other side of the grindstone, sheathed his knife, and began sharpening a lance.

"We might need sharp weapons," he said, "when we come to the
islands."

At 4:00 P.M. we saw an island; and Captain Smith prepared a boat
to land that we might secure water and provisions. But at 4:30, when
we were not far off shore, large numbers of natives came out in their
canoes. It was evident by the way they carried their spears that they
were hostile. Every man armed himself with a lance. Captain Smith
had a musket loaded and held it ready.

The captain tried to barter with the natives. Beads for cocoanuts.
But, while he was still talking, two spears were hurled at us. One
nipped Peter Kidder in the leg. Another just missed the captain's
chin. Gilbert fired. One native, who had been standing up in his
canoe, fell sidewise into the water. Smith reloaded, and ordered us to
fill the sails and alter our course. As we sailed off, we left a hundred
or more hostile canoes zigzagging behind us.

No cocoanuts. No water. God help us all.

MARCH 13. Scarcely any wind below. The sun rose bright, and
the tar bubbled in the seams of the deck. We have hardly enough
water to wet our lips; but Joe Thomas was discovered with a flask
half filled with rum. He swallowed it before Captain Smith could
take it from him. Half a flask in one swallow!

"If we be a-dyin', says I," he remarked genially, "I'll be a-dyin'
happy, thankee."

Stephen Kidder's shout of "Land ho!" ended the incident, and we
prepared to go ashore. We anchored half a mile off the island—bare
hilltops surrounded by rocks and shoals—and Smith ordered me to
explore the island with Hanson and Peter Kidder. Peter's wound
was still not properly healed, however, and, to my surprise, Joe
Thomas volunteered to go in his place.

"Straight ahead m'lad," he said to me, "and mind the rocks, says I."

Alas. It was truly a desert island. It had not a single tree. It held
not a man nor a beast. Hoping to find at least a turtle we ventured
into a small cave near the beach. Just inside lay five skeletons, and
near them was a board on which someone had written: "Whaleship
Ulysses. Nantucket, Mass."

I remember that ship. She sailed out of Nantucket when I was but a child, and no word had ever been heard from her since.

We stood appalled. All except Joe Thomas. Joe Thomas laughed, and we swung around to gaze at him in horror and amazement.

"Whaleship *Globe*," he said. He pointed at the nearest pile of bones. "That be Captain Smith, damn him," he said. "That be Stephen Kidder nigh him. That be Peter Kidder yon. And those be Anthony Hanson and young George Comstock, says I."

From the recesses of his jacket he produced another flask of rum; and he was about to drink from it when Hanson knocked it from his hands. It smashed on the rocky floor. Hanson clutched Joe by the shoulders and showed him another skeleton lying near a small stove in a corner of the cave.

"And there's what's left of Joseph Thomas," he said, almost with a ring of triumph in his voice.

Thomas' face blanched, and he stepped backward from the awful sight. He tried to say something but his lips moved without sound. Then he straightened up, as though ashamed of his fright.

"Ah poor Joe Thomas," he said. "Beaten with a rope's end by a devil's pick of ships' captains, marooned, starved, treated like a dog by his own shipmates, going home to be hung!"

"Poor Joe Thomas," Hanson repeated, but in tones of such awful irony and disgust that Thomas almost attacked him. "It was because of poor Joe Thomas that Sam Comstock killed his bloody fill. Sam was your friend. He could not bide to see you whipped."

"And he killed the poor blackamoor too, account of me?" Thomas asked with some degree of dignity.

"Belike," said Hanson. "One thing I know of that. No man was sorrier for Humphries' death. Did you note how savage he was about it, how blasphemously he swore? Think you not he was so savage but to hide his pity? Aye, there was them that cried at the hanging of the black man; but not a one of them felt as bad as the man who ordered him hung. That I know, and so do you, Joe Thomas. You whine of poor Joe Thomas, and you besot yourself with rum, you shirk your work, you steal our water and our food. Well, I, for one, will not say 'poor Joe Thomas' when I see you hanged for mutiny on the seas."

Thomas was silent. We were all silent as we rowed back to the ship, and Thomas rowed as hard as any of us, despite the liquor he had drunk.

I wonder much about Joe Thomas. Did he come ashore that he might maroon himself on that island, and thus save himself from the noose that waits us all? And what was in his mind, giving our names to those white skeletons in the cave? Is he planning to kill us all, that we may not testify against him at the trial? Was it our bones he saw there in his mind?

I could have given names to those skeletons too. Worth, Beetle, Lumbard, Fisher, Humphries. And the one beside the stove—my brother Sam.

I wonder somewhat, also about Anthony Hanson. It was not so long ago that I feared him as much as I feared Oliver or Payne. Perhaps it was because Hanson so reminded me of a shark, what with his quick graceful movements, his gleaming teeth, and his chinless dark face. Now I discover a friend in him; an intelligent friend.

I must be growing up.

MARCH 14. Cool and sunny. God has sent us water and food. Late yesterday afternoon we sighted an island. It looked barren and uninhabited, and on our port side was a great volcanic peak. Smith sent two men to explore it. Stephen Kidder and Anthony Hanson. They failed to return, and all night we worried about them. But they returned soon after dawn. They were haggard and weak, so weak they could scarcely climb aboard.

They had crossed the island a dozen times or more, it seems, looking for the boat. But always we were hidden from them by the volcanic peak; and they feared we had been forced to sail away. They were sure they were marooned.

During the afternoon they had found some small turtles, which gave them water. There is a pouch inside the turtle, close to the stomach, as every whaler knows; and one can drink the water in it without any ill effect. In a big turtle there may be as much as two gallons or more of this water.

When they were convinced we had left them they made themselves some sort of shelter and went to sleep. They woke before the stars began to pale, made their way to the beach, and saw our rigging. They also found a pool of rain water in the rocks near the shore and managed to put about a dozen gallons into the cask. A dozen gallons of water and four small turtles!

Captain Smith offered thanks to God for the return of our lost shipmates, and for the gifts they brought back with them.

MARCH 15. We are in a violent storm. I was at the wheel some hours ago when it began. First I observed a halo about the moon. It was of such vast diameter and breadth I gloried in the sight. Suddenly lightning flashed across the sky, and there came the most frightening clap of thunder I ever heard. Immediately moon and stars were blotted out. A fearful wind came from the NW, roaring with fury. Then rain began to pelt the deck. I confess I trembled at the awful malignity of this storm. And I had a thought. About Sam. He had placed a halo around his head. He was a hero. He was going to be the king of all the islands in the Pacific. And then, fury threw him into darkness and mad ruin. Let me place no halo about my own head.

MARCH 17. The storm continues with unabated severity. Heavy seas break over us. The wind roars so loudly and so continuously we cannot hear Captain Smith's orders. We have all stripped ourselves naked, the better to fight the gale. We have not even had time to eat.

MARCH 18. The storm continues, but the anger has gone out of it. Last night, after I had made a hasty entry in my diary, I took my turn at the wheel; but the force of the wind jerked it out of my hands. I tried to recover it, and was tossed from starboard to port. It was remarkable that none of my bones was broken. Smith rushed to the wheel. He too was knocked over. He cried to Hanson. But Anthony had gone aloft to help the two Kidders. They were in the rigging, flattened by the wind, fighting with fingers blue from cold, to subdue a sail that had broken loose. Seeing that Hanson was unavailable, Smith called for Thomas. There was no answer. By this time I was able to take and hold the wheel without too much trouble.

The sea rose higher and higher. It swirled above the clouds. Peter Kidder and Hanson managed to put out a sea anchor, and we began to ride out the gale a bit more easily. Later we found Thomas, below in the hold. He had found another small cask of rum!

Smith named his punishment. No food nor water for twenty-four hours.

But the penalty was not imposed for we found that a leak had flooded the forehold. Water was coming in fast, and all of us, including Thomas, went to work. Captain Smith and I, with lanterns, crept about along the ribs of the ship inspecting the hold to see where the water entered. We found several small leaks, and quickly stopped them, but we could not discover the main leak. Meanwhile, the others manned the pumps, in relays of two. I had my turn. So did Smith. We pumped for hours.

Yet the water keeps rising.

MARCH 19. Stormy and overcast. The pumps have been going all night, but the water has risen further. Also, it has entered the aft hold! A cask of rum swam about dizzily there for a time. Joe Thomas made an effort to capture it, but it was smashed against the side of the ship, and the rum was mixed with the brine, to Thomas' profane chagrin. Luckily we have retrieved our precious cask of water, unharmed.

Perhaps we shall have to abandon ship. We are exhausted. We could not light a fire during the storm; so we have eaten nothing that was cooked. We have scarcely slept, Thomas excepted. We were unable to make any observations because sun and moon and stars were obscured by inky clouds. We are lost.

But we continue to fight.

Chapter Twenty-Nine

MARCH 20. The storm continues but its violence has decreased. We have discovered the source of the big leak, at last, and have managed to stop it up. The water is rapidly leaving both holds. The wind keeps blowing, but there is no rain. And there is no rest.

MARCH 23. We have had an adventure; and, although it is somewhat difficult for me to write, and extremely painful, I must enter it now in my diary lest I forget any of the details.

It began three days ago, after we had managed to stop the leak. At noon of that day, March 20, the dark clouds hurried away across the sky, and we could see; not clearly, but with better vision than the storm had afforded us. And Peter Kidder, looking through the glass, shouted that he could make out an island, with trees on it; trees moving with the wind.

Captain Smith ordered me to bear up. Hanson sounded fifteen fathoms; and shortly after that eight fathoms. At this time we were about a mile from land at a point to the northeast. We could hear heavy combers breaking against the shore. The sound was distinct above the roar of the wind.

We tried for a passage through the outer reef; and it seemed to me the old Globe must break against the rocks at any moment. We could not save her by anchoring, and we must needs run along shore as near the land as we could. Our rigging was hanging loose, we were at the mercy of each wave that crashed upon us; and the thunder of the sea on the outer reef was unnerving.

"Close thy eyes, George Comstock," Captain Smith bade me, "and say thy prayers. There be hope for us only in prayer."

Ever since we left the Mulgraves he has scrupulously refrained from calling me "Friend George"; and I have always—or nearly always—addressed him as Captain.

While I prayed, the whaler suddenly lifted on an upsurge and shot through the rollers into a great cleft formed by two tall outthrust pinnacles of rock. It was as though we sailed through open gates into a safe harbor. We were wedged rather tightly between the rocks but were safe from immediate destruction. When the tide turned we knew we would be borne to sea again.

Presently the force of the sea subsided, the wind veered off shore, and we were able to clear the rocks without injury. We sailed about a mile off shore, and then dropped anchor.

The storm had eased up to such an extent that we had no trouble launching a boat, and Captain Smith and I went toward the beach, in search of all we could find. We stowed the boat among some rocks above the shore; and I accepted gratefully the chance to rest while Captain Smith unloosened the boat line, tied one end over a harpoon handle, folded the line into several lengths, and then swung it over his shoulder.

" 'Tis like we might meet a wild boar," he said by way of explanation; "or maybe a savage man."

We found a path; and so we realized that the island was inhabited. We went cautiously along the path, through hilly country, then through a narrow defile between huge cliffs. As we ascended, we found a few cocoanuts, which we hastily broke open. What a joy it was to drink the milk, and to eat the firm white meat! There was no rationing here; and nobody watching to see that we took only our fair share.

After this most refreshing meal we found a medium-sized turtle, placed him comfortably on his back so that he would be there when we returned, then put our mouths into the trickle of a stream that seemed to drip from the summit of the hill.

"Give thanks for clear, cool water," Captain Smith said. "Ah well, them that prefer rum to water have their own hell on earth, George Comstock. And if thee had on thy conscience the things that cling to Joseph Thomas, mayhap thee too would seek forgetfulness in rum."

We went on up the path. We saw the remains of a palm-thatched cottage; but we didn't stop to investigate it, for at the same time we saw a dozen or more natives peering over the rocks above us, watching our approach.

I don't know when I have been more frightened. Those men were hostile, and some of them had spears. I think I know now how the early settlers felt when they suddenly encountered Indians in their war paint.

Captain Smith, however, showed no sign of fear. He walked boldly up to the savages and tried out some of his island dialects. I sauntered after him, tensed, ready to run if I had to, yet trying to appear as cool and unconcerned as Gilbert.

They were of medium size, these men, except for one, who seemed to be the chief. They were all naked save for their loin cloths, and they were greased and painted. I was so frightened that I don't remember exactly how they were painted; not even in my dreams. But I do recall the horrible yellow blotches I saw on some of their faces; and I remember distinctly that their hair writhed in plaits or coils, like so many venomous black serpents.

The big man—he glistened in the sun with sweat or oil, or both, his teeth were like a dog's, and part of his nose had evidently been bitten off—put an end to the captain's attempt at peaceful talk. He came forward slowly, brandishing a huge club, and tried to grab the captain's hand. Smith stepped back, as though he hadn't noticed the man's hostility particularly, and hallooed to the ship. He was trying to make the natives believe he was summoning an army; and he was partly successful, for the chief stood still.

For a moment or two the savages were undecided. They kept looking at the ship and then at us, then back at the ship again, making gestures that were meaningless to us, but not uttering a sound.

"Get thee on thy way to the ship," Gilbert said to me, "and God speed thee."

But I could not leave him thus.

"Run," he ordered, seeing my disobedience. "I will be on thy heels."

I don't think any two men ever ran faster down a hill. We reached the defile in the rocks before I believed it was possible. And there I had to stop to catch my breath. The long weeks of work, sleepless nights, and scanty food, and then the long hard climb up the hill against the wind, had sadly sapped my strength.

"Get thee down," Captain Smith ordered.

I threw myself flat on the earth and a spear whizzed over me. Had I remained upright I should surely have been killed then and there.

Evidently the savages had hesitated some little time about pursuing us; perhaps to equip themselves with spears. But they were coming toward us now, the big man in the lead. The big man had a spear instead of his war club.

Smith was smiling. He was actually smiling. He had picked up a large stone with a jagged center, and had wrapped the end of the harpoon line firmly about its middle. Before I could ask him what he was doing he bade me run to the boat and get it ready.

As I left him, he darted behind a boulder in the path of the savages and prepared for battle. I was so curious that I turned and looked back. I had to know what he was doing. I was just in time to see him deal with the first of our pursuers, the big man with the mutilated nose.

I saw Captain Smith lift the haft of his harpoon handle, and sling the rock into the air above his shoulders. I saw the savage rush down at him, ready to transfix him with a spear. I saw Captain Smith thrust the harpoon handle upward and forward from the shoulder, saw the rock go true. It hit the savage's skull with a loud crack, and the big man fell.

I turned again, a little further down, to watch the destruction of another savage, then busied myself getting the boat into the water. Before I had shoved it more than a few feet from the shore, the captain was wading out to me.

"It is a most un-Christian deed to kill, George Comstock," he said, as we rowed to the ship. "Peace to their heathen souls! Yet when a man is responsible for other lives than his own—mind thee the tale of David and Goliath?"

"David also used a stone," I said.

"Aye," he answered, and no more was said until we neared our vessel.

Then, to our consternation, we observed that the natives were in possession. Anthony Hanson, high up in the rigging, gave us the details.

The savages had taken the crew by surprise. Stephen Kidder had slain at least three of them with musket shot; then the gun had jammed. He was now in the captain's cabin. Peter Kidder had jumped overboard, and was probably drowned.

Where was Joe Thomas? Hanson didn't know. Dead, perhaps.

"Cut the halyards of the mainmast yards," the captain shouted. "Then slide along the forestay to the foremast and cut the halyards on the foremast yard."

"Aye, aye, sir," Hanson answered.

At least the savages could not operate the ship.

But we could not board it. Neither could we return to the island.

"Let thee pray, George Comstock," the captain said, "and let thee not be afraid. We shall ply the oars gently until nightfall; and when it be dark enough, we shall retake the ship."

I rowed, most of the time, staying out of spear range of the ship. Captain Smith seemed to sleep, but whenever a shark came near the boat he opened his eyes.

"Friend," he said to one that came quite close, "it be dark meat thee wants. Our flesh be white."

When night at last had covered the sea, Gilbert bade me give him the oars and get some sleep. I felt too excited for any such luxury as slumber, yet I must have dozed, for I felt the captain shaking me; and at first I did not understand what he was saying. I made him repeat it.

I undressed then, and I went into the water with my sheath knife in my teeth and swam toward the ship. Whether there were hungry sharks around me, or whether I just imagined there were, I am not sure. But if there were, they did not attack. I swam under the counter, chinned myself onto the rudder, and clambered up through one of the cabin windows. There was a musket there, the captain had said, and a canister of powder hidden in a cabinet. I groped around until I had found them. I loaded the musket, went to the window and looked out.

The captain was moving in close with the boat. He had muffled the oars. He made no noise. He was only a shadow, moving in the dark. In a moment, I knew, he would tie the boat alongside. I was ready.

Just as I turned, the moon began to emerge on the port side, lighting up the cabin enough to show me a lance. Would it also show the natives on deck the boat being tied alongside? Surely there would be someone on deck who would see it.

As I started toward the door, meaning to go up on deck, I heard the sound of someone coming down the companion ladder. What stark terror there was in that moment! Was it a savage coming down to me, or was it one of my friends? I waited at the foot of the companionway, lance in my right hand, laying musket and canister at my feet.

Whoever was there above me wore no shoes. I thrust the lance into his chest. He fell with a scream of pain; and where he had been standing there was moonlight, and, up above, a spatter of bright stars.

As I withdrew the lance from the darkness at my knees, the moonlight and the stars were blotted out again. I hurled the lance upward.

As it left my hand, something struck me with such force on my left shoulder that I spun around and dropped.

I awakened as from the dead, with an excruciating pain in my shoulder. My head was throbbing. And I was so weak I could not rise. I looked up to see the companion ladder filled again with darkness. I managed to crawl through the cabin doorway, but I could not shut the door. Neither could I crawl back for the musket I had loaded.

In the subdued splendor of the moonlight I saw a naked brown man raise his spear to kill me. There was a savage ecstasy on his face; and perhaps that is what saved me, that ecstasy, that heathen desire to watch me suffer. I was naked, unarmed, helpless, entirely at his mercy. There was no need for him to kill me quickly. He wanted to enjoy the kill.

That ecstasy gave Joe Thomas time to come to my rescue. He came in his bare feet, creeping out of God knows what hiding place, with a belaying pin in his right hand. The savage heard him, and turned around, no doubt believing, at first, that Thomas was one of his friends. But when he saw the bewhiskered white face he acted on impulse. He hurled the spear. At the same moment Thomas hurled the belaying pin.

The native's skull cracked as though it had been no harder than a ripe cocoanut. He was dead before he fell. But his spear had wounded Thomas. I could see him stagger. And I could see that he was bleeding. I managed to get up and to help him through the door, which I bolted.

" 'Tis only the drink pouring out of me, lad," Thomas said as I eased him down onto the floor, "only the drink, says I. Blood, says ye. 'Tis your blood falling on me, though, thankee. Tend yourself, lad. Ye need aid far more than Joseph Thomas."

I snatched a sou'wester from the wall, made a pillow of it, and thrust it under his head.

All the ill will I had borne Joe Thomas went out of me, all the fear of the man, all the suspicions I had held against him.

"I'm sorry, Joe," I said, "I wish I could do something for you; but I must leave you here. I have a job to do. But, if it hadn't been for you—"

I think I began to blubber, so immense was my gratitude to this man, my admiration—yes, even love—for him.

"Don't worrit, lad," he said. " 'Tis but a scratch in the leg the heathen gave me. But the cut in your chest, Joe Thomas, says ye, that's the sore one. Aye, says I; that's the cut I'm feared of."

Thomas had been with Stephen Kidder when the natives came

aboard. He had been wounded and left for dead. For hours he had lain on the companionway, the natives going up and down over his body. The native who came so close to spearing me had stepped on Joe's wounded leg, and so brought him back to consciousness.

There was nothing more I could do, either for him or for myself. I went out, cautiously, bidding him bolt the door after me, if he could. I found the musket and canister, and made my way up to the deck, accidentally kicking something as I went toward the rigging. It did not stir. I groped about, to find the end of the rope which Captain Smith said he would dangle from the rigging. I probably would not have found it, except that I hit it with my head.

I looked around me. There were natives everywhere, it seemed, but I was in deep shadow. I hastily fastened the canister and the musket to the rope, and then yanked the line three times, the signal we had agreed upon.

Nothing happened; and I wondered if the captain had met with an accident up there. I pulled again. The line jumped upward.

I was more elated, I think, than I would have been at the chance of sinking a harpoon into a whale. For now the ship was ours again.

The captain was aloft, out of spear range, and able to pot the invaders at will, with ample time to take aim, and to reload.

I started to go down to Joe Thomas. But I never got there. I must have fainted. When I came to my senses, I was in the mate's cabin; and the ship was proceeding on its way.

On its way to Sally, and to a hangman's knot around my neck.

Chapter Thirty

MARCH 25. Puffy winds, the sea slightly choppy. This morning we sighted an island which Captain Smith believes to be one of the Nimrod group. Not bad for dead reckoning, provided that we actually have fetched the Nimrods. If the captain is correct, and my figures are likewise, we are, roughly speaking, about halfway to Valparaiso, the port we hope to reach.

For three days I lay in the cabin with my head bandaged, my left arm bound up, and my whole body feeling as if it were held down by a heavy anchor. It was a cutting-in spade that struck me in the left arm and shoulder, Captain Smith says; but what caused the injury to my head nobody knows, least of all myself.

My head has cleared, but the arm still pains.

Today I was allowed to go on deck for an hour or so, and there I met Peter Kidder. I had thought he was dead, and I was so glad to see him I could have embraced him, as though he were a girl. How close we have become through our troubles, we few men and boys! He was knocked over the rail during the fight with the natives. He swam ashore, hid himself in a cave, and swam back to us after Captain Smith had shot four of the savages and chased the others off into their boats and on to shore.

Tomorrow I shall be allowed to see Joe Thomas.

MARCH 26. Clear and hot. Wind from the northwest. I have seen Joe Thomas; and the purposes for which I was born are beginning to make themselves known to me. As yet, they are somewhat incoherent.

Yesterday the two Kidders went ashore. They saw great numbers of doves, and killed a mess of them with stones. They also obtained some fine green turtles and several casks of fresh water. Later I was permitted to bring some of the meat, and a bowl of turtle soup, to Thomas.

I was startled at seeing him. He had returned to the state in which he was when I first met him. His eyes had the same dead look when he acknowledged my presence. But he spoke.

"Away with ye," he said.

I tried to tell him I was his friend, that I owed him my life; but he didn't hear a word I said.

"Take a sip, Joe Thomas, says ye," he murmured. I had to bend low to catch what he was saying. "What is it, says I. Poison, says ye, to save ye from the hangman's bit of rope. Thankee, says I, drink it yourself, young George."

I went away thinking. Here was a man who had spent most of his life at sea, an American who had been whipped by more than one ship's captain; who had been marooned; who had suffered for days in an open boat; who had been cruelly ill-treated even by his friends; and who had evidently gone mad from this abuse.

Surely there must be something I could do for him, and for men like him. Surely there is something I can do for all those who go down to the sea in ships. Maybe the Lord wants me to become a lawyer, that I may protect them legally from the brutalities of the masters and mates of American ships. Maybe He wants me to help make the laws that will save them.

There isn't one among us, now, who wouldn't go to any length to help Joe Thomas. It is too late, I fear. A few days ago we held him in contempt. But because he fought so well, because he saved my life, and because he suffered most, our attitude toward him has changed radically. For the first time we are kind to him! Naturally, he doesn't understand our turnabout. Naturally he is suspicious of us.

Poor Joe Thomas! I wonder what would have happened had we treated him decently, as one of ourselves, from the day he came to us out of the sea. It is possible that Captain Worth and all the rest of our dead would be alive and well today—and we would be sailing home with all the "ile" the ship could hold.

"The ways of the Lord are beyond all comprehension," Captain Smith says. "It was foreordained thee should pick him up out of the great wide sea, warm him back to life, and take him aboard us— thee and thy brother—that he should save thee from the heathen's spear. And it was foreordained, I am sure, that it is thee who will rescue him once again from his insanity, and from his peril."

How Gilbert Smith has changed!

MARCH 27. Calm and hot. We are anchored in a small bay, still— we believe—in the Nimrods, close to a rather large inlet, and at a point we call Cahill's landing. We obtained that name from a tall, wild, yet rather good-looking white man, a very odd character. He is redheaded, but his beard is grizzled; and there is more beard than face to stare at. He dresses in a style that might be termed inter- national, since his wardrobe displays the colors of many nations. He is Irish, he says, and his name is Pat Cahill. But his eyes are as American as my own, and as blue as the blue in Old Glory.

I was, naturally, amazed to see a white man standing on the shore when Hanson rowed me from the *Globe*; but my amazement doubled and trebled when he shouted English words.

"A hundred thousand welcomes," I heard him cry. And, before I had digested the fact that he was a white man, and that he had spoken English, he had dashed through the shallow waters to grip my right hand, and Hanson's, and to shower us with further greet- ings and a spate of happy tears!

I thought then that he had been marooned on this island, even as Joe Thomas had been marooned by Captain Worth. But, not so. No indeed, not so.

"Ain't I the happy one now to have ye here!" he exclaimed, after he had helped us out of the boat and led us a little way across the sands; "sure 'tis the answer to prayer ye are. No less than that. Saint Patrick himself sent ye this way he did."

"Saint Patrick," he said. "Saint Patrick himself. On his own feast day," Pat said, "I asked the good saint to send me a Yankee ship. And on the ninth day, lo and behold, here ye comes to anchor at me own private landing!"

By this time I had recovered my senses enough to note that the man's nose had been flattened somewhat, and that his left ear had been hammered out of shape.

He saw what I was thinking; for suddenly he grabbed my right hand again and almost crushed it, and he winked at me and laughed.

"Ye guessed it, son, seeing me crumpled ear. 'Tis a great man I was in the prize ring. In New York mind ye. And in Boston. Ah yes; maybe ye've heard of Paddy Cahill, and me fight with Jem Mace. And I was a champion wrestler too! But then I went to sea."

All this before either Hanson or I could say a single word.

"Feel me muscle," he said suddenly to Hanson.

"Hard as a rock," Anthony said as he fingered Cahill's arm. The next moment he seemed to leap high into the air, to land on his back and lie on the sand, blinking and gasping.

" 'Tis a trick ye must learn if ye wrestle, lad," Cahill said as he lifted Hanson up with a jerk. "But ain't I the sorry host to two such fine Yankee lads? Sure 'tis ashamed of meself I am."

Behind me I heard a woman laughing. I turned and saw an island girl; a pretty savage with dark red hair and beautiful white teeth.

"This is Noneeta," Cahill introduced her.

It was because of this girl that he had prayed for the advent of an American ship. He intends to marry her; and, inasmuch as there are no missionaries in this part of the world, he must ask the services of a ship's captain.

"But none of your Britishers," he said. "Sure I'd sooner ask the blessing of the divil himself than that of the skipper of any ship carrying the R'yal George."

Pat told me he had been a sailor on a British ship. He met the girl on a nearby island; and then he had deserted.

"Me and my man, Otis," he said.

Otis is a West Indian Negro, and possibly the tallest of his race. He is almost as tall as I am. I record this fact with some incredulity. Yesterday I did not regard myself as being above the average in height. It had seldom occurred to me to take note of my growth since leaving Nantucket.

When did I begin to shoot up? And why did I never notice that I had to stoop to go through doorways? The fact came to me only this morning with a sudden start, when I saw Otis, noticed the gigantic stature of him, and then realized that he was looking up to meet my eyes.

I must be six feet, three inches. Or even taller!

Otis was as remarkably dressed as his master. He carried a musket in one hand, and a violin bow in the other. A fiddle was strapped on his back. Shades of William Humphries! Do all our Negroes play the fiddle?

Otis had jumped ship with Cahill, taking the musket with him and a few charges of powder; and he had helped Pat escape. Now Pat was king of this little island. He grew sugar cane, tobacco, potatoes, and pumpkins. He had sheep and goats, obtained by trading with merchantmen. He had built a comfortable hut, planted a vegetable garden, and, with a string of wooden boxes, had diverted a down-plunging stream into a reservoir for an adequate water supply. He pulled up a slide in the box nearest his home, and the water rushed into a bucket. Pat was king, and Otis was his prime minister, his army and navy, his man of all work, his royal orchestra, and his jester.

"Sure we have everything here," Pat said, "even rum and plug tobacco."

To add emphasis to his words he spat a brown stream at a fiddler crab a dozen feet away and all but drowned it.

"Tell your captain," he said, "the entire half of the rum is his for the joyful task of making a Christian wife of Noneeta, and con-founding her heathen father."

Everybody aboard is quite excited about Pat. Even Captain Smith. But Gilbert is troubled about the matter. He is not sure he has the legal authority to perform a marriage ceremony.

My arm is paining me again.

MARCH 30. At sea. Valparaiso bound. A calm, tropical, reposeful day, the sails flapping idly, the gulls mewing mournfully above our wake. But the spell of Pat's magic island is still on me.

Captain Smith finally made up his mind to marry Pat and the island girl. They came aboard, like Mr. and Mrs. Noah to the Ark, bringing two goats, two chickens, two doves, two turtles, two small casks of rum, two baskets of fresh vegetables, and a dish of flat cakes made by the bride-to-be.

Smith ordered Peter Kidder to broil the two chickens, make a pot of turtle soup, and broach the rum. That was the wedding feast. The vegetables were served as dessert. When I get back home, and if I escape jail, I shall order a dinner of nothing but vegetables fresh from the garden. And I shall follow that with a boiled supper!

Captain Smith, holding his Bible in both hands, looked solemnly at the overclad man and the underclad woman standing before him, and addressed them in the fashion of a minister.

"Patrick and Noneeta, with the grace of God, Who hath thrown the mantle of His protection over us all, I have decided to make thee two one in His eyes."

A voice from below startled him.

"Ahoy, Cap'n. Don't hold any ceremony without the prime minister!"

The voice was followed by the apparition of an ebony face shining with white of eye and white of tooth; then Otis came over the rail, still burdened with musket, violin, and bow.

"I'm the best man," he explained, and did a few steps of a jig.

Captain Smith smiled, then resumed his solemn mien. He began reading from chapter seven, First Corinthians: "It is good for a man not to touch a woman. . . ."

After he had ended the short ceremony he hurried into the cabin, wrote out a marriage certificate, and presented it, with something of a flourish, to the bride. Anthony Hanson tolled the ship's bell; the rum was passed around; we drank the health of the bridal couple; then Peter Kidder announced that the wedding feast was ready.

It was the first really joyous event that had occurred since those idyllic days in Oahu before the mutiny; and I am sure it gave us strength and courage to continue on our perilous way home.

Incidentally it is worth setting down here that, though he must have seen how shorthanded we were aboard, and must have sensed that we had suffered some sort of trouble, Pat Cahill made not a single comment, asked not one embarrassing question.

"Be what he may," Captain Smith praised him, "the man is a gentleman at heart. But there will be gentlemen aplenty aboard us before long, I am afeared, who will not be so considerate."

Shortly before we sat down to the wedding celebration I fetched a flask of rum to Joseph Thomas. He looked at the liquor with languid eyes and waved it aside.

This morning, after he had treated my arm—which does not seem to be getting any better—and had put a fresh bandage on it, Captain Smith took me in to see Joe Thomas.

Joe was dressed and sitting on a chair, his face turned upward, his eyes staring. There was a rope suspended from an iron ring in one of the rafters. It was swaying gently, and that was what absorbed

Joe's attention. By the light of a sperm candle on the table I saw a noose at the lower end of the rope.

"What's all this?" I asked.

"Poor Joe Thomas," Joe mourned. "He hanged himself. For mutiny, says ye. For murder, says I. He's gone to hell at last. Poor Joe!"

I had an inspiration.

"That wasn't Thomas who was hanged," I said. "That was Silas Payne."

"Was it, now?" Joe asked, looking at me with wondering eyes.

"It is only the cowardly man who takes his own life," Captain Smith abetted me. "And Payne was ever a coward."

"Aye," said Thomas. "Now I can sleep, Cap'n Smith, young George."

He fell into his hammock and slept. We have hopes that he may recover; but every sharp-edged instrument has been taken from his cabin; and we all, in turn, keep strict watch over him. He has become the baby of the ship; and we his willing slaves.

Few ship's crews have ever been beset by so much work as we. We are but four now; or at best four and a half, for my left arm is still in such condition that I can do only half the chores I should do. But no matter how hard or how long we work, we still have time to nurse Joe Thomas.

APRIL 4. Continues calm, as though we were in the doldrums. This morning Joe Thomas ate everything set before him, and complained that we were starving him.

APRIL 7. Sky overcast. Boisterous wind. The storm pounced on us with screams of anger just as we reefed sails.

APRIL 9. Storm continues. This is Captain Smith's birthday. I managed to join him at the wheel that I might give him his present, a pipe I scrimshawed out of a whale bone months ago. He tried to thank me, but his teeth were chattering with the cold. So, for that matter, were mine.

I had a few minutes with Joe Thomas. His fever has gone. He seems rational. But he is sure he will not live to see port. He is just a skeleton covered with skin and hair.

APRIL 25. Fair winds blowing. And we are no longer alone in the liquid desert. This morning we fell in with the French ship, *Versailles*, Captain Lefevre, bound from Calais for Valparaiso. Our skipper told the Frenchman we had been in some trouble, but did not elaborate on the statement, and that we were short of rations and seriously undermanned. The Frenchman looked suspicious, but he sent us plenty of provisions, fresh water, an officer, and several sailors. We go fast to the hangman now.

The *Versailles* has a dozen or more women passengers aboard her; most of them destined to be employed as governesses or maids in Chile. I confessed the sight of them stirred me mightily.

One of the girls, Rosita, seems to have taken quite a fancy to "le Capitaine Geel-Bare Smeet"; to his excruciating embarrassment. She is, or was, a teacher of languages, and has offered to teach him French. Her thin and merry voice comes sharp and clear to us from the railing of the *Versailles;* whereas the voices of the other girls are indistinct, and usually confused with hysteria and laughter.

I am, of course, not the only one affected by the nearness of these women. Both the Kidders have shaved since the *Versailles* hove along our starboard rail; and Anthony has forgotten there is work to do aboard the *Globe*, while his face wears a perpetual grin.

APRIL 28. A brisk wind from the southeast. We are following in the wake of the French ship. Captain Lefevre has generously loaned us three men to help us; and I have been excused from all work. I think my wound is infected.

APRIL 30. Warm winds. Sultry on deck. I have been sleeping overmuch these last days. My arm throbs at times, but not too painfully. Captain Smith is worried about it. Yet he pretends not to be.

The man has changed radically since we met the *Versailles*. He was treating my wound this afternoon when he glanced up suddenly, and blushed. I saw the girl then. Rosita. She was standing at the stern of the French ship, waving her kerchief. I could not help laughing at Gilbert's fond confusion.

MAY 5. Fair and cooling breezes. I lay on deck for an hour or so this day, with the sun on me; and it seemed to me, looking at the soiled white sails, that the *Globe* was a tired and dirty old eagle skimming over the sea to its nest, fearful it would get there, fearful it would not. I closed my eyes and tried to sleep, but I could not. I kept seeing the French language teacher waving to Smith from the stern of the *Versailles;* only, as always in the last few days, the girl seemed to be Sally, not Rosita. She was standing at the end of the pier in a far-off port, and she was waving not to Smith but to me— welcoming me home.

MAY 26. Today the old and tired eagle sailed into the port of Valparaiso, folded her dirty wings, and waited, with drooping head and discouraged feathers, the punishment expected.

We have come to a haven, and to judgment; a whaler with the oil of countless whales dried on her deck, but not a drop of oil in her hold; a strange ship in a multitude of many cargo carriers, a vessel bringing to shore only the tale of a long, fruitless, and bloody flight. Captain Smith helped me on deck, made me comfortable, and eased me onto a coil of rope near the rail, where I could look down on a crowd of people gathered on the dock.

Evidently news of our troubles had reached them. They were staring at our bedraggled ship as at a monster. It seemed to me they were fascinated with horror; and I am sure that some of the women there would not have been surprised if the old whaler had growled and attacked them.

Suddenly there was only one face there below me, a tearful face, a face I knew, a face looking piteously, for my brother Sam.

Perdita! Perdita with a baby in her arms.

We said no words to each other, save in the way we looked at each other. Then she was gone.

Exactly what happened afterward I cannot say. I must have fainted. Yet one thing I remember clearly. I remember looking up at the American consul, my friend Michael Hogan, and seeing the indignation and the deep concern in his gray eyes.

"Who is this man?" I remember his asking. And I remember his astonishment when he learned my name, and his insistence that I must be taken forthwith to the hospital.

I must be made well, it seems, before I am handed over to my executioner.

Chapter Thirty-One

MAY 28. I am getting better. My wound has been cleansed. The fever has abated. The pain no longer bothers me. The arm has quit throbbing. And I no longer want to sleep all day and all night. Also, the future is not so dark as it was a day or two ago, thanks to Michael Hogan.

"Don't fret," Mr. Hogan told me this morning. "We'll not hold any sort of inquiry until Captain Percival arrives. That's a whole week off at least. By that time you'll be a new man."

"What about the others?" I asked. "What about Joe Thomas?"

Mr. Hogan blew out a savage breath.

"Damnation!" he said. "I had to put them all in custody. Against my will, I assure you. Nothing else I could do. But don't fret about them. At least they are being fed."

Thank God for Michael Hogan.

JUNE 13. The examination has ended; and I was able to testify. Captain Smith, Hanson, and the Kidders, will be taken home as material witnesses. Joe Thomas will go home in irons, since the court—and even Mr. Hogan himself—was convinced that Joe was "sympathetic to the mutiny."

There will be a trial, eventually. But first, it was decided, the rest of the crew, those we left on the Mulgrave Islands, must be apprehended and brought home, either as witnesses, or as co-defendants with Joe Thomas. As for me—I know not yet what fate is mine, since the court has not determined it, due to the fact that I am still a patient in the hospital.

I pleaded for Joe Thomas, reminding Mr. Hogan how he had been marooned by Captain Worth. Hogan swore a great oath; but I did not condemn him for it.

"I remember that hell-cur well," he said. "No more damnable creature ever lived than Captain Worth. Still, it was murder, and Thomas must answer for it, if he is guilty. However, I will go easy with the chains. The man will have every care until the trial is over."

"And what about me?" I couldn't help asking.

"I can't tell you now," he said. "I must talk that over with the captain. But, don't fret. Get some sleep now. I'll see you soon again."

JUNE 16. I have made the hardest decision of my life; and I do not know whether to be sorry or glad.

Mr. Hogan came to the hospital this morning, with Lieutenant Paulding of the U.S.S. *Dolphin,* a very smart-looking naval officer, and after asking for my health, inquired how I would like to return to the Mulgraves.

Before I could answer, Lieutenant Paulding put the proposition to me.

"I want a volunteer to go back with me to the islands where you left Payne and Oliver and the others," he said. "We will sail as soon as we get word from Washington authorizing such a cruise. We don't know anything about the Mulgraves, I must confess; and we would waste a lot of time going from one island to another, no doubt, before we found the right one. We must have a pilot. The consul has spoken for you; and I assure you that you will not go aboard the *Dolphin* as a prisoner—if you volunteer."

"Let me think it over," I pleaded.

"Very well," Lieutenant Paulding said, as though he were offended at my hesitancy.

"The boy is still sick," Mr. Hogan came to my defense. "He has been through hell. He has a sweetheart back in Massachusetts, I understand. He wants to go back to her, hangman or no hangman. And we are asking him to make another long voyage, to stay away from the girl for another year or more. Give him time to make up his mind."

"Of course," said Lieutenant Paulding. I could see he was some-what mollified. He even smiled as he said good-bye to me.

So, for hours, I debated the matter. I thought of Sally; and I thought of Columbus Worth, and William Lay, and Rowland Coffin, and Cyrus Hussey, and Rowland Jones, and Oliver, and Payne, and Liliston. It was true the *Dolphin* might sail the South Seas for years without finding the proper island. What did the navy men know of that part of the world? It was only the whalers who ever sailed to the South Sea islands. I had no doubt I could find the Mulgraves without any trouble. But to make another long voyage, to suffer long periods of calm, hurricanes, monsoons and sudden nasty squalls, to go hungry again, perhaps, when provisions ran out and no friendly islands were near, to be worked to desperation again, to throw myself again down to sleep with my clothing drenched with cold salt water, my teeth dancing and chattering, and my whole body twitching in an effort to find warmth!

Oh yes, it may be I would go not as a prisoner, but assuredly there would be times when I would have to take my place with the crew.

Perhaps I have become soft, lying here, with people waiting on me, bringing me food and drink, reading to me now and then, making me comfortable. I dread another voyage, almost as much as I dread the thought of going another year or more without seeing Sally.

And suppose I do not come back!

Yet, when I considered the plight of Hussey and Jones and Coffin and Lay and Worth, when I thought that I might be the means of saving them from Oliver and Payne, when I realized that it was my duty, and perhaps my destiny, to do something for "my fellow mariners," I decided I would go aboard the *Dolphin*.

When the lieutenant and the consul returned this evening I told them of my decision. They were pleased, and quite gracious.

I took advantage of their good nature to ask a favor—that I might see Gilbert Smith before we parted, and that I might see him alone. The request was granted.

So, now, I am at peace. Doctor Rodriguez assures me I will be able to use my arm fully; though he considers it strange I did not lose it altogether, or that I did not die of the infection. Perhaps I should have died, or been a cripple, had it not been for Gilbert's constant attention, and my own astonishing health.

I grow more and more surprised every day at my incredible stature, my unbelievable strength. With my right hand today I crushed an orange, not deliberately, but through sheer carelessness. No one was more astonished than myself.

JUNE 17. I said good-bye to Gilbert Smith this morning, and gave him long letters for my father and for Sally. He is glad, it seems, that I am going to the Mulgraves; and he is confident we will find the rest of our crew and "bring them back to justice."

Gilbert said no more because, just then, my nurse announced a visitor, one Rosita Bonheur!

She affected to be overcome by finding Gilbert with me; but I am convinced she knew he would be there. It delighted me to see her, the more so because of her effect on Gilbert. The good Quaker stammered, blushed, coughed, cleared his throat, wiped his face, dropped his kerchief, picked it up, dropped it a dozen times again, kept shifting on his chair, and showed his misery—and his happiness —in a hundred other unmistakable ways. It was a delicious torture for him, and it lasted until a nurse came with my dinner and furnished him a good excuse to take himself away.

The girl went with him when he left, talking to me over her shoulder as she strode to the door, keeping tight hold to Gilbert's arm all the time, and pretending not to notice his embarrassment and delight.

God be good to all my friends. Shall I ever see them again?

Chapter Thirty-Two

JULY 4. This is a great day at home, with all the old men bragging about their exploits in our wars with England, and all the young men pretending those exploits weren't much. Bonfires burning. Orators burning too. And cups spilling over in the taverns.

I have left the hospital. My arm is nearly as good as it ever was. Mr. Hogan has promised to let me go home on the first available ship, since it may be half a year or more before the *Dolphin* will get orders from Washington, D.C., to set forth for the Mulgraves.

Fortunately the cargo vessel *Excalibur*, bound for New London, needs a second mate. She sails tomorrow! Captain Gideon House of the *Excalibur* is an old friend of Mr. Hogan's; so it was simple for the consul to arrange everything.

Was there ever such a Fourth of July before? One minute I was pitying myself as the sorriest of exiles. The next moment I was trembling with apprehension—having learned of the *Excalibur* and being afraid I should never be taken aboard her even as able seaman. Yet here I am—as second mate!

I am going home. I will be spared the ordeal of explaining Sam's black deeds to Mother and she will be spared the heartbreak of listening. She lies in the family plot in the Friends' Heavenly Rest, high above Judith Chase's Lane that overlooks the harbor. I don't think the news should come as a terrific shock to Father. For he often said that anyone who could cause the wine to evaporate in the casks in the cellar with such cunning as to leave not a single trace on the floor would never come to any good end.

But Sally. How can I break the news to her? How shatter the shrine that she had built up in her heart with such tenderness and adoration? I must tell her in my own way before the news reaches the public ear.

DEC. 25. I had silver in my pocket when I stepped ashore at New London. I had a deal of it, enough to buy me a fine suit of clothes, new boots, a new hat, and any number of good linen shirts. But I was in such a hurry for Nantucket I had no time for any Connecticut tailor. I must home at once, and in my sea rags.

And grim reality, of course, must have it that I run, in this rude fashion, into the crowd in Nantucket gathered to proceed to see Secretary of State John Quincy Adams in Washington. And all of them in their Sunday best!

I could not believe it for some few moments, this reality, this crowd of old men, this group of distinguished citizens, this collection of old sea captains, shipowners, bankers, and ships' chandlers, this gnarled, bent, corpulent, gray, and important committee bound for Washington with a petition!

I shook my head in disbelief, for I knew all these wretched and respected gentlemen, and I knew they hated and distrusted one another cordially. What could have brought them all together here? What could have given them such unity of purpose that the same look was in each face?

So I stood gawking at them, like any country boy at his first sight of the city and its representative citizens, minding not my manners, until a flash of purple brought me to my senses—a flash of purple silk and the splendor of a dimpled elbow.

I darted then into the crowd, with the impulse to seize the purple silk waist in my two hands, and lift it high. But in my blind joy at seeing Sally once again, in my haste to reach her, and in my blundering awkwardness, I unwittingly thrust my hip into the softness of old Barnabas Starbuck, her grandfather. I could not help seeing that he spun completely around, with such force that his gold-headed Malacca cane went whirling high above the heads of the crowd, and his high silk hat rolled crazily in the muddy street.

I was aware of the disaster I had caused, but at the moment it meant nothing to me, because of Sally and the sudden happiness that flooded her eyes. I had meant to pick her up and hold her high that I could look at her, yet, somehow, I did nothing more than pick up her hands and hold them.

There was such commotion in her that she could not talk; and I must confess I was as emotionally upset as she, and as inarticulate.

It was Sally who recovered first. She withdrew her hands from mine—but for a long time afterward I could still feel the warm blood pulsing fiercely through them.

"It is George, Granpa," she said. "George Comstock."

If she had said, "This is Pontius Pilate," she could not have made a greater sensation.

So I stood there in the muddy street outside the Elm Tree Inn, facing men I had known all my life—most of whom I had liked and respected. I was home; and these were my neighbors; and this was Sally, the girl I could not live without. Yet, for a long moment, this was not true. I was a stranger in a strange community; and strangers were looking at me as though I were some sort of fearful and loathsome monster.

They stared at me with wide, round eyes and wide, round, open mouths; fearful, for a time, that I might suddenly attack them. And then they glared at me in dumb fury.

I shall never again feel so helpless, so naked, so hated, so feared, despised, and menaced.

But there was a look in Sally's eyes that bade me not to mind what I saw in the eyes of the others. And she spoke to me, softly.

"Your father will be glad to see you, George."

Someone handed Barnabas Starbuck his fancy cane. Somebody else rescued his silk hat from the mud, brushed off the rim, and presented it to him with an apology. A funereal line of carriages drove up the street and the first of them stopped in front of the inn. Starbuck, without glancing at me, got in. Sally followed quickly. And, in a little while, I trudged down the empty thoroughfare to my father's store.

My father was wearing the Quaker gray. That was the first thing I noticed. He had not worn it since my mother died. He was smaller than I remembered, and much frailer. Indeed he seemed another man entirely.

It was quite evident that the news of Sam's red crimes had struck him a vital blow.

He looked up at me, but did not recognize me. He went on talking to Samantha Welles, Nehemiah's widow, who stood before the counter, her plump back to me; and he thee'd her as though he had never abandoned the plain speech.

"Nay, woman, I have no kind thoughts for yon important committee; nor for Barnabas Starbuck, its important chairman. Thee knows they go to Washington, not in mercy, but in vengeance; not in the cause of justice, but for the sake of their own business."

"But Thomas—"

"But nothing. Their petition asks that a public armed vessel be sent to the islands. Aye, it mentions there be boys marooned there by murderous companions and there be kinfolk here sorely wanting to see them again; but the main purport is that the mutineers be apprehended, and be brought back here to be hanged.

"These men, I tell thee, care little for the life or death of any ship captain or officer. They care only for the jeopardy of their business through such crime. And they think that by hanging a passel of men and boys by the neck until they are dead they will frighten other whaling crews into slavish submission, and so make sure their property is not destroyed."

"But Thomas"—Samantha interrupted again. "But Thomas, is not thy feeling colored by the persecution of yon men? Let thee be not bitter, Thomas. Thee canst sleep o' nights. These others—dost think they sleep as soundly? Perhaps thee shouldst pity them that they have such reverence for their property, and such foolish hate of thee. As if thee were to blame for aught that happened!"

I had been so full of worry at my father's appearance, and so full of sorrow and love for him, and I was so hard put for the right words with which to reveal myself, that I had paid but little attention to the woman. Yet I was annoyed when she called him by his first name, as though she had a right to. Also, I was irritated with her thin and querulous voice, and the fact that she was arguing with my father.

But I checked my anger, remembering there was a deal of goodness in this woman. Half the boys in Nantucket had learned to call her Aunt Samantha, and more than half had eaten her oatmeal cookies and stolen apples from her orchard.

I waited, again a stranger, listening to these two, and trying to find the best way to make myself known; but when I heard her saying, "They blame Sam for everything, and thee because of Sam; yet I feel sure there were worse than Sam aboard the *Globe* . . ." When I heard her saying that, I put my hands about her waist, turned her, lifted her willy nilly onto the counter, and kissed her cheek.

"God bless you, Aunt Samantha," I said. I turned to my father then, who was staring at me strangely, and hugged him. "Father, it's George. Don't you know me? I've grown a foot since I saw you, but I'm still George."

He wept at that, like a woman in pain. He mentioned my name weakly, he pressed my hands, and he looked up and down the length of me with his red watery eyes. Then he hugged me and wiped his face dry against my shirt. He motioned me to look at Samantha, and to take her down from her high perch.

"George," he said, "this is your new mother. She may not be the prettiest woman in Nantucket, nor yet the finest cook, but she is the best woman in Massachusetts, and a tower of strength in my disgrace and sorrow."

This time I kissed Samantha on the mouth.

It will not be hard for me to leave now, since I know that Father has someone to look after him. She is a very stubborn, argumentative, and contentious woman; but as good and as comforting as an all-wool blanket.

I know now that Samantha gave Sally Starbuck my log to read. Sally knows what I have written in it. Who else could have shown it to her? Yet, somehow, I do not mind too much, for it shows that Sally has not entered into the village-wide conspiracy to avoid all contact with the awful Comstock family. It is patent either that she comes privily to see Samantha, or that Samantha goes privily to her.

Actually I have seen Sally only once since that first day, and that by accident. And she said but a few words to me before she hurried on.

"It is a good story you have written, George. But how does it end? I suppose the hero goes back to sea again. Does he marry the girl in Valparaiso? Or is it the little island savage he loved so much? Motake, Mr. Comstock. Motake."

First George. Then Mr. Comstock. And she was gone. Without a good-bye of any kind. Yet this morning her Christmas present—a new log to replace the one I had completed—came to the house before the dawn, and Samantha brought it to my room and left it outside the door before I woke.

A quiet Christmas, but not a sad one, even though the people in the Meeting Hall did not seem to see the three of us. I wonder what sort of Christmas Gilbert had, and the Kidders, and Hanson, and Joe Thomas—and those shipmates we left in the islands.

I wonder how they all fared this blessed day.

Chapter Thirty-Three

JAN. 1, 1825. The year begins without bitterness on my part. May it end that way. The problems before us can never be solved unless we see them clearly; and who, with eyes dimmed by bitterness, can see at all?

There are so many problems.

There is the fate of Joe Thomas, the only one of us imprisoned on his return.

There is the attitude of the town toward my father and his wife.

It is not easy to be the father of such a murderer as Sam Comstock —nor to be my father's wife. Not when neighbors and old friends turn against them so quickly and treat them with such cruelty and contempt. It may be they will have to sell the store, or lose it. Nobody comes there any more to trade. Nobody comes even to gossip.

There is the problem of our shipmates in the Mulgraves, who must be found and brought back to Massachusetts justice.

And there is my own particular problem—Sally.

I have seen Joe Thomas. He is well fed, he says. He is well treated. He sleeps most of the day and all the night. And he is getting fat. Few people visit him. He doesn't mind. He is not lonely.

"For the first time in me life, young George," he said, "I've servants to do for me. And, if I rest a bit in the daytime, mind ye, no hell-spawned bucko mate rebukes me with fist or marline spike or cat; no captain swears at me, or maroons me on a pile of sand and ashes. Poor Joe, says ye, he's in prison. Lucky Joe, says I, he's safe from all them as hate him."

I have not seen Gilbert Smith, nor Hanson, nor the Kidders. They are at sea, though not on whaling ships. That life is closed to them forever it seems, thanks to Starbuck and his friends.

And I have not seen Sally since she mocked me with "Motake."

JAN. 2. Correction. I have seen Sally.

I had finished entering the above item in my log yesterday afternoon, and had taken up my favorite work of Shakespeare, *Romeo and Juliet,* intending to read it through again, when Samantha knocked at the door of my room and entered.

She was all apologies for intruding, but she had an errand for me —if I would be so kind.

"Will thee go to my house, George—that is, Nehemiah's house—of course it is mine too but I've always thought of it as only Nehemiah's —well, anyway, there is a Bible in the library I want, George. A big black book. Right next to all those law books Nehemiah used to pore over at night."

"Law books!" I said.

I guess it was the way I said it that made her open her eyes and smile.

"Bless the child," she exclaimed. "Does thee like the law? Nehemiah never was a lawyer. That is, he never practiced law. But a smarter man never lived—unless, of course, it be thy father. I declare, George, if thee wants those books, take them. I assure you I have no use for them at all. But do bring me the Bible. Law books! What a man sees in them I don't know; but they just fascinated Nehemiah. Maybe he should have been a lawyer instead of a cooper."

She thrust the key into my hands and hurried away.

I lost no time in my stepmother's errand. I almost ran to Nehemiah's house. Law books! I cannot even yet appreciate to the full the wonder of owning them.

The door of Nehemiah's house was not locked; but I thought nothing of the matter at the time, being filled with the joy of my new acquisition. I went headlong into the library, a tiny room built between living room and kitchen, a square room lined with shelves from floor to ceiling, and books on every shelf. And there, standing on a chair and looking at a row of books on a high shelf, was Sally Starbuck.

I don't know which of us was the more surprised. But it was Sally who spoke first.

"If you tell me you also have come for Samantha's Bible," she said, trying to keep her voice steady and her eyes from dancing, "I'll scream. I'll run out of this house screaming. I'll run through all Nantucket; and when I see that cute, that scheming, that adorable Samantha, I'll scratch out her eyes. To think she fooled me so easily!"

"A woman who would do a trick like that," I said, trying to match her voice, "probably never owned a Bible."

Sally got off the chair and gave me her hand.

She did it quite simply, without any sense of pretending. "Hello, George," she said. "Welcome home. That's what I wanted to say when I first saw you, in front of the Elm Tree Inn. I'm really glad you're home safe. I couldn't say anything, though, under the circumstances, could I? You don't give a girl much chance to talk, George Comstock, do you?"

She seemed to be entirely unembarrassed, entirely unemotional.

I was alone with her, in a house secluded from all neighbors. Nobody knew we were together, except my father's new wife. I had only to put my arms around her. I had only to lift her up to my lips, as I had once thought of doing. I had only to say that I loved her, that I needed her, that I wanted her. She could not have escaped me!

And yet I couldn't talk. I couldn't move.

I suppose I was afraid that by too abrupt or clumsy a word, or movement, I might jeopardize what little chance I had of being loved by her.

She gazed up at me, and there was so much starshine in her eyes that I could not even look at her.

"What—" I managed to ask, "what happened when you met President Monroe?"

She walked away from me, into the dark living room; and from the motion of her shoulders it was plain that she was provoked. Something unpleasant, I gathered, must have happened in Washington; something she did not want to remember.

Certainly nothing else could so definitely have affected her.

"Sit down, Mr. Comstock," she said. Even her voice was different. "Sit down and I will tell you all." Her voice was flat, and the light was gone from her eyes.

It wasn't much of a story. The President was smoking a pipe with a long stem all the time the petition was being read to him. He was very kind to Grandpa Starbuck and to Sally and the others, and very solemn. He said he had been advised of the details of the mutiny by the consul at Valparaiso. He was glad, therefore, to act on the petition of the worthy citizens of the great commonwealth of Massachusetts. He would send the *Dolphin*, Captain Percival, into the South Pacific, next summer or fall, if the vessel could be got ready by then.

"Grandpa started to read the petition," Sally said, "but when he got to the words about the American flag—"

She jumped out of her chair, contorted her face into something of the semblance of her grandpa, and acted out his part.

She strutted, she spluttered, she shouted, she whined. She boasted, she pleaded, she threatened, she predicted doom.

"The American flag, through the enterprise of the owners of whaleships, is now seen in every port of the world! Our commonwealth of Massachusetts has become great because of the whaling industry! What then, sir, would become of us if the crew were allowed with impunity to kill our sea captains and mates, and run away with the ships?"

She made me see Barnabas Starbuck standing before the President of the United States, puffing and panting his way through the petition, angry purple stretching across his cheeks, his eyes flaming, his hands shaking so that at times he could scarcely read the script he held before him.

"Grandpa's voice suddenly foundered with all hands aboard," Sally said. "After he had talked about crews running away with ships he couldn't go on. I had to finish the petition. Then the President mentioned your name. He said the consul at Valparaiso had recommended you as a young man of high principles; and he agreed that you should go aboard the *Dolphin* when it sailed."

"I am practically on my way," I told her. "The *Excalibur* sails next week out of New London for China. I shall go second mate in her as far as Chile."

Sally didn't seem to hear me. She was still playing the role of her grandfather.

"Grandpa was quiet until he got outside," she said. "Then he exploded. He banged the end of his Malacca cane four times against a rock. 'High principles!' he said. 'Dum it, dum it, dum it, dum it!' The fourth time he said 'dum it' and hit the rock, the wood splintered as though it were sugar cane and not Malacca at all. Grandpa looked at it as though he were clutching a bunch of straws! He dropped it in the muck and left it there."

I don't know which moved me more; Sally's excruciatingly funny mimicry, or her shocking profanity. I had never heard a woman swear; never expected to hear one, especially Sally, use such language. I was not prepared for the words, nor for the sulphurous tone in which they were reproduced. And I suppose I showed all this in my face; for she gave me a look and a gesture of disgust, and went back into the library.

"Help me up onto the chair," she said. "I'll have another look."

I obeyed innocently enough. I thought she actually expected to find Samantha's Bible on the top shelf, but she kept looking at my face instead of at the books above her. It bothered me, and it confused me so much I started to move away.

And then came the greatest shock of all.

"Hold still, damn it," she said, and in her own sweet voice—not in any imitation of her grandfather's. "Hold still, damn it." And with that she quickly put her arms about me, stooped, kissed me, and fled.

Before I recovered my complete senses she was running down the street.

JAN. 3. I think I know now why Sally kissed me. It was not in pity, nor in derision, as I at first suspected. Nor was it because she had discovered my lifelong love for her.

Doctor Pelligrew, stopping on his round of patients, gave me the clue this morning. He greeted me casually, as though he had seen me yesterday and the day before and the day before that, as if nothing had happened to make me one of the three pariahs of Nantucket.

It was too cold for much chatter, but I was compelled to thank him for his civility, and to point out how much we valued an old friend's greeting, now that Sam had cost us so many friends.

"Not Sam's doings, George," he said. "Not Sam's doings at all. Not a soul in town didn't know Sam. Not a soul in town blamed your pa. Everybody knew what a heartache Sam always was to him. Not a soul in town didn't sympathize with Tom and Samantha. But when folks heard you was sticking up for Joe Thomas, and wanting to study law so you could save him, and all that—well, George, that was a cat of another color."

"So I'm to blame," I said. "Not Sam!"

" 'Bout the size of it," Doctor Pelligrew said. "But stick to your guns, young fellow. Easier to live with yourself if you're right. Happy New Year. And, just between us, I'd rather be young George Comstock, town pariah, than old Barnabas Starbuck, town potentate."

With that he whipped up his horse, and was gone.

So my problem has become at once simple and complex.

I have only to go call on Barnabas and assure him I have abandoned Joe Thomas, that I believe in the sacredness of property—especially his property—and that, if I ever had any quixotic notions of bettering the lot of the common American sailor at sea, thus increasing the cost of operations and reducing the amount of dividends, I have decided they were impractical, indecent, a threat to the interests of shipowners, and distinctly un-Christian.

I have only to make friends with Barnabas, and everything will turn out right. My father will not lose his store. Trade will return to it instantly. If my father should need a loan, it can be arranged through Grandpa Starbuck's bank. Should I want to enter college and fit myself for a career, that too could be arranged. And as for Sally—well, I don't think Grandpa would forbid such a match.

All things could be adjusted if I made my peace with this furious old gobbler of a man.

But I will see him in hell first.

Let my father lose his store. Some day, somehow, I shall make up the loss to him. Let Nantucket continue to treat us as though we were lepers. What is Nantucket after all? Let Sally cling to her grandpa and avoid all sight of me. I shall not desert Joe Thomas, nor any others of my fellow slaves of the sea.

Probably Sally knew this about me; and, undoubtedly, that is why she kissed me. I should like to think she was somewhat proud of me because of my stubborn attitude—or my firm stand as Samantha calls it. But I do not fool myself. It was in farewell she kissed me. In renunciation.

JAN. 4. And now it begins. The long journey away from Sally, away from my home. But it isn't the same as it was two years or so ago, when I sailed out through the harbor on the *Globe*. There is no thrill now to buoy me up, no hope of adventure, no feeling that things will be different—when I come back—because I will make them different.

There is in me only the sterile realization that I have a job to do, that it will take long months, perhaps long years; and that I shall still be a moral outcast when the job is done.

Not so long ago I felt I should be hanged when I reached home— if ever I were fortunate to reach that blessed place. The fear vanished at the consul's greeting in Valparaiso. I know now it was an unreasonable fear, though it was real.

But which is worse—to be hanged or to be tabooed, to lose your sweetheart, or to lose your life?

JAN. 12. Calm all morning. Light winds from the northwest. But we are nearing Hatteras, and we must be on the alert.

Calm in my mind too. Work absorbs me, and Samantha's law books—and, at odd moments, lessons in navigation from Captain House himself. I thought I knew a lot about navigation. How I boasted of bringing the *Globe* to the Nimrod Islands! And how little, actually, I knew of the science.

Odd, but true. The more one learns the more one realizes the profound depths of his ignorance!

Poor Samantha. There were tears in her eyes when I lifted her up from the floor and kissed her good-bye. And she thee'd me as she thee's my father! Yet I think, secretly, she was glad to see me go—to escape from the oil-adoring atmosphere of Nantucket, to live free and untabooed again. I felt released too.

It will be better there for them, with me far away.

JULY 4. Last year at this time I was more than homesick. I was in despair. Then, in an unexpected moment, I found myself headed straight for home. Today, again in an unexpected moment I am told to prepare once more to go to sea; this time to join the staff of the *Dolphin*, at Chorrillos, on the coast of Peru. My friend, Lieutenant Paulding, will accompany me from Valparaiso.

The lieutenant's father, Samantha told me, was one of the three patriots who captured Major André. I must ask him if this is so.

I have arranged, through Lieutenant Paulding, and through Consul Hogan, to bring part of my law library aboard the *Dolphin;* but I have not yet made up my mind which volumes must be included, and which left behind at the consulate.

I feel I have made some little progress in the study of the law, though it is only six months since I started. But lately I have had the benefit of Mr. Hogan's teaching.

Mr. Hogan says that if I perfect myself in the law as I have in the Spanish language, the world is mine—or all that I want of it.

In this I think he was not quite serious, though he said it solemnly. All I have ever wanted of the world, since I was old enough to want anything intensely, was, and is, Sally Starbuck.

What if I gain the world, and lose her? What matters then to me the law, the science of navigation, the use of many languages, or anything else save the knowledge that I did what I thought was right?

Mr. Hogan feels as I do about that. Also, he promised me he would appear as a witness for Joe Thomas at the trial. No matter where he may be at the time, he will come to us at his own expense.

After Mr. Hogan speaks his mind about whaling captains and whaling shipowners in general, and Captain Worth in particular, I shall be even less popular at home than I am now. But then—

AUG. 18. Boarded the *Dolphin* yesterday; and this morning, early, we sailed for Casma, for wood, water, and such provisions as we could find. I am snugly but suitably billeted aft. I am neither an officer nor one of the crew. Nor am I ranked as a mere civilian passenger. Mr. Paulding explains that I shall, however, be treated as an officer unofficially, inasmuch as my coming aboard the *Dolphin* was sanctioned by no less a person than the President of the United States.

That means, he says, that I will have all the liberties of an officer, but none of the responsibilities. I shall have ample leisure, he assures me, to study. I may also, at times, read for pleasure, if I care to, since there is something of a library aboard.

Captain Percival greeted me cordially enough. "Glad to have you aboard, sir. Mr. Paulding will show you around." Percival is a younger man than I expected to find him and it is evident he thinks the men of the United States Navy are a cut or two above the boys who go down to sea in whaleships. But I don't suppose I can dislike him for that. Each man for his own.

The big thing is that, at long last, we are going back to the Mulgraves. I wonder what we shall find there, besides my brother's grave.

Chapter Thirty-Four

SEPT. 22. Wind fresh and steady; and still from SSE.

"Queer thing," Lieutenant Paulding keeps saying. "Queer thing, Mr. Comstock, how the wind increases in force when it hauls to the southward of southeast." He insists on mistering me. I suppose it's because I am a whaler, not a navy man. There is evidently a caste system on board. I mister him back.

We were gazing at a comet together, Mr. Paulding and I, when Doctor Rodriguez came up behind us. He said something about the system of creation, and made various other comments about the order of things. I remember one remark that has a strange comfort in it.

"He marks the comet's fall as surely as He notes the sparrow's, as certainly as He follows the path of a ship through stormy seas."

Doctor Rodriguez is, I believe, the strangest man I have ever met. I was delighted to see him again, when I came aboard the *Dolphin* at Chorrillos. I had not expected to find him in any ship, being accustomed to thinking of him only as part of the hospital in Valparaiso. And I certainly wasn't prepared to find him the surgeon of an American man-of-war.

I expressed my delight at this meeting, boyishly, I suppose. And I also told him how grateful I was for the improvement in my arm. He merely smiled, nodded his big gray head, said it was nice to see me too, offered me a soft limp hand, and left abruptly. Since then I have seen him only twice. He stays in his cabin most of the time, I believe; and usually has his meals brought to him.

He never smiles; he seems always to be thinking profound thoughts; frequently he walks by one without, apparently, being aware that he is doing so. He is not "sociable"; yet no man aboard is better liked.

It was the doctor who first drew my attention, incidentally, to the young mulatto everyone calls either Buff or Blue-Belly. Thus, indirectly, he provided me with an eager servant—even a slave—and a most devoted friend. There is nothing I need that Buff does not contrive to furnish. There is nothing he *thinks* I need he will not try to procure for me.

It was in late August, when we were anchored for half a day or so in the roads of Huanchaco [possibly the modern seaport of Huacho—AUTHORS] that I made this boy's acquaintance. I had gone ashore with the crew to see what I could see. There was nothing to interest me, and I started back to the beach.

Such a surf had arisen I could scarce believe it. The waves were running fierce and high, and the thunder with which they broke appalled me. They exploded, really, into geysers of foam that shut out the light of the sun. I was wet through, standing high above the shore and quite distant from the water. We were marooned, I knew, until the fury of this sea abated. No boat could live in it. I saw that our boat had been drawn up on the shore; and that the doctor was sitting in it, talking to the crew.

As I started in that direction, I noticed, far out to sea, little specks shooting swiftly in. At first I thought they were birds flying over the crests of the waves. Then I saw they were boats of some kind and there was a man sitting in each, a naked man with a paddle.

I saw them through the breaking wave tops, the descending jets of foam, the confusing mists above the water. Now and then I caught the glint of sunshine on a paddle.

These men were coming peacefully, easily, swiftly, evenly over those raging combers. They were riding the whitecaps without effort. They were laughing at the anger of the sea. They were enjoying themselves as men were meant to enjoy themselves, in work and play, in courage, in skill, in supreme confidence, and in ecstatic triumph.

My heart hammered with excitement as I watched; and something deep inside me ached with the beauty of the scene—the broken lines of the whitecaps surging in, the shock and tumult of the foam, the naked men riding their bundles of reeds, the clouds in the blue, the gulls flying in erratic patterns, the sunlight on land and sea.

I had somewhat dreaded this trip, thinking I should be melancholy all the time, if not bored; thinking I should be ever mindful of my lost prestige, my lost sweetheart, my lost career. Yet, sitting on the sands beside the boat, I was the most thrilled and happy man in all the world. When I began to realize this I was more than grateful to the men of the balsas.

One of them, I saw to my extreme astonishment, was not an Indian but a mulatto, who was a member of our crew. He was tall, though not so tall as I am, and magnificently built. He was like a statue carved in amber, and he had that mark on him, the bluish streak that is like a satin sash across his flat hard stomach.

What happened then happened so swiftly I did not see it all. A young midshipman named Ember rushed past me in drunken anger, and attacked the mulatto. One moment the boy was a magnificent statue, dripping with sea water, and smiling with all his startlingly beautiful teeth. The next he was falling in dismay, blood on his lips.

I sprang up. But I slipped and fell. I lay for a stunned moment, floundering in the wet sand. Before I could rise, the doctor was in command. He had ordered Ember back to the boat, and was examining Buff's hurt.

Ember stood wavering, undecided, shaking his lowered head. He had lost his cap, and his black hair fought stubbornly with the wind. His hands were still knotted, and there was blood on the knuckles of the right one. He staggered away. He has avoided me ever since.

I have no malice against the man. In his inebriated state it may have seemed that Buff had committed something of a crime in leaving the boat to disport with the Indians in the surf. I have no liking for him, however; nor, apparently, has the doctor.

SEPT. 27. Wind still southward of southeast.

This morning we reached Nooaheeva and anchored in a refuge known as Comptrollers' Bay.

Some of the officers went ashore. Buff and I had a long swim. I am learning to make great speed through the water. But I shall never be so fast nor so powerful a swimmer as he.

Buff began coaching me the day after we quitted the roads of Huanchaco. We had anchored, for a few hours, off the Lobos Islands. The crew went after seals. There were thousands of them basking in the sun. I couldn't stand to see them wantonly slaughtered. Neither, it seems, could Buff. It was very hot ashore. So we dived into the sea.

I thought, in my innocence, that I could beat him to the ship. When he realized what I was trying to do he laughed, dived under me, swam around me, leaped out of the water over me, turned and dived under me again, and continued, swimming circles around and under and over me all the way to the *Dolphin*. How he manages to spring out of the water like that I cannot explain. He is like a porpoise in his antics, and, I am sure, as much at home in the water.

SEPT. 29. Buff's lips were puffed up and bleeding this morning. I suspect Mr. Ember. The white man's superiority? Perhaps. Or Mr. Ember's sense of inferiority?

Buff's father, as Doctor Rodriguez tells the story, is a Spaniard who made himself virtually king of the island of Owyhee, and emperor of many other islands. A fabulously rich man. Buff's father is said to have thirty or forty wives. A little Solomon. Buff's mother was a Negro woman, coal black, the doctor says, and the daughter of a tribal chief. I wonder what Mr. Ember's parentage may be. Whatever it is, it did not bring him the joy of life that enriches Buff. Even with his bruised lips he smiles joyously. I must speak to Mr. Ember.

SEPT. 30. Spoke to Mr. Ember. In private. He is a poor fighting man, but not by any means a coward.

OCT. 1. At last my swimming has won a word of praise from Buff. I was not trying to make speed. Suddenly my arms and legs began to move in a beautiful rhythm. Curiously enough I had never thought of swimming as being rhythmical. But it is. It most certainly is. There is more rhythm in it than there is in a dance. It is impossible to describe the sensation I felt when I realized I had mastered Buff's method.

What a university the sea has been to me!

OCT. 30. Calm and hot. We have encountered a different type of native. These people are bold. They come aboard us in numbers, or alone. They steal whatever they fancy, dive overboard, and climb into their canoes or swim ashore with the booty.

Yesterday, after we had sighted the Duke of Clarence Island, and were skirting many small islands clustered together, more than a hundred canoes swarmed about us, evidently bent on doing us harm. They showered us with cocoanuts, pieces of coral, rocks, and even heavy war clubs. One of these clubs struck Doctor Rodriguez on the head. He was unconscious when I carried him below; but he soon regained his wits.

NOV. 10. We anchored this morning on Byron's Island, another beautiful coral Eden in the blue seas; and again we have fallen among thieves.

Men and women rushed into the water to meet the first boat sent ashore. They were armed with spears and stones. Mr. Ember wisely decided to turn back before he got too close—when it might be impossible to negotiate the surf.

The natives dived into the water, seized hold on the boat, and tried to drag it ashore. They were thrown off. They dived deep this time, and came up with rocks and pieces of coral, which they hurled at the oarsmen. One of the sailors fired his musket and wounded a native before the trouble was ended. Some of our men were badly hurt by the natives' missiles. Doctor Rodriguez is busy with them now.

NOV. 11. Shortly after I entered the above item in this log I had one of the most thrilling adventures of my life.

It happened that, while I was below with the doctor and the wounded men, a native on board the *Dolphin* wrested a musket from somebody, probably a sentinel, and swam ashore with it. Many shots were fired at him, but he was unhurt.

The captain was so angry he determined to get the musket back. He ordered several boats lowered, and went in pursuit in the first boat. This was swamped before it had gone far through the surf, and all the ammunition was made useless. The captain landed on a coral bank and sent two men back for dry powder. But a heavy sea pitched the craft against a hidden rock and stove in every timber. The oarsmen had a perilous moment or two negotiating that water before they returned to the coral ridge. The other boats, at the captain's order, put back to the ship.

The captain then signaled Mr. Paulding to fire a cannon at a large hut some distance from the shore. Evidently this was the chief's hut.

The cannon fire produced results. A small party of natives, led by a very old man—at least he was bent and bearded enough to make him seem an old man—advanced toward the captain and the boat's crew stranded on the coral. The two parties conferred in sign language.

Eventually the natives understood. One of them ran away and came back with the musket. However the lock and the bayonet had been taken off. By signaling the ship to keep firing, the captain managed to retrieve the lock. But the bayonet is still there. I don't think those people would give up that treasure if we leveled every hut on the island.

The old man retired, and other natives crept up close and threw stones at our men. They stood behind trees, or took refuge behind boulders, and they threw with accuracy.

We kept them from attacking openly and in force, breaking down trees with our cannon fire, throwing sand in their faces, and filling the world with terrible noises.

But it seemed that, in spite of all we could do, the sailors on the coral were doomed. As soon as it was dark enough hundreds of natives would sally out to murder them. There was no way, apparently, for the captain to escape. The surf was getting worse. Boats couldn't go through it. He couldn't swim. Neither could most of those with him.

Suddenly I had an idea. I went to Mr. Paulding.

"Buff and I could take a light boat to that coral bank," I said, "and bring everybody back."

"Impossible," he said.

"We are not intending to row," I said. "We will swim."

He turned from me to Buff. I think it was Buff's grin that decided him.

"Well," he said, "I still say it's impossible; but I can't see any other way."

We had no trouble at all conveying the boat to the coral—or should I say we convoyed it? But we had plenty of trouble getting the boat safely back to the ship, since this time it was deeply laden. Buff and I clung to the boat's quarters on the return trip, swimming with one arm and kicking hard with both feet.

The boat was almost filled with water when we maneuvered it alongside the *Dolphin*. If we had had one more breaker to go through, I confessed to Mr. Paulding, the boat would have been swamped, and everybody would have been drowned. Everybody, that is, except Buff.

"For a whaleman, Mr. Comstock," he said, "you're all right."

To Buff he said nothing at all.

Mr. Ember was in the captain's party. He said nothing to Buff either—nor yet to me.

But Captain Percival, I know, would make me a midshipman at least. If he could, and I were willing.

Chapter Thirty-Five

NOV. 12. We are anchored off Drummond's Island. And again we have fallen among thieves, which caused Mr. Paulding to become slightly sarcastic.

"I am beginning to think you were correct in saying that wherever we might go we would find whalemen had been there before us, Mr.

Comstock," he observed. "Assuredly somebody taught these people their infernally bad manners."

Of course he said it with a smile; but I could not answer him.

NOV. 14. Violent storms above and about us, and furious and strange currents in the water beneath us. Doctor Rodriguez is ill. Most of the time he does not know me, nor any of those who come to attend him.

NOV. 19. We have reached the Mulgraves at last.

I knew it, at once, when I saw the first native on board. He was handsomely built. His long hair was tied up neatly on top of his head. His ear lobes hung down almost to his shoulders. And he was rigged fore and aft with the "horse tails" of the typical Mulgrave Islander.

NOV. 20. We have located some wells, and the water is good. Time too; for most of the drinking supply aboard has become foul.

NOV. 21. Exploring an island today, Mr. Ember found a whaler's lance and a piece or two of canvas. I examined the lance. It was not from the *Globe*.

Mr. Paulding was standing by while I held the lance. Groups of native men and women were looking on, all wearing wreaths of flowers. The girls were also rigged fore and aft with grass mats. All had bundles of green leaves thrust through the slits in their pendulous lobes.

"It is a whaler's lance, Mr. Paulding," I said, "which proves that whalers were here. By the way, what do you think of these people?"

"They behave well," he admitted. "Still, suppose they are only dissembling, Mr. Comstock? Suppose they are but politely spying out our weaknesses so that, commanded by your mutineer friends, they may come aboard us some dark night and slit our throats before we can use our six-pounders?"

The Mulgraves form an irregular circle of coral islands, most of them connected, at low water, by long narrow reefs. They enclose a sea that is, perhaps, twenty miles across at its widest. I have not been able to determine exactly which island the *Globe* visited. It will be necessary, therefore, to have a search party hunt through each island while the *Dolphin* keeps abreast of them, outside the chain, or keeps in contact with them by small boats.

There is no break in the coral reef wide enough to let the *Dolphin* into the enclosed sea, nor deep enough even at high tide. Otherwise we should have anchored inside the chain and used the ship as a stationary base of operations. We must keep moving. We must keep the searching party supplied with food. Yet we also must maintain some sort of force aboard ship, in case of an attack.

If the mutineers have control of the natives, and are in possession of many canoes, they might, as Lieutenant Paulding fears, attack us with impunity. They could swarm aboard us, on a dark night, before we could see them.

NOV. 23. Early this morning we saw four large war canoes to the south and west. Later our shore party saw them hauled on the beach. On them, Mr. Ember told the captain, he found the lids of several sailors' chests, pieces of cloth never woven on this side of the world, and a number of ash spars.

Ash spars! They came out of New Bedford or Nantucket. Nowhere else.

We are getting close to the mutineers—and their allies?

NOV. 27. Doctor Rodriguez died today. God be good to him.

He was unconscious when he went. He had not been in his right mind for some time. We had all expected him to die soon; yet the realization that he had died was a shock to all of us.

NOV. 28. A day of sadness, and of fear.

This morning we buried Doctor Rodriguez ashore. We dug the grave in the sand, under the wide-spreading branches of a bread-fruit tree. We fired a volley over his remains and left him there.

The natives watched us curiously. They were decorous and silent enough, until the muskets were discharged. Then some of them shouted and ran away. Others laughed in glee.

At the head and the foot of the narrow grave we planted seeds. Orange, lemon, and cherimoyer trees some day will grow there. On the tree above the mound we fastened a brass plate, made last night in the forge, with the doctor's name on it, the name of our vessel, and the day of his death.

That was all, save the prayer that Captain Percival read. I wish I could remember it. The words were majestic and solemn and just as disturbing as they are consoling. But all that remain with me are these—"and in mine own flesh I shall see God." Why don't I read the Bible as I should?

As I came away with Buff I thought it was symbolic, our planting seeds about the grave. What good seed the doctor must have sown during his long life! Surely it must not be hard for a man like him to look at God, and let God look at him. Me—I am not ready yet for so terrible a sight.

As we neared the shore we saw an old man, a native, pushing a tiny canoe into the winds and the waves. There was a sail on the toy craft, and we could see pieces of cocoanut meat and some bits of breadfruit on its platform.

Buff talked to the man. It is the custom here, he said, to send forth one of these little boats every time anybody dies. It bears the spirit, the soul, far enough away from the island so that it will neither trouble the living, nor any more be troubled by them. And, of course, the spirit must be fed until it becomes accustomed to its new life.

A cocoanut tree is usually planted over the grave of a native, and the place is tabooed. The fruit is never eaten, save in time of severe famine. If a man is detected stealing one of these forbidden cocoanuts he may be punished in various ways. For a woman thief there could be only one penalty. She would be killed. Even to be found at or near a grave would be misfortune for any woman.

The old man blew on the sail, and the brave canoe took off.

I watched it for a time, sliding up and down the liquid green hills, turning and twisting in the white foam, going further and further out to sea.

I turned, meaning to go back to the boat, and it was then I saw the mitten lying half buried in the sand near my feet. I picked it up, brushed off the sand, and saw the name written there.

Rowland Coffin.

My heart stopped beating, and did not beat again for a moment immeasurable by time. I felt like one walking through a strange graveyard who suddenly sees a dear and most familiar name carved on a granite shaft.

Rowland Coffin.

There is no indication that he is dead. I have merely found a mitten he dropped here sometime in the last twenty-odd months. It signifies nothing. And yet there is that fear abiding in me that I shall not see him again, nor any other of the boys we left behind.

Payne, Oliver, and Liliston, if they are in control of the natives, as I suspect, would naturally do away with the boys, knowing they would not fight against us.

We shall know soon.

NOV. 29. We have found the island we sought, but not the men.

At Mr. Paulding's request I joined the shore patrol yesterday afternoon. I was little inclined for the task; but, overhearing Mr.

Ember's remarks as he was about to shove off with his men, I readily agreed to accompany him and the lieutenant.

The exact words I do not recall.—It was something to the effect that I was too noble to help track down the murderers who murdered my murderous brother—especially in this heat. That was what stung me into action, not his irony about my nobility, but his sarcasm about the heat.

It is about five or six degrees north of the equator in this region, and naturally it is hot. Yet there is a wind forever blowing, tempering the heat. We feel this wind more, of course, aboard ship, than in the groves of towering palms and breadfruit trees. I had to confess there was some justice in the midshipman's remarks. So I pretended I had not heard them.

We were set ashore upon a small atoll, and proceeded over a long reef to the north and east.

Mr. Ember, going well ahead of the party, found the staves of the pork and beef barrels we brought ashore from the *Globe* almost two years ago, the rags of clothing, the litter of rubbish we had left, and all that remained of the tent Sam had erected.

I stood there, for a long time, as one in a dream, remembering all the horrors of this place, the work of unloading ship, the quarrels I had had with Sam, his angry departure from us, his return, his terrible death. Over there, I thought, was where they had buried him. And I remembered how gleefully Oliver and Liliston had stomped upon his grave.

Over there, I said. I mean I had a certain place on the sand picked out as the site of the grave—perhaps in the same way Sam had in mind the sites of his palace, the community hall, the church, the school, and the homes of his loyal subjects.

But I could not be sure.

I tried to orient myself by saying, "this is the spot where Payne whipped the native girl . . . this is where I kissed Motake . . . this is where Gilbert Smith and I made our last plans to take the ship." But all I saw was a waste of sand strewn with barrel staves and rags and rotten twists of rope.

I sauntered toward the spot where I thought Sam had been buried; but I never reached it, for I saw Mr. Ember standing a little way off, with a skull in the palms of his hands. One of his men, I learned later, had unearthed a skeleton which had been buried with a box of Spanish dollars. The bones had been barely covered by the sands. A sailor's boot had easily uncovered them.

The skull was Sam's, I thought. I went up to Ember, meaning to claim it.

But something about Ember stopped me, fascinated me. He stood there absorbed with his find, shaking his head in wonder, like an actor on a stage. Perhaps, for the minute, he actually was an actor.

" 'That skull had a tongue in it, and could sing once,' " he quoted. " 'How the knave jowls it to the ground, as if it were Cain's jaw bone, that did the first murder! It might be the pate of a politician, which this ass now o'er-reaches; one that would circumvent God, might it not?' "

" 'It might, my lord,' " I answered.

Ember looked at me then with a startled awareness. And the stage was gone, and the actor. And there was only the white sand about us, and the blue and white and green and yellow sea beyond it, and the wind in the trees, and the unhurrying white clouds in the blue above us, and two boys staring at each other, saying nothing, one of them holding out a skull. But the lines of Hamlet would not let go of me.

" 'This fellow,' " I said, " 'might be in 's time a great buyer of land, with his statutes, his recognizances, his fines, his double vouchers, his recoveries; is this the fine of his fines, and the recovery of his recoveries, to have his fine pate full of fine dirt?' "

Ember shifted the skull into his left hand, and offered me his right.

"I'm sorry," he said.

I shook his hand.

It probably was not Sam's head that Ember found; yet it has made us friends.

Chapter Thirty-Six

NOV. 30. Hot and still. No wind this morning. I woke, troubled by dreams of Preacher Coffin. He was standing in the pulpit of the Methodist church, talking of his son, talking of bones and an old mitten found in the shifting sands of a South Pacific island, talking of bits of Spanish gold pieces, and of hostile savages, and of a young midshipman looking at a skull.

Then he was preaching from the top of a pork barrel, then from the sand—and the staves of barrels were all around him. There were acres and acres of staves there, white as bones, gray as bones, black as bones. Then it wasn't sand I saw, but snow. There was a cold wind. It was coming in through a broken windowpane; and I turned to see if Sally were cold too.

When I woke I went on deck. The sunrise was dazzling. I had scarce begun the entry I intended to write when Ember came by to summon me to action.

The shore party, he said, was sure the natives were hostile, had gathered all their forces, and were preparing for battle. They had armed themselves with spears and stones. They had sent the women and children away. And they were quite busy with their canoes, coming and going in fleets.

"Mr. Paulding's been out all night in the launch," Ember said. "He's just come back, for dry powder, food, and you and me. He advises you to wear a pistol."

We left almost immediately, heading across the lagoon toward the northern islands. We were seen by hundreds of unfriendly eyes, and our direction noted. Presently native canoes began to set out from half a dozen different points, all going toward the island for which we steered. They went much faster than the launch; and Mr. Paulding was angered to see them getting ahead of us.

As we were beating up to weather an intervening reef, two canoes came close to us. There were twenty savages in each, every man of them armed, every man of them showing signs of hostility.

At the lieutenant's orders we swung the launch around so as to block the natives' way. We were sixteen against forty, but the lieutenant didn't hesitate.

"Tell them to stop and be searched," he bade Buff, "if they want to live and flourish."

His voice was calm. There was even a jest in it. But there were no jests in his eyes. Nor in his tight-shut lips. Buff sang out something. The canoes stopped. And forty savage warriors submitted tamely to Mr. Paulding's intrepidity. When they were allowed to proceed they did so with alacrity, almost with gratefulness. They were plainly overawed by the white man's daring. Perhaps too they reasoned that we should never have treated them with such supreme contempt had we not weapons much superior to theirs.

We continued our own way. As we neared the island, we saw at least twenty canoes, all of them larger than the two we had stopped and searched. Any one of those craft could have carried forty men.

"A fleet," Mr. Paulding said. "We shall have to destroy that, Mr. Comstock, before it can destroy us."

"The navy," I could not help but comment, "has its exciting moments too, even as the brotherhood of whalers."

The lieutenant yawned—to put me in my place, I am sure—and showed me the hint of a smile. "Excitement, Mr. Comstock? Well, we may drum up some for you before night falls. We try not to bore civilians."

"Thar blows," I answered. "Dead ahead, sir."

"A sparm whale, Mr. Comstock?" The jest was back in his voice again, and the grimness was back in his mouth and eyes. "We'll get no ile of this fish, Mr. Whaler. There must be three hundred men or more there."

He raised his voice in a command.

"Straight ahead. Stand by to lower the kedge."

We lowered the anchor just outside the line of breakers, and were veering in through the surf with our anchor dragging, like a blind man tapping his uncertain way through strange territory, when Ember came close to me.

"Here's your excitement, Horatio," he said. "And I'm glad to see you are as frightened as I am."

Some men ashore were driving their women and children to the huts in the breadfruit groves. The others, a small army, were, clearly, making ready to attack us.

" ' 'Tis conscience,' " I answered Ember, " 'doth make cowards of us all.' Where we go from here depends on how we've lived."

"Then this is good-bye. I sorrow for thee, Horatio. Yet, I dare say, you will have more friends where you are going, than I shall ever find. There are so few in heaven."

His mouth said one thing, his eyes another. I don't think I have come closer to any other human being than I did to Ember in that moment. He was what Sam had never been, a brother. He was what Gilbert had never been, another self. He was what Sally had never been, the half of me.

How could a friendship grow between two boys so surely and so swiftly? Was it the few lines of Hamlet that engendered it? I do not think so. It was Hamlet who revealed to us the friendship that was there, which we had not acknowledged but had denied with word and fist. That I am sure of.

So we stood together in the prow of the launch with Mr. Paulding, talking lightly of heaven and of hell. And the shore of the island came slowly toward us, lifting and falling, roaring with surf, showing us more and more warriors every minute.

One of them detached himself from the group and came forward, almost to the water's edge. He had oiled his tall thin body, so that it gleamed in the sun. He was unarmed. He watched us a little while, then made a megaphone of his hands and shouted to us.

The shock of it still lives with me. He shouted English words.

"Don't come ashore unless you mean to fight. The Indians are going to kill you."

"One of the mutineers," Lieutenant Paulding whispered.

We went on through the surf with the anchor dragging, coming closer and closer to the shore.

"Do you know him?" Mr. Paulding asked me.

"No," I said. "He looks like a native, with his hair fixed on top of his head that way, with the horse tails hanging from his belt, and with that black skin."

Mr. Paulding shouted to the shore. "Who are you?"

"My name is William Lay."

"Don't hail him," Mr. Paulding bade me, seeing I was on the point of doing so. "You might endanger him."

"And us too," Ember added.

"Don't land," Lay shouted again. "The natives will surely kill you. They want me to entice you ashore. Then, when you least expect it, they will attack and kill you."

"Come to us," Paulding bade him.

Lay shook his head.

"If I do," he said, "I'll stop a spear."

We drifted in a little nearer. We could hear the natives now, asking Lay questions. And we could hear Lay answering in their own tongue. I was sorry Buff was not close enough to interpret for me.

"Would you trust Lay?" Mr. Paulding asked me.

"He's only a boy," I said. I had never known him very well, but had always liked him. I said I thought he could be trusted. I prompted Mr. Paulding to ask him if Payne or Oliver or Liliston were with him. The lieutenant did so.

"Are there any white men with you?"

"No. Not here."

At Mr. Paulding's command we discharged our pistols into the air, and then reloaded. We landed, marched up to Lay, and Mr. Paulding held his pistol close to his head.

"Now tell your savage friends that the first man to stir will be struck dead by the white man's lightning," he commanded.

Lay, weeping with sheer happiness, managed to translate the words into the native tongue. Not an islander moved.

None of us moved either, save the men at the boat. We stood, pistols in hand, ready to fight if need be, determined to rescue Lay at any cost. His tears had convinced us, more than his words could have done, that he was innocent of any plot against us.

"Tell them," Mr. Paulding bade him, "that we are taking you away; and that we shall kill any and all who try to prevent it."

Lay spoke again, almost hysterical now.

Two or three men jumped angrily to their feet. But in another second there was only one of them erect, and he was coming toward us. He was not armed. He was very old. And his eyes were as watery as Lay's.

"Let him come, please," Lay begged the lieutenant. "He's been good to me. He and his wife saved me from the massacre. He's been like a father to me. I guess he wants to say good-bye."

The old man was allowed to come as close as he wished. He took Lay in his arms and hugged him. He wept like a child. Lay patted his naked shoulders, his cheeks. Lay clung to him a minute, then told the old man something that made him weep more violently than ever.

"That's enough, son," Mr. Paulding said. "We took these fellows by audacity and surprise. But they're not going to sit like this forever."

Lay released himself and went with the lieutenant to the boat. Ember and I sauntered after them, turning now and then as though to study the sky or to observe the wind—never directly looking at the natives behind us. Had we shown the least sign of fear I am sure we should have drawn a rain of spears and stones. The backs of my knees remember yet the queer weakness they felt in that so-nonchalant withdrawal.

We got to the launch without difficulty, negotiated the surf, pulled in the anchor, and set course for the *Dolphin*—then at the *Globe's* old anchorage. I wiped the perspiration from my forehead, and sat down quickly, lest I fall.

Lay was weeping and laughing, and in no condition yet, it seemed to me, to greet an old shipmate. It was only after he began to talk that I spoke to him. Even then I was cautious. He hadn't recognized me. I doubt if he had even seen me. All he knew, at this time, was that he had found white men again, and Americans at that. He was like a drunkard becoming sober enough to remember and appreciate the good fortune that had made him drunk. And he was, at the same time, like a man found dying of thirst, to whom a little water—a few drops at a time—is a godsend. If he drank too much, all at once, it would kill him.

"My name is Lay," he kept repeating. "William Lay. I'm from East Saybrook, Connecticut. Anybody here from Connecticut?"

"That isn't far from Falmouth, is it?" I asked. "Or New Bedford or Nantucket?"

He looked at me, but apparently all he saw was a blur of white skin.

"Not far," he said. "Not far at all. You from Falmouth?"

"Nantucket," I said.

"My name's Lay," he repeated. "I've been in Nantucket. I sailed out of Nantucket in the *Globe*."

"Captain Worth," I said.

"Yes. That was his name. You knew him?"

"I knew him. And Sam Comstock. And his brother George."

"You've never been in East Saybrook? You've never been in Connecticut?"

When his mind was a little more steadied I said:

"Sam Comstock once bunged up a boy named William Lay, on the whaler *Globe*. He thought Lay was a spy sent by Barnabas Starbuck. It seems Comstock and his friends were having a party in Starbuck's warehouse, and didn't want spies. Lay had as much oil on him then as he has now."

Lay looked at me a long time. He began to weep again.

"George," he said. "George! I didn't know you. So it was you who got the navy to rescue us! You got back all right, George. And you didn't forget us. You came back for us."

"You're all right now," I said. "Cry it out, Willie. It's been bottled up a long time. Who else is here that I know?"

"Only Hussey," Lay said. "All the rest were killed by the savages. Only Hussey and I are alive. Will you go for Hussey, too? You won't leave him here?"

"Don't worry," I said.

The tears came again. "Thank God," he said. "Thank God. All the rest of my life I will thank God. Let us go for Hussey now, right now."

"Where is he?" Mr. Paulding asked him.

"Lugoma's Island," Lay said. "Lugoma is the chief." He stood up and pointed to the northeast. "That's his island." He sat down and wiped his eyes. He turned to me, speaking at the top of his voice—not exactly as though he thought I were deaf, but as if he wanted to be more then sure that I heard.

"We knew you were here. But we couldn't warn you. We were kept hidden. The natives made a hundred plans, if they made one, to capture the ship, to kill you all, and to save us from you. We kept telling them it was no use. We kept telling them your six-pounders could sink any one of these islands, if you used them. We kept telling them they were helpless against you. But they were determined to lure you ashore and murder you—to overwhelm the ship at night—or to swim out and knock a hole in the hull. They had a hundred plans if they had one. They would have killed you all, except the Negro."

"Buff?" said Ember.

"The Negro," Lay said. "Whatever his name is. The chiefs want him badly. They like him. They have heard him speak our language." He laughed suddenly. "Did you hear that? Our language, I said. My God, my God, I thought I was doomed to spend my life here!"

We landed on a dry reef a few miles from the island Lay had pointed out.

"We've got to give the crew a rest," Mr. Paulding explained. "And something to eat. Then we'll go on. Don't worry. I know exactly how you feel, son. You think we'll never get there, or that we'll get there too late to rescue your friend."

I was afraid, too. I felt, then, as nervous as Lay. Hussey was a very dear friend of mine. I couldn't bear to think of anything happening now that would leave him marooned on these islands.

"How is Cy?" I asked. "Is he as tanned as you? Is his hair as bright as it used to be? Or has the sun whitened it? Is he in good hands?"

"He's still got that golden hair," Lay said. "I think that had as much to do with saving his life, and mine, as anything else. That and his Bible."

We were still talking about Hussey when we came to Lugoma's Island. This time we arrived unobserved. Just as we were landing, however, the chief and a number of women came running to the beach. Apparently, they had just awakened. Their consternation at beholding us so close, and so well armed, was plain to see.

Hussey was with us in a few minutes, black as Lay, naked except for a blanket tied around his loins, tall, thin, laughing and crying as Lay had laughed and cried. His hair was still a brilliant yellow. The yellow of dandelions in spring. The yellow of goldenrod in autumn. It fell in ringlets about his shoulders.

"Hussey," Mr. Paulding said, "how would you like to go home?"

His voice was stern, but, for once, his face was soft. I think it was the sheen of Hussey's hair that affected the lieutenant, and the sight of the Bible clasped in his right hand.

Before Hussey could say anything the chief began to speak.

"He's afraid you'll hurt Hussey," Lay said. "He says to kill him, not Hussey."

Mr. Paulding managed, through Lay and Hussey, to reassure the old man. But then the chief began to entreat the lieutenant not to steal the boy from him. He would weep his old eyes blind without his yellow-haired son, he said. He would lie down and wet the sands with his tears, and weep his very life away.

"Tell him," Mr. Paulding said, "that I'll bring you back, if your mother gives her consent."

"I'll tell him," Hussey said. "And may I also tell him that you will give him some presents for letting me go?"

"I'll give him an axe," Mr. Paulding promised.

But it seemed expedient we should do more. We should permit the old chief and his young son, a boy of eight, to accompany us back to the *Dolphin*. Nothing less would satisfy the chief.

So we set out, Lay and Hussey sitting close together with Lugoma and his son. Hussey had not recognized me, and Lay had apparently forgotten I was on earth. I waited. There was plenty of time to greet Cy Hussey. We would have all the rest of our lives to talk.

Ember sat near me, eying me oddly.

"These friends of yours," he said—"are they Quakers too?"

"Hussey is," I told him. "Lay may be. I don't know."

"And you all believe in the brotherhood of man—that all men are equal? Don't quote the Constitution to me. I know it by heart. I mean, you Quakers really believe these people are the same as we are?"

"Maybe not so intelligent as you and I," I said. "But the same otherwise. You saw how those two fathers wept at losing their adopted sons?"

"That's what I mean," Ember said. "It spun my little world around so that I'm dizzy."

He took out a red bandanna handkerchief and wiped the flat little nose of Lugoma's son. The boy smiled at him shyly, and Ember gave him the kerchief.

You would have thought, from the looks on the faces of the chief and his son, that Ember had given the child half a kingdom.

Chapter Thirty-Seven

DEC. 13. Surely the words of Scripture have power to thrill, to frighten, to encourage, to console. And they stick in a man's mind like burrs in the hair of a dog.

Do what I will—read law, sit with Lay and Hussey and talk of Indian Row and Stone Alley and Orange Street, or of the Straight Wharf, or of Judith Chase's Lane, converse with Mr. Paulding about winds and currents and the habits of aborigines, or simply stand at the rail and wonder about the stars—I keep hearing some of the words of the burial service.

"I am the Resurrection and the Life."

"Greater love hath no man."

"The Lord is my shepherd, I shall not want."

I keep hearing the captain's voice as he read from the Book. And I keep remembering the sight of Hussey, his yellow hair flying in the wind, his fingers working at top speed on the dog-eared pages of his Bible, standing near the captain, to help him with yet another passage.

Hussey's fingers, finding the place, are as quick, and as constantly moving, as the paw of a cat. A cat scratching herself. Every now and then the cat stops to lick her paw. Every now and then Hussey stops to wet a finger.

And I keep remembering, also, the face of Buff, who stood far off from the rest of us. That face was raised to the skies all during the ceremony. It was so wet I was half afraid it would melt. And I had the queer distraction of wondering which was the shinier, the tear-washed cheeks or the gleaming white teeth.

Buff wept not only with his eyes, but with all of his body, it seemed to me. And he moaned so terribly, and so oddly! He made me think I was listening to a hundred hives of angry bees.

According to Mr. Paulding's diary, it was 4:00 A.M. on the 9th of December when we left the Mulgraves and stood to the westward. I have no private recollection of the day. It might have been anytime last year. On the Mulgraves, the captain had heard of a great chief living on South Peddler's Island, who was the king of all the island chiefs in this part of the world. He felt it imperative, therefore, to visit this potentate. Also, of course, the captain wanted to add to our food supply. So it was on the 11th that we anchored in the bay and went ashore. Two days ago! It is unbelievable.

The captain preceded us, with Hussey, in the gig. He had donned his best uniform, though the day was blistering hot. I imagine he would have given a day's pay if he could go visiting in as cool an attire as the natives. His best uniform and his sword!

We followed the gig in across a coral bank to the village which was hidden in the shadow of a large forest of cocoanut palms. We had arranged to take Lay with us; but he had contracted a bad cold, and the captain thought it advisable for him to remain aboard the *Dolphin*.

The chief of chiefs was a very old man with white hair and a long white beard. He made us welcome, after the captain, speaking through Buff, had explained his errand. Hussey stood by, as ordered, listening to everything that was said.

The natives seemed to be friendly, but the captain must have had some doubt of them for he bade Hussey to tell him what they were saying.

"The chief says," Hussey reported, "that his men are not to do anything until tomorrow. The white men, he says, just want to look around a little today. Maybe they will see something they like. To-morrow they will come back to trade. Then—"

"Then what?" the captain demanded.

"Then they will attack and murder us all," Hussey said.

"Speak to the chief in his *own* language," the captain ordered him. "Ask him his name, the name of the island, how many islands pay tribute to him, things like that. I don't care what you say. I just want to shock the old son-of-a-gun."

Hussey spoke, and produced a greater effect than any of us had believed possible. The chief and his men looked as if they had been blasted by lightning from the blue skies.

"Good," the captain commended Hussey. "Now tell the old so-and-so I have some presents for him, and some for his friends; and that we want cocoanuts and bup. All we can carry."

Hussey obeyed with a smile. But the smile waned when the chief began to talk to him.

"The old boy will take your presents, Captain," Hussey said, "but he has neither cocoanuts nor bup to spare. He says he heard there were two white men being kept in the Mulgraves, and he was pre-paring to send a fleet of canoes to bring them here, where, he claims, we would be much better treated. He wants to know where the other white man is who was with me. He says, 'Is he on board your ship?' He is much interested in Buff, too."

"He has no cocoanuts to spare?"

"He has only enough, he says, to feed his own."

The captain frowned, and tried to shrug off his exasperation. He bade Mr. Paulding get the presents from the boat. Then he presented the chief with a battle axe. The old man looked at it, and his eyes gleamed. But he wasn't eager to take it.

Through Hussey he explained he couldn't accept the axe as he had nothing in all the island valuable enough to give the captain in return; he had only a few mats.

It was getting dark and the captain decided to return to the ship. He transmitted his compliments to the chief, bowed, made signs of amity and respect, and started with Hussey and some others to the gig.

Mr. Paulding, Ember, Buff, our oarsmen, and I followed. But to our intense surprise, and alarm, we discovered that our boat was not where we had left it.

Buff saw it, half a league or so down the beach.

"No drift," he said. "Ladrones move him."

"Ladrones?" Mr. Paulding put in. "Thieves?"

"Of course!" Ember said. "You notice, Lieutenant, they have sent their women and children inland."

While we were standing there, and before we had decided what to do next, two of the chief's messengers ran to the gig. They told the captain the old man had found another mat for him, a very beautiful mat. He would give it to Hussey, if Hussey would go for it. The chief wanted to put it in Hussey's hands, nobody else's.

The captain ordered the oarsmen to shove off. And we went, half running, along the curving beach in the direction of our boat.

"They want Buff, Lieutenant," Ember said. "They'll be waiting in that clump of breadfruit trees opposite the boat. Why don't we let Buff swim to the ship?"

"Slowly, gentlemen," Mr. Paulding called, checking our impetuous march. "It will not do for us to reach the place winded. Nor with our powder wet. If we go too fast, the natives will suspect we're on to them. They'll ambush us before we get near the boat. Let us walk along as if nothing had happened. Don't touch your pistols. Don't look into the forests."

Hardly had he finished speaking than a figure sprang out of the deep shadows under a cluster of palms and caught me around the knees.

"Motake," I heard. "Motake. Motake."

It was the girl I had kissed the night we sailed away in the *Globe!* Buff talked to her.

She had come to warn us of a war party waiting in the breadfruit trees near the boat.

"Them hombre want me only," Buff said. "Think me hombre blanco. Think me white hombre mucho sun-tanned. Think me hombre smart like dickens. This girl be kill for talk. She come 'long us too."

I lifted her up. She threw her arms about my shoulders and held me, looking up into my face with an expression that said many things. It said, "Are you glad to see me?" It said, "I knew I'd find you again." It said, "Please don't leave me this time." It said, "I'm awfully afraid." It said, "I've betrayed my husband, I've betrayed my king, I've betrayed everybody on this island, but I have not betrayed you." And it said, "Hold me, hold me, hold me; never let me go."

Pain came into her eyes even as I looked at them. A monstrous agony. She trembled. Her fingers gripped my flesh until they hurt. But only for a second. Then they relaxed. I saw that her eyes were glazed over, as with a film. I didn't understand that. Not until I saw the shaft of the spear sticking out of her back. The blade of it must have pierced her heart. Had the arm that threw it been much stronger, the blade would have gone through my heart as well.

"Down," I said, instinctively. "Take cover."

I lowered the girl to the sands while everybody else threw himself flat. Everybody, that is, except Midshipman Ember.

"Sir," Ember said, "I suggest again that Buff swim to the ship. It's him they want. Not us. He can beat even their fastest canoes in the water. Me, sir, I'm going to make sure they don't get our boat."

He was sprinting down the beach before Mr. Paulding could answer, or anybody else comment. In a few seconds, we were spread out, running after him.

I didn't see the spear thrown that took the life of Motake. I did see the one that slew Ember. It rose slowly out of the shadows. It fell slowly. Ember was still running when it struck him. He stopped, but only for a moment.

There were two men in our boat. Ember yanked the spear out of his middle, cast it away, drew his pistol, and ran toward the boat. He wanted to be sure he was in range. He wanted to be sure he did not miss.

He stopped, aimed, and fired.

One native fell dead. The other dived into the water.

"Fire and reload," Mr. Paulding commanded as he came dashing up.

I gave him my pistol, and caught hold of Ember. He stood wavering, shaking his lowered head, exactly as I had seen him on the beach at Huanchaco, after he had pummeled Buff. Again he had lost his cap, and his black hair stirred in the breeze. Again I saw blood on the knuckles of his right hand.

He staggered as I reached him. I threw my right arm around him. Somebody else held him on the other side. I was not surprised to see that it was Buff.

"You're hurt," I said. And only then did I see the frightful wound the spear had made. The sight of it almost unnerved me.

" 'That rat-catcher,' " he said. " 'That king of cats. Didst see him pounce, Benvolio? A scratch. Marry, 'tis enough. Where is my page? Go, villain.' Get me into the boat and let me rest."

I was in no mood for Shakespeare, but I spoke the lines as they came to me to speak, knowing that would please him.

" 'Courage man; the hurt cannot be much.' "

" 'No, 'tis not so deep as a well, nor so wide as a church door; but 'tis enough, 'twill serve.' Is that you, Buff? You're all right? They didn't get you? 'A plague o' both your houses. Zounds, a dog, a rat, a mouse, a cat, to scratch a man to death.' Help me into the boat, Benvolio, or I shall faint."

Mr. Paulding tells me the natives fled in panic after our volley was emptied into the woods. One was killed, he says, and two were badly wounded. And this morning, he adds, when the captain went ashore, and our six-pounders showed their power and their anger, the chief had every man in the war party put to death.

"The captain gave the chief a lecture on treachery," Mr. Paulding says, "and on respect for white men. If we weren't so hard up for food, and so pressed for time to look for fresh supplies of it, the lecture would have been long and harsh."

What does it matter?

We held Ember in our arms all the way to the *Dolphin*, Buff and I. His face was ghastly pale, even in the darkness. He had no weight. That was the horrible thing. He had no weight. When I picked him up and carried him aboard, he had no weight at all.

We had no way to stop the bleeding. We had no knowledge of how to stop the pain, except to give him great quantities of rum. We had no means of reaching him, except, at times, through Hamlet.

" 'Alexander died,' " he whispered, toward the end. " 'Alexander was buried, Alexander returneth into dust, the dust is earth; of earth we make loam; and why of that loam, whereto he was converted, might they not stop a beer-barrel?' "

" 'Imperious Caesar, dead and turned to clay,' " I prompted.

" 'Might stop a hole,' " he said, " 'to keep the wind away!' George, don't cry. And don't let the old man know I died to save a Nigger. It would bust his bile. He'd die. But I did that, didn't I? George, I really did."

Two days ago! And last night at sunset, there was the captain praying over him; and Buff weeping with his whole body; and Hussey fingering his Bible to find another verse.

There was Ember, neatly sewed into the clean old canvas. There was the flag, the waiting plank, the little knot of sailors mourning over—over Hamlet.

And there was the gorgeous background for this last act in our heroic drama—the clouds that loomed like purple hills against the dim horizon, the white sails gently breathing over our heads, the straining webs of ropes, the towering masts, the grim and silent cannon, the tinted waters, the tinted sky.

I half heard, half saw, the splash the body made. It dulled the glory of the dying sun. But it lit the evening star.

Chapter Thirty-Eight

DEC. 15. Bright. Southeasterly trade winds. We are heading for the Sandwich Islands.

Mr. Paulding and I have been talking again about winds and currents. He insists that a diarist should make daily note of wind, sun, stars, rain, and other natural phenomena. He chides me for my neglect in this and other entries.

Mr. Paulding keeps his log up to date that someday it may be read, and appreciated, by men of science—astronomers, geographers, mariners, biologists, even ethnologists. I keep mine for my own pleasure—and perhaps too, someday, for the pleasure of intimate friends.

It is with an effort that I write today. I have forced myself to the task only in the hope of ridding my mind of a ghost. The ghost of little Motake.

When I wrote of Ember here it was as though I had dug a grave for him with my hands and placed him gently therein. It was as though I had covered the mound above him with flowers, and had found resignation in their fragance. His death was no longer a harsh reality to me. It had become a hallowed memory. It was not now a grief to banish. It was a treasure I might keep until I die.

So too, I hope, it will be with the little island girl. Yet I doubt it.

Lay does not know her name, nor does Hussey. Lay is inclined to be somewhat vulgar about the girl. "Your elephant-eared sweetheart," he referred to her. I was offended and walked away.

Elephant-eared! This is, of course, an exaggeration. Her ears were long, but so were the ears of all the other natives on the island, especially the women. It is considered a mark of beauty. I am told that in China little girls' feet are kept tightly wrapped so they will be small for life. Tiny feet are the sign of beautiful Chinese women. I suppose there are other weird customs in other parts of the world.

Her ears were slit when she was an infant, so that the stems of flowers might be inserted. As she grew, the holes were enlarged and stretched.

She was married to the son of a chief on Peddler's Island. Did he bury her beneath a cocoanut palm, in a grave tabooed like others? Did he mourn her? Was it he that killed her?

"I never saw any marriage ceremonies or anything like that," Lay said. "Marriages are arranged by the parents. Without any fuss. Then boy and girl start living together as man and wife. No divorce either.

"When this girl of yours got married there was a hullabaloo. I thought sure it was a funeral. Everybody smeared with oil, decked with flowers and shells, shouting, dancing, drumming. But there was a feast. And then everybody ran to the beach. And there was your girl in the canoe with her new husband—and his ears twice as long as hers, or maybe longer."

DEC. 16. Yesterday, both Lay and Hussey reminded me last night, was the third anniversary of the day we set sail in the *Globe*.

Perhaps that explains why, subconsciously, I thought of Sally's pink mittens yesterday. Shall I ever forget their waving to me as the ship moved out of the harbor?

I thought then, as I think right now, and as I have thought many times in the last few years, that I shall never see her again.

We talked also of Joe Thomas last night. I learned, not through them but through Mr. Paulding, that in their sworn statements to Captain Percival, both Lay and Hussey said they regarded Joe as one of the instigators of the mutiny, and just as guilty as those who murdered the captain and the mates. This fact, however, I carefully avoided mentioning.

I did not say much but let them know my own views on the subject. I shall have many opportunities during the voyage to show them how wrong they are. I was perturbed only because of the effect their statements seem to have had on Mr. Paulding, especially on his attitude toward me. He must believe they are right, and I am wrong. He must think that I am deliberately trying to protect the prime instigator of the mutiny because he was my brother's friend.

But all this will pass.

Our rescued friends have had their hair cut, have been shaved, and have been fitted out with decent clothes. Yet there is still something most singular about them. Not their color. I do not mean that.

I have seen white men just as tanned. It is in their attitude, in their demeanor. They break out suddenly into wild laughter. As suddenly they weep. They look at each other, and nobody knows what they are thinking—nobody but they two. And each knows perfectly what is in the other's mind.

It is almost like having two tamed and civilized natives aboard. Sometimes it is impossible to realize that neither of the two is a stranger to me, and that Hussey was once my best friend.

Twenty-two months of exile have changed them almost completely.

They have told their stories over and over; so that, in my mind, I have seen the things that have happened to them as clearly as though I had been present when they happened. I can, therefore, understand something of the change in them.

The story they tell of the massacre is especially vivid.

There was a panic when it was learned that the *Globe* had sailed away. Payne nearly poisoned himself with his anger. He exercised his resentment on the woman he had taken for his own, and on the crew members we had had to leave behind. I imagine he suspected all of them would have joined us had it been possible.

He beat his woman savagely again. The crew he put to work, tearing one of the boats apart that they might make a more substantial vessel of the other. He wanted a boat with a deck. He wanted a boat, he said, that would take him and the others away from the islands in safety and with speed, should they be forced to flee.

"The natives were well-disposed toward us," Lay said, "and Hussey and I made a number of friends among them. We were especially fortunate in meeting Lugoma, Ludjuan, and a few others."

I had a mental picture of Lay and Hussey treating these new friends to some of the ship's stores we had landed on the beach. I remembered the cranberries especially; having managed to steal a few spoonfuls of them one night when no one was looking.

It was Payne's treatment of the woman that led to the slaughter. She ran away once too often. Or Payne recaptured her once too often. At any rate the natives began to retaliate. First they stole some of the tools and weapons in the tent. Then they began attacking small parties Payne sent out in search of the stolen goods.

"Along about the end of February or the first of March," Hussey said, "Payne sent Coffin, Jones, Liliston, and me to the nearest village. We each had a musket. We each had powder and some fine shot. But none of us had anything like a musket ball. Payne thought all we had to do was to make a noise with the guns.

"This day we were after a hatchet that had been stolen. We got it all right, and started back. Natives hidden behind trees threw stones at us. We ran. You could hear me panting a mile away, I ran so fast. Rowland Jones tripped and fell, and before anybody could help him there were half a dozen natives around him beating in his brains with rocks.

"Payne tried to pacify the natives after we got back to his tent. I saw him jabber with one of the chiefs. He made some sort of a dicker with him. Then he came back to us, scared green.

" 'We got to give them beggars all we got, if we want to live,' he said. 'They outnumber us one hundred to one. Don't contrary them in any way. Let them help themselves.'

"They helped themselves all right. They pulled Payne's tent down. They broke open the barrels of beef and pork. They pawed over all our provisions, kicked them around, or threw them in the sand. Then suddenly, and for no reason at all, a woman of sixty or so, a wrinkled old hag you would have sworn was too feeble to stand up, jabbed her spear right through Columbus Worth.

"I thought I was going to get it too. I saw Worth down, the spear sticking out of him, and people throwing rocks at him. And the faces! It reminded me some of hog butchering. You've heard pigs squealing when their throats were cut. It was like that. We were the pigs this time, we were squealing.

"Then—I still don't know how it happened—Lugoma was sitting on my back, and I was eating dust and sand, and he was talking soft, and keeping the spears away from me.

"Afterward he took me by the hand and brushed the sand off me. We ran. My shoes was cut to patches on the sharp coral. I fell. I was winded and tired to death. But I was more scared than tired. I took my shoes off and we ran some more. I cut my soles. But I slept well that night. I woke up crying, thinking everybody was killed but me. And there was Lay, with Ludjuan and his old woman. We both broke down and cried like a couple of whipped kids."

Hussey and Lay were separated soon after this meeting; and, though they had occasional glimpses of each other, they were kept far apart. Probably so they couldn't plot against their masters. They were treated more or less kindly. They were fed when there was food. When there was famine they had to rely on their own resources, like everybody else. Lay stole the cocoanuts on the tabooed graves, daring the consequences. Hussey, whose patron depended more on the sea for his food than on the trees, learned to eat raw fish.

"We went back to the scene of the massacre sometime later," Lay said. "We helped bury the bodies." A spasm of pain showed in his eyes. "We were both sick as dogs afterward. Then we gathered up some flour, bread, meat, our Bibles, a blanket apiece, and a decent pair of shoes for each of us."

Lay didn't keep anything long. Ludjuan and his wife liked the bread and ate most of it. The pork and beef, however, though it was considered fit enough for American whalemen, they could not abide. It was only a little spoiled, Lay said. It didn't last long. Neither did the shoes, nor the clothing.

In due time Lay was made to conform to the habits of his betters. His Bible was taken from him before he could think of anything to do or say. He couldn't save it. It was torn to shreds before he had a chance to read even one passage from it. Hussey managed to keep his by saying God would smite whoever touched it. That was a taboo the natives understood and respected.

"There was a big powwow one day," Hussey said.

"We thought we were going to be cooked and eaten," Lay chimed in.

Everybody on the island had come to see the white captives. They had greased themselves with cocoanut oil. They had put on their best mats, and their finest strings of beads or shells and they had put the most fragrant plants into their ear holes.

"They took us to a flat piece of land about half a mile from where Payne's tent had been," Lay said. "There they gathered around us. There were about thirty girls with wooden drums. They started beating them. Then they began singing. Then everybody began shouting and screaming and flinging their arms around and dancing."

"And when they were all tired out," said Hussey, "they came and touched us, ran their fingers through our hair, and felt our ears. Most of them went away laughing as if they were sick. We must have been a funny sight to them, and both of us so scared we could hardly breathe."

"They liked Hussey's golden hair," Lay said. "Especially old Lugoma liked it. I guess if my hair was as pretty as Cy's they wouldn't have made me wear it the way they wear theirs. They'd have let me carry it natural, like he did."

Several times the natives were tempted to kill the two white men, believing them responsible for pestilence, famine, or other calamities.

"Once," said Lay, "there was a funny disease. It swelled the hands and feet, and sometimes it puffed out a man's face so that he was blind for days. We got blamed for this.

"The witch doctors—I suppose that's what you'd call them—or the medicine men—they were bent on murdering us. But Hussey worked over his Bible, like a man strumming on a hurry-up banjo. He told them if we were harmed the sick men would swell up all over and bust. Before they could decide whether or not Cy was a Sunday School boy or just a lying Yankee, everybody begun to get well."

Both boys had learned the native language by the time the *Dolphin* arrived; they had been accepted as able and respected citizens; they had achieved a real place in the society of the islands, and might, in time, have become chiefs—carrying Sam's dream into drear reality.

The *Dolphin* wasn't the first ship they had seen, but they knew she was an American man-of-war. They knew her business in these waters. And they knew that soon or later they would sail home aboard her. But, as Lay put it, they nearly died of "gangrenish anxiety" just the same.

"I was on the beach when your first boat came ashore," Lay said. "I was in a hut, though, guarded by a lot of old women. And I had only to let out one squawk if I wanted to die. I didn't want to die.

"After you left, the chiefs all got together and decided to make a sortie by canoes some night when there wasn't any moon. You wouldn't have had a chance. Then I told them about your six-pounders."

"Lay fired the *Globe*'s swivel for them once," Hussey said. "He loaded it with a charge that should have blown it to bits. When it went off the island seemed to rock. There sure was a panic!"

"All I had to do," Lay resumed, "was to tell them your cannon were a thousand times as powerful as that little swivel. I told them you could sink the whole chain of islands if you ever let loose."

"So they decided to lure you ashore and get Lay to talk you into an ambush," Hussey said. "You know how that worked out."

"It would have worked, I think," Lay said, "if you didn't seem so cocky and cool, so absolutely sure of yourselves, and so contemptuous of anything the natives could do against you. That broke their nerve. You didn't have to fire a shot."

JAN. 5, 1826. Something is happening to Lay and Hussey that I don't understand. They no longer seem cordial and Hussey actually irks me since he has resumed the plain speech.

JAN. 9. At daylight, coming out of a thick woolly fog, we saw Bird Island lying close; and Mr. Paulding asked me to accompany him ashore.

Thus at daylight, on the ninth day of this new year of the Lord, I came out of my own particular fog to see that I had lost the friendship of the two shipmates I came so far to find.

"Thanks for thy invitation, Friend Comstock," Hussey said when I bade him come along, "but we are sick of islands."

"What's really the matter, Cy?" I said.

"Since thee must know," he said then, with some hesitation, "it is thy attitude toward Joseph Thomas."

"My attitude? I will not see him hanged. You will?"

"Aye," Hussey said. " 'Twas he used thy brother, as the devil a willing tool, to kill the captain and the mates, and maroon us all on the island. This I know. This will I swear to on the witness stand. I will see Joseph Thomas hanged by the neck 'til he is dead."

"And," said Lay, "if ever man deserved to die with his neck tight in a noose, that man is Thomas. He planned the mutiny and all that followed."

"I see," I managed to say. "And so we are no longer friends?"

Hussey answered for the pair.

"Them that connive to deliver murderers from justice, Friend Comstock, are no friends of ours. And let me ask thee this—will thee stand up in the box and perjure thy immortal soul to save Joe Thomas, when thee knows as well as we that he is guilty?"

Perjury or not, they shall not hang Joe Thomas.

Chapter Thirty-Nine

JAN. 12. Off the island of Oahu. Weather fair. Light winds. I have again become something of a pariah. Even Mr. Paulding seems to be avoiding me. It is not at all astonishing. If people believe someone a murderous scoundrel—Joe Thomas, for instance—they believe his friends are scoundrels too.

One good thing about this is that I have now much more time to devote to my law books, and to the task of teaching Buff to speak better English. But Buff isn't at all interested in English. He is interested in nothing but seeing his father again. "Mi padre," he keeps saying. "Mi padre."

The voyage ends for him when we come to port. He will then

be paid off for his services as interpreter, and will hurry home, by boat, by balsa—or maybe even by the power of his own swimming arms and legs!

JAN. 20. Fortune is still with me. I have acted as an attorney in a real court of law! I have made a satisfactory settlement! And I am going home in the brig *Harbinger,* which sails in a week or two to Boston, via Valparaiso!

Home!

"We can raise the coast of Chile in nine or ten weeks," Captain Abner Jackson assures me. "And from there to Boston, twelve weeks at the most."

I shall see Nantucket in July!

And whom have I to thank for this? Buff.

As soon as the *Dolphin* docked—the first American man-of-war ever to sail into any port in the Sandwich Islands—we discovered how badly she needed repairs. It will be late in April before she can continue her voyage. Like others aboard, I was appalled at the idea of remaining here all that time. Therefore, even before the masts were taken out, I had asked, and received, permission to make my way home independently.

The captain was most obliging. "You are not a prisoner," he reminded me. "You are an honored guest, sponsored by the President of the United States. You have conducted yourself as a gentleman. You have served with us, under fire as it were—the fire of native spears at any rate. You have aided the Navy materially. We are sorry to lose you. But I understand your hurry to get home. She is a very lucky young lady, sir."

It was almost immediately after this that Mr. Paulding came looking for Buff and me, one or both of us.

"I came to request one last service of Buff," he explained. "Now that he is no longer a member of the crew, I cannot command him."

"Mi padre," Buff said, grinning delightedly at the lieutenant. "I see him mañana. Mañana, mañana."

"What do you want of Buff?" I asked.

He answered obliquely.

"There's an American shipmaster in trouble. A very decent-looking little Yankee. Captain Abner Jackson of the brig *Harbinger.* Boston man. It seems some native thieves have robbed him of a deal of linens, calicoes, and other dry goods. And there's some sort of trial. Karamoku thinks it proper to have an interpreter."

"Karamoku?"

"They call him Billy Pitt too," Mr. Paulding said. "He was the

High Carney, the great friend, of Tamahamha. Tamahamha, I gather, was a great king, a great warrior. Karamoku was his chief adviser, his best general, his ablest lieutenant. Now he's old and sick, but that doesn't matter. The governor and the main chief are away somewhere, so Karamoku has to serve as the judge. He's the law. All the law. The only law. And he suggested I engage Buff."

I looked at Buff and saw that he was willing.

"All right," I said. "We were going for a long swim today. But that can wait until Buff comes back."

Mr. Paulding made me an awkward bow. Then something of the rigidity went out of his body, and something of the chill I had observed in him the last few days went out of his face.

"We'd like to have you along too, Mr. Comstock," he said. "I know you are interested in legal matters. These proceedings may interest you exceedingly."

Karamoku's hut, like most of the other houses in this part of the world, was an awkward assembly of poles and rafters, thickly covered from ridge pole to foundation with native grass. It was situated on the edge of the town of Onaroora. It rose up out of a wilderness of weeds. And it had a wicker fence around three sides of it.

A tremendous man was asleep in a swinging cot when we entered; and I saw that he was suffering from dropsy. He reminded me of my uncle, Shadrach Mills, who died of that disease.

This was the law!

There were a lot of naked and half-naked and three-quarter-naked men in the long narrow hut, and one of them was fanning Karamoku as he swung to and fro. Lamps burning whale oil lit up this quaint courtroom in a fantastic way.

Karamoku woke as we came in, and, in excellent English, made us welcome. He pointed to the piles of mats lying in a far corner, and bade a servant place some of them for us. Thus, presently, we sat on either side of the dropsical judge, Mr. Paulding and I. Buff stood near me.

In front of us, in a ragged line, stood half a dozen thin, dirty, naked, trembling men—the thieves. Facing them, at Mr. Paulding's side, stood the Yankee captain, a neat little man with the baldest head in Christendom, I fully believe, and one of the most flourishing beards.

"I had more hair on top of my head once, Mr. Comstock," he boasted later in the day, "than you have now. But, what with one thing and another, it went right down through the skull and came creeping out through the chin."

A servant lifted Karamoku gently into something of a sitting position, and placed a quantity of mats behind him. The chieftain took the opportunity to remove a garment from his upper half—an English major general's uniform jacket—and became as naked as any man before him.

Despite his nakedness, his sickness, his unnatural obesity, there was a grave dignity about him, an urbanity that would have made itself felt anywhere, and a solemnity that more than awed me. There was nothing comical about him—and there was nothing pretentious about him either. He was not entertaining us. He was not trying to impress us. He was simply administering justice.

He spoke first to Captain Jackson, and it became evident that, in his time, he had been an orator of no mean quality. His voice was resonant, deep, freighted with richness of character. It was emotionless, yet it begot emotions. It was calm, unexcited, yet mysteriously stirring.

"You have asked this court for justice, Captain Jackson," he said. "I shall work, to the limit of my poor mental and physical powers, to see that you obtain it. State the case against these men."

Captain Jackson used few words. He had removed a quantity of his goods from the hold of his vessel into a certain store, from which it was stolen. The thieves were pursued. They threw away some of the loot in the taro fields through which they ran. The remainder they concealed in filthy oil casks. All the materials—linens and calicoes, mostly—were recovered. But they had been so damaged they were worthless.

"And you want the thieves punished?" Karamoku asked.

The captain wasn't at all interested in punishment, he said. He was interested solely in getting recompense. Karamoku asked many questions about the punishments meted out to thieves in the United States. I imagine he wanted to get an idea of justice, as we practiced it, so that he might make up his mind fully as to justice in this case.

Then, through Buff, he questioned each of the six natives. He was quite gentle with them. He made me think of a father putting questions to his children.

Each man stepped forward as his name was called. A servant held up a lamp so that Karamoku could not fail to see the defendant's face clearly, and in order that each defendant could clearly see the face of justice.

Each man in turn confessed his guilt and threw himself on the mercy of the court. And when Buff couldn't put their words into English, Karamoku did his own translating for our benefit. Yet he never tried to shame or embarrass Buff, nor to imply in any way that Buff wasn't the finest interpreter in the kingdom. On the contrary, he made Buff proud of himself.

When the last native had confessed, Karamoku turned again to the Yankee trader.

"They have all confessed, Captain," he said. "And they are willing to make restitution, but powerless to do so. As you see, they are extremely poor men."

It came to me with a sudden sense of shame that most of the natives on this island were poor. It was only the white men, especially the English and Americans, who were wealthy.

"I quite understand your wish for compensation," Karamoku continued. "You are entitled to it. But where are you going to get it? Not even the chiefs of the village, who feel responsible for these poor thieves, can ever repay the worth of your goods so foolishly and wantonly destroyed."

The judge swung a little while in silence. All you could hear was the swishing of the fan. Suddenly he appealed to Mr. Paulding.

"What would be the American idea of justice here, Lieutenant? Justice for the captain, and justice for these six foolish and hungry thieves?"

Mr. Paulding shook his head. "Unfortunately," he said, "I am not an attorney. But my friend, Mr. Comstock, who never travels without a law library, might be able to advise Your Highness."

I found myself suddenly warm and flustered and altogether too young to be where I was. And I had an insane desire to step close to the boy with the fan. My cheeks were burning.

But I did have an idea, and I meant to voice it, come what might. I got up quickly.

"May it please the court," I said, "neither Captain Jackson nor this court wishes to work a hardship on anyone. All that is sought here is compensation. Like for like. Goods for goods. Perhaps the court could free the prisoners if they would promise to help provide the complainant with, say, enough sandalwood to make up for his losses. Perhaps the village chiefs might also aid in having this cargo put aboard the captain's ship."

Karamoku smiled at me, pleased with the solution, then looked at Captain Jackson for comment.

"By jingo," the little man said. "By cracky! By crackety crackety crack! Your Honor, nothing could be more fitting than that. Sixteen piculs of sandalwood. That's about a ton. Maybe a little more, a little less. Eminently fair. The young man couldn't have spoken fairer."

Karamoku questioned the defendants, each in turn, turning their fear and anguish into incredible joy.

"So be it," he said then, signaling the servant to remove the mats from behind him. "Sixteen piculs will be placed aboard the *Harbinger;* but it is only right that the men be paid for the work entailed." He smiled at me again, in his fatherly way. "You will be a great judge someday, Mr. Comstock," he prophesied.

He was asleep before I left the room.

The captain was waiting for me outside the wicker fence. He stopped me as I came through the gate, ignoring Buff and Mr. Paulding entirely.

He asked if I would sail as supercargo in the *Harbinger.* Of all things! And he has included a few piculs of sandalwood for me. Boston! I keep telling myself it's all true.

We'll be at sea before the month is out.

JAN. 21. Buff is gone. He left with half a dozen friends—or were they his brothers?—in a long outrigger canoe. He was standing up amidships when I saw him last, waving me good-bye, and crying. I am glad I did not hear the sounds of his weeping, nor see his face too clearly.

I stood on the shore until the long narrow craft was only a dot far out in the waters. Then the dot took wings and came back to me. It flew overhead, crying. A white gull, crying like Buff! A bird that took flight from that point in the wide blue sea where his canoe had vanished! I felt like weeping myself, knowing I would never see Buff again. How crazy all the people I know would think me, did they guess how much Buff meant to me. What a hilarious joke it would be to all of them. All of them, that is, save Sally Starbuck.

FEB. 1. At sea. Hot and bright. Light winds. We are headed SSE for the Society Islands, thence farther south to catch the westerly winds. We expect to reach Valparaiso by the end of March, even if we have to spend a week in the islands stocking up with wood and water and fresh vegetables and fruits.

We sailed out of Honolulu on Jan. 27, just as the moon was coming up. We expect to be held in Valparaiso for at least a week. From Valparaiso to Boston is ninety days at the most, Captain Jackson swears.

I looked for Constant Lewis and Holden Hewman and other old shipmates who might still be somewhere in or around Honolulu. But I found no trace of them. Nor of Lia-Lia.

Neither Lay nor Hussey has forgiven me my determination to appear for Joseph Thomas; yet they no longer feel that in my desire to help him I am betraying them.

Both have loaded me down with mail for their parents and their friends, and with instructions in how to break the news to those I meet. I imagine they envy me, going home ahead of them. But, if so, they managed to conceal it.

MARCH 30. Valparaiso again. My first foreign city. How young I was, walking with Gilbert Smith through these narrow streets, overcome by the queerness of everything, especially the rolling grogshops, the llamas, the cockfighters, and the shrines.

It hasn't changed at all. It exercises the same charm over me; elicits from me the same words of wonder.

Yet it has changed immeasurably in my affections. It has lost so much! Captain Blanco is no more. His daughter has gone, no one knows where.

At the American consulate I met only strangers, who told me Michael Hogan is in Boston. I shall see him soon. Him and Joe Thomas.

Valparaiso may be the most enchanting city in the world. But the friends who helped to make it enchanting have vanished from it. And I shall be glad to leave it, too.

Chapter Forty

APRIL 6. Homeward bound, with a fine breeze speeding us on our way. And I have more mail to deliver when I reach Boston. Mail for "Geel Bare Smeet."

I didn't know the lady at all when she came aboard the *Harbinger*. I had forgotten there ever was such a person. And she didn't know me either. Not at first. Something about her reminded me of Perdita. She was dark. Maybe that was why. Dark and lovely.

She understood, she said, that we were sailing to Boston, in the United States of America, and that we might deliver mail to someone there.

"Rosita Bonheur!" I shouted.

I introduced Captain Jackson then, who invited Rosita to stay aboard for dinner. And after we had talked a long time about Gilbert

Smith, the Quakers, the shakiness of the new Ramon Freire regime, the sturdy qualities of that grand old warrior, Bernardo O'Higgins, the absence of Michael Hogan, and the speed and beauty of the brig *Harbinger*. I spoke of Captain Blanco and his daughter Perdita.

"I knew Perdita," Rosita said. "Gilbert once took me to her house. She married a Peruvian shipmaster last year, I understand."

"I didn't know," I said stupidly.

"You could have known, George," Rosita said. "You were here then. You were at the American consulate. But you never tried to see her—or any one else. Now, just passing through as it were, it occurs to you to find her again—maybe to say good-bye to her and nothing else. And you are puzzled and angry that she went away. How like a man that is!"

She was suddenly contrite and sympathetic.

"George, you weren't in love with her? Don't tell me I've said something cruel."

I reassured her.

Whatever little affection I may have felt toward Perdita flickered out as Rosita's intelligent black eyes searched through me. I had sentimentalized the girl because of her innocence and youth and beauty, because of her gay laugh and her liking for me, and because of a cross thrown into the sea and a quarrel with my brother Sam. I had dramatized her. I had made her the heroine of a tragedy more terrible and more shameful than the mutiny and the murder on the *Globe*. I had almost persuaded myself that I was responsible for the sorrow and shame that cankered her innocence and youth. But Rosita's eyes, keen, intelligent, and somewhat mocking, brought me back to realities.

Her look confirmed the truth I have always known. I have never loved any woman but Sally.

I never shall.

We are a whole day's sailing away from Rosita as I write, and that much closer to Sally. Yet I cannot help but feel I am farther away from Sally—hurrying home to her—than I have ever been.

Before she left, Rosita handed me a packet of letters for Gilbert. There must be at least forty of them, the whole tied together with red silk ribbons, and reeking of scent.

I was astonished to be entrusted with such a bulky package.

"I write him every day," Rosita said. "When I learn a ship is going to Boston, I make up the package and ask the captain to take the letters to the city of Boston. It must be the most wonderful city in the whole world, for Gilbert says it is."

"By jingo!" Captain Jackson cried, "the lad is right. And, say the

word, lassie, and I'll make room for you somewhere on board. I'll
carry you to Boston. No charge at all. By cracky, Miss Bonheur, it'd
be a pleasure to have you."

Rosita blushed and laughed.

"Next year, Captain, if you come again to Valparaiso, I shall travel
with you. But, Gilbert Smith has not yet asked me to visit him. Are
all the Quakers shy, and slow?"

Perhaps we are.

JUNE 25. Boston at last. Eighty-one days out of Valparaiso, including the week spent in Barbados. It is impossible, but I am home
again. I am home, this time, to stay. Tomorrow we shall begin unloading cargo. Surely I shall be in Nantucket for the Fourth of July.

But this is the Fourth today, the glorious Fourth. This is the Fourth
of July, Thanksgiving, Christmas, New Year's, and Easter all rolled
into one. This is one of the days I shall never forget. June 25, 1826.

Sally, I've come home!

JUNE 27. Saw Joe Thomas today, and wish I hadn't. He looked
Spanish or Portuguese again—or some sort of foreigner. But his skin
was bleached. The same long nose. The same abundant whiskers.
The same skinny arms. I thought of Gilbert Smith's phrase as I
reached to shake hands with him—"Thy card-playing fingers."

But he wouldn't shake hands. He almost spat in my face. Prison
has stolen away his wits again. He thought me an enemy, though he
knew who I was.

"I'll have no words with ye, Friend Turncoat," he said. "Nor ye
with me. Be damned to ye, George Comstock; ye haven't hanged
me yet."

JUNE 29. And now I know who has embittered Joe Thomas against
me. I talked to him today as he stood on the packet boat *Pharaoh*,
Boston to New York, of which he is the mate. Gilbert. My great
friend. My hero. Gilbert Smith.

I would have gone aboard, but he saw me running down the dock,
and halted me.

"Stay where thee be, Friend Turncoat," he said. "Thee be not
welcome higher."

Friend Turncoat! Joe Thomas' name for me. Acquired from Gilbert Smith! I stopped, as I would have stopped against a solid wall.

"Gilbert," I said, believing for the fraction of a moment that he
must have mistaken me for somebody else, "it is I, George. George
Comstock."

"Aye," he said, looking down on me with more scorn than I believed possible for him to engender. "I know thee. I know thy name. Whoso named thee George did not forsee thy future, else had he called thee Benedict Arnold Comstock. Begone! I have no time to dally with thee."

"But I have mail for you, Gilbert," I could not help saying. "I have a packet of letters from Rosita."

"Leave them on the coil of rope there near thy feet," he said.

"But it's tarry," I objected. "Do you want the letters dirtied?"

"They be dirtied enough already with thy carrying them," Gilbert's voice lashed me out of any self-deception, out of any belief that this was not reality. "Drop them on the rope, and go—lest I lose my patience and my temper."

I went. I walked away. I don't know where. I don't know why. Who has turned even my best friends against me?

Maybe I shall find the answers in Nantucket.

JULY 5. We unloaded the last of the cargo this evening. I shall leave for home tomorrow.

JULY 6. I am leaving for Nantucket with more than $1500. Captain Jackson's "extra few" piculs of sandalwood, which he said he sold for me, brought more profit than he had expected.

"The laborer is worthy of his hire," he said when I began to protest at this unheard of generosity, "and the lawyer his fee. You don't know how much money you saved me, by jingo, with your sandalwood proposition. You deserve it, sonny. And if you change your mind about staying ashore—I say, if you ever hanker to go to sea again—there's always a berth waiting for you on the speedy *Harbinger*."

At least I have one friend in the world. One friend and nearly $1600. I don't think my father ever made $1600 in one year, clear of all expenses. The money should help him start in some other business, if he has to. He's welcome to every dollar of it.

JULY 11. Nantucket—a muggy day. We are living in Samantha's old house. The library has become my bedroom, odd as that seems. Here Sally kissed me, a year and more ago, and swore, and dashed away. Here I sleep, and dream of her; here I spend hours reading, and wondering about her. She is in Boston. She has been there several weeks. She was there all the time we were unloading the square-rigger; but I never had a glimpse of her.

AUG. 28. I have decided to enter the Harvard Law School, if I can pass the entrance examinations. The money I brought home will help me through the course. Should I have need for more, there is the money from Uncle Shadrach's marble quarries in Vermont which had been willed to me upon my uncle's death.

The marble is beginning to move, as table tops, gravestones, cenotaphs, and crosses. Barnabas Starbuck, of all persons, is moving it. On commission.

"The stone was lying there idle," my father explained, "and I thought to put it to some useful purpose, such, for instance, as feeding thy father and thy father's wife. 'Tis thine, of course, son George; yet I doubted not thee would wish me to employ it in thine absence.

"Friend Barnabas was not averse to helping in this, inasmuch as it would help him too. So there's marble going to far countries, George. Even as far as China. Mayhap, someday, thine Uncle Shadrach's dream of a thousand marble churches may come true—a day I shall not see, but thee may."

SEPT. 15. Boston—My birthday. Nineteen, going on twenty. I feel much older than nineteen. That makes Sally twenty, going on twenty-one. Why did she go back to Nantucket the day after I arrived in Boston? Did she know that I was here?

I have been tempted to write to her. But what is there I can say?

Have not yet located Mr. Hogan. I did hear, though, that he too was once a student of this law school. Somehow that brings him a little closer, no matter where he is.

OCT. 30. Boston—Letter from Rosita Bonheur. The U.S. Frigate *Dolphin* sailed into Valparaiso harbor during the last week in July. My friends Lay and Hussey were aboard. She does not mention Gilbert Smith.

DEC. 25. Nantucket—Christmas with only the three of us in the house. We are still tabooed by the better citizens—even by Judge Hussey who wrung my hand so hard last July, when I told him Cy was alive and well, and who swore he owed me a debt of gratitude for "directing" the navy to the "jungle islands."

But I did exchange greetings with Sally and her grandfather, as they were coming from the Methodist church.

Sally, in white and blue, was so much more lovely than I remembered that I could not get my breath. I could only mumble, "Merry Christmas, Sally."

"Merry Christmas, George," she answered. Her eyes were as brilliant as the new-fallen snow in the sun, and as blinding.

If I see no more of her for another year, I will not think fate too unkind. A little of her goes a long way. She is strong drink. She is more potent than the most powerful of drugs.

"Mmm," said her grandpa. "Mmm Christmas!"

Then he looked closer and saw who it was he had wished a Merry Christmas. He gathered the dark clouds around him. But Sally hurried him along before he could even shake his cane.

Preacher Coffin was just behind. I nodded to him in all friendliness; but he pretended not to see me. The same preacher who broke down and wept in my arms. The same bereaved father who kept saying, "I know how you loved him, George; I know how he loved you!" The same red-eyed man who kept stroking an old mitten I had picked up on the sands of an island thousands of miles away! He passed me by as if I had been a stranger and a tramp.

JAN. 2, 1827. Nantucket—Another letter from Rosita, forwarded from my rooms in Boston. It explains why the castaways are still in transit. The *Dolphin* did not stay long in Valparaiso. In August she went looking for the captain. He was in Callao. The *Dolphin* went to Callao. Lay and Hussey were there transferred to the frigate *United States*. When they will start home Rosita does not know. Again she does not mention Gilbert.

I told the news to Nathan Pickens, the postmaster. I know no one who can spread it faster.

"If the news is as reliable as the puffume on that letter," Pickens remarked, "them boys won't be home for another half a year. How does she know they've been transferred? Callao right near this Valparaiso?"

He knew how far Callao was from Valparaiso. He had been a whaler once himself.

Somehow I feel I have not acted wisely. Sally will know all about that "puffumed" letter before the sun goes down tomorrow.

FEB. 14. Boston—St. Valentine's day. No mail. No valentines. I think I am studying too hard. Or maybe it's just this long hard winter.

APRIL 9. Boston—Up and around again, after a long siege. The doctors thought at first it was pneumonia. But, if they found out it was something else, they didn't give it a name. I am going back to Nantucket for a few weeks' rest. I wonder if the violets are up yet in the woods.

APRIL 15. Nantucket—Another letter from Rosita, "in the same kind o' puffumed envelope, I see."

Gilbert has written her about meeting me on the dock that day in Boston. He thinks I have gone back on Joseph Thomas, that I am going to testify against him. That explains his attitude and Joe's. But it doesn't explain why either of them should think so badly of me.

Lay and Hussey, Rosita writes, returned to Valparaiso on the frigate *United States*. They were put aboard the frigate *Brandywine*, which is fitting out now to bring them home. "It is expected to sail in a few weeks."

The letter was dated January 1.

I suppose I must spread the news again, through Nathan Pickens. At least Nathan talks to me and lets me talk to him.

APRIL 20. Nantucket—Another letter from Rosita. The *Brandywine* will proceed to New York, not to Boston. "She will leave within a few days." This letter was dated January 15, and must have been brought home by a whaler, since it smells of "ile" as well as of French perfume.

Lay and Hussey may be in New York this very minute. If it took the *Harbinger* eighty-one days to make the trip, surely the *Brandywine* will not take longer.

It is probable the two may come home on the *Pharaoh*. Wouldn't that be wonderful? Gilbert would be as overjoyed as I was to see the pair; and he would indubitably find out from them how I stand on the matter of Joe Thomas' innocence or guilt.

I must see Nathan after supper. We'll get everything ready for a welcome-home celebration that nobody in Nantucket will forget.

Chapter Forty-One

MAY 2. A week ago the little *Pharaoh* sailed proudly into the harbor, white chevrons shining beneath her bowsprit! The whale ships gave warning of her arrival, sounding their fog horns madly. Bells rang in the town. Men and women scurried from their houses, children from their schools. Merchants left their stores untended.

The butcher, the baker, the candlestick maker, the printer, the black-smith, the undertaker went rushing to the docks. I think everybody was there that morning, except the babies and their nurses.

She came in slowly, like fog, with the reflection of the sun on the water playing madly on her hull. Yet, something seemed to be wrong. The craft was bringing home two boys long ago given up for dead, but she seemed neither to be elated nor excited in any way.

The bells were still ringing as the gangplank was put in place. The fog horns were still crying. The people were still cheering and shouting. And a thousand gulls were circling overhead, mewing like hungry cats.

There were the heroes, standing at the rail, one on either side of Mate Gilbert Smith. And there, on the dock below, waiting for the gangplank to be made steady, were Judge and Mrs. Hussey, both of them crying. Near them stood Barnabas and Sally, the two Kidders, and Anthony Hanson. Thus, all the survivors of the *Globe* were present, except Joe Thomas.

Lay and Hussey were crying too; and for once Hussey was not using a wet finger to find a Bible text. He was waving to everyone. He was shaking his right hand with his left. He was blowing kisses to his mother. He was making motions to his father, to Barnabas, to Sally, to me.

Before we realized it, a crowd of men and women was surging up the gangplank, and another crowd was trying to surge down it.

Then Gilbert Smith had swung me around with his rough right hand and was glaring at me in most un-Quakerish wrath.

"I've heard of the perfumed letters thee gets from South America," he said. "Aye, even in New York, I heard the news, Friend Stab-in-the-Back. And I'll not abide it."

He did not realize, perhaps, how loud his words were, how distinct above the clamor of the crowd. I did not realize it either, until I saw Sally's head swing sharply around, until I saw her grandfather turn my way.

Gilbert raised his hand to strike me. I made no move to stop him. But Samantha did. And so did my father.

But before the blow could fall, or my parents speak a word, a man shouted from the deck of the *Pharaoh:* "Who'll buy Sam Comstock's bloody skull?"

The voice was loud and terrible; and in the hush that had been created by Gilbert Smith's mad jealousy, it was all but paralyzing.

Gilbert dropped his fist and turned to look. Probably there were not more than half a dozen in the crowd who did not immediately forget what they were doing, who did not become absorbed in the scene that followed.

A man in sailor's clothing, a stout coarse man without a hat, a man who looked both drunk and idiotic, was holding up a skull and a cross-hilt saber.

"I got Sam Comstock's skull here, friends," he shouted. "I got his blood-stained sword. Who wants 'em? What am I bid for the head of the foulest murderer of the seven seas? What am I bid for the sword that killed so many men?"

Nobody spoke for a long moment. Nobody moved.

"Speak up, ladies and gents," the monster called to us. "Who'll say twenty dollars? Who'll start it at twenty dollars?"

We saw the captain coming toward him, marlinespike in hand. The would-be auctioneer saw him also. He darted away. He was unsteady on his feet, but he managed to evade the captain. He gained the gangplank; and I moved to apprehend him when he got to the foot of it.

He saw me waiting for him below. He started to turn and go back, but he didn't complete the maneuver.

Suddenly the man was falling. I did not see what caused him to fall. He was simply falling, and the skull was rising in the air—a ghastly white balloon. Then it too was falling, and the point of the naked sword was threatening both falling skull and falling man.

More quickly than the eye could follow, the blade went through the sailor's body. The skull sent up black water and scum oil from the space between the packet boat and the pier. And the sailor's body was falling, in a sort of a half circle, after the skull.

The man's shoes showed clearly for one moment. The soles were patched. The heel on the right was missing.

Women all around me were screaming. Samantha was screaming. My father sagged against me, smiled at me, and died.

His heart, Doctor Ashley explained. He didn't have to explain, but he wanted to. "Thank God he went that way, George. Without pain. There was a shock, yes. But not a twinge of pain."

The doctor called me George. It seemed to break the spell. So many others, after that, called me by my first name. They forgot their hatred and their fear of me, in their remembered love and respect for the man who begot me.

Had the sailor who tried to sell the skull been a Nantucket citizen, things would, no doubt, have been different. But no outsider may come here to blaspheme Nantucket's dead, or to slander Nantucket's living, without making the whole community gather together in defense.

I did not see Mr. Paulding at the homecoming. Yet he was waiting for me at Samantha's house when I bore my father's body thither. And he took charge of arrangements that had no meaning for me.

He had come on the *Pharaoh;* assigned, I imagine, to shepherd Lay and Hussey back to the town where they could be held as witnesses, in three hundred dollars bond, like the rest of us, pending the trial of Thomas.

"Did I kill that man?" I asked him.

"You may have wanted to," he said, "and nobody would have blamed you if you had. I don't know what was in your mind—nor in the captain's. I think the captain of the *Pharaoh* would cheerfully have killed him too.

"What actually happened is that he slipped. There was a slippery place on the gangplank. I think somebody had spilled oil on it. The fellow lost his footing. He was holding the skull in his left hand. He let go of it—tossing it upward. He tried to recover it with his right, forgetting he had the sword. Trying to recover his footing, and the skull, he ran himself through. A clumsy accident. Call it retribution. Call it justice.

"This was no enemy's doing. I don't believe the fellow knew this was Nantucket—or, if he did, that he realized Sam Comstock was born and raised here. You see, George, when we came ashore in New York, opposite the West Battery, there was a crowd waiting for us. They knew all about the mutiny on the *Globe.* They gave Lay and Hussey a great cheer. Then some of our boys, the devils, went among the crowd peddling skulls and swords. Every one, of course, was a relic of Sam Comstock. They sold fifteen skulls. And fifty swords.

"The fellow on the gangplank must have been one of those New York dupes."

The thought came to me—but I did not voice it—that even in death, my brother had not ceased to kill.

Preacher Coffin begged permission to preach my father's funeral sermon; but I had already asked Elijah Goodyear to do that. Preacher Coffin sighed, and he shook his head sadly as he walked away. I felt sorry for him, knowing—I thought—a little of the shame he must feel at having treated my father so coldly during these last few years. It was a pity I had to deny him the melancholy pleasure of speaking at his old friend's grave. There would have been solace of a kind in this—and a measure of reparation. He walked away with head bent, his thin hands rubbing each other as though to furnish themselves with heat and comfort. He made me think of a man chafing his hands above a fireplace in which the fire had died.

He, too, like Lieutenant Paulding, had, for the first time, called me George.

And how often since have I pondered the words of that wonderful old Doctor Goodyear, "The only successful man is one who loves, and is beloved by, his neighbor and his God."

Even as Elijah Goodyear finished speaking, the children of Nantucket were gathering fresh wild flowers to heap above my father's humble grave.

MAY 3. Letters of condolence from Captain Percival and Mr. Hogan, both of them in Washington, D.C. Also a summons to appear before Mr. George Blake, United States Attorney in Boston, as speedily as possible.

I visited Joe Thomas' lawyer, James Trecotheck Austin, an old friend of my father's, before going to see Mr. Blake. And after we had talked for some little time of my father and his tragic death—"despite his untenable views in favor of abolition, he was a fine and staunch and sturdy citizen, George"—Austin warned me against Blake.

"Don't tell the man everything you know," he said. "The fellow is sharpening his knives. Don't lend him your whetstone. You'll get your throat slashed.

"Ambition, George, is a more horrible disease than any known to medical science. Blake would trample over your body, and mine, and a hundred others if he had to, to seat himself in the chair of the governor of Massachusetts. This is Blake's ambition.

"Don't give him any harmless little interview—unless you want him to indict you and try you with Joe Thomas."

"Me?" I exclaimed. "You don't mean he'd think of indicting me?"

"He has an idea that if he hangs Thomas he can be elected governor. He is sure that if he hangs you, too, and any others of the *Globe* survivors, the job is his for life.

"You'd be surprised to know how many men have been duped, politely, into giving Mr. Blake too much information. He sucks news out of people as a weasel sucks blood. You'd be surprised to know how even a few pretty compliments can be woven into a rope by Mr. Blake. If I weren't his good friend I could say some mighty unpleasant things about this Mr. Blake!"

"He's a hangman, then?" I said, not sure Austin wasn't fooling.

"In the last sixteen months," Austin said, "he's led thirty men to confide in him. Of these he's hanged only twenty-six. So far. The others are in the death cell. Don't say a word more to him than you have to."

After that, Mr. Austin began asking me questions. I was with him nearly two hours. I told him everything. He never once jotted down a word or a fact. He never asked a question the second time.

His thin pockmarked face was serious when I left him, and most solemn.

"Remember," he warned me again, "don't pick up snakes, don't fool with fire, don't trust George Blake."

After that I called on Warden Jeremiah Doane and asked if I might see Joe Thomas. I thought Thomas might have changed his attitude toward me, or that I might manage to assure him I was still his friend.

The warden didn't rise to greet me when I came in. He merely lifted his red face from a ponderous book, in which, evidently, he had been recording some ponderous statistics. Then he blinked his little eyes at me.

"Impossible," he said. "Joe be reading Scripters." He shifted his cud to the other side of his mouth, with much working of jaws and facial muscles. "Good day. Close the door."

I did not visit Mr. Blake until late in the afternoon. He looked at the clock, meaningly, as I entered, but he seemed affable enough. And he might have got up to greet me had he not been encumbered with two little Negro boys, one on each leg, who were polishing his boots with blacking, with rubbing, with spitting, with hard breathing, and with exclamations of sheer joy.

"Sit down, Mr. Comstock," he said. "This will not take long."

He is a thin man with a massive head, a very wide mouth, a bulbous nose, and a pair of eyes that protrude out of his skull like an insect's. His skin is a pale, pasty color. Almost a greenish white. I should say he is a sick man. But he does not appear to be sick. He has taffy-colored hair, fine hair, fine as a baby's. I wonder if it's always rumpled like that.

He spoke in a dulcet voice, asked if his pipe smoke bothered me—which might have been a way of calling my attention to the beauty of the pipe, or to the fragrance of the tobacco burning in it—then took up a bunch of papers and began to read them.

One of the Negro boys looked suddenly up at me. He dropped his polishing rag.

"Mmmmmmmmmmmm mp!"

That's what it sounded like. With the eyes getting bigger and whiter all the time, the face darker, the gleaming teeth more wondrous shiny.

Impelled by his brother's expression of so much admiration, the other boy looked up.

"Mmmmmmmm mmmmm mmmmmm!" he said.

"You a mudra?" the first one said.

"Don' look like no mudra," the other said.

Mr. Blake laughed. "Of course he isn't a murderer. Get on with your work. Call that a shine? Pay attention now."

The boys worked, but only for a few seconds.

"How big is you?" the first one asked.

"Guess you's de bigges' man in de whole state of Boston," said his brother.

Mr. Blake took his feet down from the boxes, on the tops of which they had rested—the heels lying snugly on plush cloths so they might not lose their luster. He stood up then and scowled at the pair. "All right, imps," he said. "That'll have to do. Get out of here. Can't get a decent shine with you two jabbering all the time."

He looked at the polish critically. So did I. I wished my own boots had ever been as bright.

Mr. Blake waited until the boys, laden with their brushes, rags, blacking, and boxes, were almost at the door of his office. Then he tossed a copper coin up into the air so that it would fall somewhere between them. He seemed amused as they dropped everything to watch and catch the flying penny. He laughed when they smacked their kinky heads together.

I was with them in an instant. I couldn't help myself. There was something in the woe on their faces, something in the disillusion I saw in their eyes, that I had to repair. Immediately, I picked up the coin and magically it was changed into a silver piece.

"What are your names?" I asked them.

"I'm Fustus," said the first one.

"I'm Justus," said his brother.

"I was the fustus to come, day we was bo'n. We twins."

"And I's justus big as he is, justus pretty, 'n' justus dear to ol' Mammy's hot."

"You is as big as God," Fustus told me. "You is as good as God." And Justus said, "You is God!"

I forgot that such a bugbear as George Blake existed, until those beautiful children had gathered up their impedimenta and sped away.

Mr. Blake chose to be subtly derisive.

"Charming, Mr. Comstock," he said. "Most charming."

He thrust into my hands the papers he had been scanning.

"I brought you here," he said then, "to tell you that, as a witness for the United States, the city is yours. Gin, giggles, and guitars, and all the rest of it. I've drawn up this little statement, compiled from the testimony of other witnesses. Just sign it, and don't worry about a thing."

"Did Gilbert Smith sign one of these?" I asked.

"That pious psalm-singing Quaker?" Mr. Blake sneered at the idea. And that brought out the Quaker in me. I became another Gilbert.

"Thee despises psalm-singing, Friend Blake?"

He didn't answer that. Not exactly. He entwined a finger in his fine taffy hair, loosed it, entwined it again.

"Mr. Comstock," he said with some severity, "there is no power on earth that is going to stop me from hanging your friend Joseph Thomas. He's a murderer and a mutineer, and he shall hang. You can help or hinder me. To some extent. To the extent that you help or hinder yourself."

I reached for the pen. I inked it carefully. I signed the last paper and handed it back to him. But I didn't sign my own name. I signed it "Hangman Blake."

He didn't look at it. He folded it up carelessly, and put it in a drawer. He locked the drawer, and put the key in the lower right pocket of his beautiful robin's-egg-blue waistcoat.

He jingled some silver coins in his right pants' pocket, and I thought I knew the reason why.

"And if thee offers me the usual thirty pieces of silver, Friend Blake," I said, "I will punch thee in thy ugly and most un-Quakerish mouth."

Chapter Forty-Two

JUNE 15. Nantucket—The trial of Joseph Thomas, though it raised such excitement in New England, has been almost forgotten by this time. Thomas himself is forgotten.

Who remembers him, or all the emotions he churned up in the drafty courtroom of the United States Circuit Court during that first week in May? Who remembers the battle that swirled around him, the hope, the despair, the desperate efforts we made to keep the red blood pulsing through him?

It was my intention, long ago, to put down every word that should be spoken at the trial; to record every ruling of Mr. Justice Story and Judge John Davis; to make notes on the strategy of the government and the defense, on the handling of witnesses, on the building of a case for and against Joe Thomas, and on the methods of presenting evidence to the jury.

Had I done this, I should have spent many nights without sleep.

I was happy to learn that Justice Story would preside, inasmuch as he is one of my professors and the author of some of my favorite law books. He is another Karamoku, a man of ripe wisdom and mellow justice. I had confidence in him. I knew that Thomas would be given a fair trial, in spite of Mr. Blake. Joe knew it, too, I'm sure.

I have waited these many weeks that I may write calmly, without bitterness, without exaggeration, and without cluttering up my log with unimportant details.

It was a glorious day, the first Monday in May when the ordeal began.

I remember distinctly the white clouds swirling in the Prussian-blue skies, the lilacs and hyacinths that scented the air, and the fishing smacks and packet boats and idle whalers and impatient merchantmen making white lines upon the blue-black waters of Boston Bay. I remember the sea gulls gibbering and gossiping together about schools of little fish. I remember the saucy robins strutting on the lawns.

I was up long before the time set for the trial. Samantha, who had just arrived from Nantucket, contrived to get me some breakfast.

"A beautiful morning," she observed. " 'Tis an omen, Long George."

Ever since my father's death she has been calling me Long George.

"When a body saith 'good morning,' " she went on, "he meaneth 'God's morning.' It is a way of thanking the Creator for the new day He hath made. It is a prayer of appreciation and of thanks."

She talked me into a sanguine mood, then sent me forth. But she would not accompany me to the courtroom. Not that day, she said. She would come later. She would be there when I took the stand.

The courtroom was packed, but room had been reserved for me and other witnesses. I spent half an hour or so looking idly at the plain oak panels, the rostrum with the leather-backed chairs behind it, the dusty American flag draped on the wall above it, the dustier clock, and the people who had come to see the contest for Joe Thomas' wretched life. And all the time I kept pretending I was a stranger, seated among strangers.

There was nobody in the courtroom familiar to me, save the witnesses nearby me. The spectators were mostly women. Old, middle-aged, young. Here and there I saw a man among them; a reluctant escort, I suppose, fetched there by some wife or daughter. I hoped to find Sally Starbuck somewhere in the room, but I was disappointed.

It was shortly after ten o'clock when both sides answered "ready." The clerk read a list of names from pieces of paper he took out of a little box—after he had spun the box on a wheel. As they heard their names called, twelve men walked clumsily and self-consciously into the jury box.

I looked out the window as the lawyers questioned these men, trying to calm myself, trying to be philosophical about all this. Yet my nerves kept torturing me, making me squirm in my chair, drying up my mouth, putting odd thoughts in my mind.

Here I was with a group of my old shipmates. Hanson. The Kidder brothers. Hussey. Lay. My best friend, Gilbert Smith. But I was anathema to each and every one of them. When their eyes met mine—a catastrophe that could not be avoided—they looked quickly elsewhere. I felt as though I were a wall, at which they threw little stones. Little stones that struck lightly, and hurt terribly as they bounded off.

And not six feet away was another friend, Joseph Thomas—who also hated and despised me.

This was a worse ordeal, I thought, than setting out in a little boat to harpoon Leviathan. Here Leviathan hunted you. You did not hunt him. You tried to escape him.

And Leviathan's weapon was not a harpoon that would go through you sharp and clean, bring you a quick and not too painful death. Its weapon was a rope; and it would dangle in front of your eyes for weeks, perhaps for months, before it was placed about your neck, skillfully knotted, and you were dropped from the gallows for a drunken crowd to see, and to applaud.

One didn't look for oil in this courtroom, nor cocoanuts nor bread-fruit nor bup nor poi nor turtles for your crew. One sought political preferment, money, fame—all to be gained in the snuffing out of a fellow creature's life.

I had told myself I would profit greatly, as a law student, by paying close attention to this legal contest. But I was too deeply moved to give more than ear service to the proceedings, and too disturbed by the attitude of those silent friends who sat beside me. It seemed to me that it was I, not Joe Thomas, who was on trial.

Before very long I had put away the scratch paper and the pencils I had brought with me; and I would have tried to sleep—as Joe Thomas seemed to be doing—had I dared.

I listened, but only half hearing, as the soft voice of Blake tried to qualify the first few talesmen he examined. Were they opposed to capital punishment? Did they have any scruples against hanging a man convicted purely on circumstantial evidence? If they found the defendant guilty of murder in the first degree, would they hang him? Should it transpire that others—or another—of the *Globe* survivors were equally guilty, would they hang him too—or them?

Hang him. Hang him. Hang him.

Monotonously, repeatedly, the words sounded in the room.

Hang him. Tick-tock. Hang him. Tick-tock. Hang them. Tick-tock. Hang Joe. Tick-tock. Hang George. Tick-tock. Hang one. Tick-tock. Hang all. Tick-tock, tick-tock, tick-tock!

I got up suddenly and made my way out past the long row of knees and feet. I couldn't help myself. The dulcet voice stopped. I turned, instinctively, to see Blake grinning at me. In a meaning way. In a pleasantly sinister way. He seemed to be enjoying what he considered my precipitate flight. He did not resume his work until I had left the room.

The trial proceeded quickly after the jurors were sworn in. Mr. Blake read the indictment. Then a funny-looking little man, the clerk, stole in—like a timid husband creaking quietly late at night into his bedroom—and got ready to preserve, with a quill pen, the address Mr. Blake would make to the jury.

Mr. Blake rubbed the hair on his head, that fine shining hair of a baby, twisted a strand of it in his fingers—doing this for good luck, I thought, as sailors sometimes touch a hunchback's spine. Then he thrust his right hand deep in his pants' pocket and placed the other hand meticulously over his heart. He looked intently at the gentlemen of the jury, and, with a sad little smile, plunged into his rhetoric.

I can still remember his white hand resting on his robin's-egg-blue waistcoat, a blue ring on his little finger. That hand moved occasionally, to touch the heavy gold watch chain that traveled from the right upper pocket to the upper left, or to make some dramatic gesture. But mostly it rested tranquilly above the heart.

And I can remember his highly polished boots. Sometimes the right one was poised daintily over the spittoon in front of the jury foreman. Sometimes it was the left that was exposed.

I thought it was in danger—for the foreman chewed his tobacco with as much relish and as much vigor as anybody else in the courtroom, including Joe Thomas. But I forgot about that after Mr. Blake began to talk. So did the foreman.

The other hand now and then jingled silver dollars in the sanctity of Mr. Blake's pants' pocket, but it stayed hidden.

"May it please the court, and you gentlemen of the jury," he began, "it is my most painful duty . . ."

Ah yes, his painful and his solemn duty! He must, through these witnesses here, relate the story of the crimes that happened one awful January night aboard the whaler *Globe*. And so forth, and so on!

Blake gave us a graphic and most gruesome account of the killing of the captain and the mates; sparing us no detail of barbarity or blood; keeping his voice level, without inflection, without emotion—so that it played its devilish part to perfection.

Only when he had told of the death of Lumbard did his voice change pitch. He cried out then, in a voice that sent shivers through me, the plea that Lumbard made for his life.

" 'I'm a married man and a father, Sam. I just got a letter yesterday. I'm the father of a little girl. You won't kill me, Sam. For her sake, Sam.' "

He paused. He looked around him, as though he had wakened from an evil dream and were not sure of his surroundings. There was sweat on his pasty face. His long thin lips quivered, as though with terror.

"And I shall prove to you, gentlemen of the jury," he went on, "that, in answer to this pitiful plea for mercy—I shall prove it through these witnesses, including Sam 'Comstock's beloved brother, George —I shall prove that one of the conspirators jabbed a bayonet through the father of that new little baby girl, saying, 'I am a bloody man; I've got a bloody hand!' "

The last words were a whisper. A whisper meant to chill the blood.

But Mr. Blake was not through with Lumbard.

"They thought he was dead, gentlemen of the jury. But he wasn't. He had been stabbed more often and more cruelly than Julius Caesar. Yet he lived. He still wanted to live. For that new little girl. For that daughter his wife had written him about! For that tiny mite that God in His infinite goodness had sent him! In spite of all his agony, he wanted to live! For her!

"He caught at the plank, and clung to it, when they tried to kick him overboard—when they tried to kick him into the sea, as some slovenly sailor might kick a fish's entrails off some spotless deck! And once more he begged for mercy."

Now Blake shouted.

" 'Comstock! For my baby's sake! Mercy!' "

Joe Thomas, who had sat unmoved all that day, with his eyes

half closed, and his hands in his lap, jumped to his feet in evident terror at the anguish (and the menace) in the prosecutor's voice.

He sat down quickly again; but he had harmed himself. Even against my will, I saw that in the eyes of the jurors. There wasn't a man of them who didn't believe, then and there, that Joseph Thomas was one of the men who had so terribly tortured that helpless baby's helpless father.

Mr. Blake's loud voice had upset the decorum of the court. I mean he had roused such anger, such horror, such despair, and such violent indignation among the spectators that they could not contain themselves.

Justice Story rapped three times for order before quiet was restored, and those women who were standing up, crowding into the aisles, or seemingly on their way to the chair in which Joe Thomas sat —to tear him apart with their hands, for all anybody knows—moved back to their proper places. They all sat down again. All except one, a young lady who was taken sick, evidently from too much emotion, and who had to be carried out.

Mr. Blake had made his point. He went quickly to the close of his oration; stating that he could prove, beyond all shadow of a doubt, that Joseph Thomas—and perhaps one or two others, now in this courtroom as witnesses—should be numbered among the mutineers.

Mr. Blake lifted his boot. The foreman shot a long brown stream into the cuspidor, and wiped his mouth with the back of his hand. Mr. Blake inspected his boot, saw it was unsullied, and gave the foreman a look that complimented him on his patience in waiting, and on his accuracy.

He bowed to the jurors. He removed his right hand from his trousers' pocket, wiped his greenish-white skin with a spotless handkerchief, and walked slowly to his chair. He sat at his table and pretended to busy himself with a sheaf of papers. The left hand, still pressed against his heart, fluttered in distress. He was, one thought, still suffering for Lumbard.

Justice Story looked at the clock and seemed astonished—as I was myself—to realize that Blake had taken less than an hour for his talk. He told Mr. Austin he might proceed for the defense.

"And the court will appreciate it," he added, "if you will try to make your talk as brief as your adversary's."

"I'll do my best, Your Honor," Austin said.

He stood awkwardly before the jurors, shaking his head in humility and shame.

"Gentlemen," he said, "I don't know what to say, how to begin, what to do. I am not an orator. I am not even an actor. I'm afraid

I have no tricks at all with which to entertain you. I can't shout. I can't whisper. And I can't make you see, so vividly as Mr. Blake has done, the terrible crimes perpetrated at sea, on the whaleship *Globe*, on the night of January 26, 1824.

"But I have the same set of facts to give you as has Mr. Blake. Perhaps I should stick to them.

"Mr. Blake has told you those facts will doom this poor sailor, Joseph Thomas—"

"Oh, now," said Mr. Blake, quickly springing up and appealing to the two judges, "I object to that phrase, 'this poor sailor.' Counsel must realize the impropriety of attempting to excite the jurors' sympathies by such twaddle. 'This poor sailor' indeed!"

"I accept counsel's correction," Mr. Austin said, still awkward and humble. He spoke without waiting for a ruling from the bench.

Mr. Blake was too astonished to comment. The judges bent forward in their chairs.

"You gentlemen," Austin went on, "will pardon a country lawyer for trying to evoke some sympathy for a man who has waited more than two years for this brief bout with justice. I should have tried to evoke sympathy for Lumbard's baby, for Lumbard's widow, for the widows of all the men killed that night on the *Globe*, and all their orphans. I should have tried to wring tears from you for Worth, and Beetle, and Fisher, and Lumbard. For all the dead.

"Pity for the dead, gentlemen. Not for the living. Pity for everybody but Joe Thomas. If I feel sorry for Joe Thomas, that is my own personal sorrow; I should not inflict it on you. If you hang him—that will be Mr. Blake's sorrow, too. Mr. Blake is always sorry when a jury hangs a man. But he puts this feeling aside when he sets out to prosecute the next one. It is his duty so to do. His painful and his solemn duty!"

Austin had turned from the jury. He was facing Blake. His voice was not so loud as Blake's had been, but it was loud enough, and bold enough to thrill the court anew. And he was looking at Blake with such contempt and anger that Blake did not dare stop him.

Abruptly, Austin swung around.

"I said 'this poor sailor.' Forgive me. We do not come here for your pity, gentlemen. We do not come here for your mercy. We have come into this court for one thing only. We have come for justice. Will you give us that?"

One of the jurors nodded his head up and down. The one who had spent six years at sea when he was a boy. The others stared at Austin as though he had lightning hidden up his sleeves.

"I called him 'this poor sailor,'" Austin began again, "only because he has waited so long, and so patiently, for trial. The other survivors of the *Globe,* gentlemen, have not had to wait these weary years in jail. They have been free to come and go. For, until this morning, there was no slightest suspicion raised as to the guilt of any of them.

"You have heard Mr. Blake say what he expects to prove to you. I have no quarrel with the prosecutor there. I have no quarrel with the facts. Captain Worth was brutally and most foully butchered, gentlemen. And the mates were slain, with him, in as wanton and cruel and dastardly a murder as any we know of in modern times.

"Mr. Blake believes the sailor Thomas was one of those who inspired or planned the mutiny and murders. He is sincere in that belief, gentlemen; as sincere and as stubborn as I in my belief that my client did not dream there was a conspiracy until it had burst into this unnatural, unholy, and unutterably fiendish massacre.

"But—if he did know there was such a plot—a plot to take the ship and let the red blood fill the scuppers—if he was aware of it and if he consented to it—if you can believe him guilty after you have heard all the evidence for and against him—if you can find him guilty beyond the peradventure of a doubt—then I might be justified in saying 'this poor sailor.' Then I might be excused for asking clemency for him.

"That must sound strange to you. And to this honorable court. And to Mr. Blake. Perhaps it sounds strange to Thomas himself.

"Let me explain. There was a duel between this sailor and his captain, if you can call that a duel in which one of the antagonists has all the advantages and the other none. There was a duel that ended only in the captain's death.

"Mr. Blake has described the captain to you. A noble, benevolent, sober, generous, God-fearing father to all his crew! Why any gang of murderers could bring themselves to do away with so saintly a character I do not know. Yet they did kill him—and apparently with glee.

"I shall bring you witnesses who will paint another picture of Captain Thomas Worth. They found him a besotted, tyrannic, stingy, murderous, demoniac beast!

"And they will give you some idea of the unequal struggle that developed, from the very first, between him and—and this sailor Thomas. Excuse me. I almost said again 'this poor sailor, Thomas.'

"I shall put witnesses on this stand to show you that, from the very first, Thomas was mistreated by Captain Worth. He was locked up below, on suspicion. He was marooned—put on a desert island without water or food or clothes enough to keep himself warm at night—with nothing but a knife, which would end his miseries if he chose to use it. He was spread-eagled and scourged.

"If a man such as this entered into any conspiracy to kill the captain who hated him—and whom, I grant, he must have hated—then he did so only in the hope of saving his own life.

"I repeat, gentlemen of the jury, if Joseph Thomas entered into the conspiracy to murder Captain Worth, and the mates—which I deny—then he did so, purely and solely, in self-defense."

Mr. Austin looked at the clock and saw that he had much more time than he needed.

"Gentlemen, you heard Mr. Blake say that Joe Thomas, after he had been flogged until the blood poured from his back—I am not trying to excite your pity, remember, but blood did stream from that terribly scourged flesh—blood as red as that of the captain's or the mates—after he had been flogged, Joe Thomas, being carried below, was invited to the captain's cabin.

"The implication is that Joe was being asked to come along and help with the mutiny and murder. Mr. Blake did not tell you what Thomas answered, if he answered anything; but he intimated that Thomas knew what would happen, yet did nothing to prevent it.

"Mr. Blake wants you to believe that a man consents to murder, even if he is too weak—by reason of having been beaten half to death—to stagger up the nearest companionway and inform on the men meditating vengeance.

"Mr. Blake would have you believe, first, that Thomas was aware of the conspiracy; second, that he consented to it; and third, that he did nothing to prevent it.

"I shall endeavor to show you, first, that Thomas had no knowledge whatsoever of the conspiracy; second, that, if he did discover there was such a conspiracy, he was too weak to do anything about it, either to take part in it or to prevent it; and that, if he consented to it—which I again vigorously deny—he did so only to save his own life. He knew those men, his friends, would surely kill him if he tried to thwart them. He knew that if he knew anything.

"I am sorry I cannot tell you that Joe Thomas said to his friends, 'No, no; you shall not kill the captain. Even though he half killed me, you shall not touch him. Nor the mates. I must get up, if I can. I must go tell the captain you plan to kill him—so that he can kill you. Be quick, dress my wounds, that I may the sooner accomplish this most noble errand.'

"No. I will not tell you any nonsense of that kind. You would not expect me to—any more than you'd expect me to ask pity for Joe Thomas. Nobody ever pitied him before. Why should you?

"Let Mr. Blake pity Thomas, when he has started him aswinging. Mr. Blake pities all the victims of his oratory and his actor's skill. But not until they are dangling on their solid ropes.

"It is his duty, gentlemen, his painful and his solemn duty, not to pity them until then.

"I ask justice for Joe Thomas.

"If you have pity left to spare, give it, in your charity, to Prosecutor Blake."

Chapter Forty-Three

JUNE 16. I am not sure whether it was the third or fourth day that was so critical for me. I do not recall whether it was a Wednesday or a Thursday. But I do know it was a dark, foreboding morning. Black clouds and biting rain. A wind in the harbor that was almost a gale. And in the flat, desolation of spirit.

Samantha was sitting at the breakfast table when I rose, the King James Bible spread before her. With the help of a work-wrinkled finger—God bless her—and the light of a sperm-oil lamp, she was reading out loud from the Seventy-Seventh Psalm.

" 'I cried unto God with my voice, even unto God with my voice; and he gave ear unto me.

" 'In the day of my trouble I sought the Lord: my sore ran in the night, and ceased not: my soul refused to be comforted.' "

I have memorized that particular psalm, and sometimes the verses visit me, even unasked.

"Will the Lord cast off for ever? and will he be favorable no more? . . .

"Hath God forgotten to be gracious?"

Samantha had not been able to sleep all night. Her fear for me had ceased not. Her soul could get no comfort, save in prayer.

This because of Mr. Blake's skillful handling of his witnesses. Slowly, but surely, it had seemed to me, and to Samantha, the prosecutor was working my destruction. And this through the words of my old friends.

Bits of his devilishness come back to me at times—and probably will continue to come back so long as I live.

Mr. Blake: Do you know this of your own knowledge?

Witness: Uh, well, sir, not exactly. No sir.

Mr. Blake: Somebody told you this was so.

Witness: Yes sir. Mr. Comstock, sir. George Comstock told me.

Mr. Blake: Meaning the same George Comstock now here as a witness, the beloved brother of the murderer, Samuel B. Comstock?

Witness: Yes sir, George Comstock.

It mattered not who the witness was. The same questions elicited the same answers.

Mr. Blake went especially deep into the matter of Joe Thomas' coming to the *Globe* out of the fog.

Mr. Blake: You saw Thomas come aboard?

Witness: Yes sir. Everybody seen that, sir.

Mr. Blake: You are positive the Comstock brothers found him and brought him aboard? That is, Samuel B. Comstock, the red killer of four peaceful men, and his beloved brother, George?

Witness: Yes sir. Sam and George.

Mr. Blake: Was that the only time you saw these three together?

Witness: No sir.

Mr. Blake: Where did Joseph Thomas, this defendant, come from? Do you know of your own knowledge? I understand—you have already testified that he came out of a fog—but what I want to know is, what ship did he come from, if he came from a ship—or if the Messrs. Comstock, who were so often seen in his company— Scratch that out. I'll reframe the question.

The poor little clerk scratched out a lot of things Mr. Blake said. But, of a certainty, he could not scratch them out of the minds of the jurors. Mr. Blake kept within the law. Mr. Austin, always waiting an opportunity to object, never was given the chance.

"Be patient," Mr. Austin had bidden me. "No man who keeps hitting below the belt is of champion caliber, George. And there are referees who are not blind. Suffer Blake another day or so."

It was soothing to hear Samantha reading those verses.

" 'Thou art the God that doest wonders. . . .

" 'The clouds poured out water: the skies sent out a sound: thine arrows also went abroad.

" 'The voice of thy thunder was in the heaven: the lightnings lightened the world: the earth trembled and shook.' "

The clouds were indeed pouring out rain and the lightnings were at play. But despite the deluge and the storm the courtroom was packed again that morning.

Sometime before noon, perhaps about eleven o'clock, Mr. Blake concluded his case by summoning Barnabas Starbuck to the stand. As he stood up and began striding forward to take the oath, I saw his granddaughter, Sally. But she did not see me.

It was just about this time that Michael Hogan, sopping wet, but smiling mysteriously, squeezed his great bulk onto the bench between me and Cyrus Hussey.

"Have lunch with me," he whispered. "Got something wonderful to tell you. We'll ask Justice Story too. And Captain Percival."

"The captain is in town?"

"We got in together, about an hour ago. Who's the pompous individual on the stand?"

Starbuck didn't sit long in the witness chair. Mr. Blake had put him there only that he might tell us how great a sea captain, how noble a man, and how fatherly to his crew was Captain Thomas Worth.

But Mr. Austin utterly demolished Starbuck's arrogance, took away even his importance. And this blandly, briefly, insolently, almost carelessly.

Austin: How often did you speak to this captain you have so highly praised, Mr. Starbuck?

Mr. Starbuck: Why, ah, I don't remember I ever did see the man. Knew him by reputation. Only time I see a ship's captain, sir, is when I'm compelled to.

Mr. Austin: How often did you visit your ship, the *Globe?*

Mr. Starbuck: Never set foot in her.

Mr. Austin: Yet you have raised your right hand, sworn to Almighty God that you would tell the truth, the whole truth, and nothing but the truth, and you have told this court and this jury that Captain Worth was a good and honest man, that he was sober, that there was no rotten meat forced down the throats of his crew, that he was not a skinflint, a bully, a despot, or, in any way, a disgrace to his owners, to his calling, to the whole human race. You have sworn that, Mr. Starbuck! And you have also sworn the man was a stranger to you! That is all.

He turned his back and sat down.

Poor Barnabas flushed, then paled until I thought he would drop dead. Then the flush returned. He gathered himself up with some dignity, and made his way slowly back to Sally.

It was just before noon, when—Mr. Blake having finished his case —Jim Austin called me as his first witness.

He did not question me very long. The story of the mutiny and murder had been told and retold many times since the trial began. I was asked to clarify only a few details.

Austin led me swiftly over that too familiar ground, made me tell about our retaking the ship, and about our voyage to Valparaiso. Then he asked innumerable questions about Joe Thomas.

Q: Did you, at any time, on the night of January 26, 1824, see Joseph Thomas with your brother Sam, or any of his accomplices? A: No.

Q: To the best of your knowledge, was Thomas in the captain's cabin at any time that night? A: I know he was not. He was lying in his hammock.

Q: Have you any information as to Joe Thomas' participation in these crimes—that is, in any way whatsoever? A: None. Had I thought he was one of the mutineers I never would have brought him home.

Mr. Blake objected to my answer; and the court directed it be stricken from the record. I didn't mind. I had picked up one of Mr. Blake's tricks and used it against him. The jury would not forget.

Q: Do I understand you asked Joe Thomas to help you retake the ship? A: I asked Gilbert Smith to recruit the men to take back the ship. I was not in touch with Thomas or the others at that time. I was kept ashore by Payne. Gilbert came and went to and from the ship.

Q: You did not ask Smith to include Payne, Oliver, Liliston, or others? A: I certainly did not want Payne, Oliver, or Liliston included. I did have the opportunity to see Hussey, Lay, Coffin, Jones, and Columbus Worth and I did ask them to join us. I wanted only the innocent with us.

Before Mr. Blake could object, before he could tell me that it didn't matter to the court what I thought, felt, or wanted, Austin had turned to him, saying, "You may cross-examine."

Mr. Blake began gently, bringing out the fact that Sam liked me, that he always tried to protect me, that he confided in me; and that I had liked Sam, had "hero-worshiped" him when I was a small boy, and had done many things for him that I would not have done for others.

Then he asked a few questions about the murder of Captain Worth. I answered them readily enough.

Suddenly Blake glared at me. His voice grew loud. His pop eyes seemed to take on a reddish tint. His right hand played with his baby hair.

"It is significant to me, George Comstock," he said, "that everything about these crimes revolves around you. You were at the wheel. Nobody else. You reached for the rattle. Nobody heard it sounding.

We have only your word for it. Humphries was holding a light. Who saw this? Nobody but you. We have only your word for this.

"You put Payne, Oliver, and Humphries at the scene of the crime, with your brother Sam. They saw you too. You were a witness. But they did not harm you in any way. Doesn't that seem significant, even to you?

"You are the only living witness to what happened that night, George Comstock. I charge that you have not told us the full truth of what occurred that night. I charge that you have lied to this court, and to this jury. I charge that, like the poltroon you are, you were one of the conspirators, and that you are shielding yourself behind their dead bodies!"

I was so stunned by this outrageous accusation that I could not speak. And so weakened I could not get up.

I heard Justice Story say, "It is nearly one o'clock, Mr. Blake. The court will recess now until half past two." I wanted to thank him for this respite he had afforded me; but I was ashamed to look at him.

"You will be present at that time, Mr. Comstock," he said.

"Yes, Your Honor," I answered. It was then that I saw Captain Percival and Michael Hogan making their way to the bench. And it was also about this time that I saw Samantha elbowing through the crowds toward me. I couldn't face her.

I slipped away, trying to escape the notice of those between me and the door. But my stature was against me. Everybody saw me. Some of them booed. A woman with more than the average paint on her cheeks ripped a white feather from her hat and tried to jab me with it as I passed. It might have put out my right eye, had I not jerked my head away.

Where I walked in that most terrible hour and a half I do not know. But wherever I walked, the verses of the psalm pursued me. In the rain and the lightning and the thunder and the wind, they spoke to me—as, no doubt, they have spoken to millions of other harassed and troubled human beings in the centuries that have passed since King David first sang them to the Lord.

"Will the Lord cast off for ever? and will he be favorable no more?

"Is His mercy clean gone for ever? doth his promise fail for evermore?

"Hath God forgotten to be gracious? hath he in anger shut up his tender mercies?

"And I said, This is my infirmity: but I will remember the years of the right hand of the most High."

That phrase captivated me. I repeated it over and over as I

plunged through the dark cobblestoned, rain-splashed, puddle-filled Boston streets. "The years of the right hand of the most High."

That right hand had upheld me in all kinds of peril, until now. It would uphold me no longer.

"The waters saw thee, O God, the waters saw thee; they were afraid: the depths also were troubled."

I cried the words aloud, inaccurately no doubt, but as accurately as I could remember. And after a time I saw the symbolism in them. The waters of my soul had been stirred to their depths. They were afraid. They were as troubled as the waters of the sea. And there was nothing that could calm them—save Him who had created them.

I must have gone home and changed my clothes, though I have not the slightest recollection of doing so. At any rate, when I found myself back in the courtroom my clothing was comparatively dry. And the waters of my soul no longer were afraid—nor troubled.

I stood up when court reconvened, meaning to resume the witness chair; but Justice Story bade me keep my seat.

"You will notice," he said, "that the jury has been excluded for the time being. There is a reason for this. A very good reason." He looked away from me, studying those around me and behind me.

"This," he proceeded, "is a court of justice. It must give justice to all. It must give justice to those, especially, who have, rightly or wrongly, been accused of serious crimes.

"Perhaps it is not the regular procedure to halt the trial of one man, so that justice may be tendered to another. But then—" and now he looked at Judge Davis, at Mr. Blake, at Mr. Austin, and at Captain Percival and Michael Hogan—"but then it is not the regular procedure for any United States Attorney to convict one man without a jury, when he is, ostensibly, trying to convict another before a jury."

He paused, evidently waiting for an objection of some kind from Mr. Blake. The latter sprang up angrily, hesitated, sat down again. The justice called Anthony Hanson to the stand.

What happened after that still amazes me; still strains my powers of remembering.

The examination went something like this.

Justice Story: Mr. Hanson, you have known George Comstock a number of years. You have been quite close to him, according to the testimony here. Do you consider him a poltroon, a coward?

Hanson: George Comstock? He's not afraid of anything, Your Honor.

Justice Story: Is that so? Interesting! But, on what do you base this statement, Mr. Hanson? I mean, do you remember any certain episode, any occasion on which you saw his courage tested? Tell us in your own language. Don't be afraid of any interruptions. This court is not concerned now with nice distinctions of the law. It wants the truth.

Hanson: Well, I seen him once go overboard with a lance, trying to kill a mad whale.

For a moment I thought that Hanson was lying, out of sheer friendship for me. I was touched but indignant. Then it came to me. Joe Brown, the poor frightened native we had shipped in the Sandwich Islands, the one who spent that Christmas day saying, "Christ born, Christ born," and grinning at everyone.

Joe Brown killing the baby whale. Joe Brown standing in Fisher's boat. The mother whale charging through the water, jaws wide open. Joe Brown lifting his second harpoon. His foot must have been caught in a rope. He couldn't get away. He had to die. But he chose to die with a weapon in his hand!

Hanson brought it all back to me.

"George seen the native was a goner, unless he could divert that whale. So in he dived. Never seen a white man swim like that, Your Honor, before nor since. But didn't do no good. Whale swallied Joe Brown, boat, and everything. Took 'em down with her to the bottom of the sea. George Comstock, he got scolded some by his brother. And then Captain Worth scolded him."

One by one my friends were thus called to testify.

The Kidders told how Gilbert and I retook the ship after the natives had captured it, on the way back from the Mulgraves. Both of them gave me all the credit.

"There was twenty savages aboard her at the time," Stephen Kidder swore, "but George Comstock didn't keer about that."

I don't remember that there were twenty savages on the *Globe* at any time. There may have been no more than ten. And if I killed as many of them as the Kidders say, I must have killed them after my head was injured. I do not remember. I killed only two, to the best of my recollection.

Gilbert Smith was called. He corroborated the testimony of the Kidders in every detail—not glancing once in my direction.

"I should like to tell thee, also, Your Honor," he said, "that this be not the only time George proved his intrepidity of heart."

"We are listening," Justice Story reminded him.

Gilbert then spoke of my fight with Liliston, and my rescue of Motake. "At that time," he said, "he was but a boy. He had not yet begun to shoot up; and Liliston towered a full head and more above him. Yet Comstock did not hesitate to attack."

"And?" That was from Judge Davis.

"Almost broke Mr. Liliston's jaw, Your Honor."

Some in the crowd began to titter, others to laugh. Some rose up for a better look. At me. Justice Story rapped his gavel smartly on the bench.

"How old was the girl?" Judge Davis asked.

"Twelve, thirteen," Gilbert said.

"Pretty?" The judge smiled when he asked that question; and the women in the court again had to be quieted by the gavel.

"Yes, Your Honor," Gilbert said, "in her heathen way, Motake was a pretty girl. Even with clothing on her—"

The tittering burst into a medley of laughter and screams that drowned out the thunder of the gavel for a moment or two, then hushed. In the middle of the hubbub Gilbert left the stand and Michael Hogan took his place.

His testimony went something like this. He was Michael Hogan. He was the American consul at Valparaiso. He had served in that capacity for seven years. Yes, he did know George Comstock. Yes, he had an opinion about Mr. Comstock's poltroonery or courage. Mr. Comstock was one of the most valiant, heroic, and unselfish young men he had ever met.

He even went into details, telling, for instance, how in the hospital at Valparaiso I kept my fever up by raving about a girl named Sally.

Sally was listening. Sally had heard this. I should have been overjoyed. Yet I still could not lift up my head.

After a time I became aware that Captain Percival was in the witness chair, and that he too was testifying for me.

He told of how Buff and I rescued him, swimming through the surf.

Then he spoke of Ember. He was so excited, I was alarmed. He told a fantastic story of the adventure on South Peddler's Island. Then he said President Adams had written Congress a letter about me, citing me for "courage and intrepidity above and beyond the call of duty." He ended something like this:

"This is the man whom the President of the United States of America wishes to honor with a medal that shall have the approval and the blessing of the Congress of the United States.

"This is the man the President of the United States wishes to brevet a lieutenant in the United States Navy, if he wishes it.

"This is the man whom a slavering lawyer, who never in his life saw danger, dares to brand a poltroon!"

I had a vision of Sally and Samantha together, standing on a bench, looking with horror and dismay at the women trying to kiss me. I ran, in absolute panic.

Chapter Forty-Four

JUNE 17. There was a celebration in our rooms near the common that May night of my triumph. Jim Austin was there, and Captain Percival, and Mr. Hogan, and Captain Jackson of the *Harbinger*, and several others. Samantha gave them buttermilk and her own cookies. It was almost ten before they left. Captain Jackson, incidentally, promised he would ask Gilbert to sail with him next trip as mate. Now the jealous man, I thought, would have a chance to see Rosita, and discover he had no cause for jealousy. At any rate we should, some day, be friends again, I hoped.

Late that night I woke with a feeling that something was terribly wrong, some danger was threatening. I lay for a long time in bed, unable to account for this peculiar sensation. I tried to rid myself of it. It stuck to me like a burr. What was wrong? I had to know.

I dressed and ventured out, realizing that I could think better on my feet than on my back. The storm had ended. The air was clean and cool and sweet. The moon was sliding down a mackerel sky toward the horizon, frightening the baby stars. Boston was a clean and exciting and beautiful city, even in its sleep—but I could not dissolve my troubles in her wandering streets. I must have the sea, the swaying masts, the smell of tar and fish and oil and lumber, the musical slapping of the water on the sands, the feel of immensity, timelessness, infinity.

So I drew the sea deep into me, sitting on a wet rock above the harbor, and let my mind drift back to the courtroom.

I was in the witness chair before the noon recess. Jim Austin was standing in front of me, a day's growth of stubble darkening his face and deepening his scowl. There was a rip in one of his unpolished boots. There was ink on the fingers of his right hand.

Back of him, to his left, Joe Thomas sat, dead to all intents and purposes save for his masticating jaws. Over to the right, further back of Austin, was the prosecutor. He was seated at his table, smoking his handsome English pipe, his head in clouds of blue-gray smoke.

"On the night of the mutiny and murders," the voice of Jim Austin repeated, "did you see Joe Thomas with your brother or any of his accomplices?"

My own voice returned to me. "No, I did not."

"You are sure of that?"

"Positive."

I recalled, now, the queer look that came into the prosecutor's face at this, and the open terror that flashed in the eyes of Thomas. At that time I knew only that one man was astounded to anger by what I had said, and the other frightened to despair.

That was what was wrong. That was the danger.

Here, with the sea whispering to me, I realized the truth. Blake must have thought I had deliberately flouted him. He had written a statement for me, and I had signed it. Evidently he hadn't yet noticed that I had put his name, not my own, in the place for signatures. I had said one thing—to his way of thinking—in the statement. I had sworn to the opposite on the stand.

No wonder he had attacked me so ruthlessly, and with such confidence of working my destruction!

And, for the first time, I saw a trap into which I might have stepped.

Had Justice Story not suspended the trial for the noon recess, the trap would have closed relentlessly on me—perhaps around my neck. Blake's attack had so stunned and confused me I would have kept stubbornly to the testimony I had already given—if only to spite the man further, to defy him, to show my contempt of him. I would have continued to swear Joe Thomas was not with the mutineers that night, at any time that night.

And so, innocently, but very stupidly, I would have perjured myself beyond all help. For I had seen Thomas with Oliver and Payne that night!

I remembered now. I had seen Joe on deck, shortly after the bodies had been thrown overboard to the sharks.

I had not seen him spit in Lumbard's face. I had not heard him jeer at Lumbard's plea for pity. I had not seen him crush the mate's enormous fingers under his boots. But I knew he had done all these things. It was common knowledge.

I had been below when the bodies were disposed of. But I had come on deck shortly afterwards, and I had seen Thomas then—with two of the mutineers!

I had forgotten, completely, the brutality that finished off Mate Lumbard. And that was the key to the prosecution.

Blake had no hope of hanging Joe for the murder of the captain, nor of Beetle, nor of Fisher. But he knew he could hang him for the death of Lumbard.

He had showed us all that key at the opening of the trial. He had waved it at us, defiantly. He had told us its terrible importance in his repetition of Lumbard's plea for pity. Then he had hidden it, so to speak, in one of his pockets—that it might be ready when he needed it.

He had not brought out from his witnesses any details of Lumbard's last moments. He had led us to believe, either that he had forgotten Lumbard's heroic efforts to maintain his life or that he did not know how Thomas had thwarted them.

In his opening statement he had said "they" stamped on Lumbard's fingers—not "Joe Thomas stamped on them."

He had been waiting, I realized now, until it was time to cross-examine Gilbert Smith. He hated Smith, "that pious psalm-singing Quaker." He wanted to hang Joe Thomas with the testimony of his "best friend," Smith!

Also, the jury would be more convinced of Thomas' guilt if the truth could be wrung, reluctantly, from his "best friend." The more reluctantly, the better.

If Smith said he did not remember, or if he denied the truth, Blake would call enough witnesses in rebuttal to jail him; perhaps to hang him too.

Joe Thomas knew these things. That's what the flash in his dead eyes revealed—I realized, now that I had meditated on it. Joe knew. And he was horribly afraid.

I must have walked many miles after I left the beach, for I was wet with perspiration when I returned home. The birds were singing; the flowers were straightening themselves in the sun; the grass had almost dried itself of the dew.

As I entered, two little Negro boys flung themselves at me with shrieks of welcome. Each had a clean white napkin tied about his neck, which enhanced the beautiful lacquer of his black cheeks. Fustus carried a big spoon in his right hand. Justus had egg and porridge near the corners of his mouth.

"I do declare," Samantha scolded. "I was worried half to death. Art thee not well, Long George, that thee walketh in the night?"

"He God," Fustus explained, his voice acid because I had been reproved. "Mista Thomas say he God. Ol' Mammy say he God. Big judge say he God. Ev'ybody say he God. God walketh in the night, Aun' S'antha, who we to say he caint?"

"The boys say that Joe Thomas wants to see thee," Samantha said.

"And what were you doing in jail that you met Joe Thomas?" I asked the twins. "You mudras?"

Samantha answered that too. "They live there. With their mammy. She is the warden's housekeeper and cook. She is a freed woman, and her children were born here. In freedom. In Boston. Her husband is still a slave, someplace in Virginia. And—prepare thee for a shock—she knoweth our Sally!"

What on earth, I wondered, could bring Sally into such a fetid, reeking, cold, wet, filthy, slimy, vermin heaven as the Federal jail in Boston? Samantha must have been mistaken.

The warden fawned on me that morning when I presented myself at the jail, and led me straightway, and with some little ceremony— as though I were a most distinguished visitor—to Thomas' cell.

I was astonished. This was not the dark, narrow, fusty, musty, chilly niche in which I had seen him the last time. This was a spacious room, with calico curtains on the windows—to soften the shame of the iron bars—with a real bed in it, with soft chairs, and with books and checkers and chess, and many other comforts.

"Sit ye down, young George," Joe greeted me. There was no particular warmth in his tones. And he did not get up from the bed on which he lay. Yet neither was there the chill I had felt on that former meeting.

Joe had been scrimshawing an image of the *Globe* on a sperm whale's tooth when I was announced. He put everything aside; but he did not give me the courtesy of a glance.

"Yon Quaker captain," he said, "warned me I could not trust ye. Friend Turncoat, he called ye. But ye've given him the lie. Damn all sea captains again, says I. All save one, that is. All save Captain Percival. But 'tis the exception proves the rule."

"Don't blame Gilbert," I said. "He's simply jealous."

"Nay," Joe said. "He be afeared. Ye gave your log to Sally, Gilbert says; and, when the time comes, the lass will rise up and swear my life away. There be things in that log, says he, will hang me sure."

"So that's it," I said. "He thought I had turned traitor. He thought I was afraid to tell the truth myself, and that I'd strike you through Sally! You needn't be afraid."

"Thankee for the word," Joe said. "Thankee most kindly, m'lad. I be not afeared of Sally. Who else would get me such a room as this? Who else would bring me candy and books and whale bone and tobacky? Who else would bribe the jailors to be a little kinder to me than they would be otherwise? I be not afeared of Sally. And Gilbert be a fool."

He bade me kick the spittoon nearer to him, and asked if I thought there was a God, and if God would punish him for Lumbard's death. He was afraid to die if there was a God, he said.

"To be cheated twice, young George . . . to be so foully done in this life, and the next, too—Aye, I be feared! But Lumbard! He et the hams we didn't get that Christmas day, him and Beetle. What they couldn't stuff down they give to Lay and Hussey and to young Worth. 'Pity,' he asked me! Pity for his baby. I gave him pity. I danced on his well-fed, thieving fingers until he dropped into the sea. Lumbard, yes. His ghost haunts me, young George. But the mutiny, no. I be as innocent of that as any of ye. Go along now, young George. I don't need your lanthorn any longer. But don't let go of it. The sharks be after you as well as me.

"When ye take the stand again today, don't tell no lies for me. Don't stretch the facts, young George, lest ye stretch your neck, with mine. Blake made his brags last night. And laid his plans."

"How do you know that," I wondered.

"A body knows everything in prison," he said, "especially when his little friends be shining the devil's shoes. I warn ye, mind the rocks."

Chapter Forty-Five

JUNE 18. The trial resumed. Mr. Blake wiped his pale, moist brow with his kerchief, rested his thumb on the top button of his blue waist-coat, and stared at me a long time.

"How many men have you killed, Mr. Comstock?"

Before I could answer, or Austin rise with an objection, or the court make any ruling, Blake transferred his boot from the spittoon in front of me to that below the chair of the jury foreman, and took the panel into his confidence.

"I am sorry for the abruptness of that question, gentlemen. I should have prepared you for it. But, in the heat of getting at the truth, I forgot to tell you. Yesterday, when you had been excluded from the courtroom, His Honor, Justice Story, brought out the fact that Mr. Comstock is a hero.

"You remember I was hasty and brash enough to call him a poltroon. I ask your pardon, and his, publicly, freely, sincerely. I was woefully ignorant of his worth. It transpires he has killed many savages in his young life—and oh so many ladies!" If it was feminine titters he stopped to hear, he was disappointed. Nobody even snickered. He went on, eulogizing me in a suave left-handed sort of way that made me feel a simpleton and a lout.

I saw a juror purse his mouth, take aim, and fire. But Mr. Blake had seen him too, in time. He removed his boot from its exposed position, without appearing to notice anything unusual, and turned again to me.

"How many men have you killed, Mr. Comstock? As many as your beloved brother Sam?"

"Perhaps," I said, fighting to keep my head. "Perhaps not. But certainly, in all my life I haven't killed as many as you have in the last few weeks, Mr. Blake."

He was so shocked at my impertinence that he forgot the jury's ambush. This time it was the foreman of the jury, spitting from an angle and a distance hard to calculate with any nicety, who tried for the shining mark—and who almost crowed with delight when he saw he had not missed.

A sudden feeling of elation gripped me. The jurors must have learned, overnight, to hate and detest the dandyish Mr. Blake. Otherwise they would most certainly have held their fire.

It was unbelievable that they deliberately spat at his boots, with Justice Story and Judge Davis looking on. Yet that's exactly what they were doing.

I began to feel, then and there, that Joe Thomas might not get his neck stretched after all.

Like the judges, Mr. Blake ignored the spitting. The pupils of his pop eyes enlarged and reddened. But he managed to rein in his temper. His voice was gentle when he spoke to me again, and very, very tolerant of heroes.

"In comparing yourself to me," he said, "you were referring no doubt, Mr. Comstock, to the number of unfortunate criminals found guilty in this courtroom, by juries such as this one; and who were sentenced by judges, no different than those here today, to be hanged by the neck until they were dead.

"These men, Mr. Comstock, were justly executed. They murdered, and they lied. They fought and they lost. It is not proper to infer that they were killed as you, let us say—or your brother—might kill. Nor is it proper to impute their deaths to me. I am not a red Indian, taking pride in scalps.

"Had any of those thirty you refer to spoken truth from the chair in which you sit; had any of them confessed his guilt, and all the circumstances of his crime, I say to you, George Comstock, that man would not have tasted death. At least it would not have been here offered him to taste!

"But I will withdraw the question, and ask another."

He pondered a moment, looking ruefully at his sullied boot.

"Did you kill Captain Worth, or contribute in any way to his death?"

"No," I answered. "I did not."

"Nor Mate Beetle, who once rope-ended you? I think that was the term used here, was it not?"

"Nor Mate Beetle, who taught me astronomy and navigation, who was my friend, and who had a right to rope-end me because he was my friend."

"Just answer yes or no, Mr. Comstock. Did you kill Mate Lumbard, or Mate Fisher, or in any way contribute to their deaths?"

"No."

"And you maintain that all those who did murder these four men are themselves now dead—all except the defendant, Thomas?"

"They are all dead," I said. "And Joe Thomas was not one of them."

"Joe Thomas, you say, had no part whatsoever in the murder of the captain?"

"None whatever."

"Nor in the murder of the mates?"

The question was rolled slowly up to me. I rolled it slowly back, having seen it coming from a long way off.

"None whatever. Joe Thomas was below when the captain and the mates were attacked. He came up to see what had happened. He did spit in Mate Lumbard's face, thinking him dead. He did stamp on the mate's fingers when Lumbard came to and caught hold of the plank. But Lumbard was dying before Joe saw him. And he would have died, anyway, with all the stab wounds in him, no matter what Joe did!"

Blake had made no effort to stop me. He listened quietly, too quietly for my nerves.

"Joseph Thomas spat in Lumbard's face?" he asked then. "Lumbard was bleeding, dying, apparently dead? And Thomas filled that face with spittle?"

"Yes sir."

"Then the mutineers started to roll Lumbard's body off the plank, into the sea, into the school of sharks that had been attracted by the blood from the other bodies. Is that right?"

"Yes sir."

"But Lumbard wasn't dead? He came to life? He caught the plank? And, though his throat was cut, he managed to cry out in a loud voice? Is that correct, Mr. Comstock?"

"Yes."

"He begged for pity. He begged for life, for his baby's sake. That is true, is it not? And Joseph Thomas said, 'I'll give you pity.' And he jumped on those desperate, bleeding, life-clutching fingers! Isn't that true?"

"He stamped on Lumbard's fingers," I said, "and Lumbard fell into the sea. But he wasn't dead. He began to swim."

That stung Mr. Blake into another roar. "Will the court instruct the witness to answer questions with a simple yes or no?"

But Austin out-roared him, and out-maneuvered him.

"Your Honors," he shouted, "I am taken by complete surprise by this testimony; and I must ask time to study it, and to prepare some proper sort of defense."

"Your client has concealed this from you?" Justice Story asked.

"My client has consistently refused to talk to me," Austin replied. "And my witnesses have, until this hour, made no slightest mention of the incident Mr. Comstock has just testified to. I am overwhelmed. A man's life is at stake and I have no proper way of fighting for him."

"How long will you need?"

" 'Til Monday morning, if the court please."

That was Thursday or Friday morning. I am not sure now which it was. And I confess I have forgotten what I did, not counting my conferences with Jim Austin, between the adjournment of court and its resumption. Perhaps I went back to Nantucket, in the hope of seeing Sally. If I did, I did not see her.

I knew that Joe was sick when I saw him leave the court that day; but I was not prepared for the change in him when he appeared the following Monday morning. He shambled to his chair then and sprawled in it as though he had spent the week end in a morgue.

Austin asked and was given permission to withdraw me, temporarily, from the witness stand, and to swear Joe Thomas as a witness in his own defense. This after some legal chitchat at the bench, and before the jurors entered.

Joe sat straight in the chair, a hairy, sharp-faced, bony dummy, with dead eyes and thin grim lips. I wondered, for a fantastic moment, what sort of wires propped him up.

The only sign of life I saw in him was the movement of his jaws. He was chewing his tobacco, but without joy. He spat it out too, without exhibiting the slightest hint of pleasure.

For some little time he answered questions readily enough. Then he began to hesitate before he answered, and to squirm. He made queer motions with his head, and slow strange gestures with his hands. His knees moved wide apart. He drew up his legs until only the tips of his boots touched the floor. He made everybody in the vast courtroom feel uncomfortable—and worried.

It was so evident the man was sick! Yet it was not until a little after eleven that any notice was taken of his condition. At this time Jim Austin was trying to make him testify to the circumstances of the flogging.

Q: First, Mate Beetle laid on with the rope end?

Joe stopped moving entirely. There was a film over his dead eyes. His hands, resting in his lap, were suddenly white, and sharp. You would have said they came to a razor-blade thinness around the palms.

Suddenly his mouth twitched, and he said "Aye."

The court, hushed as a tomb, heard the sound plainly; and hushed again that it might hear more.

Q: Then Lumbard, a much younger and stronger man, took the rope from Beetle. And he opened your back. With how many lashes?

Joe did not answer.

"He's dead," women in back of me whispered. "He's dead," they whispered in other parts of the room. "Why don't they get a doctor for him? Will they let him die? They tortured him to death. I wouldn't treat a dog that way. They killed him. I don't think his heart was good. I tell you he is dead!"

Austin, sweating freely, assured the court his client was not shamming.

"I knew he was ill," he said. "I begged him to let me bring a physician to his cell. But he refused. He would not be dosed to death by doctors, he told me. That's the way he put it. And he wasn't going to be delayed by them, nor kept from testifying here today. He's been waiting too long to be set back by anybody."

While Austin was speaking—and shaking as though he himself were ill—two fat little men, each equipped with professional-looking Vandykish beards, and one of them carrying a round black bag, were projected through the crowd—now hissing like a lot of geese—by court attendants.

One of the doctors reached for Prosecutor Blake's pulse when he had been ushered inside the railing, asking, "You the patient?"

"There, stupid," Blake said testily. "The man in the witness chair. We want to know whether he's alive or dead. Are you sober enough to tell us?"

"Certainly, certainly," the doctor squeaked, his voice grating on every taut nerve in the courtroom. "The man in the chair, you said? Mister, what chair you mean?"

Within a few seconds they were kneeling on either side of Thomas, one trying to detect a heart beat, the other concentrating on the pulse.

"Well?" Blake asked.

"There's no heart beat," one doctor said. He straightened up, stuck a finger into his ear, agitated it, took it out, shook his head, and placed his ear again over the region of Joe's heart.

"No pulse," the other doctor said. He opened his black bag and fingered the jumble of bright instruments therein. "Anybody got a piece of looking glass?"

"He's dead," cried Austin, starting forward as though to sweep away the doctors.

"Dead," said the doctor who had listened for a heart beat.

"Dead," said the other, shutting up his bag.

And then the dead man's eyes fluttered, and his hands moved.

There were few screams; though, I heard later, more than a hundred women fainted. They must have done so, quietly, in their seats, without falling to the floor. If they did fall nobody heard them.

There was too much horror in the miracle, and too much awe, to provoke many screams. And it came too unexpectedly.

The eyes fluttered. The hands moved. The feet moved. The arms moved. A tired old body shot up out of the witness chair. The doctors turned white at this ghastly resurrection; and then sat down, in silly postures, on either side of the man they had pronounced dead.

"Avast!" he said to them.

That was another horror, another cause for rigidity and chills, this voice of a dead man, sounding in the awful silence of the sepulcher.

Color came back into Joe's cheeks. Warmth returned to his white marble fingers. Fire re-entered his soul. And fury. And the epic defiance I had encountered in him once before.

"Hah," he said, looking down at the cringing physicians. "What jackass rolled these beer kegs here to meddle with my flesh?"

He bent closer above the two.

"Aye," and his voice was stronger, and sterner. "I ken ye. Dr. Simeon Haprib. Dr. Shebley Parr! Street-walking medics as seek young drunken sailormen to practice on! To dope and physic and cut as it may please ye. And to rob! I ken ye well. What brought ye from the alehouse here, with the alehouse odors on ye? I be no prey of yours. And I have eaten corpses more alive than ye be now—and scraped their bones clean with my teeth. Loose me, and be off, ye carrion croakers, lest ye draw a plague of flies! This be my hour in court. Ye shall not spoil it."

He didn't wait for them to go. He didn't know they still existed. He stood with his raised hands clenched. His dead eyes—still dead, they seemed to me—were looking at the bench. His feet were wide apart. His legs were braced as though there was a heaving deck beneath them. And every hair on his hairy face stood out distinct—intent and menacing.

His voice was pitched in the shrill scream I had heard the night he cursed the chained head of the whale. But in the profound stillness in the court it had the force of thunder.

Joe opened his clenched hands, and his fingers were white bones that frightened a man to look at. White bones so thin you felt they would cut paper. The little clerk whose duty it was to transcribe every word that Joe might utter, looked at those hands, and swooned. Nobody noticed him until later, when he crawled out from beneath his table.

"Ask no silly questions of me now," Joe cried. "Did I do thus or so? Did this poor sinner lie? Or that one? I come to speak the truth. The sands of life run swiftly out of me. Let me say here what I have come to say—what I have waited years to say—before it be too late to say it.

"Hear me and act," he cried, "for that is justice.

"I had no hand in the mutiny or the murders. Save for Mate Lumbard! Him I denied pity. Him I spat upon. Him I cursed. Him I forced to drop into the sea by jumping on his fingers. I confess it freely, before God and man. That is the truth of it. That is the whole truth of it. That is nothing but the truth of it.

"Persecute me not now with your lawyers' fiddle-faddle. Weary me not now with the bull-like roar and the bullfrog face of Blake, with the worried look of Austin, nor with the nice punctilio of the court. Like Saul of Tarsus, 'in stripes, in imprisonments, in tumults,' aye, and in squalor and filth and vermin, I have waited overlong for justice.

"Hang me decently and quickly, Your Honors; or decently and quickly set me free."

He collapsed into the chair, and looked as dead as he had looked before the doctors came. His bony fingers curled into tight fists. One leg sprawled out in front of him, rocking a cuspidor. The other was drawn up until the knee almost supported his chin. His head fell back against the back of the chair. And slowly, like curtains being drawn, his dead eyes closed.

Before the renewed whispering and stirring had been quieted by the gavel, Jim Austin was asking for a directed verdict of not guilty; and Blake was shouting at him, "Shame!"

"Order," Justice Story demanded. "Order, or I'll clear the court-room. Mr. Blake, if you have an objection, make it in the proper way."

Blake bowed to the court, and turned his face to the jurors.

"May it please the court," he said, "we have heard testimony, during this peculiar trial, that only a few of us believed. We were told of a man who had been stabbed to death, who came to life again, and who died the second time while swimming for his life.

"Did you believe that? I did.

"We were told that this man, Mate Lumbard, had had his throat slashed so terribly that he could not talk—but not so seriously as to keep him from crying aloud for pity.

"Did you believe that? I knew it to be true."

Blake, I thought, was stumbling blindly through his thoughts, not sure where he would go. His face was as waxy as Joe's, and as sweaty as Austin's.

"Now—we here in this court—with our own eyes and our own ears, we have seen another dead man come to life, and heard him cry aloud. We have heard him cry, not for pity, gentlemen, but for justice.

"Maybe we don't believe that either; though we know it happened."

He wiped his brow with a fine white cambric cloth, and looked to the right of him, and to the left, as though he wanted to speak not only to the jury, but to the world.

"What men these whalers are!" he shouted.

He raised his hands, as though to fend off any applause that last remark might have engendered.

"Joe Thomas, rotting in his chains, lying in his filth, eating out his heart for years, while his shipmates go blithely about the world, comes, dying, here to demand the justice due him.

"And his counsel asks the court to direct the jury's verdict.

"Again do I say 'Shame!'

"If the defense will rest its case now, the people will do likewise. If they will waive the judge's instructions to the jury, so will we. It is the free verdict of the jury Joseph Thomas asks for. And, so far as the people are concerned, that's what he shall be given—not the directed verdict of the court."

He scowled angrily at Austin's look of suspicion.

"I am no longer interested in the verdict," he went on. "The man is dying. I am interested in the man. No person coming here for justice should be permitted to die here for lack of doctors. Neither should he be permitted to die without his meed of justice."

As Blake finished, the jury foreman caught his unblemished boot abeam, and spattered it from stem to stern with yellow venom—but without intent, without being at all aware of it. Then, without waiting for another word, he began to poll his fellow jurors.

Like the foreman, they too relieved themselves of their fine-cut charges, shifted uneasily in their seats—they had become stiff with awe and excitement, it appeared—and whispered, one to another, half aloud, "Not guilty, not guilty, not guilty."

Before the last juror could be heard from, the foreman was on his feet, saying, "We the jury, find this here defendant, Joe Thomas, not guilty!"

Joe died in the hospital an hour or so after he heard that he was free.

"Your friend was with him," Austin told me. "That minister, Elijah Goodyear. A fine old chap. Wasn't it he who preached the sermon at your father's grave?"

The lawyer looked gravely out to sea, following the wake of a whaleship, bound on a long, long cruise.

"Thomas died peaceful," he said. "He died listening to the preacher. I wasn't there. I was in the alehouse down the street, trying to make myself believe this hadn't happened.

"It's as though I'd tried to defend a spook. He was a spook. You found him in a fog at sea. In a whaleboat that was empty except for him. He's gone back into that fog—as mysterious a cuss as he was when you first saw him.

"He was an educated man, Joe Thomas. Or Thomas Joad. Or whatever his right name was. He might have been a lawyer, or a doctor, or a minister, or anything you please. Why did he make himself out such an ignorant rum pot, such a humble dolt?"

"And why," I asked in turn—also watching the white wake of the whaleship, and the gulls above it, and the way the west wind fell upon her sails—"why, at the age of twenty-seven, did he look like an old, old man?"

We buried him on the hill, in Nantucket, not far from the end of Judith Chase's Lane. Elijah preached a sermon at his grave; and little children searched the fields for wild flowers, as they did at my father's burial.

I did not listen to Elijah. I was wondering about Joe Thomas; and about the justice or the mercy he had found.

God must have seen him lying in the empty boat of life, adrift on the misty sea of death. What happened? Did the Almighty pick him up and warm him and feed him and give him clothes from the slop chest and sign him on as one of the crew?

Or did He let him drift?

Chapter Forty-Six

JUNE 19. The long drought of ostracism broke after the trial, and friendship began to spatter again, first in a bashful sort of rain, and then in great drops.

But perhaps my heart has been numbed. Perhaps my appreciation of this friendship is at fault. Or perhaps it is just because of Sally that I feel so neutral toward all my friends. I came close to scolding the twins today. That's how cranky I have become. They had been playing with Samantha's pet Rambouillet ram, and had almost let it get out of its pen.

It was on that fell day when the crowds of women were trying to kiss me that Sally went away.

"She went to New York," Samantha said, "on the coach, with two friends, and Charity Gantry for her maid."

It is good to have Samantha's sheep to look after, as well as my books to study. Otherwise, I could not stand it here. I might even now be with Gilbert bound for Havana in the *Samaritan*.

I chanced to meet Gilbert after Joe Thomas' funeral, and we became good friends again. He offered me the chance to go along as first mate.

"We know," he said, " 'twas whaling and whaling captains killed poor Joe. What we are just beginning to realize, Friend George, is that whaling be dead, too. Aye, as dead as Joe Thomas. Whaling as we know it. It has become now only a shabby business. But an old salt need not bewail all this. Barnabas Starbuck is readying a vessel for the China trade. The *China Star*, she is. And, right now, the schooner *Samaritan* be loading in Boston with a cargo for the Cuban city of Havana. She sails within the week. The pay be good. The food be good. The slop chest will rob no one. Barnabas Starbuck has made me the skipper, Friend George. And you—?"

I had no heart for the venture, but I did not tell him so. I interrupted him.

"But I thought you were going to Valparaiso to bring Rosita here."

He blushed, and he shuffled his feet in a way I had never noticed in him before. He looked, somehow, like a boy caught in some embarrassing scrape and unable to lie his way out of it.

"There be money in the venture," he said. "And I shall need it. Havana is not far. I may be back before Miss Bonheur arrives. Will thee come?"

I told him no.

"Then, will thee look after her in my absence?" he asked. Even his jealousy was dead.

"Yes," I said, and started away. But he called me back. And he was even more embarrassed than a few moments before.

"Let thee not trouble thyself too much about a certain person," he said. "It was not exactly pity that caused her to help Joe Thomas in the prison. Nor yet curiosity, Friend George. She knew he had saved thy life."

"Then why did she run away?" I could not help asking. He shook his head, nearly as perplexed as myself—and walked off.

The *Samaritan* sailed on May 15, her striped flag fluttering on her mizzenmast. A stately craft. Hussey and Lay and Hanson and a dozen or more others were aboard. I envy them, in a way. They are free. They are not dependent on the whims of a girl. They do not have to wait here—for years, it may be—for a woman to return.

JUNE 25. Rosita arrived in Nantucket a few days after the *Samaritan* had left. She is staying with Gilbert's parents, but I have seen little of her. The ram was sick, the day she came, and it was not for several days that I felt it safe to leave him. It was just as well, perhaps, as Rosita was suffering from seasickness. She was thinner than I remembered.

It is strange that I feel so little the tragedy of my friends. Perhaps I am not human, after all. I cannot understand myself.

The captain of the *Star of Asia* reported that the *Samaritan* had been wrecked in a gale off Cape Hatteras and had been abandoned by its crew. The barkentine *Nestor* had later news. It had picked up four survivors and heard the full story from them.

Cyrus Hussey had been washed overboard. Lay and Hanson and Gilbert Smith had remained aboard the *Samaritan*, with one or two others, determined to bring the wreck into some Virginia port.

Judge and Mrs. Hussey were on the dock when the *Nestor* was made fast. They were stunned by the news. Their boy had sailed half around the world, he had encountered a thousand perils, and come home safely. Now going to Havana—and Havana was only around the corner! They kept saying "only around the corner."

Rosita tried to comfort Gilbert's people. "He is not dead," she insisted. "I tell you he will come back. Have faith in God."

Am I made of wood that I feel so little for these friends, that I mourn only for myself?

JUNE 28. Rosita has become one of the most popular persons in Nantucket. Everybody thinks she is the niece of Napoleon Bonaparte. There are stories that she escaped from France after incredible hardships, and with more than a hundred thousand dollars in jewels. Mr. Starbuck is especially fond of her.

What most people like best about her is her faith in Gilbert and in God.

Mr. Starbuck has promised her, or so Samantha says, that if Gilbert does manage to salvage the *Samaritan,* he shall have command of the *China Star.* Not only that. He will have a bridal suite installed, so that Rosita may go with her bridegroom wherever he takes the *China Star.*

JULY 1. The ram escaped early this morning. I found him, after a long search, in the brambles near "Old Fiddle-Head" Hewman's woods. He was quite worn out with his fight to free himself—and I had to let him rest a while before taking him home. Also, there were many burrs to be picked out of his black wool. He had hurt his right front leg, so I had to carry him.

I saw Mr. Starbuck and Rosita as I came across the common. But apparently they did not see me. Rosita was talking about sheep. "Not the sheep that go baa-baa—but the sheep that sails the sea." And she was looking up into his face with such patent admiration that the old man positively glowed.

I was half tempted to say something, by way of greeting, but suddenly I felt weak and dizzy. The stagecoach had stopped and a man had got out of it. He looked like Gilbert Smith. I almost believed, for an unholy moment, that it was merely a sign, a bad sign. That it was the ghost of my friend come to tell me he was dead. I was sure of it!

Then a man who looked like Anthony Hanson got out of the stage, and I began to breathe again.

It was an eerie minute or two. The common was full of people. But nobody was talking. I guess nobody could talk.

Suddenly Rosita ran to Gilbert, and her wild sobbing broke the silence.

I couldn't take a step forward. My legs were still too weak. I could only watch the stagecoach. A tall Negro got out of it. Charity Gantry got out of it. She had a purple hat that kept bobbing up and down.

And then I saw Sally. Anthony was helping her from the coach. I was still rooted to the earth.

So she had gone to Virginia. She had gone to buy that Negro slave! I knew who he was immediately I saw him. The father of the twins. He couldn't possibly be anyone else.

She had gone to Norfolk, and she was there when Gilbert brought the wreck of the *Samaritan* into port. Naturally, she had taken Gilbert and Anthony to Nantucket with her. Lay and the other survivors must be in Boston by this time, I suppose.

I let go of the ram. I don't remember doing so, but that's what must have happened. I dropped him and forgot him. Sally had seen me and was coming toward me. Sally in blue and white. Sally cool and sweet despite the heat of the day. Sally spotlessly clean in spite of the dust. Sally, more beautiful than ever, was coming toward me.

The ram took that precise occasion to charge. Without a warning of any kind, he hit Barnabas Starbuck full astern and knocked him, cane, high hat, frock coat, snuffbox, and all, into the only mud puddle in all Nantucket.

I shut my eyes.

"Thar blows!" a boy shouted maliciously. "Buh-lows! Buh-lows!"

Sally said, "Grandpa, are you hurt?"

Suddenly, I heard Barnabas' loud voice shouting maledictions. I opened my eyes then, and saw him, cane raised high, chasing a couple of boys. I saw also that Gilbert and Rosita were clasped in each other's arms, and that the twins and their mother were rushing up to claim the tall Negro. I saw that he was, like myself, unable to move. And I saw that Sally was coming toward me again.

And now her eyes were blazing!

She stood in front of me, at last, and all I could do was feast my weary eyes on her.

I tried to say something. But I was as dumb as I was powerless to move.

She was evidently provoked, and I don't blame her.

"What must I do," she asked, "to keep you from trying to maim my grandfather every time you see him?"

I tried, desperately, to say I had not meant to hurt him ever. I tried, hopelessly, to explain that I was just holding the ram, and that I didn't know how he got away. I gave it up. Her eyes upset me.

"What do I have to do?" she demanded. "*Must* I marry you, George, for my poor grandfather's sake?"

Her eyes blazed again, but I saw, this time, that it was not anger that had lit the flames in them.

Queer how that ram, striking at the right time, and in the right place, had brought matters to a head. I don't think I shall ever again know such a blessed moment. I don't think I could stand it.

There was life only in my arms. I reached out and grabbed her. And I shall never let her go so long as we both shall live; I shall hold her much more securely than I held that blessed ram.